# THE WOMAN WHO DID

# THE WOMAN WHO DID

## LOU ALLIN

**FIVE STAR**
*A part of Gale, Cengage Learning*

GALE
CENGAGE Learning·

Farmington Hills, Mich • San Francisco • New York • Waterville, Maine
Meriden, Conn • Mason, Ohio • Chicago

**GALE**
CENGAGE Learning®

**LIBRARY OF CONGRESS CATALOGING-IN-PUBLICATION DATA**

Allin, Lou, 1945–
    The woman who did / Lou Allin. — First edition.
        pages ; cm
        ISBN 978-1-4328-3057-1 (hardcover) — ISBN 1-4328-3057-0 (hardcover) — ISBN 978-1-4328-3054-0 (ebook) — ISBN 1-4328-3054-6 (ebook)
        I. Title.
    PR9199.4.A46W66 2016
    813'.6—dc23                                                                2015024245

First Edition. First Printing: March 2016
Find us on Facebook– https://www.facebook.com/FiveStarCengage
Visit our website– http://www.gale.cengage.com/fivestar/
Contact Five Star™ Publishing at FiveStar@cengage.com

Printed in the United States of America
1 2 3 4 5 6 7 20 19 18 17 16

# THE WOMAN WHO DID

# CHAPTER ONE

*1896, Vancouver Island*

The dramatic new Parliament buildings on this magical island were a strange place for a murder, but even Paradise had a serpent.

Detective Sergeant Edwin DesRosiers chafed his hands against the bluster of the raw night. It was threatening to sleet, and wild southeast winds from Puget Sound buffeted the port. He hopped a cab from his home to Belleville Street on the Inner Harbor.

The vehicle wheeled off, the horse's hooves muffled on the hard-packed road. Edwin found his way to the constable who had reported the death. "She's over there, Sir," the man said, pointing.

Edwin walked over to the shadowy spot, removing his bowler hat as he knelt, and though he wasn't religious, he whispered a brief prayer for her soul. The broken marionette on the grass would find a pauper's grave. Yet there was something . . .

He edged closer, his heart bursting. It was Vicky. How calm she looked, how unmarred her luminous face, except for the trace of creases edging her eyes, unchanged in fifteen years. Born a farm girl, Vicky took good care of herself. A sound diet, no beer, wine, or opiates. Only her profession had betrayed her.

What had brought her to this bedraggled bower in a small park meant for strolling lovers? What twist of fate sent *him* to her side? When he'd gone north to seek his fortune, he had carried the tintype she'd given him as a lad. During a bunkhouse fire, he'd lost it and mourned in mute despair.

*Ave atque vale.* A dead language useful only in law, medicine, and obsequies. His bruised mind whirled as his lips betrayed him.

"Pardon, Sir?" Constable Lester Eales moved the bull's-eye lantern closer. A welcome heat radiated from the glass. The woman's eyes were open, the pupils wide and unseeing. Their aquamarine depths had been like the Georgia Strait on a calm, sunny day. Now a cloudy film was developing.

"Nothing. I said nothing." The middle-aged constable was a decent soul, but thick-headed as a beast of burden, a good footslogger who would never make corporal, nor care.

"Wagon's on its way soon as the boys at the station can hire one at this hour," Eales said, standing tall in a Prince Albert–style uniform with a double-breasted, brass-buttoned jacket and bobby hat. A billy club was tucked into his belt. Quieting a prisoner without cracking his skull took a skilled tap. "No fit night for a dog. Say, you got here in jig time. Without that corner call box, it would have taken hours with the old tin tooters. It's a new world, innit?"

Edwin looked up, wiped the rain from his face. His short-brimmed hat did little to keep off the frigid drops of late April. Cold as he was, he could feel those long, supple legs drawing him into warm female mysteries, Eve, Salome, and Cleopatra rolled into one sweet, devilish spirit. Victoria had laughed and kissed his burning cheek, red from a close shave. *Able horsemen go slower and enjoy the ride, Neddy, my brave virgin warrior. Girls are going to swoon for those black curls. Now best leave my rooms. I have an appointment.* The Cadogan Hotel. A delicate *muguet* perfume from the cut-glass bottle on her dresser. Lace curtains rustling in the breeze. The soft feather bed with red silk sheets. On the wall in a gilt frame *The Blue Boy.* Her pet name. He'd worn his best suit even though an inch of ankle showed.

Eales gave a cursory grunt. "The togs look on the posh side for a chippie."

"Show some respect, Eales. A woman is dead."

"Sorry, Guv. I mean, she's a looker, ain't she? Those clothes and baubles cost a pretty penny, too. Not your average dolly. But what would a real lady be doing out here at night? It's not far from where the other two girlies—"

"Damn your common slang out of a penny dreadful. Get down to business. When did you find her? The exact time. It had better be in your notebook," Edwin said. This was no road accident, stroke, or heart attack. They were fifty feet onto the grass, and a stocking was looped around her neck. Even Blind Jake hunkered in his begging spot would have known by touch alone that she was dead at someone's hand.

Edwin felt her wet wrist, still supple but slightly stiffening. The jaw would have been less flexible, one of the first places for rigor. Temperature was only one indication, and the night was cold after a mild sixty-degree-Fahrenheit afternoon. A light rain had begun to fall over an hour ago, when he had lowered the sash on the parlor window. After supper, he had been reading the *Daily Colonist* to check the mining stocks, wondering about the risks of a copper venture on Texada Island.

Had it been eight o'clock? She'd been mortal clay by then. Why hadn't he felt the string between their hearts tauten and snap? He shifted her full skirts to examine the ground. Wet. So she was left after the rain began. In darkness. The checked gabardine dress with a short coat was subdued and tasteful. Her kid shoes, soles barely worn, were still polished, unspattered with dust from the paths tramped by picnickers who flocked to the popular waterway on Sunday. She hadn't walked here. A thick barberry bush hid her from two directions, leaving the chance that she might have been seen. Had she had been killed someplace else? The proximity to the other attacks made some sense. In the last three months, two prostitutes had been strangled with a plain black cotton stocking. Snatched from behind and losing consciousness, the women could give scant details about their attacker. Thanks to noises of approaching carriages, the man had run off before raping or killing them.

"Never assume. Makes an ass of you and me. The letter *u*, get it?" grizzled old Sergeant Dempster had said when Edwin had been a rookie. Edwin needed to leave open all possibilities.

Given that the other two women had come from the dark underbelly and survived, the first attacks had gone unremarked. Local murders were largely domestic affairs or barroom brawls. As for Vicky, he looked at her left hand. No ring. No white mark. No husband.

Where ever she'd lived, she'd done well enough. Jet bead necklace and a silver pin on her coat. Tasteful but not lavish. One detail looked wrong. She was dressed for the afternoon with no cloak for plummeting evening temperatures.

During all those years, if he'd wanted to look at Vicky, he could visit his mother's boudoir. There she kept her paintings too risqué for the parlor. Vicky was reclining, like Goya's *Naked Maja*. Naomi's works sold to saloons, under the wry-wink name of "William Bonny," and to exclusive gentlemen who paid handsomely to memorialize their mistresses. This colonial island antipodes was a backwater for any avant-garde artist. She dreamed that someday she might find her way into an exclusive New York or Montreal gallery or even a grand museum in London. Edwin knew the folly of her dream, but a nod was wisest.

The constable snapped open a pocket watch, tapping the glass with one stubby finger. "It's gone ten. I came through here three hours ago on the dot, and she wasn't here, I swear on my mother's grave. Then an hour ago, make that fifty-five minutes,

I was starting my rounds again. Broke up a fight between those bums dossing down near the junk buildings. First thing you know, there's a fire and half the city's cinders. Roust them all out, I say." He made a broad gesture at dark forms down-shore huddled in the distance. Likely Eales earned a coin or two from the warehouse owners for his efforts as a sporadic watchman.

Who would blame the poor devils, looking for a place out of the rain? Gaslights in the distance shimmered haloes in the fog blowing in with the tide.

"Give me the lantern." Edwin walked a precise circle twenty feet around the body, shining light on the ground. Nothing.

"Her personals, Eales?" No woman left home without a reticule if not the more capacious modern handbag. Perhaps something lay in her deep pockets. He'd leave that for the coroner. Jones had cautioned him never to meddle with the corpse. On the other hand, why would an ordinary thief risk the gallows for a paltry sum?

The constable shook his head as he spoke, and moisture feathered his mutton-chop cheeks. "Didn't see nothing laying about. Do you think that she was robbed? Or interfered with, God forbid? That around her neck ain't *her* stocking either." He pointed to her buttoned shoes.

"She's dead, man. Money nor virtue matter not to her now." Eales had made a good point about the stocking. Someone, presumably a man, had come prepared. Vicky would have fought another woman. She was tough as a mother cougar. And her face had no marks. Her clothing bore no obvious rips or tears. The area was quiet and deserted. A scream would have carried several hundred feet.

A large arbutus spread its skirts upward, the chestnut bark peeling from the pale greenish-white trunk, blighted winter leaves drooping on the evergreen. Leafy rhodo bushes provided more cover twenty feet away. His faint hope that someone had seen her began to disappear.

"I've been on this beat two bloody years and haven't laid eyes on this gal. Her fancy get-up don't fit with the usual trollops in the alleys or hanging out the windows in Chinatown, yammering for custom. Could be she worked for one of the fancy houses where she could bide indoors. Making a living on your back isn't that rough if you've got bed and board and a fair madam."

"You sound as if those places are your second home. I thought you were married." Edwin arched a questioning eyebrow.

A round of coughing delayed the answer. "Of course not, Sir, I—"

"What gives you the impression that she's on the game, Constable?" Edwin felt strangely protective. His objectivity was compromised, but no one was taking him off this case. What they didn't know . . .

Eales shrugged his shoulders and blew his craggy beak on a red-patterned handkerchief. "Goes without saying, it do. A lady wouldn't be out here without an escort. A fool knows that."

"It's only ten minutes' walk to where the other women were attacked."

"True enough, Sir. The others were on Wharf Street in the alleys where the Jack Tars like to troll for sardines. But this one . . ." His voice trailed off.

Where was the damn doctor? Edwin shivered under his mackintosh, envying the constable's rubber cape, sweaty but waterproof. "Thank God the rain has stopped. Small mercies."

They turned at fast-moving footsteps. A street urchin, his wool cap pulled low, ran by as Eales stuck out his arm and caught the scruff of his neck. "Hey, now, slow down. You near crashed into the detective sergeant here." The boy wore shabby knickers with holes in the long stockings. His shoe soles flapped with cardboard repairs. A hand-me-down coat hung to his knees. Shadowy circles around his eyes and the dirt line ringing his neck testified to his homeless, or at best, catch-as-catch-can, life.

"Whoa! What's all this? The lady drunk? Dead? Ho-ly." The boy bent closer for a look, but Eales yanked his collar.

"That's enough out of you, little pup. Stand back. You're always hanging around here, Ben Conrad. Probably looking to pick a pocket."

"Says you, copper." Ben squirmed and pulled free, smoothing down his coat.

"You'll be in the dock before you're twelve, dancing on the scaffold not long after." His look was stern, but Eales had a soft spot. He was a father of three hellions with one in the warming oven.

Edwin folded his arms and locked his gaze onto the boy. In a town of five thousand, everyone has eyes. "Did you see anything, son? Have you been around here all night? Do you know this woman?"

The boy put one hand on his snake hip and pushed back a greasy lock of hair with a mittened hand. "I were here all right, but I din't see nothin' and I don't know her from my own gran. Got a nickel? I'm mighty hungry. Ma's been gone all day gleanin' coal and she ain't come back yet."

"Tell the truth, you. We're not paying you to make up lies," the constable said, then looked at Edwin. "Sorry, Sir. He doesn't have a mother or father, do you, little monkey? His older brother's a runner for the Fan Tan Alley gamblers. You should hear him squawk that pidgin jabber."

Edwin fished for a dime and flipped it to the lad. No doubt the sides of his stomach were meeting. "Get you something to eat and come right back. Another might be waiting for you."

"Aye." Saluting smartly as he backed away, the urchin ran off.

Eales gave Edwin a dubious look. "You'll never see that scamp again." He clapped his arms together in the cold. Under the old wooden James Bay Bridge in the distance, the glow of a small fire warmed the night. The roof was noisy, but for some it was a home.

"If he's as hungry as he looks, he needs it to clear his head. While we're waiting, get over to that camp fire and find out if anyone saw or heard anything. And leave the lantern here. Speak before you approach or you'll scare them off. A soft word does more than a rough hand."

As the constable walked off, his hobnailed boots squishing on the grass, the rumble of an open wagon sounded on the bridge. Complaints were rife about the lack of an official vehicle for the department. The mayor had said, "The budget's tighter than a constipated bull's butt. Maybe next year." Vicky's last ride would be bumpy, not that it would matter.

Dr. Timothy Jones, one of several coroners, heaved himself out of the wagon, worn black leather bag in hand, then plucked a small lantern hooked on the side pole. "Lord dyin' Jesus, it's a cold wet night to call a man out. I left Come-by-Chance for this?" He fumbled in his heavy tweed overcoat pocket for a flask and offered it to Edwin. "*A votre sante,* my favorite froggie. You'll catch your death instead of criminals." Having been to medical school in Montreal, he spoke French to Edwin when he wanted a matter private.

Edwin took the jibe good-naturedly. He'd been called worse things. French Canadians here took their places in line well after the English and the Scots. He'd arrived on the coast too late. In exploration years, sixty percent of the area had spoken French.

"After you, Sir." Jones had already had a few, as his bulbous red nose testified. But he never missed an hour on the job, day or night. Even at fifty, he was fit and spry like a boxer.

Jones drank deeply, then wiped his mouth and the silver flask before passing it. Edwin took a warming swig. Kentucky bourbon. He preferred cognac, but the widower favored the American drink. Jones's young wife and baby had gone down with another two hundred and fifty souls during the sinking of the SS *Pacific* in late 1875. The ship was charging through a storm thirty miles south of Cape Flattery, Washington, when it struck the sailing vessel *Orpheus*. In the dark confusion, the *Pacific* sank with all hands but two. The disabled *Orpheus* drifted and ran aground on remote Tzartus Island, losing the ship but no lives. Jones never spoke of it, nor was he the type for self-pity. His work became his life. Edwin was glad that he'd been on the rota for Vicky.

The spavined white nag pulling the wagon shied at the shriek of a pair of fighting cats. The horse looked five breaths from the glue factory, but tonight was Hobson's choice. "Hold that beast, young Dick. Move the wagon back a bit to shield us from the wind off the water. I've got a devil of a rheum already," Jones said. Dick gave a cluck and the mare shuffled her feet. Dick was a mute, a "dummy," some called him. But he harkened like a little bat, making good use of signing and a small slate for writing.

"More light," Jones said, kneeling by his open bag as Edwin moved the lantern closer. "Hold it there. Our lady has much to tell us, and she's been waiting for her last gentlemen callers." He gently pulled aside her clothing at the neck. Large purple bruises stood out as if thumbs had pressed down on either side and across the front of the windpipe. A stocking fell slack below the marks.

"Like the other two attacks, Tim. This time he used his hands to finish her. That stocking's five cents a pair in the Sears catalog." Cleaner than knives or guns but just as deadly. Edwin couldn't imagine the pure evil in slowly and quietly squeezing life from a beautiful woman. Cheap cotton or silk, what did the fabric matter?

Jones wiped aside a drop of rain hesitating on the end of his nose. "Sign of a temper, but a devil to prove. Doesn't leave evidence like stab wounds or bullets. Everyone has a pair of mitts ready-made to kill. Any identification? You didn't—"

"I know enough not to disturb the body. We have her name. Victoria Crosse."

The doctor scratched his square chin. "That's an early break. Who is she? Who was she? What did she hope to be?"

Whether it was better to have a philosophical bent in this job or not, Edwin couldn't say. The knack got the doctor through the night. Edwin filled him in without the personal details other than that she had posed for his mother, probably earned money on her back, and been gone from the city for years.

Jones nodded. "Would there be something you're leaving out? You're a bit solemn. I've known you too long, Edwin, not to notice. And I'm no alienist, just a student of common sense and observation."

Against his will, Edwin felt a sigh leave his chest. "I was young, but old enough. She went away with a small piece of a boy's heart. I never thought I'd see her again."

"Now I understand. And you do have an alibi for this evening, of course," Jones said. At Edwin's surprised face, he thumped him on the back, then took another drink. "A black jest for a black moment. Fellows like me whistle past the graveyard. We'll all drop our dust there someday."

Edwin heard the peeps of frogs down by the water. During the day this grassy expanse was popular for strollers. People popped by to see how the new Parliament buildings were progressing, cheap entertainment. At night it might attract rough trade. The Gorge, an estuary from the strait, floated many bodies out on the tide, especially in high winds under the right conditions. And once on the open water, busy red and Dungeness crabs waited away from industrial outpourings. "I'm wondering why she was left here for us to find instead of in the water. It seems like a stupid mistake."

"Interrupted, perhaps." The doctor fingered her dress gently. "No silks or taffeta, but tasteful. The shoes look brand-new. And the jewelry. If this was a robbery, why leave it?"

"The jewelry's common jet and silver. No gold or stones." Living with a mother who dressed well, he had some ken of women's fancies. The doctor examined one of her hands. "Manicured. Same care as her clothes. No wedding ring or sign of one."

"She had such hope for the States. I'm sorry to see her end like this." Without a man, what could an impoverished and uneducated woman do that was legal and lucrative? Starting a business took capital. Then came the dangers and consequences of pregnancy.

"So she modeled for your mother. Quite the temptation to peek through the keyhole. I've never known any models or actresses, more's the pity."

"I was fifteen and taller than you. Usually I was at school during the prime hours for light. Miss Crosse posed for four or five portraits over a few months." His voice trailed off. Naomi liked to talk to her subjects to help them relax during the long sessions. The more she knew about their lives, the better she could capture the soul on canvas. As for his . . . hour alone with Vicky, Naomi had arranged it for his birthday, and never mentioned it again. He trusted that Vicky hadn't told her about his dim performance.

"Now you have me intrigued. I've never met your mother, remember. And where are these pictures? At the art galleries back east or in Seattle?"

Edwin gave a wry laugh. "In every other saloon in the Pacific

Northwest. This city is a hard sell for an artist. They want pretty landscapes or portraits. My mother should have lived in Paris."

"Ah, but then we two would have missed out on a beautiful friendship." He removed a thermometer from his bag, and Edwin turned away. They became quiet for a few minutes.

After reading the result, Jones motioned to a burly man in work clothes who hunched next to the driver. "Karl, *kommen sie hier.*" He looked at Edwin. "German. New immigrant from the Palatinate. Knows his stuff. I've taken him on as my diener. Assistant. About bloody time for what they pay me."

"Time of death will be important. Her eyes had started to cloud. Where was she killed?" Edwin asked. "I'm thinking not here. The grass was wet beneath her. I was finishing supper when the rain started."

"Basing on the internal temperature and the fact that it's about forty-five degrees out here, you could be right. I'll check the lividity with more accuracy before we get her iced down. Come by the morgue tomorrow. I have another autopsy in the morning. Natural causes, but there's an insurance payment involved, so needs must. One-thirty should be good."

"*Es ist traurig. Schoene mullerin.*" As Karl lifted the woman gently in his arms, the doctor opened the tailgate of the wagon and they placed her on a piece of clean canvas, closing it over her like a winding sheet.

"What's he saying?" Edwin asked. " 'Beautiful . . .'—I can't make it out." His mother spoke some German thanks to the similarity to Yiddish.

"A romantic is Karl. I think Schubert wrote a piece of music called *Die schöne Müllerin*—'the beautiful miller girl.' " Jones prepared to join the wagon, then turned. "Give you a lift as far as the morgue?"

In a strange way, Edwin felt like a father surrendering his daughter to her final escort. Seeing her tomorrow would be brutal. Edwin waved his hand. "You go on. I have a few things to finish once Eales gets back from inquiries at the bridge." Where was that boy? Had Edwin been cheated like a country bumpkin?

The wagon clattered away. Nothing could be heard but the soughing of the water on the pilings. Something splashed into the water with a squeak. Probably a lusty Norway rat. Now *there* was a survivor.

The constable returned as the wagon pulled off. "I took names by the firelight best I could, but everyone's mum. Drunk or blind as old Jake."

The young boy was running toward them with something in his hand. He skidded to a stop and took large bites from a hot, jacketed potato, gobbling as if it had been his only food all day. "I'm back, Sir. What about that other piece of silver?"

Edwin smiled. "Not so fast. Did you see or hear anything in the last few hours? I'm assuming you were around here."

"I was dozing off under a tree, having me a kip to fill my belly. I heard the Saint Andrews bells strike eight." He took the last bite of potato and gulped it down whole. His cheeks were pocketed like a chipmunk's.

"Did you see the young lady?"

"I seen a carriage or a wagon. Then shapes moving in the darkness is all. A man with a deep voice said 'Ab-b-bott.' Or 'about.' " He creased his small dirty brow and gave his head a scratch to chase the nits. "Sorry, Sir, I was thinking about my brother. I should have saved him a bite."

"That's all? And he stuttered?"

"Yes, Captain. A stutter. Just like I'm telling you. That's all I heard."

"I'll need your address, boy."

To that, a shrug. Edwin closed his notebook and tucked it away. No use turning Ben in to the Orphan's Home. He wouldn't stay long and Edwin wouldn't envy him the constant prayers and boring regimen. Ben had an older brother keeping an eye on him and he knew where to get enough to eat. Sometimes that was all a child could ask. He was thin, but not unhealthy. If his clothes were shabby and ill-fitting, at least they were warm.

The hot food had put a sparkle in the boy's eyes and a snap in his posture. "Find me down at the wharves where the U.S. steamers dock. Plenty of rich Yanks need a message sent, and there's good handouts. I knows all the cooks, I do."

# CHAPTER TWO

The grandfather hall clock bonged two as Edwin entered his home on Amelia Avenue, a quiet lane between Blanchard and Quadra. It had taken him a full hour to walk in near stupor from the death scene. Cabs were off the streets anyway, but he wanted to clear the cobwebs. Not only his first official murder as a detective sergeant, but the loss of an old friend, if those simple words described what he'd felt for Vicky.

The last time he had seen her, he had been on his way to school. She and a toff were crossing Douglas Street. That trim step. The lilt of her bustle. No one moved like Vicky Crosse, poetry in motion. She'd caught his eye and winked. His heart had jumped.

The man had strode down the street to hail a cab. Edwin stopped to be mannerly, feeling common in his knickers and loose cotton shirt. He doffed his cap and crushed it in his hands. Words wouldn't come. His lips grew numb and clumsy.

A smile almost put him at his ease. "My regards to your mother, Edwin. I hope she is well, and you certainly are growing into a fine man. Even a year has made all the difference. You must be over six feet now," Vicky had said. Her bow lips were rouged delicately, and she wore a blush of powder under a light veil trailing from her pink-ribboned hat. On her lapel was a fresh sprig of violets. One tapered and expressive eyebrow raised in a flirt. If he'd owned the world, he would have placed it at the feet of this darling girl. But she wasn't the marrying kind.

He owed her his shuddering entrance into manhood, no light debt. And she never patronized him by calling him Master Edwin, like a youngster.

"I'll . . . pass on your good wishes." He drank in her face like an intoxicating liqueur. Those laughing eyes looked as if they had never lied, but he doubted that. "Miss Victoria," he added like a pledge. "Please take care of yourself."

"You're not to worry none about me. I'm leaving for the States on the next steamer to Californ-i-ay. I have prospects, Edwin," she added with confidence, offering him a curtsy. "I may be on the Barbary Coast at first, but I will climb Nob Hill and no mistake. Perhaps I will send you a penny postal card, my blue boy."

She reached out her hand toward his cheek, but stopped as hoof beats neared. Her escort held the cab door. His narrow wolverine eyes gave Edwin a suspicious leer. He seemed about thirty, carrying an ivory-handled cane. A spindly beard didn't add dignity, nor did the spectacles with smoked lenses. The man pulled a cheroot from his pocket in leisurely fashion, then lit it with a wooden match struck on his thumbnail.

That postal card never came, and after five years of hard laboring on land and sea, Edwin had been nine more years with the police, rising from the ranks thanks to his pluck and initiative.

Now his mother had to be told. Hers was a spirit as independent as Vicky's, merely born in a better place. Naomi had been the only daughter in a wealthy family in Montreal. Martin and Sarah Grossman had hoped she'd marry one of the Jewish businessmen Martin brought around. After a year studying art at the Sorbonne, Naomi had returned briefly only to fall hard for a bootstrap French Canadian lawyer with a magnetic smile. He'd helped her out of a snowbank during a blizzard, and they hadn't made it home until midnight. Despite their pleas, the wedding took place a "respectable" year later.

Serge DesRosiers had been left on the doorstep of an orphanage in the Gaspé. A kind priest recognizing talent had seen that he got a thorough Jesuit education and a working scholarship to law school. By the age of twenty-six, Serge had made a name for himself.

Edwin had dim childhood memories of a rich butter *kuchen* and his grandfather's beard tickling his chin. There was Shabbat, the lighting of the candles, touching the *mezuzah* on the door. Then the Panic of 1873 had wiped out much of the Grossmans' investments in railroad speculation, and though Jews were a rare commodity in Victoria, Serge and Naomi agreed that more opportunities lay west. Their "mixed" marriage might raise fewer eyebrows in the new empire.

Making a fortune was not a priority. Unable to resist someone in trouble, Serge had more *pro bono* clients than those who paid, and the brick home on Michigan Street ended their upward mobility. As funds dwindled, their cook and housekeeper left. Edwin's extra tutoring ceased in addition to thoughts of law school. Creditors began rapping at the door. Then one day shortly after Edwin's thirteenth birthday, he had found his father shot in the temple in his office on Yates Street, a pistol on his desk. *Je suis désolé,* the scrawled note said. Naomi had always joked about Serge's poor penmanship, but this was nearly unreadable, according to the attending doctor, more proof of his mental distress. For a while they subsisted on the sale of the house and furniture, then moved to a boarding house. Desperate and ashamed at the privation, Edwin had gone north to find manual labor to help his mother survive. Naomi's nudes, his eventual job on the force, and the generosity of a friend had earned them a mortgage on the small row house.

Number 55 was in the middle of a row of two-story brick workingmen's houses from the 1880s. Downstairs were a parlor, kitchen, and dining room, with three bedrooms and a bathroom above. Rudimentary plumbing in an enclosed box ran up the outside of the house and connected to the new sewer and water system. The houses were multicolored, trimmed with white, some with a bay window. Back on the long narrow lot, their man Wong had his garden next to the old privy for his use.

A gaslight in the hall flickered in feeble welcome, but Edwin didn't tiptoe. His mother rarely went to bed before three or got up before noon. That left the bright afternoon for her painting.

As he turned the latch, he heard a squeaky bark upstairs: Gladdy, short for Gladstone, their spoiled King Charles spaniel. Edwin would have preferred an Alsatian, a man's dog, anything but this useless, flat-faced toy. He left his hat and coat on the hall tree and his boots on the mat.

His ghostly image scowled at him from the large hall mirror and the wooden compartment of the new telephone gave silent reproach. Only hours ago, shortly after dinner, he had held the receiver to his ear, surprised at the late call. Then the world had turned upside down on Belleville Street. Vicky gone. How could he break the news to Naomi? If by a miracle she was sleeping, he wouldn't have to tell her until late tomorrow. By then he could cushion the sad news.

"Is that you, darling?" a gravelly voice called. An apparition floated onto the landing in a blue silk gown trimmed with rabbit. At a statuesque five-ten, his mother carried a few extra pounds with a regal bearing. "I heard the telephone hours ago and then the door shut. What kept you out so late? Are you newly enamored of some young lady, planning to age me by making me a grandmother?"

"Sorry. I was . . . gone longer than I'd thought I'd be." While his mother spent windfall dollars on caviar and champagne, he had inherited his seriousness and frugality from his father. Someone had to take charge. Dilettantes didn't pay the bills.

"You worked regular hours when you were a constable and looked so handsome in that uniform. I'm not sure I like this change even if you're paid more, which heaven knows makes our life more comfortable. Are you hungry? There are a few morsels in the icebox." For dinner, they'd had one of Wong's concoctions. Rice and vegetables with a trace of meat, usually leftovers, which helped their budget. In Cantonese it was called *tsap seui,* or "miscellaneous scraps."

He straightened his shoulders to ease a stress cramp in his taut back. No use postponing the inevitable. Naomi could see through any man. If anyone had loved Vicky as he did, it was his mother. "There is something I need to tell you. Why not come down here to the—"

"Nonsense. The fire's out by now. It's warmer in my room." She waved him up. "I'll pour you a brandy. All that dreary rain. I miss Montreal winters. Isn't that strange? Speeding along in a sleigh with the horse bells jingling. Hot chocolate and toast and cheese on a long fork. Do you remember doing that with your *zayde*? You caught his beard on fire."

He removed his scarf and smoothed back his hair with his hand. Coal-black corkscrews and thick as black lamb's wool—he couldn't tame it into the slickly parted modern style, even with pomade. He marched slowly up the steep, narrow stairs, remembering how he had once been mesmerized following Vicky's inviting hips as she entered Naomi's studio. Questions tormented him. Where was her cloak? How long had she been back? Did she know her killer? What was the motive? Blanks to be filled in a report now took an agonizing personal turn.

In her boudoir, which harbored what small luxury remained from her marriage, Naomi was reclining in an overstuffed pasha chair, her long legs on a brocaded ottoman. A tiger skin, a present from a Punjab rajah visiting Montreal, lay at her feet. "He promised me that he'd never shoot another," she had said.

"Animals should run free." The floor was covered with a threadbare Persian carpet. Heavy, swagged brocade curtains with patches shut out the cold.

Relieved of watchdog duty, Gladdy snored on the bed on a plump velvet initialed cushion, expelling pungent farts from too many sweetmeats. His rhinestone collar reflected the gaslight. Naomi's lush titian hair, tinged with gray at the temples despite the monthly henna rinse, was braided for the night and coiled down the side of her aristocratic neck. A wispy cloud of Russian tobacco floated from the Sobranie in her ivory holder, sent from Old Bond Street in London by another former flame.

"It's been a bad night, Mother." He traced a finger along the row of his father's law books. Naomi devoted a corner of her room to her husband.

"Let me guess. Your first murder. Is that what's bothering you so much? You always get so involved with your profession. Just like your father. 'But it's such an interesting case, Naomi. And who will help if I don't? They'll pay when they can.' That was always his excuse. But don't hold back. I'm a woman of the world. Use me as your sounding board like he did." She leaned forward expectantly and flashed proud eyes at her son.

Another faint sweet smell met his nostrils, but he'd leave that alone for now. A fresh sandalwood incense stick had been lit. A brass statue of the jovial and tubby Laughing God sat on the dresser next to a blue glass Kwan Yin and a precious medieval triptych, a miniature altar, all saved with her tears from the auctioneer's gavel. "The artistic spirit needs food as much as the belly," she'd say.

Pouring himself a drink from the sideboard decanter, he took a seat in an armchair by the smoldering coal fire in the grate. Next to the stove hung a pair of bellows along with a shovel and poker. A handsome portrait of Serge in his barrister's robes and wig held pride of place over the mantel. "Father and I serve justice in a different way." Odd, he thought, that he'd lived over half of his life without him. And yet Serge was as corporeal as the woman who faced him, waiting for his reply with a mild crease on her ivory brow. Naomi hated delays, but he was in no mood to start.

"You look so troubled, Edwin."

He took a large gulp of brandy and felt the warmth infuse his core. It was tempting to obliterate his memories, but he needed a clear head. Still, his thoughts whirled.

"I'm guessing that a woman was involved. *Quelle horreur.* Another of those pathetic streetwalkers assaulted? How else are they to make their living? The world will never be free of men's lust and women's accommodations. It's the world's oldest profession and it ought to be legalized and regulated for health and safety, not run by bribes. Everyone knows the police get their *gelt* by turning a blind eye. You told me that yourself."

He gave her a slight bow of the head. "I don't know how else to say it. Victoria Crosse is dead. She was found by the Parliament buildings. I saw her. There's no mistake."

"Vic . . ." Her voice trailed off. Stillness filled the room. Naomi stiffened, then she slumped like a gallant oryx pierced by a fatal arrow. She hugged the shawl closer. "That's impossible. If she'd returned, she'd have come to see me. She was almost like a daughter."

"She can't have been back long. I'll be setting the information net beginning tomorrow."

She gave a small moan and half turned. The ebony bust of Nefertiti on the table shadowed her profile. "So young, so alive. That spirit."

He shook his head. This was harder than he'd thought. He drained his glass, squeezing his eyes shut at the burn down his throat.

"A daughter," Naomi repeated in hushed tones.

And to me, he thought? Another kind would have gone looking for her, starting in San Francisco. But he had had duties, and he'd needed to go north to work. Suppose he'd seen her here weeks ago? What would his feelings have been with her on the other side of the law?

"Edwin, I must know what happened. An accident? Was she run down by a carriage? Not a fire, surely. Her beautiful skin." Brick and stone were replacing wood after every blaze, but the town remained a tinderbox. The clang of the pumper engine chilled for a reason. "Cholera or influenza?"

He spread his large hands. "This is all I know, Mother. It happened down on Belleville in the park. Sometime after dark. She was strangled with a common black stocking. Similar to the other attacks."

"Worse and worse. And you saw the body. What a shock for you." Smoke dribbled from her lips.

He tried a manful shrug he little felt. "She was untouched for the most part. She could have been sleeping."

"A small mercy. Then it was fast." Naomi sat up and crushed the butt into an abalone shell. "Was there a witness? Has anyone been arrested?"

"At that time of night? Of course not. We've only begun the investigation. As for her profession, you know the risks and so did she. Someday it was bound—"

He stopped abruptly when his mother stood and marched toward him, fire in her emerald eyes and nostrils flaring. Her hands set on her hips in defiance. "Don't play the self-righteous prig with me. Women have to do what they have to do. It was your great luck to have been born a man. You should be down on your knees to quixotic fortune for that gift."

He looked up. "Forgive me. That wasn't my intent. I'm not judging her."

"Aren't you? Victoria was no common tramp. She was always

a lady and she didn't deserve this, your heartless sermons aside." Naomi flung herself back on the chaise, and waved a slender hand, the nail beds never quite free of paint. "So she took the occasional favor from men. A bracelet. A stole. Don't be provincial. Rich men love to give things to beautiful women. It's their character . . . and their pleasure." Her gaze fell upon a ruby ring on her finger. It had appeared suddenly after she attended a performance of *Lohengrin* in Vancouver.

They turned toward the portrait on the wall over her dressing table. Victoria was reclining like an odalisque, one leg demurely crossed to conceal her pubis. Satiny cushions and swaths of silk and tulle surrounded her, and Naomi's previous King Charles spaniel, Dizzy, slept at her feet. She was lowering a ripe July cherry into her mouth, a symphony of pinks. Naomi used to say, "Not as risqué as Courbet, of course. Even I wouldn't put his *Origin of the World* in my drawing room. The perspective is a rich joke. The delta and the alpha and the omega."

Brandy was blurring the edges, but his bones sagged under the weariness of a long day. "Tell me everything you knew about her. Clear your mind and think. Where was she living? The Cadogan Hotel burned a few years ago." He paused. "Her personal life will figure. This was no random killing. That doesn't happen here to women as worldly wise as she was."

Naomi's face softened, and a tear glinted in her eye. She gave a shaky yawn, then fluttered her eyelids. "I'm far too upset. We can speak of it at breakfast. My eyes will look like black holes tomorrow."

He stood and put his glass on a table. His desk would be waiting when the sun came up. Constables would be displaced to gather information. He pushed on. "She was born here, you told me. Some of her friends might still be around. And her family. Out of town as I recall. Where?" He needed to close his eyes in a dark and silent room, even if he didn't sleep.

Silence greeted him.

"Breakfast for you will probably be noon, Mother. Why can't we talk now?"

"Because I've been . . . my head's in a muddle. I simply can't, Edwin." She gave the chaise a pound with her strong little fist. "How callous you are. Sometimes you don't seem to be . . . your father's son."

Edwin admired her spunk. She was fighting back against her grief. "Fine, then. By the end of tomorrow I may know more. Jones promised fast work. He's as good as his word." Did she know that he was speaking about an autopsy? That part of his job she never probed.

"I'm not that ignorant about the process. Now I *won't* get to sleep. Ripping her to pieces. Like they did to your father just because he . . . Robbed him of his dignity, the last valuable he had. *'Az dos harts iz ful, geyen di oygn iber,'* Mama said. When the heart is full, the eyes overflow." She blinked back tears.

"I'll need your help. We both . . . cared for her. Who else will help her rest in peace?" he whispered, getting up to hand her a handkerchief.

"Sorry I lost my temper. You're right about putting our heads together." She reached up to lower the gaslight, leaving them in shadow. "Perhaps it was a woman who killed her. It wouldn't be the first time." Not all females were frail flowers with impeccable ethics. Some had the muscles of a washerwoman and the spirit of a Tasmanian devil.

Now there was a different perspective. As he left the room and shut the door behind him, he heard the sobs start. Models came and went, but Vicky's pictures sold more than any others. Naomi painted her from memory now, frozen at twenty. She liked few women. Queen bees never did. Did she see part of herself in the young girl?

In the bathroom, he gave his face a quick splash, then toweled off and went to his room. Reflected in the shiny brass headboard, a bright full moon was silvering the edges of the clouds. Hadn't the other two attacks come at the same time of the month? Moon, lunatic, a connection predating Bedlam itself. He'd talked with enough medical staff to know that the concept was no superstition.

Down the block, a time-challenged rooster crowed. Fit only for the pot, that one, Edwin mused. Cold sweat streaked down his back as he undressed and climbed beneath the sheets. Prone to tossing and turning as he was, nightshirts wrapped him like a shroud and barbaric wool union suits itched. So he slept in a silk singlet and silk drawers that reached half way down his thighs.

It was never hot here, even in summer droughts. The Japanese current brought a Three Bears perfect-porridge climate to Vancouver Island. In its mad march from being a Hudson's Bay Company post to a gold-rush portal to the capital of Canada's newest province in 1871, the city of Victoria had grown up. And that meant crime. Edwin gripped the bars behind him until his hands ached for release. As the dark corners of his mind merged in the middle and brought him peace, he whispered, "My darling Vicky, I'll see your killer hanged in Bastion Square."

# CHAPTER THREE

Edwin shook himself out of his feather bed, rubbing at a neck stiff from a restless night, awakening on the hour. The ship's clock from his father's old office read seven o'clock. Was this what it was like to turn thirty? At the timber camps, he had caroused until midnight and greeted dawn by ignoring the buzz of a hangover.

He rubbed gritty sleep from his eyes, stretched, and dropped his feet onto the cold floorboards. A partial splash in the bathroom sink revived him. Attacking his stubborn curly black hair with a stiff brush, he thought how much his life had changed. When he'd been a laborer or a beat constable, his days were laid out by others. Now he faced unpredictability and challenge. As a corporal, he had attended two murder cases. A husband had stabbed his unfaithful wife. Two drunken bluejackets had quarreled over a wager. One had used a belaying pin to stove in the welsher's head, then pushed him off the docks. Within an hour, both killers were in a cell. This case would not be the same.

He had an uneasy feeling about Victoria's death. A lack of witnesses and her questionable social status might send her case into a dusty file cabinet filled with records of the hapless poor, even their corpses unclaimed. Would the *Daily Colonist* milk the story American-style to boost circulation? Doubtful. The public's thirst for sordid affairs went unslaked in the staid capital. To shake things up, he might need to have a wee word with Liam O'Neill.

O'Neill had come from the Seattle papers to make a splash in a smaller pond. Edwin admired his fearless commitment to the truth. O'Neill had broken a story on a gold-mining scam that had fleeced more than twenty island investors. A flimflam man had bribed an old prospector to salt an area around Lake Cowichan, then spread the word to sell thousands of shares. The tippling reporter had turned up the fact that the man had tried this scam before on the Olympic Peninsula. The police had made a quick arrest in Duncan. Sometimes reporters had the resources and nerve to do what the police couldn't.

Edwin put on a clean shirt, celluloid collar and cuffs, a vest, and then his discreet gray suit. Instead of the long, formal coats from his father's day, he favored the new look. A maroon silk cravat was carefully tied at his neck. Looking good but not ostentatious was important.

Wong had sewn up a small rip in his shirttail. When did the man ever sleep? His corner in the low-ceilinged basement was tidy and warm beside the coal and provisions. A secondhand cabinet and orange crate held his few possessions. Twenty dollars a month were generous wages, and Naomi, loving her evening soirees, gave him the entire weekend off from Saturday noon.

Like most Chinese, Wong had crossed the ocean to climb the Mountain of Gold, only to find himself working as a servant. His wife and son lived with his parents on a farm near Nanking. The earnest look in his eyes promised that someday he would bring them over. Would there be another mouth or two to feed when they arrived? That happened.

One child had been enough for Naomi. Serge, on the other hand, was always seeking a game of catch or mumblety peg, putting his boy on his lap to read the news together or quizzing him on Latin legal terms. Naomi confined herself to an occasional pat on the back. "Edwin, don't clutch me," she would say, straightening her dress or her hair when he sought to give her a toddler's hug. She was not a demonstrative woman. A baby was more a requirement than an occupation. Nevertheless, her love ran deep. As for his own inclinations, Edwin had no time to indulge whatever paternal instincts might lie in his heart.

Edwin preferred not to sit alone at the ornate dining room table with the credenza, china cabinet, and silver candelabra. The kitchen was the coziest room. Wong was especially proud of the Nugget nickel-plated woodstove and the coal gas–fed water heater. To one side was a Hoosier Special cabinet with a flour bin and niches for eggs, beaters, and graters. At an oilcloth-covered table in the corner, Wong ladled out steaming oatmeal, followed by sunny-side-up eggs and crisp bacon on a plate from the warming oven. Fresh coffee bubbled in the pot. Wong rarely spoke, coming and going in padded slippers like an agreeable ghost. His English was improving. This morning he had circled in pencil a notice for coal. Another uncircled ad stated, "White labor only employed." Having felt the double sting toward French Canadians and Jews, Edwin had a fellow feeling for the man.

Wong wore dark pantaloons and a plain, collarless blue-cotton shirt. His pigtail originated with the Mandarins, the masters who rode with the "reins," and the caste tradition persisted in Canada. The thin white cotton gloves were possibly a custom from earlier service. He stood quietly, hands folded in front of him. An indefinable twitch on the broad Oriental face suggested that his employer needed a shave.

Edwin scratched at his stubble. "I'll be getting a shave downtown. Our family reputation is safe." A hot towel with his feet up and a relaxing scalp massage would give him a calm, reflective start.

Like a buzzing hive, the station would be restless about the murder. Twelve precious hours had passed. Everyone knew about the critical nature of the first few days in a murder case. The spotlight would be on Edwin and the way he commanded his "troops." To his superiors, however, laying charges and a successful outcome was more important than actual guilt or innocence.

Toast accompanied a large pot of lemon marmalade. Edwin took a slice of "boughten" bread from the silver rack to sop up the egg yolk. Wong was a cook, not a baker.

Setting down his serviette after finishing, Edwin left the kitchen. He passed the elephant-foot umbrella stand in the hall, put on his gleaming boots and coat, and headed out the door, hoping to outrun a shower. After his years pounding a beat under a rubberized cloak, he found bumbershoots effete.

The sky was gray and glowering, as if in mourning for Vicky. Streets were mud from November to April, punishment for a mild climate in the temperate rainforest. Life in this damp was one long process of getting warm and staying warm. Moss grew on anything horizontal. Mildew wasn't as particular. Every ten years, Victoria got a blizzard of several feet to remind it that the island was part of Canada.

The postman was beginning his rounds, riding a bicycle, the latest fad. He zigged and zagged, pulling up to each box and ringing his bell for punctuation. Edwin turned right on Cormorant and walked at a brisk pace to Douglas, where he made a left. At a striped pole, he entered Sulo's Barber Shop, happy to find the place empty. He saluted the balding proprietor, hung up his coat, and took a seat in the swiveling chair.

"Just a shave. Trim the moustache, too, please."

"Heard about that doxy killed last night." A white sheet snapped over him, and a hot towel from the steamer spread comfort over his face. Sulo began stropping his razor with a *whap whap whap,* as Serge had done. On one occasion when Edwin had lied about taking a neighbor's horse for a ride, Serge's leather had pinked his bottom. Naomi had flown into a fury in opposition to any corporal punishment.

Sulo continued in the void of silence. "Blind Jake told me as I went by his corner. Do you think we have a West Coast Ripper on our hands, Your Honor?"

Nothing could beat the urban telegraph. It hurt Edwin that they had labeled Vicky a whore already. Because she wasn't from the upper classes? Because they assumed every woman out alone at night was a harlot? At least the stocking detail hadn't made the news. Edwin's muffled reply caused Sulo to whip off the towel and begin soaping with aplomb. "Don't take this the wrong way, but folks are saying the police don't know their arses from a hole in the ground. Present company excepted, of course."

"Is that so?" Edwin knew that the Finn liked his jokes, but he was in no mood this morning, not with the indelible picture of Vicky cooling on the mortuary table. With a taste of soap from the words he had risked, he shifted.

"Hold still, man! Do you want your throat cut like Sweeney Todd's customers?" Squinting over work he could do with his eyes closed, Sulo began edging the sharp blade down the sides of Edwin's cheeks and onto his throat like a lover's deadly kiss. Now and then he cleared the lather, and Edwin swallowed, bouncing his Adam's apple. Finally Sulo used miniature scissors for the trim, then stood back with a proprietorial assessment.

"You do look a treat. The ladies will love that baby-smooth face. At least for the next four hours. Oh, the hearts you will break." He started whistling "After the Ball."

Edwin merely smiled at the compliment. It was common gossip that Sulo had a yen for adolescent males. Every other year there was a new helper sweeping up. Then the young man would be seen in a decent suit and sent on his way with a ten-dollar U.S. gold piece. Probably a lot kinder than an orphanage. And they were never younger than fifteen. The poor were on their own at that age.

Before Edwin could reply, Sulo applied a trace of Russian bear-grease pomade, combed his hair with a "tsk" for the stubborn curls, and then slapped his cheeks with a powerful lilac aftershave that made Edwin sneeze. "There's talk about getting up a posse to patrol the streets, keep things safe for our women."

"A posse. Christ. That's a damn stupid idea, and you tell them so. This isn't Tombstone," Edwin replied, his voice rising. The romantic wild American West captured the imagination. Every poker game had a joke about a dead man's hand.

Sulo nodded vigorously, his wattles jiggling. "The pretty penny we pays in property taxes and that fancy mayor's palace downtown leave you wondering."

Hoping that the perfume would dissipate outside, Edwin added a tip to the quarter. Sulo often had good information. But a gang of vigilantes? Normally Edwin didn't even carry his Colt unless he was serving a warrant. This was the land of peace, order, and good government.

The Victoria Metropolitan Police, the oldest local force west of the Great Lakes, began life as Victoria Voltigeurs in the 1850s, mostly Metis accompanying the Royal Navy expeditions. The force now numbered over thirty, including clerks, jailers, and one matron. Henry Sheppard was chief of police.

As raindrops pocked his hat, Edwin welcomed the wooden sidewalks with their overhang shelter. The rain wasn't sideways . . . yet. Edwin bought a *Daily Colonist* from the boy on the corner of Douglas and Pandora, giving him a generous five cents, still thinking of little Ben. The eight-page paper had been founded in 1858 by the eccentric Amor de Cosmos, provincial and national legislator and second premier.

The Bastion Square armory had sufficed as the first jail and government building. Then came the city hall, under construction since 1878 in John Teague's Second Empire style. With three distinct facades and a tall clock tower, the red brick building was hard to miss, but to some, it was "an ornamental abortion." Pigeons cresting on the mansard roof got a prime view to snag a peanut from the boardwalk.

Edwin entered, heading for the Police Department. A gilded portrait of the jowly old queen glowered from the wall, like the Hudson's Bay Company's unofficial motto: "Here Before Christ." On the coinage she seemed to have aged from a girl to a matron to a portly old woman with no legs. He passed by the chief clerk with a wave, through the "barnyard" where the constables and corporals were located, and went straight to his new office with a frosted glass door. The door sign, *Edwin Des-Rosiers, Detective Sergeant,* had filled him with pride and he had lingered to trace the letters as soon as they dried. Now he was charged with anger and, even worse, self-doubt.

He hung up his overcoat and hat on the rack and sat at a battered oak desk covered with a pristine green blotter. An array of pencils and a pen knife for sharpening sat at the ready, as did an inkwell, gold-filled fountain pen, and a date stamp. A wire tray held his latest business, the dreaded paperwork only Chief Sheppard worshipped. "An army travels on its stomach, gentlemen, but good police work steams along on thorough doc-u-mentation."

An hour later, in the drift of Craven pipe tobacco, Reggie Thirkstan eased through the door, stepping as if on eggshells. His thinning caramel hair was brushed back with oil. Dark pouches under his eyes and an uneven shave testified to another late night. He had taken to chewing Tutti Frutti gum to sweeten his breath after his cheroots and mid-morning pick-me-ups.

Wearing a striped shirt and suspenders over his trousers, carrying his coat over his arm, Reggie was the very picture of a dissolute Gibson-model man.

"Say, Rozzer, old chap, haven't got a drop I can borrow, have you? Hair of the dog." Reggie rubbed his temples and gave a theatrical eye roll. He had learned the slang term for a police officer from his undergraduate studies in England. "Rozzer" might have come from Rosseretario (the Venetian count upon whose ideas Robert Peel founded his groundbreaking police force). To Edwin it was better than some French Canadian slurs, and admittedly, it fit his name.

Edwin gave him a shrug. "Myers keeps a bottle of port for his lumbago. Try him."

"I've got a head like a poisoned pup. Up late playing billiards with the lads. Damn Cardinal took me for thirty dollars. If the Pater knew . . ."

Flipping his jacket onto the rack, he emptied a spoon of Eno's Fruit Salts into a glass of water from the office pitcher, and with a bleary eye, watched it fizz. Then he drank it, tapped his chest, and burped. Twenty-five-year-old Reggie had been "sent down" from Cambridge during his third term and had been dispatched as punishment to manage a rubber plantation in Malaya. When he fathered half-native twins, he was packed back to Victoria where his family could keep an eye on him. His father the councilman had gotten him a job to "shape him up," insisting that Reggie skip the lower ranks on the basis of his "education." He'd been appointed only a month ago, and Edwin had been designated as his mentor and officemate, losing a straw draw.

"I heard about that murder in the park. So you're in charge, are you? Any progress?" While Edwin was making a "fair" copy of his previous night's report, Reggie plonked himself into a chair. He dumped his pipe dottle into a potted violet on the windowsill and took up his pouch and tamper, his manicured hands shaking.

"We know her name, not much more."

Reggie whispered, " 'Who was her sister, who was her brother, had she a father, had she a mother?' "

"Did you make that up? It's very bad." Reggie often burst into verse, having "read" literature at Corpus Christi College. Edwin imagined that he read only the racing form. To relax, Reggie often shuffled a pack of French playing cards, marked discreetly, counting on the pictures to distract the other players.

" 'Fatherly, motherly, sisterly, brotherly, take her up tenderly, treat her with care.' Thomas Hood. They're finding a body in the poem. How's that for real life? In his 'Poetic Principles,' Poe called it the 'truest' poem ever written. Not like that pap from Wordsworth, tra la the daffodils." From his bookshelf he pulled a leather volume and extended it.

Edwin waved it off. "Get serious, you fool. Her name was Victoria Crosse. This is real life, not a damned poem."

Reggie colored and stood up, ash dropping onto his tight fawn trousers. Georgian breeches perfect for showing off his legs and family jewels would have pleased him more. He rubbed at the dark marks. "Bloody hell. I just wore these for the first time today. Savile Row."

"Why so nervous? Did you know Miss Crosse?"

"I've . . . heard of her. Can't say just where at the moment. The Union Club perhaps. The usual braggarts in their cups." He coughed almost demurely. "I still kick over the traces for a fortnightly lark. My altar date with Carrie's coming up."

"Miss Crosse was a bit old for your tastes. Thirty-five." For a moment, Edwin wondered if Reggie was lying about knowing her, but he was a very transparent fibber. Chances were that his nerves were raw from the boozefest.

"True enough. I like my cherries ripe, not fallen from the tree." He shifted a bit. "Before diving into the marriage bed, I need a date with the doctor to check out the old winkle. There's a bit of a . . . well, never mind. As for your Victoria, once I've been into the sauce, every cat looks alike in the dark. Some even improve, as you can ima—"

"I'm reaching the end of my tether with you, Thirkstan. Many years ago, she was a . . . friend of my family." Edwin's sharply defined dark eyebrows had their own stormy language. "She came back to town only recently, so I doubt you've met her."

Reggie held up his hands in surrender. "I apologize. I didn't know this was personal. That's different. But why would the boss give you the case, then?"

Edwin kept mum. He didn't want any suppositions from Reggie as to why he was upset. His past with Vicky would disqualify him from pursuing the case, and he wanted her killer to pay. "I met her a few times. That's all. My mother knew her professionally. And I'd prefer that you kept quiet about the connection, understand? Solving the case is very important to me."

"Sure, Rozzer. Mum's the word." Reggie fingered the fabric of Edwin's coat on the rack. "Hello, what's this? Nice stuff. Where did you get it? Not in this provincial backwater, I'll warrant. San Francisco?"

"London. Aquascutum. The company designed coats for Crimean War officers. Perfect for our eternal rains." His mother had ordered the coat as a birthday present. She liked to see him look good and flattered herself that despite their difference in hair color, one myopic geezer at a concert had thought that they were brother and sister.

"The Big Smoke, eh? Pater might send me and Carrie over to make the rounds of the superannuated relatives at Christmas. Sort of a late honeymoon. He thinks he can get me a two-month leave. I'll have to bring one back." He crossed his legs and smacked one knee. "A coat, I mean, not a relative."

A muscle in Edwin's jaw twitched. *What kind of pull did*

*Reggie's father have? Commenting would only make him look petty.*
"So who at your Union Club might know something about
her?"

"It could be one of a dozen wags. You know how fellows
bandy about girls' names. Half the time it's all baloney. How
did the poor creature die? Not stabbed, I hope." He gave a the-
atric shudder.

"She was strangled with a stocking. Needless to say, I mean,
of course, we haven't released that detail." Summoning these
memories made his throat constrict so that the words tumbled
upon themselves for want of breath.

"I say. Do you expect it's the same as grabbed those two
other dollies? Just moved up a notch?" He reached for his newly
translated copy of Krafft-Ebing's *Psychopathia Sexualis* and
started thumbing through, wiggling his eyebrows at places he
had underlined. "Fetishism. That's the ticket. Whooo hooo. Using a stocking could signify that—"

"Or it could just be a damn stocking. As for the connection,
Belleville Street is several blocks away. For strolling and picnics,
not hunting for paid female company."

Reggie tore himself away from the chapter and tapped his
pencil on his hand. "The first two weren't quite in the same
class, were they? Eales said your girl was dressed well. I passed
him on the way in."

Mamie Blake and Rosie Rochette were overblown, cut-rate
whores who plied the trade around the wharves. They were
thirty pushing sixty, and sported a black eye every other week.
In dark and stinking alleys they delivered ten-cent knee
tremblers in a metropolitan tradition dating back to Rome.
"Victoria was no common streetwalker. She posed for my
mother and may have had rich . . . clients. That was fifteen
years ago. Apparently she went to the U.S., following prospects.
When we find why she came back, we'll know more. Soon as I

got in, I telegraphed San Francisco to see if they had a record on her. No word as yet."

"A good-looker, eh? Posed for your mother? Wish mine had the same hobby. If the girl had married some old plute for his dough, she'd have been rolling in the proverbial and standing to inherit. I knew one Russian doll who—"

"We have no reason to believe that she married. I told you to take this seriously. You're wasting time with this speculation. Do you want this jackass attitude to appear on your monthly report?" He pounded the table with his fist.

"Sometimes, you are such a stiff." Reggie pulled a hand over his face and changed expressions like the masks of comedy and tragedy. "No more. I promise. What else? I'm all ears."

"What are those marks on your hands? It can't be a work injury since you do none."

"I tried to move Carrie's cat off my coat. Damnable beast." Reggie gave a nervous laugh. "So in sum, that's all you have to go on?"

"If Vicky had a handbag, it was taken. We have no idea where she was living. The first order will be to find any contacts, now or in the past. Jones may come up with something helpful regarding place of death. I'm heading out for the autopsy later."

Reggie's elbow knocked over a picture of his fiancé, the only item on his desk other than a dish of toffees and a copy of *Blackwood's*. "Oopsy daisy." He gave the picture a loud kiss and righted it.

"How *is* Carrie, the chosen one?" Carrie Palmer's father owned provisioning stores in Victoria and Vancouver. Plans had been made for an elaborate wedding at Craigdarroch Castle. The Thirkstans had powerful friends in government and business.

Reggie put his hands over his ears. "God, what a tongue on her. Can she slam a man. In private, of course, thank heaven.

I'll be as short as Rumpelstiltskin by the time we've been married five years. And all the ankle biters scrabbling on the carpets and drooling on my suits. Still, Pater had to put up with Mater and her mater as well. Oh, my aching balls."

"Knock knock," said a voice as the door opened. The matron came in with a Brown Betty of tea and two cups, along with a small plate of unusual biscuits. "Thought you could do with a bit of this. Thanks for the gift, Reginald. The tea tin is a beauty. I'll keep it for special." The older woman, wearing a plain navy dress similar to a housekeeper's costume, poured for both men.

"You make a heavenly cuppa, loveliest Eliza," Reggie said, flashing a gleaming smile as she fluttered her lashes. Matron Elizabeth Crawford, Irish, unmarried at forty and unconcerned, was the only female officer. Women were rare at the holding cells, mostly drunk and disorderly, but she handled them with gentleness and tact. More than once she had taken them home, cleaned them up, and helped them find respectable positions.

The aroma of bergamot floated in the steam. "A trifle strong for morning, Reggie, but I know what you were probably up to last night, you rascal." She passed the biscuits. "Try one of these. My da brought them all the way from Philadelphia on the train."

Touching his stomach, Reggie turned paler, but Edwin took one of the square pieces of golden cookie. "Jam inside. That *is* different."

"They're called Fig Newtons. Gives an old recipe a fancy touch. Wonder if they'll catch on here."

When she had left, Reggie managed half a cup of tea, inhaling the steam like a tonic. He coughed loudly into a snowy handkerchief embroidered with his initials, then pounded his chest theatrically. "This catarrh will be the death of me."

"Stick to cigars. And don't inhale like you do with those coffin nails."

Reggie took his German silver hunter watch out of its fob pocket and flipped the lid. "How about you do the honors for the both of us with Jones? Not sure I have the stomach for it. Anyway, I'm due at the wine merchant's to check on the wedding order. We're getting a special shipment of Château Margaux 1887 that came through the Panama Canal, and I'll need to sample it in my usual meticulous oenophile fashion. The old man spent a bundle of dough."

"I'll have some chores for you when you return. Don't be holding up the wall by then."

Reggie slapped Edwin on the back. "You're a brick, old chum."

"Chump is more like it." As Reggie left, Edwin buried himself in paperwork, his pen scratching in determination. He blotted his work carefully and inspected it. Reggie was about as much use as tits on a bull. He wouldn't last long. As soon as he was married, his unsuspecting in-laws would bring him into the business. Father Thirkstan entrusted the family firm to Reggie's older brothers, paragons of commerce and character with four perfect children each already.

Near noon, Edwin grabbed a bite at the Grotto in Trounce Alley, a narrow pedestrian street between Broad and Government. For the price of a ten-cent glass of beer, plain food was complimentary. In the United States, the baseball season was under way, and as many men were talking about the New York Giants and Yankees as they were the cricket match results.

As he munched his ham sandwich and pickle, three businessmen at the next table were arguing politics and the economy. Fallout from the Panic of 1893 and its twenty percent unemployment rate still haunted investors. Who would have thought that the Philadelphia and Reading Railroad would go belly up? People were selling stocks to buy gold-backed securities. The conservative monetary standards of the Populist presidential candidate Bryan were worrying the establishment. Things weren't as bad in Canada, but when the sleeping elephant rolled over, life got tricky for the mouse.

After paying a visit to the lavatory, Edwin walked to Fort Street. At his spot near the Masonic Hall, Blind Jake was playing his ocarina, his white cane beside him and a tin cup with change on the edge of the burlap mat. Edwin dropped in a dime. Despite his handicap from a horse kick as a child, Jake had a finger on the pulse of the city. Not much happened that didn't reach him. There was a sharp brain behind those dark glasses. "Your health, Jake."

"Afternoon, Mr. Edwin." Jake recognized any voice from twenty feet and gave a snappy salute.

"Can you keep an ear for information about the woman killed over by the Gorge last night? And does the name Abbott mean anything?"

"Used to be a longshoreman called Abbott at the outer wharves. I'll ask around. Poor sparrow to go that way. I had a little sister once who . . ." His voice trickled off in bittersweet memories.

With scarcely enough time to check on the lead from Jake and still make the appointment with Jones, Edwin caught the streetcar. When the trolleys had arrived in 1889, the first electric railway in the entire world was only six years old. With their electric lights, bells, and hand-painted advertising signs, they made a colorful addition. This car advertised Morris, the Tobacco Man. The National Electric Tramway and Lighting Company's lines ran downtown and out to the new Royal Jubilee Hospital, more recently out to Esquimalt over the Point Ellice span. Regular stopping places had been established, instead of letting the cars halt at will. Traffic kept to the left, a nod to England which flummoxed Yankee visitors.

A young man hopped on and ignored the conductor's fare

demand by shoving to the other end of the car. At Edwin's gruff "Hey, there!" the scoundrel jumped off a block later, jostling a woman in a dark dress. Her rich brown hair was loosely pinned, and she was carrying what looked like a large notebook or sketchbook. As she struggled to keep her feet in the crowded car, Edwin reached out a hand and steadied her, giving a sharp look to a chubby youth in a sailor suit. The boy stood with embarrassment. "M-mam," he stuttered, "take my seat."

The woman tossed Edwin a smile that galvanized his body. Was his face as flushed as it felt? He glanced at her hands, but the left one remained underneath the pad. He touched his hat brim in respect. Her intelligent gray eyes were the color of mourning doves. Who was she? Should he be bold enough to make conversation? Surely this happened all the time on public transport. Manners were changing quickly as the new century approached.

The car eased to a stop at Superior Street and she got off. Did she live around here? It had all happened so fast. Reggie wouldn't have let business interfere with pleasure. Edwin had no time to track her, nor would that be seemly. What an irony that he was heading for Vicky's autopsy.

# CHAPTER FOUR

The car lurched around St. Lawrence, and then Erie on the way to the outer wharves. Edwin finally located the foreman in a shanty by the water. A cheeky seal was bobbing for handouts, his whiskered face resembling a fat old rummy.

"Abbott? Old George? Damn me if he didn't take off for Sudbury out east six months ago to join his brother digging for nickel. Can't see the money in that. Can you? Godforsaken place in the damn bush. Freeze a man's pecker."

Nearly two o'clock. Edwin made his way to the morgue, located in the city market next to the fire hall and the terminus of the Victoria and Sidney Railway. Convenience had put it there. Cost had kept it.

The low ceilings made him duck his head, but he entered Dr. Jones's cold bailiwick with more than the usual trepidation. Bare electric lights hung at intervals illuminated without the cozy feeling of lamplight. Antiseptic warred with reek. Corpses were preserved by ice blocks before being taken to Hayward's Funeral Home, or one of the smaller parlors sprung up to deal with the increasing population. The embalming process, begun not long after the American Civil War, retarded death's metamorphosis, but not everyone could afford it. The poor quickly found pauper's graves. Burials in the pioneer cemetery downtown had ceased, and Royal Oak, overlooking the Georgia Strait, was getting the custom. In the Chinese Cemetery on Gonzales Bay, bones were retained in a crypt for decades before being sent "home."

Jones was puffing on a noxious cigar, tamping the ashes onto the rude wooden planks. "I was wondering if you might turn up. Poor sods like you who aren't used to this should skip lunch. I'm finished with the lady. Take a look?"

His last and most important appointment with Vicky. That her final moments above ground would be here appalled him. "What a hellhole, Tim. Why not move the facilities to the Jubilee? Having a morgue adjoining a public market is not only blasphemy but a health hazard."

"You're a man of sense, even if you're not a doctor. Look at the filthy wooden floor. It should be cement, all those bodily fluids and waste. Impossible to keep sanitary. And the water hookups are medieval. We need slate tables. Don't even ask me about the lack of soap and towels no matter how much I complain. Once before my diener was hired, I came in to find bloody rags piled in the corners. The other coroners have been screaming blue murder."

Edwin nodded, breathing through his mouth. "It's bad all right." At the spider-webbed window, young boys crowded for a look, tapping on the glass and giggling. "No privacy either."

"Get up there and put the fear of God in them, Edwin. You little bastards!" he yelled, waving his fist.

Back upstairs, Edwin threatened to take the boys to jail, then call on their mothers. They skipped away, one of them sticking out his tongue. "Dirty copper!"

As he reentered, Jones handed him a dingy cut lab coat with a suspicious smear. "We've been complaining for years. It may take a serious catastrophe to get the city to move. Maybe cholera." Some thirty years ago, a smallpox outbreak had struck fear into the island. Many Natives, especially susceptible, had been sent away from their reserves, spreading the disease throughout the province.

"Or a ship sinking with major casualties," Edwin said, forgetting to his regret Jones's tragedy. At last he forced his gaze down to the scarred table.

When Vicky had been young, shorter on curves, Edwin had glimpsed her posing nude for his mother, peeking through a keyhole, but even he was surprised at the lovely alabaster symmetry of her body, though pallor had overtaken the rosy blush. "You haven't made the incision."

"It's not always necessary. Frankly, I hated to mar this one. I can tell you one thing. She's given birth."

Edwin swallowed nervously. "How . . . how do you know?"

Jones tapped his temple. "Trade secret. Actually it's all in the pelvic bones. And would it matter if she were pregnant now?"

"It might if it were a motive," Edwin said. "Blackmail, for example. On the other hand, most unmarried girls would try to get rid of it." What had intervened in those fifteen years? How differently might things have turned out if . . . Did his voice betray more than a professional interest?

"I'll find out more when you leave. No sense letting you watch me during the gruesome part. It's different when you've known someone, even slightly." Jones manipulated the neck under the bruises. "Rigor's long gone."

Edwin swallowed, then reached up under his tight collar. A raw burn stung the back of his throat.

"Even without the bruises, it's easy to feel that the hyoid is fractured. See the straight line that the stocking left? When people hang themselves, the line moves up. Fools staging a 'suicide' forget that detail. And you can see where the thumbs were. Not that large. Some women have big hands. Imagine facing the person that you're strangling. That's a sick mind. Ice in the veins."

Edwin cast back his mind to the records. "That wasn't true in the other two cases. He came up from behind and looped the stocking over their heads. They blacked out. The sounds of carriages approaching could have frightened him off. Possibly those failures enraged him enough to kill full-face forward on the third attempt."

"Most likely they were pickled, easing their hard lives through the bottle. I'd venture our Victoria here never touched the stuff. Clear skin. No liver enlargement." He gave a slight smile. "My mother always said, 'Gin, gin, will make you sin. Lips that touch liquor will never touch mine.' Temperance lady, God rest her soul. Give her an ax and she would have been smashing saloons like Carrie Nation. She hectored my father to an early grave."

"My mother's a bit more liberal." *Especially when it comes to opium.* He wanted to leave, but that meant that he'd never see Victoria again.

"Upon my word. Looks like the lass fought back. See here." The coroner traced bruises on the forearms. "Defensive. But she was no match. There's a small window when your air's cut off. Most people panic. She might have had time for one hard kick."

"Vicky would have battled for her life. Did she scratch him? Women usually do."

Jones picked up a large magnifying glass and peered at the fingers. "Scrapings under the nails. She tried. Could be he was marked up."

"Do you think she was killed where she was found? In that park? The ground was wet beneath her."

The coroner shook his head. "Good analysis, my friend. Important for the timing, and it fits. Lividity says she was moved from the murder scene and had been lying on her side. Once the blood pools, that's that. As to *where* she died, there isn't any clear indication. I found nothing on her clothes like soil, straw, stains. She might have been killed in a drawing room, a theater box, or even in a carriage."

Edwin blew out a frustrated breath. "That argues against the murder being a crime of opportunity, someone attacking her in the park on the spur of the moment. How long did she lie where she was killed, would you guess?"

"A couple of hours. The killer might have been waiting for his chance to move her. Only doctors or undertakers deal with bodies. It's a very exclusive brotherhood. We're not all cut out for this." One corner of his mouth rose a fraction.

"And yet they say that the Ripper might have been a medical man gone bad."

"I've always been fascinated with that case and the way the organs were removed. He certainly made a fool out of the authorities."

Edwin forced his eyes away from Vicky. "I mean to catch this man, Tim. It's just so damnable that it's my first case. As if fate is jesting with me."

Jones firmed up his lips in sympathy. "What stands out most?"

"After dark, she was taken to a public place to remove suspicion of proximity. That doesn't argue lower class to me. I'm still amazed that she wasn't weighted down and taken out to sea. A small rowboat would do fine."

"You say she'd been gone for years, Edwin. The killer was counting on no one identifying her. Women don't go out without their fancies, a handkerchief, some money. Ordinary jewelry was left. It's very confusing." He shrugged. "Could be a third party came by for the purse. A grave robber."

"Her clothes show that she had done moderately well in San Francisco, if that's where she's been. It's a big city. I'm waiting to hear from them."

Jones got a quizzical look on his face. "There's something else I want you to see. Help me turn her over."

Edwin obliged, and they lifted her with care. With her slender size and weight, she rolled easily. Edwin gasped. At the top of her buttocks, in the small of the back was a dark blue tattoo. "What the hell . . ."

"A hexagram. Done within the last few months. You can tell from the clarity and the lack of inflammation." He moved a gentle finger around the mark. "One continuous line. Very distinctive. I'm not one for geometry, though."

"She didn't have it when she posed. Naomi would have mentioned it. Tattoos are a man's game. An anchor. Lover's heart. Homage to dear old Mother. I saw some on the Coastal Salish up north in Campbell River. An initiation rite for young boys and girls. What could have caused her to do this? It must have hurt like the devil."

"Put your men on it, then. If she got it here, we might learn more. Check the dock areas for the usual places."

"Let me make a copy. It has to have some meaning." Edwin pulled a small notebook from his pocket and tried to re-create the tattoo. Drawing hadn't been passed on in the family genes, but he captured the idea.

As Edwin finished, Jones hung his rubber apron on a peg. He turned to the only sink and began scrubbing his hands with carbolic soap. He inspected them, then scrubbed again. "God, this job is hell on skin. Lister's ideas have saved plenty of lives, though. Puerperal fever used to kill one woman in five."

Despite Jones's complaints, Edwin admitted that it was probably cleaner here than in a war hospital in the Crimea. With a fresh towel, Jones dried himself, pulled down his sleeves, and replaced black pearl cufflinks. Then he put on his jacket and straightened his tie. "One curious item. This is all we found in the deepest pocket of her skirts. It's an odd thing for a lady to carry."

Edwin stepped closer as a marble dropped into his palm. "A children's toy." He rotated it in his hand. "Plain. Terra cotta, perhaps. This little pattern of dots is unusual. Hardly a keepsake like the cat's eyes I collected. You said that she'd given birth. You don't suppose that she has a baby somewhere." A cold sweat broke across his forehead.

"The breasts show no recent sign of giving suck." The coroner shook his head. "A working woman might have farmed it out to a wet nurse. And clearly you're no parent. A mother wouldn't leave a marble near a baby."

Edwin folded his hands in self-control. "She would never have abandoned a child. Perhaps she sent it home to her parents." Suppose all those years ago, the French letter had failed. He'd been in such haste. She had taken care of the disposal, leaving him panting on the bed.

Jones took his arm and looked into his eyes with a steady gaze. "You're going off the deep end, Edwin. Stop the speculation. I thought she wasn't a close friend. Weren't you a callow youth when you knew her?"

Edwin ignored the question, and Jones wouldn't probe. "I'll need the clothes. They may yet tell us something, lead to a seamstress with information." Edwin secured the marble in a handkerchief. "She looks so cold, Tim."

"She's past feeling, man, but we treat our people with dignity. Don't worry about that. As for the clothes . . ." He scratched his head. "Dammit. I'm not sure where they are. Karl should have put them somewhere safe."

With what little they had to go on, everything was welcome. Laundry marks. Something individual. These weren't rags. If the clothes were gone . . . Edwin felt his hopes sag.

Jones disappeared for a few minutes into a back room and came back with a large muslin bag. "Thank God for that."

"Petticoats and underclothing are mysteries in themselves," Jones said with a sigh as if missing that part of his life. "Karl says this is what she was wearing, and he's very precise. The jewelry, not that it's valuable, is in a smaller linen bag inside."

Edwin took the evidence of a soul, hugging it to his chest like a baby. How ghoulish to pore over Vicky's last remains, a means to an end he might be better off not knowing.

# CHAPTER FIVE

Edwin, two detectives, and Chief Inspector Calvin McBride met in his office. An uncomfortable oak bench had been moved into the room. Edwin took a seat with the lower-ranking man, Childers, while the senior man Brush chose an armchair. A lithograph of the raising of the Siege at Khartoum flanked a bronze bust of the younger Queen. Even hinting at Her Majesty's friendship with her Scottish groom Mr. Brown was a passport to unemployment. As far as McBride was concerned, Scots Presbyterians had marched from barren and lonely hills, fueled only by oatmeal, to civilize the planet.

Bookshelves lined the room, more for show than consultation. A gilt-edged Bible. Sleek leather-bound editions of the *Statutes of Canada. Upper Canada Cases. Halsbury's Laws.* Volumes of the *Indian Act.* The only less-than-pristine edition was the *Criminal Code.* McBride sat in proprietorial fashion behind a desk as large as a small rowboat. It held a turntable of well-chewed pipes, a crystal paperweight, and a pile of papers with perfectly squared corners. "Brush has told me that this murder is yours, DesRosiers. What have you done so far, laddie? How does it fit the other two attacks?" he asked. "The public is getting restive. Those vulture reporters, including that damn paddy O'Neill have been camped by my door. I asked council for money for a fourth detective so that we'd have two men for nights and two for days. Easy street for you, so where is that fool Thirkstan?" He shifted to arc a blob from his bulging mouth into a waiting spittoon, then refit his bulk to the massive leather chair. Caterpillian tufts of hair nestled in his prominent ears.

"Reggie's making the rounds of tattoo parlors this morning, Sir, as are three other constables covering rooming houses, cheap hotels, wherever the usual suspects gather. I've taken the liberty of cabling San Francisco police for any information on . . . Miss Crosse. If she didn't come back here alone, that's one more angle to pursue."

"Any relatives nearby? Did she step out with any steady?"

"Her parents live on a farm on the lower island. I'm not sure where yet." The murder happened too late for the morning paper, and even by tomorrow Vicky wouldn't be named. "The attacks sound similar, but only on the surface."

"Nonsense. With that defeatist attitude, you'll never make an arrest. You're probably tripping over the answer right now."

"There's that strange tattoo. And her clothing may tell us something about where she took her custom. We still hope that, Sir, well—"

"Well's a deep subject. Your investigations aren't. Who the hell cares where she bought her drawers? Could be mail order for all we know. Point is that women don't feel safe on our streets. We're the capital city, not the Klondike. It's embarrassing. What about that feeble-minded fellow who used to roam the docks? How about an Indian? They get up to no good with a skinful, poor godless sods."

"Already checked on old Sam, Sir," Edwin said. Sam Boone had been in jail the last week for drunken and disorderly conduct. The hapless chap only got up to mischief when his so-called friends plied him with rotgut rum. Blaming murder on a roving tramp was as creative as the administrative minds got. He ignored the accusation against the local Salish.

"Childers has been covering the cribs, haven't you? Soft job, that. Probably given a drink at each door, if not more," Brush added with a cautious smile under his "spinach" whiskers. He'd lived in Victoria all his life and had valuable contacts in the Native community. His wife was part Cowichan. Her father had been a Scottish factor and her mother a chief's daughter. "As for me, I can guarantee you no one from the Songhees Reserve was involved. Killing a white person. And a woman to boot. There would be public riot."

Childers spoke up, Adam's apple bobbing and his hooded eyes like half moons. "Even at the best houses, the girls were worried enough about the two attacks. A murder changes things. The streetwalkers are going out in pairs. Could we increase our presence—"

McBride let out a roar. "No, we cannot, you chucklehead. It's been six bloody weeks since those assaults with no results, and now this. If you need to go back and talk to everyone again, do it. Shake the box and see what rattles. You're being paid princely wages, and I want charges laid before the week's out or I'll have the pack of you out of your glad rags, back into plain blue, and pounding the pavement and chasing pickpockets. At least our fair city will be getting its money's worth."

The room fell deadly silent. "That's all. Shove off. The lot of you." McBride's ham-sized arm made a dismissive gesture. Edwin was the last to leave. McBride's eyes smoldered.

"You'd better be right about Thirkstan. You're supposed to be teaching him the ropes. Every time I see the young wastrel, he's gallivanting about, not a care in the world. His father's married to my cousin, and I got him this damn position under pressure, but he's a washout."

Edwin cleared his throat. If Reggie passed a saloon or met a pal on the way to a card game, they wouldn't see him until tomorrow. "I expect to have him report back later today."

"I want to see his smiling mug here at seven a.m. sharp tomorrow, and no mistake. Now shut that door. I have a department to run. And don't be wasting time nitter-nattering about me like a bunch of wet hens."

In the hall, the group traded relieved looks. "That's over. Let's have a drink, fellows," said Brush. Within minutes, they were ensconced at the nearby Occidental Hotel. Glasses of beer made the rounds. A savory smell drifted over. The bartender pushed a plate toward them with strange crispy potatoes. "Try these," he said. "Saratoga chips. They're right tasty with a little salt. Cook just learned to make them. La-di-da, doncha know?"

The men dug in, spreading grease on their faces. "For the ladies, maybe. These aren't going to suit a man's appetite. Beefsteak and mashed potatoes, more like," Brush said, wiping his hands on his trousers. He looked up expectedly. "So what about asking the two chippies again?"

They sat at a rickety table in the back under flickering gaslight. An old rummy swept up sawdust and peanut shells and gulped the dregs from each abandoned glass. Childers pulled out a notebook. "The two girls cost me a chicken dinner. All's I learned was that neither one could identify the culprit other than on one point."

Edwin sat up. "They said they didn't see him. So what's all this about?"

"Once they relaxed a bit, got to chewing the fat, something occurred to them." Childers finished his sarsaparilla and swiped the foam from his lip with the back of his hand. Everyone made fun of his taking the pledge. His father was a Methodist deacon. "He had an odd smell about him, and he burped a lot."

Edwin would have guffawed, but he waited patiently instead. The first brick in the wall of a case often seemed innocuous. "That sounds like eighty percent of the city's working-class men. Can they be more precise? Garlic? Beer? Whiskey? Or something from the trades? Tar, tanning, vinegar, blacksmithing? Are we talking about his breath, his clothing, or his body?"

"Ammonia, the older one thinks. She used to be a charwoman before she wrecked her knees. Don't need knees to lie on your back. Can't be sweat or pong. Women would know."

"Ammonia, eh? That *is* specific. If we find any suspects, it's a point to work with, that and the stocking idea. Going sour like this with a killing, our man may have done a runner. He could be halfway to California by now or up to Alaska." Steamers and sailing vessels plied the harbor. Any given moment had a dozen ships at anchor with a spot for a coal shoveler or deck swabber, no questions asked.

A few jokes passed about going "around the world" without leaving the city. "That's enough clowning," Brush said "See what I have to deal with, Edwin? And you want to be lead detective in ten years? Or are you shooting for five? I'd best watch my back."

Edwin took another chip, appreciating the salty crunch. "If I can find out where she was living, I'll know more. Someone must have seen or heard something. Rooming houses and hotels are hives of activity. I have her clothes, too. And a strange marble from her pocket."

Childers said, "You know women. They pack around the kitchen sink, wag chins over tea. Could be a bauble for a child."

That reminded Edwin of what Jones had said about her having given birth. He suspected that he'd never learn the truth about that. He needed to stop dwelling on it.

"As for that worthless Thirkstan . . ." Brush signaled the barkeep for another round. Then he took a pig's foot and gave it a tentative gnaw as if it were Reggie's.

"I'll give him your regards." Edwin drained his glass. "The Crosse woman . . . knew my mother many years ago. I'm going to speak to her about it tonight. Her old friends might have information if we can find—"

"Them's on the game have short lives," Brush said. "If Jones is right about her being killed someplace else, that queers everything. And consider this. What if the two whores blabbed about the stocking?" He stood and stretched, tossing down the bone. "I'm due in court to testify in a forgery case at the Bank of British Columbia. And it's a woman. Who would have thought dolly-mops could get up to that?"

Back at the station, Edwin took the sad bundle of Vicky's clothes to the Property Room in the new quarters. Sergeant Richards was in charge of the small array of equipment, no more than a microscope, minor chemistry lab equipment, and scales. Many said that the new fingerprint method would change the face of crime solving. Comparisons of bullets and barrels were also on the horizon. But establishing a data bank would take decades and only large metro areas like Toronto were moving ahead. Still, future Lizzie Bordens might have something to think about.

"Afternoon, Richards," he said as he spread the clothes on a large table covered with brown butcher's paper. The cadaverously thin man, whose weak heart kept him at a desk, gave him a slight nod as he stared at a fish knife with dark brown stains. Dr. Jones would have measured the wound for depth and checked the edges. A pen knife didn't make the same cut as a boning knife. But how would they know whose blood it was?

Edwin sorted through the clothing, separating it. The material seemed to be gabardine, if he remembered from accompanying his mother to the dressmaker's. A white silken one-piece garment served as chemise and drawers. The crotch seams were open for access, the same reason that men's pants had buttons on the front. With the gored skirt, the matching petticoat ended in a lacey frill. Another petticoat gave the desired frou-frou, his mother's word. Then he picked up the corset, quite the mechanical contraption. How did women wear these things, laced so tightly? No stains, rips, or tears. Against the darkness of the dark dress, he noticed several long blonde hairs. The same color as Vicky's, yet her hair had been curly. These seemed straight. He rolled one between his fingers. Not as stiff as horsehair. Several went into an envelope. Who knows what might turn up under a microscope?

"See what you can get from these, Richards. The lady was strangled, the doc says. But give an eye to these unusual hairs."

"People are a magnet for hairs. Could be animal. Fine horsehair. At any rate, these are costly goods and well-maintained," Richards said, fingering the hem of the dress. Between the winter mud and the summer dust, long skirts didn't stay pristine for long. Even the most careful laundry couldn't prevent fading if it wanted to defeat stains. Cleaning was a harsh all-day process involving vats of boiling water and turning poles. The poor didn't change clothes often.

"Log them in A to Z. This is a murder case. I don't want anything lost," Edwin reminded him. Could his mother tell him where the corset had been bought? "I'll take this with me," he said, and Richards gave him an odd look.

"Mark it down, man. One corset. White," Edwin said, stabbing at a ledger. A button could lead to a garment, then to a laundry, then to a suspect. It was all part of the trail. Not that he was a religious man, but he hoped a higher power was guiding him.

Back upstairs, he found a telegram from San Francisco on his desk. "No record Victoria Crosse." So Vicky had kept her nose clean in the States, at least under that name. A closed door. But why had she returned?

# CHAPTER SIX

Edwin went home at five-thirty that afternoon. On the way, he met Wong turning the corner onto Amelia, carrying two wicker baskets of marketing. From H. Saunders on Johnson at Oriental Alley. Carrot fronds hung over the side, and brown-paper parcels had come from the butcher. Wong was humming what sounded like "When Strolling Through the Park One Day." The man faded so easily into the background, it was hard to remember that like all good employees, he had his finger on the household pulse. Brush was fond of saying, "No one knows a man like his valet."

Edwin held out a hand for one basket and got a welcome nod. Wong, short but wiry and strong, wore his blue cotton coolie suit and a conical straw hat. Orientals got looks and comments for dressing above their status, though a few like Fat Charlie Chong stuck out their double chins and sported embroidered silks on the rare times that the Chinese left their enclave en masse. Funeral processions were one example.

The first group had arrived with the 1858 Fraser Gold Rush, and by 1862, the city had a dozen trading establishments. The western push for the railroad brought another sixteen thousand immigrants and twice the "coolies" struck to improve their conditions. Chinatown had over three thousand in a six-block area, second only to San Francisco. Mumblings were rampant that the fifty-dollar head tax was going to be raised to as much as five hundred dollars. Canada had made good use of the workers and was now closing the door.

"Are you still bringing Mother opium, Wong? Don't be afraid to tell me," Edwin said as they walked briskly. Wong didn't slow his pace, nor did he answer with more than a shrug. Edwin didn't pursue the matter. Not only was the drug legal and opium factories listed on fire maps, profits helped float the city government. It wasn't as if she were bedding down in a doss house in Dragon Alley. He suspected that she'd been no stranger to the drug since his father died. The substance was common in creative circles, especially influenced by De Quincey's *Confessions of an English Opium Eater*. Cocaine was also common in patent medicines. Mothers gave their babies soothing syrup laced with alcohol, also a leading ingredient of Lydia Pinkham's helpful nostrum for female hysteria.

Arriving at their tidy front yard, where well-nurtured lucky Chinese-red rhodos were in riotous bloom, Wong took the baskets down the brick side path to the back door. After heading upstairs to his room, Edwin changed into a paisley smoking jacket. Their evening meal would be enjoyed in the formal dining room. Naomi took her *petit déjeuner* and late afternoon tea in her bedroom/sitting room.

Despite his distress over Vicky and the fledgling progress of the case, Edwin was building an appetite. Wong was a quick study, moving easily from American dishes to French and Chinese. Naomi had taught him how to make her mother's latkes, beet soup, and honey cake. Matzo had to be replaced with crackers. Halibut served as gefiltefish.

With no sign of his mother, a disturbing note, Edwin came into the parlor and poured himself a generous brandy, parking in a wide Jacobean armchair in front of the coal fire which chased off the evening chill. The small room was crowded with tchotchkes from his grandparents' home. A fragile bisque shepherdess, a miniature wooden shoe, a silver visiting-card holder, even a dreidel toy for learning Hebrew. Heavy, swagged velvet curtains kept out the night air, but the gaslight was turned up full. A blue ceramic urn of pampas grass stood in the corner.

The sliding connecting door opened, and Naomi made her entrance, her head held high with the posture from balancing books on her head during Miss Huguette's finishing school in Montreal. A wisp of Worth floral perfume followed, then Wong with champagne in ice, cold air swirling from the bottle. With a flourish, their man poured a flute and handed it to her, then bowed and left. The doors closed again, leaving them in private. Champagne was an unusual touch. A new friend?

"Some music please, darling. I've been in a brown study ever since you told me about Victoria," she said.

He got up and wound a key on the box which sat on a side table. "Believe Me if All Those Endearing Young Charms" began tinkling.

"God, how maudlin. That song always depresses me. 'And around the dear ruin,' " she said. Her ample lips, lightly rouged, gave a small pout.

"A 'dear ruin' you will never be, Mother." Was she getting depressed again? The gloomy winter temperatures and skies were behind them now. But she was immaculately groomed, and her flaming hair swept up in lustrous waves. That was a good sign. He took her hand and bowed over it. Continentals never actually kissed the hand, she had explained. Very bourgeois.

"Spoken like a good son. I wonder if women will ever achieve true equality, even with the vote in New Zealand. We live in the wrong part of the Commonwealth." She inspected her palm as a whiff of turpentine arose. "Damn. There's still some paint." Her nails were clipped short for convenience.

Then she took a brocaded arm chair and rested her trim ankles on the ottoman, soft silken slippers on her feet. A quiet evening at home meant harem wear with gauzy, voluminous trousers and a billowy low-cut top. A few freckles graced the smooth skin that belied its fifty-five years. She adjusted an alpaca shawl around her shoulders. "And now it's time for our very sad talk. I couldn't concentrate. I spent the afternoon reading the latest *Yellow Book,* which did not cheer me. Please say that an arrest has been made."

"I've hardly had time to begin," he said, curbing his annoyance. "You're an important source and last night you said you were too tired. Let's start with her name. Was it a fabrication? I need to know when I look for her friends." The Victoria Cross was Britain's coveted medal of honor.

"I always suspected that she was making a wry joke. The girl had a wit, as I'm sure you appreciated, though you were born an old soul."

He took out a small notebook and pencil. "So when you first met her . . ." He paused in his prompt, not that it would matter. Naomi would take her time, resisting normal badgering.

"Darling, champagne first. Get yourself a glass. Don't jump in, badgering me like a bumpkin. Is this the way you have been making love to all of those sweethearts?"

He gritted his teeth like his father must have for decades. After the brandy, the champagne tasted like water. He sipped at a glass, then raised one eyebrow in her direction.

"I see that in your new position, Edwin, you are trained to get to the point."

Edwin sighed. "Please do it my way, Mother. Begin at the beginning. Genesis."

Her glittering emerald eyes fixed on his. Her cheeks had an unusual paleness, as if she hadn't slept well. But she always managed eight or nine hours. "I never realized what a pedestrian job you had, now that I'm an actual part of it." A sigh.

"It's shoe leather, Mother. I wouldn't recommend it for

someone of your sensibilities. Now please . . . begin."

He suspected why she was stalling. Anything that made her abnormally sad could tip the delicate balance. Sarah Grossman, her mother, had been sent to a sanatorium for a few months after Naomi's birth.

Naomi leaned back and took a large draught of champagne, then wrinkled her Hellenistic nose. "Flat. The storage wasn't cold enough. Or I suspect the bottle got shaken. Wong should know better. We don't have champagne every night, more's the pity." She put down the glass, her full lips tight in a bitter smile. "It's painful, but I shall plunge and plod for your sake."

He fixed her eye with a basilisk stare. "Please proceed."

"We first met in Beacon Hill Park. They were firing those noisy guns for the Queen's birthday. What a din." She stopped suddenly and turned her face away. A slight sniff followed.

Edwin gentled his voice. "Go on, Mother."

Naomi took a deep breath and her eyes fluttered shut for a second. "I was painting the duck pond. We were having a glorious sunny day. Everyone was strolling, sipping the warmth like a tonic. That's when dear Victoria came along. Providential, because I needed a new model. Remember how Minerva Rombauer ran off with that Texan. All those oil wells." Naomi never passed up a chance to paint a beautiful figure, but rarely got the opportunity in the small community. "She seemed to glide, as on wheels. Bustles were in fashion, stupid things. She carried a mauve silk parasol and wore a fetching cerulean-blue caped dress. A lovely bonnet, too. Riotous ribbons. I was surprised that she was alone. She reminded me of myself. A bold, young modern woman sallying forth alone. One time at the St. Joseph Oratory in Montreal, I spent all day gazing—"

"You must have sensed her profession. You wouldn't have dreamed of asking just any girl to pose." One corner of his mouth rose in a smile.

Her stiffening showed that she had taken umbrage, an art form with her. "Don't lecture me on morals. Whatever she did for a living was hardly my concern. Beauty is my business. I am a conduit."

"So you came right out and asked her? Dressed so respectably?"

"We had a meeting of the minds. Women are subtle. A shy girl she was not. I gave her my calling card. And then you know the rest. She posed for at least five paintings in the next year. Thanks to Oscar acting as my intermediate, I sold the pictures nearly immediately. And I paid her very well. Forty dollars for a few days' work is a fortune. The fare to San Francisco is not cheap."

What of the men who bought those pictures? Or the saloons that displayed them? Was it far-fetched that someone had recognized her on her return, past her prime to all but him? An old grudge from a spurned lover, perhaps a family man? The idea of blackmail was tempting.

"I need specifics if I'm going to find her friends. Do you know where she lived before the . . . Cadogan Hotel? Did you send a note or a letter? You must have had to contact her for the . . . sessions."

Naomi got up and went to a small maple secretary. She pulled down the writing shelf and ran her fingers over one of the *pigeonniers*. Then she retrieved a leather notebook and leafed through it. "Hell's bells," she said. "I need my reading spectacles. Ugly things. Edwin, they're upstairs on my bedside table."

"Let me see. I won't pry into your little books of secrets." With a wink, he took it from her. Vicky's name was under C. "Seventy-seven Chatham Street."

"Over the butcher's, she told me. Rent was cheaper because few could stand the smell, but the place was borderline decent.

I sent a boy, of course. Now the area's gone downhill." She put a hand over her forehead. "Hers was a dangerous trade for a woman alone, yet more dangerous with an unscrupulous man in control. If only she'd been working in a high-class house with sensible protection."

The fancy brothels "contributed" exorbitant taxes. But they made equal profits on the women and the liquor they sold to gentlemen callers in parlors with plush furniture, flocked French wallpaper, crystal chandeliers, and "fine" wine. Some city fathers had investments in places their wives hurried by without a glance, tsking at the "fallen women" within.

"I can't see her returning to that kind of poverty. But it's a logical start. She might have visited, even after fifteen years."

Why hadn't he asked Vicky about her friends, her interests? Why had he been so tongue-tied, mute or stuttering to his goddess? And it wasn't as if they had spent much private time together, except for the once, and that would have to suffice for the rest of his life.

A crease fell between Naomi's dark, shapely brows. "Like many, she was a farm girl from the island. Somewhere out the west shore, or was it up Nanaimo way? Duncan? I'm not sure. She sent her mother money by monthly post. She was proud of that. A visit or two, I would think. Perhaps it was awkward for all of them. She and I spoke of beautiful things."

What about that tattoo? Briefly, he described it. "What do you make of that?"

Her hand went protectively to her breastbone. "Despoil herself? What could have possessed the girl? Her skin was flawless. Tattoos are very low class."

"But the design was complex, not the usual hearts and anchors. Dr. Jones seemed to think that she got it within the last couple of months. Reggie's looking into it." *And where the hellfire was the wretch?*

Naomi shivered and pulled the shawl closer. Then she reached down to prod the fire with a poker. "Something like that lasts forever. Imagine if you wore your sweetheart's name and then found another. And as your skin sagged from age . . . *mon dieu.*"

"Something else I wanted to show you. It's a corset."

"You mean hers?" She gave a sharp inhale and a quiver of disapproval. "This is grotesque. I couldn't imagine pawing through . . ."

"That's the way we work. It's as important as handwriting or any other clue." His gaze went to the bag on a side table. "Her jewelry was hardly pawnable. This is the only significant piece of clothing."

Naomi's eyes widened. She touched it with two fingers, and her expression changed. "My, this is a cunning mantrap. The latest fashion. Not a woman in the city has one."

"Then I've brought it to the right place. What is it telling you?"

She pored over it like a couturier. "The bias-cut silk trim says Paris to me. Notice the clever suspenders for stockings. Cruel old-fashioned garters bind the legs and leave marks."

"Where would you buy one here?" Edwin prepared to make a note.

"Silly man. You can't. We live in the wilderness. San Francisco. Montreal or New York City. Not fusty Toronto. Victoria had an excellent source of money when she bought this item."

A small gong sounded, and they went into the dining room. A lacy tablecloth was set beneath a platter of leftover beef ribs, roasted potatoes, and tired carrots. As he pushed the woody vegetable around his plate, Edwin yearned for the spring days of better produce, heralded by the first tender pea and lettuce and spinach. Wong had already tilled the kitchen garden for early planting and had made a glassed cold frame at the south side of the house.

Wong brought out a bottle of unlabeled red wine. "Dear Lord Rumming had this sent from Washington State. The grapes are far inferior to the French varietals, but those are the perils of a young country."

"I understand that growers are making great strides in California. A place called Napa." How he wished he had the time and money to travel.

Naomi ate heartily. Her metabolism was one of her gifts. "Now may we speak of happier things?" his mother asked as they were finishing their meal. "It is your birthday approaching," Naomi said, blotting her mouth demurely. "Do you have any special wishes?"

He thought back to his fifteenth birthday. Shortly after his father died, she had called him into the parlor. "What did your father tell you about the facts of life?"

He blushed, unable to do anything but roll his eyes. She pulled a packet from her pocket. "Did he provide you with these?"

Edwin examined the delicate French lambskin letters, as she called them. One tapered eyebrow arched, but no smile came. "By the time you run out, you should know how to purchase your own from a discreet chemist. Remember two things: A man always supports himself on his elbows. And never get a girl in a family way. A careless moment can destroy a lifetime. Parenthood is not merely a woman's responsibility."

Then they were back to the present. "One request," he said. "Vicky deserves a decent burial."

She took another sip of wine and moved her plate aside, depositing her serviette. "How very dear of you, Son. Hayward's, I would think?"

He nodded. Time was of the essence. Would she even be embalmed? He didn't like to imagine that.

"They're the best. We can arrange for a small and tasteful stone as well. I'm thinking that her parents may want her interred at home, wherever that is. I suppose it would look better coming as a gift from me, her benefactor, certainly not a policeman."

"Well put." He noticed her blink twice and turn away. He popped another piece of meat into his mouth. It tasted like sawdust. No fault of Wong's.

They both turned as their man bustled in with a tray.

"Treacle pudding. Now that's better," she said. A silver pourer stood ready.

"And no jokes about Spotted Dick," Edwin said as he drowned the sweet in golden syrup and forked up a luscious morsel. Knowing that Vicky would have the respect that she deserved made some difference. Now it was up to him to find her killer.

# CHAPTER SEVEN

Dante described nine circles of Hell in his Inferno, and Reggie had visited each in his nightmares, plunging to the bottom of the vortex with Satan holding Judas and Cassius in his maw. He was afraid to open his eyes, the headache was so punishing. His mouth tasted like the bottom of their late gray cockatiel Tinky's gilded cage. The discipline of the wedding band was the only anecdote. Make that antidote. He squinted at the merciless alarm clock, unset as usual, but mindlessly ticking off the minutes of his wretched life. Nine already. Late for work. Last night the bartender was too clever by half. Just back from the States with such wickedly amusing cocktails. Reggie tried every one twice, and was the last man staggering out of the Union Club. Brandy daisy, flip, Tom Collins, and that blue blazer, tossing flaming whiskey to create a theatrical arc of flame. Father had warned never to budge from whiskey and soda. The old fart was right.

He made a quick toilette, hardly caring what he was wearing, although Baines had tiptoed in to arrange an outfit on his gentleman's valet stand. What the deuce had the Rozzer told him to do today? Why hadn't he written it down? And missing the meeting with McBride. He'd pay for that. Not that he wouldn't chuck the job, but not now. Father was settling a tidy sum on him once the ring was on the finger, and a new house on Dallas Road for his wife, the nubile Carrie, would follow.

Groaning, he massaged his temples back to life. Of course!

He was supposed to make the rounds of tattoo parlors to see if they recognized the design on Victoria Crosse. Where was that sketch Rozzer had made? Some sort of hexagram. Loco-looking thing. He'd never be able to draw it with his feverish brain.

He rummaged in his trousers hanging like a dead thing on the bedstead. Nothing, except for a rip in the knee where he'd made an acquaintance with a slippery gutter while falling out of a cab. If he'd lost the drawing, he'd have to find Edwin and lay his broken body at his mercy. How humiliating. He picked up a silver brush and began attacking his hair. Was it beginning to thin into his father's bald dome, or was he imagining it? Underneath a playbill for *Romeo and Juliet* was the folded paper.

Thank Christ. His noggin was pounding out "Men of Harlech" double-time. Sticking his head out the door, he assessed if the bathroom was empty. It wouldn't do to run into Mother or Sis. Damn women. At least his father kept out of his way, as long as he thought Reggie was working. The old man ran a ship chandler's business that his grandfather had founded. Arthur Thirkstan breakfasted on steel-cut Highland oats, brown sugar, and cream, followed by kippers, and was out of the house by six. Reggie's two plodding brothers were welcome to that prosaic, grubbing life.

In the bathroom cabinet, he found a packet of headache powders and emptied it into his mouth, followed by a glass of water. A roiling commenced. He needed something to settle his stomach. "I called for madder music and for sweeter wine," he recited. "I have been faithful to thee . . . Carrie?" He chuckled at his poetry. Was it his imagination or was the old noggin beginning to hum again? Fresh air was the ticket.

Back to his room he went and rummaged in the wardrobe. His silver hip flask had . . . miracle of miracles . . . one good swallow of single malt Glenlivet. He gargled it, enjoying the pleasant heat and the way it cut the scum like a knife through pastry. Capital idea. Now to get out of the house without being seen. Everyone would take it for granted that he had gone to work early. He peered around the corner, then tiptoed down the stairs. A capital jest, slipping *out* of the house. As he oozed out a side door, which led to the cellar, he realized that he had forgotten his new fedora. Too bad.

The morning air revived him as he walked down Menzies toward the harbor, a brisker pace as the blocks went by. He cast an eye at the fledgling Parliament buildings. Farewell to the quaint old Birdcages, the original complex so vulnerable to fire. That bugger Rattenbury was in charge of the design, a bold man. But bolder yet had been the fixing of the capital in Victoria instead of upstart mainland Vancouver. Otherwise he'd be living in a backwater. His throat seized when he remembered that this park was where Victoria had been found.

Stopping in at a lunch counter for a cup of strong coffee bombarded with sugar lumps, he pulled himself into action. Wharf Street, Store Street, the fringes of Chinatown, that's where the navy went for tattoos. In all of his jolly times making the beast with two backs, he'd never seen one woman branded. What had the girl been thinking? True, she was hardly virgin territory, but that touch would have spoiled her for any man short of a longshoreman.

In the next two hours, he had no luck at the seedy shops. The proprietors, scurrilous types, shrugged and swore that they had never seen such a design, offering crude sample books as proof. Their vacant eyes testified that they hadn't the gall to lie. The design seemed familiar, now that he was concentrating. He'd avoided studies in geometry and math, preferring the arts.

Then something from an amusing alcoholic tutor returned to him. A uni . . . uni . . . what was it? A symbol favored by Bruno, a sixteenth-century Italian priest-philosopher burned at the stake for heresy. Accused of dabbling in the occult. Now that *was* a poser. Why would an uneducated, lower-class female have such a tattoo? Didn't he have some notes from the course moldering in a steamer trunk in the carriage-house attic?

Parched by his footwork, Reggie stopped in for a beer at a saloon and chugged it, followed by a prairie oyster of Worcestershire and raw beaten egg. Everything behaved itself. "Bartender," he called, and when the man reached for the glass, Reggie flogged himself mentally to keep from having more. Instead, he dropped a dime tip to an old man at a shoeshine stand. Appearances counted. One more stop, and his job was done. But how could he tell the Rozzer that he'd found nothing?

He ambled out of the dockside hotel and around the corner to an alley between Johnson and Yates, recoiling at the reek of urine and garbage. Had something died here? Anyone alone here at night might best have a will. Why would Pater want him in a job which took him to such disreputable places? Old handbills were cracking on the scuffed walls, and moss grew in the parging cracks between the bricks. He stepped in something soft and cursed, inspecting his calfskin boot. It didn't seem to be dog excrement—probably an errant banana slug. Then he came to an old door with the paint peeling. The word *Tattoo* was so faint, he could barely read it. The last *o* had been added in a different color. At last the headache had flown. He was even getting hungry if he could just escape this stinking hellhole.

He tried the door. Locked? Just stuck it appeared, as he applied his shoulder with an *oomph*. Inside, he smelled the stale fug of incense, perhaps from a neighboring opium den. He rang a bell on the dusty counter, then rang again, and through a bamboo curtain limped a cadaverous man with a wart on his nose. His seersucker suit hadn't been cleaned or pressed since purchase. The canvas apron bore traces of inks and what looked like dark blood. As Reggie flashed his identification, the man smiled broadly with stumpy front teeth and the breath of a midden.

"Sir, at your service. We are honored. You require a tattoo? It's usually the navy gives us custom. But the idea is taking hold across the pond. I understand even the dear queen has a tattoo, a very discreet and ladylike design to be sure." His wink was enough to turn a sober person's stomach.

Reggie peeled off his lambskin gloves to retrieve the thin, folded paper from his breast pocket. He hated to place them on the filthy counter. The infections this place could harbor he didn't want to imagine.

"Do you recognize this design, my . . . er . . . good man?" he asked.

The cretin shook his head so vigorously that spittle sprayed from his slack lips and Reggie stepped back. "Look again."

"No, sir. I'd remember that one. She's a poser." He affected a smile, but his eyes didn't cooperate, avoiding contact. Fake, Reggie thought. Rozzer had said that the entire face took part in a real smile. He'd bust a gut out of Reggie using his system.

"I have other pictures that the ladies would admire. Tattooing's a very old art. 'Tis said that Captain Cook brought the tradition back from the islands." He rattled other data which had Reggie's head spinning. Clearly he was trying to be evasive in hopes that the law would go away.

Was other questionable business being conducted here? The place was so bare that he wondered how it survived. Smuggling? The white slave trade? It wouldn't be the first time a pheasant was flushed in search of a grouse. A fellow had to keep his eyes open.

"This is police business. While I'm here, I'd like to see into the back room if you don't mind."

"Certainly, Sir." The relaxing of the man's shoulders showed that there would be nothing gained. So much for the clandestine "usage of a premises" threat to look more thoroughly.

He ushered Reggie through the curtain to a room that took feeble light from a large, cobwebbed window. A burly man was seated beside a table. On his extended forearm was a half-completed tattoo of the Fenian flag. The Irish never surrendered. His uniform left no mystery about his career.

"What's this all about?" he asked in a gruff voice. "Finish up, pal. I'm due on watch at the ship and I need my ashes hauled in the next half hour."

Paraphernalia was laid out on filthy tables. It was a long painstaking process, Reggie thought, and no place for a lady.

"Is this equipment portable? Can you use it anywhere?"

"I never have occasion to leave me shop, Sir. Not with my fine reputation."

"If you say so." He touched his hat and turned. Behind him, the sailor reached for a tin mug and slurped. The reek of raw rum filled the air.

You didn't need to be Sherlock Holmes to read the lie. Problem was, how to catch him off guard. Lull him into a false sense of security? Certainly he wasn't going to lurk around the corner. Some foot-slogging constable could do that. See who came in. Watch where he went. But McBride would never authorize twenty-four-hour surveillance.

As he returned to the welcome fresh air, he noticed a boy selling newspapers on the opposite corner. Reggie ambled over. "Hello, lad. Are you on this corner every day?"

The boy looked suspicious. "What if I am? I'm a newsie fair and square. And there's no use asking me to come with you. I've heard about that before. 'Course if you pays well enough—"

Reggie stepped back in alarm. "Good heavens, no. You mistake me entirely. I'm after information, nothing more."

The boy put down his papers. "What is it you want, then? I'm no rat."

Reggie moved in closer and pointed. "See that tattoo parlor over there?"

"What about it? He's a tightwad bastard. He'd sell his own ma for two bits."

Reggie folded his arms in amusement. "So you don't like him. All the better. Listen now. This is worth a dollar."

"A simoleon? Up front, then. I ain't stupid."

Reggie told the boy, whose name was Horace, that he was to watch the shop and note anyone coming or going. The boy assured Reggie that he spent the day here after collecting his papers and rarely left before dusk. An overhanging balcony gave him rude shelter during rain. His men's pants cut rough at the bottom were held up with a rope belt. A sweater from a rag bag kept him warm.

"I can already tell you something. He lives in a room upstairs. Another is that some Sundays after supper, he's usually gone. Around once a month. Walks out and goes to the river."

That sounded interesting. "To the river, eh? This coming Sunday, follow him. And be sharp with your wits. Don't make it look obvious." He took out a Yankee Liberty Head dollar and gave it to Horace. He'd bet his salary the boy had never had one in his grubby hand.

After an entire morning of clean living, Reggie's stomach finally came through like a champ. He patted his gut. "No oysters today, old bean. A good old English joint. That's what won the Hundred Years' War, along with the oak bow. Then back to headquarters. Meeting that cheeky little tad was a stroke of luck."

# CHAPTER EIGHT

None of the constables brought helpful information from the street. Vicky hadn't been back in town long enough to leave a trail. Life for the underclasses was anonymous, short, and brutish. Those who eked out a living from petty theft, prostitution, and gambling lived day to day. The more he thought about the relocation of the body, the more Edwin suspected collusion, a puppet master in hiding.

Even a simpleton knew that the more time passed, the less likely a crime was to be solved. People forgot, left town, died. Barroom brawls resulting in death were a "piece of cake." The rare upper-class murder often saw the culprit go free thanks to expensive solicitors and barristers. What about Vicky? Thirty years from now, leaning on a cane, he didn't want to hear, "The police never solved that one. Poor stupid buggers." Naomi would haunt him without mercy.

The old rooming house was his first stop. As opposed to the gilt-edged brothels around Courtney and Douglas, the chippies plied their trade north on the edge of Chinatown in the Chatham, Herald, and Fisgard areas. It was close to the wharves, so navy boys could trot across the bridge from Esquimalt. London had its Seven Dials and San Francisco had its Barbary Coast.

Like any frontier society short of women, Victoria had been plagued by prostitution from inception, first from the Natives, relegated to the Songhees lands across the Gorge, then the

Chinese, and lately the whites. The Women's Christian Temperance Union at #2 Work Street offered "fallen" unfortunates a bed and minimal job skills. A bandage solution, Edwin thought. Men would always need relief, scientific studies to explain the causes of prostitution said. And some women, by circumstance or predilection, would find that the quickest way to a full stomach was on their back or their knees. Some found a belly of another kind, despite resorting to pessaries and vinegar douches.

Like roaches, the netherworld thrived on darkness, so early morning was perfect for catching them sleeping off a stupor from the cheap drink which eased their brief path through life.

The new federal legislation in section 8 of the *Criminal Code of Canada* covered street soliciting, bawdy houses, and those who frequented them, "not giving a satisfactory account of themselves," an ambiguous line covering a multitude of sins. Fines went to fifty dollars and imprisonment up to six months, with or without hard labor. Bribes from the wealthy landlords hiding behind a tapestry of artful property-ownership papers were one circumvention.

Early spring mornings were so pure and hopeful, even in this sordid business. Roosters were crowing from the chicken pens. The sun was peeking through the budding trees. Rainbowed azaleas were taking turns like debutantes.

At Douglas he headed north and finally went west on Chatham. The newsboys were crying their wares about another famine in Russia. A keen follower of international politics discussed at her soirees, Naomi predicted that the Romanovs would agree to a duma rather than following in the footsteps of Louis the Sixteenth. Edwin wasn't sure. People ground under a boot didn't rebel. They mobbed only when they glimpsed a shred of hope.

Shifting feet to avoid a steaming pile of road apples, he left the dusty street and mounted the wooden sidewalks, passing a barber, a haberdasher, and a china store, with a saloon and lunch counter across the way. Down the muddy street rolled a milk wagon, a "float," the local Brits called it. An oafish horseman with a riding suit and English saddle passed him at a fast clip, and mud splattered onto his trousers from the heels of the red roan. Edwin stamped his feet to dislodge the clouts.

Then the buildings grew shabbier, and he turned the corner onto Chatham. A butcher shop advertised its presence. Beef and pork slabs hung in the window and the cloying reek of spoiled meat wafted from the alley. A vagrant sprawled on a pile of rags, filthy cap hiding his face, a tabby cat beside him washing its own mug. From habit, Edwin took a look. The man shifted in his sleep and released a pungent fart. Drunk. Perhaps he swept the saloons for a crust of stale bread and quart of beer. In the winter, constables picked up derelicts and took them to the holding cells for the night. Few could survive the drenching rains of winter, even at fifty degrees Fahrenheit.

Edwin entered the butcher shop, breathing through his mouth. Flies buzzed by, some trapped on sticky, curling strips dangling from the ceiling. A glass case held plump English sausages, chickens yellow with fat, thick beefsteaks, and pink bologna rings. A jolly, barrel-chested, ruddy-cheeked man in a stained white apron greeted him, cleaver in hand. He was separating meaty pork chops, chopping mere breaths from his stubby fingers. "Ah, the man of the house pays an early visit for the choicest cuts. What can I get you today, my good sir? A nice roast for the weekend? Just arrived from Cattle Point on the hoof. Prime stuff. Marbled and blue as a vein on the Madonna's breast." He tipped a wink to Edwin.

A poetic butcher. Thirkstan would approve. Edwin showed his identification. "I need some information about a girl who lived upstairs here perhaps fifteen years ago." He swatted at a bluebottle circling his head. Zipping off, it made its way to a teenager preparing working-class mince on a block. Many a poor family survived on bread and potatoes with dripping for savor.

The man put down his cleaver and smiled indulgently. His teeth were white and even like corn kernels. "People come and go. It's a decent house. I was a youngster then, learning at my father's knee in Winnipeg. But I hefted many a carcass. Ladies like a strong man." He displayed bulging biceps.

"Victoria Crosse was her name."

"Is that the one was murdered? Word's out. Why look back that far, man?" He shook his head in respect and made a rudimentary sign of the cross. "Poor lass, but I never knew her. I just bought the former owner out some five years ago."

"I'd like to talk to the . . . ladies upstairs. They may know something."

The man placed the pink chops lovingly in the case, arranged them with artful sprigs of parsley. "There is an old trout in room five been here donkey's years. You might ask her. Now's a good time. I came before dawn and saw lamps on upstairs. Be sure to knock first. Once I was collecting rent, and . . ." His cocked-arm gesture said it all.

As Edwin turned, he added, "Watch the third step from the top. Always something needs doing around an old place like this." He called to the pimply youth. "You know where the hammer and nails are, Joe. Hop to it. We don't want our law-and-order man breaking his leg."

Edwin headed around the side of the alley to an enclosed set of stairs. Back of the property leaned two rickety outhouses, targets for Halloween pranks. The way upstairs was dark, and he moved carefully toward the top. The reek of boiled cabbage and onions made his eyes water.

A shabby, unpainted door stained with dark brown led to a

hallway. Light filtered to his feet through a filthy piece of cracked window glass at the end. A tarnished tin 5 marked the spot. Edwin knocked, then knocked again. He heard female coughing. "Police. A word with you, Madame. No trouble."

A minute later, a bleary woman in her forties in a threadbare kimono and bare feet opened the door an inch, leaving it on a chain. Edwin explained his mission. With women, his politesse worked better than a strong arm and threatening voice.

"Ah, you sound like a pea souper. Just like me. You're a long way from home, you." Expressive gestures accompanied her voice, something he missed in the West.

Inside, she pointed to a half-sprung horsehair sofa with one missing leg propped up with a brick. The room was spotless, with a Murphy bed folded into the wall. A small gas ring served for cooking, and the stale smell of fried potatoes lingered. A sink with a dripping tap offered cold water. On the small deal table was a mug of dark brown tea while a whole-meal loaf lay on a board next to a wedge of dry cheese, the rind green.

Diane Lajeunesse had been raised in the Gatineau. She'd come west with her husband, a timberman, advancing to a planer. He had perished in a sawmill accident in Port Angeles, leaving her with only the clothes on her back and two *enfants* dead of influenza. With no way to make a living, she had come across to the city to try her luck. "Soon as I can save a bit more, I'm starting my own seamstress business. *Grandmere* taught me the small stitches, and I have my sight. I was doing fine until I got sick a few years back." Her shrug and delicate pat to her concave chest indicated that she bore fate no special malice. Her dreams waited around the corner, outpacing her resources.

"Why not go home to Quebec?" he asked, touched by the cultural bond.

"There's nothing for me there, Sir. My brother runs the family farm. They don't need another mouth to feed."

Once she had been pretty, he thought. High cheek bones with a Native leavening. Raven black hair like his, but straight. Chestnut brown eyes. Her skin was sallow from lack of sun, and the skin slack on her bones. Still, the structure was there, like a good skiff.

He nodded in respect. Then he took out his notebook and asked about Vicky.

A sadness crossed her eyes like a shadow, and she turned and coughed into a handkerchief. "Someone mentioned a girl dying. Me, I don't read so good. *Calice.* She moved out of here to a nice hotel after I came. No one else here would remember her, *pauvre petite mouton.*"

"Did she live with you?" he asked, looking around with discretion. "Or in another room?"

"Right here. We shared that very bed, *deux petites pois.* She came back, you say? I thought I saw her on Store Street getting into a fine carriage."

"Was she in the . . . trade then?" He knew the answer, a good test.

Diane tried to answer, but had to take a sip of tea. "She had some gentlemen friends. I won't pretend not. Don't like to speak ill of the dead." She pointed to a faded candy box. "Bought me those for my birthday all those years ago. Victoria always shared her sweets. I keep buttons in it."

So they hadn't talked after her return. Still, he needed to know about her parents. That was his next mission.

"When she left for the States on her expectations, she called them, she sent me postcards. I still have them." She turned to a shabby bureau and lifted out two pictures. One was of San Francisco harbor, the other a grand hotel called the Palace. "A friend read them to me. Here, you look."

Edwin checked the stamp side of the cards. There was no return address, merely the usual good wishes. It was tempting to think that she had lived in such a hotel, but it wasn't likely. Cards sold for a penny. He had collected them in an album his *zayde* gave him, lost in the many moves.

"Do you know where her parents live?" They might be dead, too. Were there siblings?

"Bless her heart. She sent them what she could. The old couple was better off not wondering how she'd earned it. Farmers, they are, out Sooke way, if they're still alive. She took the stage to see them." She gave a slight sniff. "They don't know nothing of city ways. And far off like that, they wouldn't hear bad about her."

"Mrs. Lajeunesse, we want to find out who killed her."

Diane gave a broad laugh. "Thank the Merciful Mary for you, then. Why would you care about a girl like that?" It wasn't said as an accusation as much as in wonderment.

Edwin swallowed back a heavy lump. "Every . . . life is important to me." He met her eyes until she blinked. She moved closer, almost touching him. A rank smell of sweat and unwashed clothes nearly made him retreat, but he froze. How could she wash, other than in a cold basin?

"Please, *monsieur*. Find out who did this." She gripped his sleeve in a touching gesture, fever in her dark eyes explaining the cough.

"Do you have any ideas that would help? People she knew?"

Her thin brows creased with reflection. "She had some rich friends then. They still might be around. Ask them."

"Give me a name." His nerves leaped at a possible lead.

"She was right close about that. Says what I didn't know couldn't hurt me." She paused and then looked up brightly. "She was as near as a sister. May she rest with *les anges.*"

"In her profession," he said, "this can happen to women. Unless they are protected."

"So Vicky said. She was smart as a whip." She leaned closer.

"Once I suggested that she join up with one of the fancy houses. Champagne, a parlor, a piano, even a maid and cook. But she was her own mistress, she was. Wouldn't have none of that."

One shoulder of her faded kimono slipped and she reached for it, shielding her modesty. She was no more than five feet tall, the product of malnutrition and hard use. Many wealthy families who needed servants would hire neither the Irish nor the French. The pungency of an unemptied chamber pot peeking from under the bed made his nostrils flare.

"It's funny, though, Mister. Something I thought of." She smothered a cough with her small hand.

He paused. From fifteen years ago? "And what's that?"

"She said that the finest man she met was a man but no man." She cocked her head and gave a nervous giggle. "Now what could she have meant by that riddle? A man's a man, ain't he?"

As he left, he handed her what he had in his wallet. Four dollars. She could eat for a month if she were careful. But he didn't like the sound of her lungs. Consumption thrived under these conditions. No cure in dry sunny California for his country-woman.

Tears brimmed in her eyes as she tucked the money into a tattered Bible on her dresser. A rosary hung from the mirror corner. "And Mister, you see her parents, please tell them that I'll pray for her, such as I am."

# CHAPTER NINE

Edwin enjoyed the smell of a clean stable with fresh feed and the floors mucked out. Sullivan's Livery on North Park Street was in walking distance, with a lush clover pasture in summer. Acreages were being swallowed by development now that the city was thriving.

Two miniature donkeys which Sully kept for his kids hee-hawed as he passed. No eternal use, the hayburners were, but the kids put straw hats on them and rode them in parades.

Pegasus, Edwin's ten-year-old dapple-gray mare, was munching prime alfalfa in her stall. Sully never cut corners by purchasing moldy fodder. At Edwin's familiar whistle, Peggy whinnied in delight as her ears swiveled. It had been too long since he'd gone for a ride, but her saddle sore had needed to heal. The stable boy Bart greeted him. Edwin always gave him a shinplaster to make sure the horse got her share of oats as well as Saanichton hay. Bart scavenged deadfall apples from the fruit trees along the roads.

Edwin took a curry comb from the shelf and began smoothing the mare's rippling flanks. She nickered and presented her velvet nose for a pat. "She looks good, Bart. Only a white mark left?" The blanket had caught on a tiny brass nail lifting in the saddle. He'd been sick with guilt when he removed her tack for a cool-down walk a month ago.

The boy doffed his cloth cap, wiped sweat from his forehead, and shook back a blond cowlick. His large plaid shirt was

Edwin's hand-me-down. Bart was barefoot, muck up to his bare calves in his patched pants with one crossed suspender. Easier to wash with a cold bucket than to clean his precious boots. Edwin wondered about the risk of lockjaw. "Got some salve from the horse man, and she's chipper as ever. Can't hardly find it now except where the hair's coming back." He took great pride in caring for the horses and hoped to be a jockey someday at the nearby racetrack.

"Miracle worker." Edwin pulled the small but tasty Gravenstein apple from his pocket and gave it to the boy to feed her. From another he took a paper bag of humbugs. The youngster was barely twelve and lived in the loft, an orphan who wandered by a hungry week after his mother died from typhus. Aloysius (Sully) Sullivan made sure the boy had warm blankets for the hay and three daily meals, including stew, soup, and bread and the occasional pie from his plump wife.

"I have a good joke for you, Sir," Bart said with a sly look as he sucked on the candy. "What did the chick say when the hen laid an orange?"

Trading funnies was their habit. Edwin played along. "I give up. That's a real head-scratcher."

"Come look at the orange mar-ma-lade," Bart said, grinning ear to ear.

Edwin ruffled his hair. Preserves would be a rare treat for the boy. He checked his timepiece. Ten already. No time to waste.

"Going far?" They both laughed as a barn cat disappeared around the corner of the tack room with a fat mouse in its mouth. Everything earned its keep.

McBride had made it clear that Edwin was to deliver the sad message in person, now that they knew where the family lived. "A bloody piece of paper is no way to tell a mother and father that their loved one has been murdered. Get used to it, Detective Sergeant. That's why you're not walking a beat anymore.

You're supposed to have a few brains. *Savvy fare.* Do it with heart, man."

For the last few hours, Edwin had been running through all the clichés. *Sorry for your loss. In a better place. With the angels now.* Dutiful neither as a Roman Catholic or a Jew, he envied the blind faithful who believed in a heaven. In this capacity, a woman might do a better job. He felt helpless dealing with tears, and so did the other fellows, if they'd admit it.

"Out to the Western Communities. To Sooke. I'll be back before dark." It was nearly twenty-five miles, hours of rough riding, best in midsummer when the mud dried up. The thought of traveling at night with the horse ready to cripple itself and its rider in a fall was not pleasant. He hoped there wouldn't be any delays at the bridges.

"What about bandits, highwaymen like Billy the Kid? Fill you full of holes as easy as look at you." He mimed a quick double draw. *Pow pow, pow.* "Why not take the stage like a gent?"

Sully had been fooling with the lad, spinning him stories. Edwin kept a straight face. "I don't have all day. This is Her Majesty's business." From his capacious oilskin coat, Edwin pulled a long Colt pistol. Precaution for the road. Normally he didn't carry it unless he was expected to make an arrest.

"That's a beauty. Can I hold it? I'll be real careful. I shoots rats with the twenty-two varmint rifle we keep in the barn."

"It's loaded, so not this time." One of his days off, he'd ride Bart pillion out to the quarries for target practice. The boy needed a man to look up to. Edwin had been scarcely that age when his father had left them.

His cheeks puffing with effort, Bart lugged in the saddle, a modified English and cavalry style, cleaned and soaped. Edwin checked it over to avoid carelessness which had hurt his mare. Adding the saddlebags with the pistol and a flask of water, he cinched up the girths while Bart shoved in the bit and led Peggy outside. "Check her sides now. She'll gobble air and then the saddle will slip off. It's her little trick, it is." A frisky gelding watched them from the paddock and neighed a greeting. Quacking geese moved aside in prickly fashion. They were as good as watchdogs as their ancient Roman ancestors. Horse stealing was a serious offense.

Giving the boy a salute, Edwin mounted easily and trotted though the gates and down North Park to Douglas at a brisk pace, keeping to the left. Delivery wagons had begun to crowd the roads. A team of oxen, rarer in town but willing beasts for the heaviest burdens, pulled a load of barrels of oolichan oil for lamps. What with one hunting ground closing after another, the sealing which had boosted the harbor was disappearing as fast as the whaling. Now they had gaslight and even electricity. When would a newfangled horseless carriage appear to scare the dickens out of the horses?

Then he headed south, passing over the bridges into Esquimalt, its fields of dairy herds the first source of fresh butter in the colony. Now all had been divided into building lots for miles.

It felt good to be in the saddle again. He advanced to a light canter. Peggy high-stepped in the open air. If only he could take her out every day like a privileged gentleman. Reggie was afraid of horses, having been kicked by a polo pony at his older brother's match.

The Craigflower farm property came into view. The new colony had established farms as quickly as possible. In addition to housing for the workers, they even had a school dating back to 1854. Only out an hour and skipping breakfast, Edwin was tempted to stop at the Four Mile Hotel, but denied himself.

The island more resembled the wilds of Scotland or Wales before forests fell to the ax to feed the sawmills. Nostalgic plantings of fierce gorse and broom by the homesick Captain Grant had helped the illusion. Local plants had been elbowed out by the pernicious if cheerful yellow blooms. Edwin loved the acres of wild blue camas that the Natives prized for its edible bulbs. Then the parcels ceased and what remained of the Constance Cove Farm began. The lands were further divided by the passing of the Esquimalt and Nanaimo Railway, which looped back north and through the wild Malahat.

Fort Rodd Hill came next, a high promontory where the military was building the latest in gun emplacements as protection from an attack by sea. Then past the Hatley property, the fields of Metchosin, and finally onto the winding road leading to Sooke, like entering another deep-green, shadowy country.

Colwood Corners sounded almost urban, but was still pastoral. The Peatts owned much of the land around Kelly Road. Wherever the land flattened, crops waved in the breeze along with daisies, another hardy transplant for spring blooms. Crossing streams, he could see the flap of a beaver tail and its V-shape wake where it made its dams and caused flooding. They hadn't yet been hunted out, because the rage for beaver hats had waned. Once he'd seen an old and faded red penny postage stamp with the diligent rodent. A feller at the logging camp had called Edwin a "beaver beater" and received a fist to the jaw.

The old Sooke Road had been begun in 1874 at the cost of nearly five hundred dollars as a wagon route to the prosperous Muir farm, Woodside. Apple orchards flanked the roadside in a few clearings, then melded into the thickness of cedar and firs, dark even in high summer. Where the sun peeked in, the shy and sinuous arbutus flourished. Even at Dewdney Flats, he was getting weary from the saddle. Then came the Summit, where snow appeared on the heights.

A farmer in a wagon passed him with a load of wizened winter swedes and cabbages. Another carried sheaves of hay for town stables. At one spot by a waterfall, the old open stage was stuck in the mud. Male passengers had been rousted out to free the vehicle and looked aggravated to be besmirching their clothes. A bonneted female face leaning over her seat warned her portly husband not to "have a bloody heart attack." Who lived way out there? The holy trinity of fishermen, lumberjacks, and farmers along with cheaper land. Timber from one built the houses, and the products of the other two filled the bellies.

At one bend atop a long hill, Edwin gazed up the mossy rocks to the heights, where a pair of intelligent ravens warbled and swooped, part of the aboriginal mythology. Sweating mercilessly, he dismounted, lashed his canvas duster and coat behind him like a bedroll, and drank deeply from the canteen. The container gave the sweet water an unpleasant, metallic taste.

Back on horseback, he passed a farm at Burnt Timbers Road, where a Mrs. Veitch welcomed travelers. Then he climbed again and found himself overlooking Cooper's Cove. From there a steam ferry moved goods around the broad Sooke harbor, people like dolls on the far wharves. Peggy needed a rest and a good rubdown later for yeoman duty.

Then as he descended through another copse of trees, the land opened again and acres of pale green oats waved welcome. This land to the north into the hills and south down to the water belonged to the Lannons. Heavy Douglas firs still stood guard, but U.S. markets were hungry for fresh wood, barge by barge chomping away the island. Herds of dairy cattle roamed in the distance. They were also passing the T'Souke Reserve, hidden by trees. The melting pot included Scots, Natives, English, and French Canadians intermarrying in the "custom of the country." One of the founding fathers, Douglas, had a mother from Barbados, and his wife was half Native.

At the Milne Store, Edwin dismounted and watered Peggy at the tank, giving the heaving flanks a pat. The village core boasted a hotel and a couple of saloons. Loggers and fishermen had heavy thirsts.

The Sooke River basin was postcard pretty, green hills across the water south and behind north into the San Juans, topped by Mount Quimper, a Spanish name from the early explorers. A small fishing boat made its way from the estuary down the strait, looking for returning salmon stocks headed up the spawning creeks. Everyone feasted on salmon, fresh, dried, or smoked, like the poor ate lobster in the Maritimes. That folks back East thought that smoked salmon was a luxury made him smile.

He fastened Peggy to the rail beside a handsome pinto pony. From his stash, he took a bag of oats, put them in a feedbag, and fastened it to her head. "Eat hearty, girl. It's been a long haul for you. Maybe we can find tender green grass at the next stop. Or cow parsnip." The liquid eyes thanked him, and her jaws chomped into action.

Edwin thumped up the wooden stairs and went inside. The floor planks creaked as he avoided new pans and pots hanging from the ceiling. Bins of flour, sugar, and other staples lined the shelves along with cans of vegetables, beans, fruit, and soup. A man was turning a crank, filling the air with the smell of fresh-roasted coffee beans. Canada loved its tea, but adopted java from its American cousins.

"I'm looking for . . ." Suddenly he felt stupid. He still didn't know if Victoria had been using another name. But Diane had said that her family lived here. "Do you know the Crosse farm?"

"You've landed at the right place, neighbor. I know every pond, puddle, and pool within fifty miles hereabouts. Care for some joe? Looks like you came a long way." The man in a white smock, his arms with sleeves pulled up with garters, gestured to a blue enamel pot on the woodstove. A corncob pipe puffed out an aromatic blend. If anyone could afford a good tobacco, a merchant could.

Edwin nodded and pulled up a barrel seat at a plank counter. Declining sugar and seeing no cream, he was handed a crockery mug of brew so strong that a spoon could stand in it. The wall was covered with a selection of animal traps, ropes, tools, fishing gear, and saddlery.

After giving his customer a brief history of the town, the clerk stabbed his truncated index finger at a rough map behind the counter. "Crosse farm's not far. Keep on the main road, but at Otter Point Road turn right. Straight on goes to Woodside Farm, where we get our mail. About half a mile on the right, there she be. Fifty acres. Poor soil though he got it cheap enough. Not much of a living, even plowing in seaweed over the years. Crosse raises a few cattle, does a bit of beekeeping for extras. When he goes, the place will turn back to bush, I expect."

"That's sad after so much work. No sons, then?" Victoria hadn't been in search of a farm boy to marry, the usual pattern.

The clerk rubbed the back of his neck and relocated the pipe into the other corner of his mouth. "That's another story. Guess you'll see when you gets there." He took down a glass jar and offered it to Edwin. "Have a barley sugar candy. We're neighborly, not like the snotty townies." He added a few more details for travelers.

Edwin didn't imagine that it took much in this mild climate to keep a body and soul alive on a small farm, not if you had a boy or two and a good wife. Chickens for eggs and meat, a few cattle, hay to cut for feed, a pig grown on scraps, then apple, pear, and plum trees and your own garden for produce. A good life if you could stomach the monotony. His mother would wither and die. Farmers didn't care if they saw the latest play, read the new books, or heard political developments as quickly as they moved through intercontinental telegraph lines.

Edwin had had enough hard work when he wildcatted around the island from sixteen to twenty, sending back every penny so that Naomi and he could escape that drafty rooming house on Pembroke. He'd worked off fishing boats as far as the wild Hecate Strait and run a trapline around Lake Cowichan. The worst thing he'd ever done was dig coal in Nanaimo. Edwin hated being dirty with a cold creek for a bathtub. The day that his fingernails were clean again and he could shave his itchy beard had been the second happiest in his life.

Crunching a scrap of eggshell left in the coffee and sucking on the sweet, Edwin left a few coins, remounted, and rode away, passing a small church. He was surprised to see a solemn funeral procession. Women in buckboards. Men and children walked behind. No fancy undertaker. No elaborate mourning clothes. A makeshift spruce coffin.

He admired the Sooke River Bridge, larger and stronger than the original. A log boom a hundred feet long directed the drift timber. On the other side was the Phillips Farm. Dogs were baying, a safeguard against cougar or bear. Peacocks strutting their stuff made him laugh. The farmer must have visited Beacon Hill Park or missed the stately homes of England. A swampy area glowed with bright yellow swamp-cabbage flowers. The Natives used the large leaves for platters and in times of hardship, consumed the malodorous but nourishing plant.

In the 1860s, a gold rush up the Sooke River at Leechtown had brought a government trail north as well as a slapped-up hotel on the harbor front near Murray Road. Then going up the long hill, he passed the substantial two-story Charters House and Charters Hall Community Centre. Then a one-room schoolhouse. He remembered the clerk saying that the Throup farm and finally the Murrays were supposed to be quite hospitable. Visitors were cheap entertainment for the price of a meal.

The village was home to a few hundred people, some clustered near the pretty harbor, others in the outlying farms.

Today's calm harbor belied the dangers outside its safety. The strait was a perilous mistress. Many ships had been lost in this fifty-mile entry to Puget Sound and the Strait of Georgia. News of the sinking of the SS *Pacific* had been unknown for days until a boy found the wreckage on the beach. Not long after that, a rescue trail was made along the telegraph line to Cape Beale and the Trans-Pacific cable, but it would take a hardy soul to survive the walk alone.

A large dark brown shape galumphed across the road, causing Peggy to shy. Edwin regained his seat and came to a halt, his eyes in the bush. A tiny bear cub hardly bigger than a dog padded after its mother. "Easy, girl. They want nothing to do with us." He leaned to pat her neck, then urged a trot.

Ten minutes later, he nosed telltale smoke before he reached the clearing. The tiny homestead held a cabin and small barn, the bare minimum. Vicky's parents would be in their fifties, at the end of their hardscrabble lives. They hadn't even clapboarded the cabin or added an addition. No wonder their daughter had wanted out. What more would there have been for her other than to marry some jughead and end up with a Mother Hubbard brood? It had been the way of the world since the dawn of agrarian society.

A large mixed-breed collie dog with matted hair raised itself to greet him, but seemed disinclined to bark and didn't bother the horse. From the unsteady look of its rear legs and its bleary eyes, it was an ancient fellow, unable to follow its sagging bollocks' urges toward neighborhood bitches in heat. Black and white hens and a rooster roamed the yard, pecking at grubs. In a fenced area half a dozen milk goats baahed and butted each other. Hardly ten acres cleared, backbreaking rocks piled in the middle of both small fields. Then there would be cutting the trees, burning the stumps, and hauling them off with oxen, sometimes borrowed. A brutal tale inviting fatal accidents.

A flourishing farm with able sons would have had a two-story house to replace the cabin, a much larger barn, outbuildings, and split-rail fences. Here, the alders were creeping back over the property. The old bull looked too tired to perform, and only two cows roamed, hardly enough to sell milk beyond the family's needs. A huge manure pile dwarfed the barn. An enormous pig grunted in its filthy pen, a cheap but dependable meat and lard source. A lard-crust pie was likely the one cheery spot in the week.

Edwin fastened the reins to a fence so that Peggy could browse the lush green grass. He took off his Stetson and made his way to the house, feeling less than professional after putting on his crumpled suit coat. A makeshift fence of bent alder twigs kept the house from the beasts. Bluebells and phlox added color, and a small garden stood at the side, junk sawmill slab for a rustic deer fence. A well with a foundation of river rock sat by the house, its oaken bucket dangling. The door to a privy with a moon on the door hung crookedly. Inside would be an inevitable Eaton catalog or worse yet, corncobs. He walked up the two steps to the porch. Not even a smokehouse at the side for the ubiquitous salmon at the nearby creeks. Reconciling Victoria's plush room at the Cadogan with this penury stretched the imagination. "Hello, the house," he called. Then a blast rang out, and he ducked.

# CHAPTER TEN

From around a corner of a chicken house came a man with a shotgun bent over his arm. "That'll teach that weasel to go after my hens. Hello, yourself, Sir. You'd best be no salesman, for there's no penny to spare here. But you are welcome to a cold drink of buttermilk," said a stooped man with a grizzled beard and a slight limp. A deep burn down the side of his face testified to an ancient mishap, perhaps at a forge.

"I have some . . . news if you are Mr. Crosse."

"That I am." Leaving his barn boots outside, Crosse opened the door for Edwin and showed him into the one room serving as kitchen, living room, and dining room. Beyond were two doors, presumably to bedrooms. A cheap cook stove warmed the building. From one room came a gaunt woman, flour on her face, cleaning her hands on her worn meal-sack apron. "Ma, my tea?" came a call from the rear.

She looked tired and careworn, but her blue-green eyes belonged to her daughter. "Pardon, Sir. Our son, John Daniel. He's not strong. A martyr to health." She tapped at her heart, then went to the stove and poured hot water from the pot into a tea pot, swirling it first to warm the pot. Then she dropped in a tablespoon of soggy tea leaves from a saucer.

"It's a pleasure to see a visitor. Are ye bound for the Gordon place down by the water? I'm George Crosse. My wife, Annie. Dearheart, get the man a cup of tea." He extended a hand scarred and scabbed with the dangerous and demanding business of farming, where an errant nail carried lockjaw or a hoof from a cantankerous cow could kick a head into eternity. Annie presented a cracked floral cup, yet probably their best. Edwin took it and chose a pressback chair by the room's only table, declining the offer of honey.

Edwin bowed his head. This part he hated. He wished that a flask of brandy were every officer's kit. Instead he took a neighborly sip of the tea, weak as a kitten. "I have no kind way to tell you this. Your daughter Victoria—"

A gasp went up, and the plain cup the old man held shattered on the floor. "Maaaaaaa" came a whiney sound from the other room.

The woman turned to George, then sank onto a chair, weeping. "Pa, can you . . ." Her voice dwindled into the hopelessness only those bereft of all comfort can know.

"Who's there? Is something wrong?" A scuffle sounded, and in the doorway leaning on a makeshift crutch stood a cadaverous man with a ghostly face. He was hollow-eyed, but freshly shaved and his narrow head bowl-cut. His nightshirt was patched and dingy. Annie gathered herself and got up to help him back to bed.

"John Daniel, you'll catch your death in this draft. You only just got over that catarrh." John Daniel blinked at the light from the window and let himself be led away, muttering. Edwin wondered if he were feverish or half-witted.

"You were saying, Sir. About our Vicky?" asked George. His hand trembled as he ran it through his hair. Crinkled eyes and leathery skin testified to a rough life outdoors. Tar paper was tacked to the wall, wet patches showing where the chinking was inadequate. Winters would be long and hard with the punishing rain. Beasts in the barn had it better, husbanding warmth in their stalls.

"I'm afraid she came to harm at the hands of a criminal. She died a few days ago," Edwin said. "We recently learned that you were in Sooke." He explained a few details of the murder, trying not to be specific. What good would it do? Of death's thousand doors, all had the same destination. Had they thought that their daughter could survive alone in the city? And yet she had for fifteen years. Anomalies around him had been purchased with her life. A fancy oil lamp on a deal table. A rocking chair, nearly new, by the fireplace. A thick red-and-black Hudson's Bay blanket.

The old man bowed his head. "Victoria would have been alive if she'd stayed. But she didn't want the life. Never encouraged the boys to court her. She learned her letters right quick at the school. I thought she might make a teacher. Had her grade eight, too. And she was a kind girl. Good with the lambs when we had them. A newborn mite seemed dead and she wrapped it and put it behind the stove, until . . ." His voice broke and he turned away. Talking about the good memories seemed to ease his grief. Edwin understood this. The scene of his father's bloodied head he didn't want to revisit, but he wanted to know the truth, and someday he would.

"I met her once a long time ago. You have every right to be proud of her." It didn't seem proper to say that his mother painted her portraits. Not *those* kinds of portraits.

His voice shook. "How did she die, Sir? Did she suffer? Was there pain? Oh, tell me not."

Edwin firmed up his lips. "It was very fast." Not exactly true, but he hoped they wouldn't ask for more.

Edwin took out his notebook. "I want to bring this criminal to justice. We need to know details about her life, such as where she lived in the city. In this way perhaps we can discover a path to her killer. Man to man, I can tell you that she was strangled, but perhaps it wouldn't be a good idea to inform your wife. Women are soft creatures."

Annie came back into the room. Crosse hastened up beside her and took her arm gently. "This gentleman, he's from the police. Victoria has lost her life sudden-like. A scoundrel took it through no fault of her own. We have to help him, Ma."

"Oh, God. The poor sparrow. That's why I dreamed of her last night. She's in God's own nest now." The woman hugged her husband for the briefest of moments, took a deep breath and sat down, her apron twisted in her reddened, careworn hands, abused by harsh alkali soaps and scalding water. She buried her face in her arms and wept without sound as the men shifted in their chairs. Her husband got up to rub her back. Then he rested, hands on his knees, shaking his head like an old soul.

At last she quieted, then gave a gesture to the bedroom with her thumb. "He's all we have now, is John Daniel. And he can't help. We wondered if Victoria might have a son . . . not that she was the marrying kind, but . . ."

Here she looked at her husband. "Even on the wrong side of the bed, George means. We would have raised him, someone to help on the farm. Keep it in the family."

"I gather she's been away for several years." How could he explain the undertaking fees and stone? Best let the tenor of the talk decide.

"Aye, yes, she was barely sixteen when she left for the city. Her christened name was Ruth, like my mother, but it was too plain for her. She picked Victoria because of the old Queen's daughter. She was known as Vicky, too. Empress of some country. Our Vicky was a big help to us before that, wasn't she, Father?" For seconds, her eyes glowed with the happiness Edwin had seen a minute ago.

George straightened his shoulders. "Mother taught her to sew and mend. When she were fifteen, she said she were going to be a ladies' maid and have her own silver comb and brush. A jolly good place where the rich live, and she could have met a fine man, even a butler. Farming is a hard lot, free though you might be. And proper enough for her kin going back these three hundred years. My pa came from Milton Damerel in Devon, in a boat across the sea in 1845. Half of Devon cleared out for Canada's free land. His cousins came to Ontario. But when we heard about it out here, he brought us all. I'm the only bairn left. This farm's been ours since 1870."

So she'd been in town for four years when she met him. Long enough to know what she wanted and what she couldn't have. "You couldn't have been able to see her very often, being so far away."

"Came one Sunday a month, she did. That was before the stage, so she had to find a ride. There's always someone going in and out, like a pretty girl to talk to. She gave us what she could. Helped her mother with the mending and John Daniel's needs." He squeezed the bridge of his nose. His hair was thick and snowy white, his best feature. Vicky had inherited her mother's small nose, not his honker.

"And then she were far away in the States for nigh onto fifteen years," Annie added. "She sent us more money as time went on. Allowed Pa to hire a lad for some of the work when he broke his hand. Otherwise we might have had to—"

"She was in San Francisco, I believe?" What she had done in a big city like that, he imagined that he knew.

"Thought she was going to get rich. Then one day a year ago, the money stopped. We were afraid that she were poorly. Our letters came back unopened. The schoolmarm helped us write them."

"And then only a few months ago . . . La, she looked grand, didn't she, Pa? A real treat."

The old man nodded and laid a finger on his potato nose to wipe away a drip. Then he thought better of it and hauled out a handkerchief, giving his beak a long blow.

"You must have been so happy that she had returned."

They looked one to the other. "Aye, so we were. And a job, too. Someone she'd met on the boat. A real stroke of luck. She was working at the Victoria Theatre, doncha know? A grand place. Making the costumes, are you, I asked? She was clever with a needle. But she told us that she was going to be an actress herself, though her pa and I didn't hold with that. We're not a churchgoing family since Sooke has no pastor, but we have a family Bible. Sometimes we share Sabbath with the neighbors and they read it." A worn King James version sat proudly on the mantelpiece.

Edwin kept quiet. It seemed strange for Vicky to be starting a career as an actress at her age. The business preferred ingénues barely out of their teens. "How many times did you see her since then?"

"Oh, one or two more. She had money for the stage."

"And the last time?"

"Was two Saturdays ago, wasn't it, Pa? Said she couldn't come on Sundays no more. That was part of her job. She brought us ever the most beautiful box of French soap for me. A razor for her pa. Chocolate creams from a shop called Rogers. A real treat for us'n glad to nibble honeycomb at Christmas. I'm ashamed to say we et it all up that very week."

Vicky had been secretive with her parents. For good reason. "Would she have spoken to anyone else around here? An old friend?"

"Naw, Sir. She kept to herself here. And as for the new friends, why bring them to this lowly place?" She swept her hand in embarrassment.

"And she didn't say where she was living?"

"Some fancy hotel. Had a room all her own. Thanks to that Abb . . . Abb . . ."

"Abbott it was." His wife pursued her lips.

George held up a finger. "That's it. Abbott. You had more words with her than did I."

"The one as got her the new blue dress she wore. She kind of laughed about that room. Right jolly she was." His wife shooed a mangy cat from under the table, and it ran out the door.

Edwin sat up with interest and made a note. Abbott again. But that was a dead end, wasn't it? "No first name for the man?"

"We don't know, sir. It was mentioned only the one time. Perhaps a beau. Her ma asked were she getting married, and she did tip her the wink. Victoria was very choosy. We thought she was going to be an old maid." At the irony of this statement, he looked suddenly at the ground, putting his hands on his heavily stained trousers with a whiff of the barn muck. His old-fashioned smock belonged in George I's Devon.

His wife's knobby, chapped hands worried themselves. "Forgive me for asking, Sir, but can we have her home? Pray God she isn't in the cold ground already, is she? We don't know how things work over there."

Edwin explained that any effects would be returned as soon as possible. He'd buy her a burial dress, not that he'd mention that. They would open the coffin and have a last look at her. People always did, embalming or not. "That will be taken care of. Official funds from the city. Don't worry. I'll send a telegram to Sooke letting you know when to expect . . . her. No more than another day or two at the most."

"La, sir, she'll be buried here in our own family ground with two little babbies that sickened before they were even toddling and both her grandparents on George's side." She looked out the window to a small plot with wooden carved markers. A pleasant place, under a large arbutus tree winding branches in upward in a prayer to its creator, pale thin brown bark peeling to reveal light green beneath.

George reached for a long, narrow notebook with a leather cover. "Sir, we none of us have our letters. Except for Victoria. Could you please write down her name and the date she passed to her Lord? This is our only record. We'd be beholden to you."

The pages chronicled, in different writing styles, dates of birth and also farm expenditures and prices for sales of the occasional animal. Ten bushels of oats. Two hundred pounds of potatoes. Paltry profit for a lifetime of cares and pain. With his pencil, Edwin added the sadness. Imagine a world where you had to depend on the kindness and ethics of someone else for tasks needing literacy or numeracy. Trust was all they had.

With a final "sorry for your loss," he took his leave, collected Peggy, and was back on the road, his stomach roiling with hunger. No time before dark to stop now. He'd have to let one side of his gut debate the other. At least it wasn't raining . . . yet.

The way back went faster, as it always did. A few miles east in Saseenos, he saw a young boy trudging along the road. He carried a bindle on a stick. His floppy boots were hand-me-downs. A painful limp signaled blisters. If traveling on horse seemed tiresome, this seemed worse.

Edwin trotted alongside. "How far are you going, son? Can I give you a ride?"

The boy looked up and brightened. "All the way to the Millstream? Honest, Mister?"

"I'm going that way. Come on up." He reached down and pulled the boy up behind him. The lad didn't weight more than ninety pounds. "You won't make it there before dark. How did you happen to be out on the high road at this late hour?"

"My uncle has a fishing boat, and I've been helping him. I earned a whole dollar hauling crabs this week. And I slept on the ship, too. In a real hammock like in the navy. We had a fry up every morning. I bet that I gained five pounds. I'm taking

my wages home to Ma, and we're going to have the best supper. She don't get but four cents a pound for collecting rags."

"I bet you missed her." At least the boy wasn't without a bed.
But at this pace, he wouldn't be home until midnight.

"I'm mighty worried. The baby died last month, and my two
brothers have had the fever. I'm the oldest, see. My name's
Charley."

"Call me Ned," said Edwin. "I don't have any brothers or
sisters." The boy mentioned no father, and it seemed better not
to pursue that. The lad's trusting arms wrapped around him.
Edwin hadn't given much thought to children. But it might feel
good to teach a boy how to fish and hunt, or spoil a girl with
dresses and music lessons. Problem was, you needed a wife.

When after another two hours, they finally reached the Six
Mile Pub at Millstream, Edwin dropped off the lad, pressing
coins into his hand. "Get your mother something special, son.
Candy or a pretty ribbon. You know how women are."

"I'll pick her some flowers, too. Those yellow daffy ones," the
boy said. "She likes to put them on the table."

The lad would probably rob a neighbor's garden. He'd done
it himself. As he got Peggy a drink at the stone trough, and then
tied her to the rail, he watched Charley hop down the street.
Kids had such resilience, but no one could go without for long
and not pay the price. If he ruled the world, no young one
would lack a bed, warm clothes, and wholesome food.

Edwin approached the pub as three sailors stumbled down
the steps, holding each other up, but laughing and not belliger-
ent. He'd broken up enough fights early on in the force,
especially when the ships docked after being months at sea with
watery grog and wormy hardtack.

The inn had been one of the first on the stage line started in
the 1880s and served as a drop-off for the Royal Mail. In 1855
it had been the Parsons Bridge Hotel, a focal point for the Brit-

ish sailors who filled ships' water barrels at the mouth. The proximity to the Esquimalt naval base guaranteed steady business.

He took a seat next to a cheery grate inside the dark roadhouse and ordered a pint of lager, finishing half on the spot after the dusty ride and, after a satisfying burp, asking for another. He imagined how Charley's mother would look when she saw the money. Where did they live? A small room in a ramshackle firetrap? A tarpaper shack cobbled from driftwood?

"What fare have you tonight, Innkeeper?" he asked the portly man with a long white apron. In the corner, sailors were tossing darts, laughing and swearing.

"Beef stew with Yorkshire. My good wife is the best pudding maker in British Columbia, I'll warrant. High and light as a cloud. Savory drippings and gravy. And I buy the beef from Craigflower Farm. None of those tough mainland steers. Swim them clear to Cattle Point, I bet."

"Any oysters?"

"New barrel from Fanny Bay. Fresh off the steamer."

"A dozen to start, then. And beef stew it is. Plenty of bread, too. I've been riding half the day." He shifted his backside on the bench, unable to find a comfortable position.

The briny oysters slaked his thirst, even with tiny grains of sand from the shucking. And the tender beef, gravy, and pudding were everything the innkeeper had promised. He felt so stuffed that he could have crawled to the dark inglenook for a short nap had Peggy not been waiting hungry. One of the men was playing a concertina. "My Old Kentucky Home." Edwin blinked at the oil painting of a lady reclining with Gladdy at her rosy feet. What would they say if they knew? He laughed to himself. It wasn't Victoria. This model was raven-haired. If he remembered correctly, she'd gone to Whitehorse to sing in a saloon and "get rich" overnight.

Nearly nodding off over a second pint, he roused himself to pay and went out to douse his head in the cold stream. A tiny green tree frog hopped to safety. It was six and darkening. So Victoria thought she was getting married? Or was she gulling her parents? And that Abbott name again. He'd combed the telephone book, the city directory, and the tax rolls with no luck. One more chore for tonight.

Back over the bridge, he detoured to the Victoria Theatre. A poster advertised the upcoming, one-night-only appearance of the famous thespian Richard Mansfield in *Beau Brummell*. Tonight was the last showing of the hit comedy *A Railroad Ticket*, with Freeman's Funmakers. At the wicket he was told by a stern, horse-faced woman with her hair in a bun to go around to the rear. Entering from the alley, backstage he found a wee gnome perched on a stool, reading the paper.

His cheek rubied by a port-wine stain, the man looked up. "No visitors backstage, Sir. It's the last night for Mr. Canfield. Everyone in town's seen him. Filled every night, just like in Seattle. You'll have to wait until after the performance unless you wants me to give some lady flowers or a note." He wriggled a fuzzy gray eyebrow.

"I'm with the police."

The man leapt to his feet. "Nothing untoward here, Sir. And we just had a fire inspection." Purged many times over by flames, Victoria took its fire protection very seriously, especially with multistoried buildings. City maps listed all businesses in colors, even opium factories. "Of course if you fancy a free ticket as an officer of the law, I can arrange—"

"It's nothing to do with that. I need to see your manager, or whoever does the hiring and firing."

The man worried a finger in his oversized ear and wiped it on his pants. "Sir, that would be Fred Appleyard, but he's ailing this last week."

"Is there anyone else I can talk to?"

He shook his wattles. "No one else has any truck but Fred. You'll find him in his rooms at the Windsor Hotel. He's damn near out of his head with fever, though. Last I heard the doctor said he might be buying the farm, if you get my meaning. 'It's not the cough what carries you off. It's the coffin they carries you off in.' " His lugubrious tone matched his poetic sentiment.

A bit of praise sometimes greased the wheel. "You seem like you don't miss much. Do you know a man named Abbott associated with the theater?"

The man pursed his thin lips. "That's my aunt's name. Felicia Abbott. But she lives back in Ontario."

Taking his leave, Edwin set out for the old Windsor, which stood at the corner of Courtney and Government and had been one of the first brick buildings in the city, circa 1859. People still talked about an explosion twenty years ago when the brainless owner had gone searching for a gas leak while holding a candle. By her slowed gait, Peggy was tiring, and he felt like a cad. She wasn't Pony Express material, just a faithful horse. "Not long now, Sweetheart. You'll be back in your stall fed and warm." Her limpid eyes gave him the lie.

Ten minutes later, Edwin approached the front desk. All but a few keys were gone from the board behind the clerk. The hotel must have been doing land-office business. "Fred Appleyard?"

The man gave a bored sigh and folded his arms. "Not another one. We've had his haberdasher, his vintner, and his stableman here already today. Word is that he's about dead. That's one way of getting out of debt. Those who plays the ponies pays the piper. Especially if they can't handicap worth a damn."

So Fred was a gambler. It didn't surprise him. But nearly dead? "My business is official." He showed his identification.

A familiar belly in an eye-watering checkered suit approached him. It was former constable Davie Crockett, given the boot from the force for helping himself to a crate of whiskey on an off day as a guard at the docks. "If it isn't our police department itself. How have you and the lads been? Miss me, do you?"

"Not the same, Davie." He looked around and nodded. "I admire your duds. So you've come up in the world."

Davie leaned over and horked up a chaw toward a brass spittoon in the corner. Then he hooked his thumbs in his vest over a trencherman's stomach. "I'm the house detective, if you can believe it. Doesn't pay well in coin, but I gets a room in the basement. Meals, too. I can sleep until ten. All the nasty stuff happens at night, doncher know?"

"I need to talk to Appleyard before he croaks. Could be he's on the lam."

Davie waved the clerk back to his duties as a middle-aged couple collected their key. "If I knew where he is, I'd tell you. His lady friend, not a bad looker for her age, came and got him and took him to her rooms to nurse him back to health. They slipped out in the night, a bell boy said. He always settled his account before, given time. Sends us the theater custom, too."

"What about the new address?"

"Haven't a clue in hell, my friend."

Dead end, Edwin thought. Maybe for Fred, too. Naomi had theater connections. But she had gone to Vancouver by steamer for a few days of shopping. Time to get a bag of oats and a rubdown for his best friend. He was so knackered that he might bed down in Sully's hay himself.

# CHAPTER ELEVEN

Except for the holding cells with the dregs of Saturday night shenanigans, City Hall on Sunday was deserted. Edwin sat in his office and reviewed his notes, scratching a new idea, only to cross it out. Several points nagged at him. The seeming similarity of the third attack, the moving of the body, and that blasted Abbott. What about that silly marble?

He'd met Jones in Bastion Square the day after he'd gone to Sooke. They sat in the courtyard as life swirled around them. "I have some news about our girl," the coroner said. "She wasn't pregnant when she died. In fact, that wasn't in her future. Scar tissue from an old abortion, maybe two. Damn butchers. What's a woman to do, though? Those old wives' tales about drinking gin and taking hot baths are twaddle, and few have the nerve to throw themselves down a set of stairs. Amazing thing is that she escaped a fatal septic infection. And in her . . . business, being barren is a blessing."

"But she had given birth." The thought galvanized him. Was it the emergence of a paternal instinct?

"Bones don't lie. Obviously before the damages. With what results, I can't say."

Edwin paled, his bedazzlement with Vicky sending him careering from one useless clue to another. He cleared his throat and gazed down the street at a small hearse pulled by white ponies. A child's funeral. All the sadder for the miniature ceremony. Some posed their dead babies in photographs with the bereaved family. The closed eyes, awkward poses, and grief-stricken faces. Appalling.

"How is the case coming? I'll be releasing the body today. I can make arrangements to have it sent to Sooke as we discussed."

Edwin looked into the doc's wise old gray-green eyes. "I told her parents. They'll grieve, but it's better than never knowing her fate. Can you set things up with Hayward's? A plain but decent casket? They can send me the bill." There went the money he had saved this year for his father's debts. His personal responsibilities took precedence.

Jones gripped his shoulder in a comrade's touch. "That's real white of you, Edwin. They'll cut me a discount. Allow me to chip in."

"I knew her in better days." Vicky was on her way home at last. He could make later arrangements for the simple stone marker.

A constable sent to the Windsor brought no further news of Fred. As for Abbott, nothing turned up in the files of arrest records. They needed someone full time, indexing and cross-referencing the information. Now there was a job for a woman with quick fingers and sharp eyes. Some said that they might soon operate those typewriting machines, but that took strength.

He munched on a banana, a treat Wong had picked up at Erskine and Wall. Imagine living where year-round you could pick your food from a tree. But without the incentive that came with having to earn a living, where was a civilization? Steps sounded in the hall. One of the cleaning staff? He flipped the browning peel into a wastebasket.

"Tennis, anyone?" Reggie pranced in wearing fresh whites, striking a ridiculous pose. "Rozzer, well met! I stopped by for my racquet. Left it up on the cabinet after I had it restrung. A few of the fellows are going to Caledonia Park this morning to watch a baseball game. Seattle is playing Victoria. Then we'll head for the Carr house to try out their grass court." He hauled over a chair and stood on it to reach to the top of the glassed bookcase, blowing dust from the catgut strings and twanging it like a banjo.

"Have a good time." Was Edwin the only one who cared about Vicky, or shouldn't a policeman take work home? "I was in Sooke to see the Crosses until late on Friday. What did you find out about the tattoo? Don't tell me you haven't started, or I'll break that fool racquet over your head."

Reggie thrust out a placating hand. "Settle down. I made the rounds. At the last place near Store Street, the man was definitely fishy. A lowlife who couldn't lie to save his soul."

"What do you want to do about that? Search his shop about an invented crime and then hit him with this one like your idol Vidocq?"

Reggie had been reading memoirs of the enterprising French thief, who began working with the Sûreté and then founded his own detective agency. His devious interrogation techniques were legion. Edwin found them somewhat unsporting, despite the "any means to an end" philosophy.

"Aren't we in a testy mood?" Reggie told him about the boy on the corner. "It's like having someone on the payroll for nothing. Am I smart, or am I smart?"

"I stand in awe of your initiative, for once." He mock-tipped a hat. "McBride was about to have your sorry hide."

Reggie perched his rump on the edge of the table. "There's something else about that tattoo. I didn't waste all my time at Cambridge, and Mother made me keep all my school notebooks, which I checked posthaste. According to an old rum-pot philosophy tutor, that tattoo is a unicursal hexagram. One line makes the design. Here's the juicy part. The idea dates back to a heretic monk, then to Rabelais himself in a fictional abbey called Thélème. 'Will and Desire prevail over Logic.' "

"What malarkey. You've been reading too much Krafft-Ebing, and probably for the wrong reasons."

"A typical Catholic, fighting against a restrictive upbringing. The more proscription, the sweeter the sin. Daresay you'll find some diddling priests."

Edwin refused to rise to the bait. "Vicky was in the business. But she was not an educated woman. What would she be doing mixed up in that scholarly stuff?"

Reggie clipped and lit a cigar, puffed a few rings, and sighed with contentment. "That's for you to find out, chum. Morris orders these for me. I'd like to go to Cuba sometime. See those señoritas." He made a dancing motion with his swervy hips. "So you went to Sooke, aka the Antipodes."

"Vicky gave her parents all that she could over the years." He filled Reggie in about the Crosse family. Every sad detail.

"Counting on coming into money, was she? Some say *cherchez la femme*. I say *cherchez l'argent*." With an eye on the Regulator clock in the corner, Reggie tucked the racket under his arm and gave Edwin as assessing look, a mischievous smile on his smooth face. His light brown hair was parted, slicked, and ready for action. Under his arm was a straw boater with a red silk ribbon. "This is Sunday, the Lord's day, at least for your Catholic half. Take a break later. We could use another man, even a stodge like you. Four men to nine ladies! Delicious odds. You do play, don't you?" He said it like a dare.

Edwin hated to admit that he was a total novice. When he'd been old enough for the game, he was off earning a living. "Of course, but I really don't have . . . I mean I'm not . . ." He patted his striped shirt and heavy trousers.

"Leave it to me, old son. I'll nip home for an extra costume and we can round up another racquet." Reggie mimed tossing a ball high and serving up an ace.

"I don't know. I—"

"Let's see those gunboats. Come on, put 'em up." He scrutinized Edwin's boots. "Same shoe size as *moi,* maybe a bit wider. You know what the girls say about big feet. Look handsome, stick out your jaw, and give a manly whack now and then. Let the girls win a few. They eat it up. My old fag from Eton who goes to Wimbledon every year gave me a tip for a tricky serve. Works magic with the rustics."

Edwin drummed his fingers on the desk. Nothing else to do right now unless he could find Appleyard . . . before he died. Did he really expect to discover anything helpful among thousands of records, the fading ink barely legible? "But I really should—"

"Stuff and nonsense. The fresh air will do you good. Shake up your brain. It's too nice a day for maundering. 'What can ail thee, knight at arms? Alone and palely loitering.' Carter's Pills is the ticket. Anyway, don't you want to meet some ladies?" He made chicken sounds and flapped his arms until Edwin laughed despite himself.

"You *are* tempting me. Nine girls?" He blinked at the window where the sun punched through the clouds. It was the best day in weeks, ten degrees warmer outside the massive building.

"Nine muses or was it seven? This might be your last chance. More infernal rain tomorrow. Come about one-ish. There will be a grand tea later. Em's sisters know how to lay on a spread."

"M who? Where's the Carr house anyway?"

Reggie looked at him as if he had fallen off a turnip truck. "Emily Carr, you silly goose. On Carr *Street,* get the picture? Down by Beacon Hill Park. Very posh but not hoity-toity. Her pater from Britannia had a mercantile business on Wharf Street. Quite the gold-rush tycoon. He sold out and then died a few years ago—the mother, too. The family has the old manse, though most of the original acreage is gone. The older sister runs things. Em gives art lessons. Quite the independent woman. And talk about a sight for sore eyes." His wolf whistle rattled the windows.

"Only sisters? What a henhouse. No wonder you need a few roosters."

"Not *all* women. Five ladies and a brother. Nice chap, but I think he's a lunger. Clara's been married, and the bounder ran off and left her with kiddies. Em is a corker, though. If I didn't have the old ball and chain with Carrie . . ." He drew a shapely form with his hands.

"You talked me into it. So where is the house?" Edwin didn't remember the last time he had gone out for a social occasion other than when his mother sent him to a concert with a colonel's niece from Kingston. Pretty girl with trim ankles, but she turned out to be a missionary heading for the Punjab and chirped on about saving brown souls.

"Go down Birdcage Walk, jog around and keep south, then take Carr and look for the gardens and court. Two-story with a porch. Italianate. Tidy but no mansion. Very tasteful. Carrie and I hope to have one just like it. With my own billiard table."

Edwin watched his friend go, and heard him bellowing "Ta-ra-ra-boom-de-ay" all the way down the hall. He pored over the material again, picking up the strange marble from Vicky's pockets and rolling it between his fingers. The idea of her having a child gnawed at him. The boy or girl could be . . . fourteen. Impossible. He must stop thinking like this.

Hours passed; sheer boredom and hunger gave him a nudge as the clock tower struck noon. He was getting a headache from the eyestrain. To go or not to go? Would he fit in? And Emily, like most girls, would hardly be interested in a common flatfoot with neither business expertise nor schooling.

*Buck up.* He entered the men's bathroom and unbuttoned for a final minute of pondering. Then he washed up and dried his hands on the towel. In the mirror, he checked his face. A hint of shadow. Taking out a pocket comb, he gave his hair a few strokes. Then he clicked his strong, white teeth. Inspecting his breath, he shook out a few licorice Sen-Sen. *Once more into the breach.*

By the time he reached the Carr property, it was after one. The yellow house had a large, shady veranda and a second story with ornamental gingerbread. Comfortable without being ostentatious. And with a woman's touch, or rather five of them. How did the brother stand it?

From the fence line, he suspected that Carr had once owned a substantial acreage, butting up against part of Beacon Hill Park to the east. Fifty years ago, fields ringed the downtown core. The gardens were English style, deliberately casual. Brits had imported their love of gardening, reveling in the mild climate. Copper azaleas were in full bloom. Colorful beds of perennials and annuals placed the house into a fairy tale. His guts rumbled and he gave his stomach a surreptitious pat. Why had he skipped his usual breakfast just because it was Wong's day off? There had been cold meats in the icebox along with boiled eggs and half a loaf. Vicky's death had dampened his healthy appetite.

A pleasant woman in the bracket his mother would call *d'une certain âge* in a floral shirtwaist dress came forward. "Hello, Mr. DesRosiers. Reggie told me to expect you. And thank goodness, for we are famished for men today." Tucking a folding fan under her arm, she cocked her head at him as they shook hands. "Yes, there is a resemblance."

"Excuse me, Ma'am?" Had Reggie called him a cousin or some such tomfoolery?

"He said that I was to watch for someone who looked like John L. Sullivan."

Heat came to his face, and he hoped he wasn't blushing. He

managed a friendly smile. "I'm no boxer, and I think I lack a few inches and pounds of muscle on the champion."

"But you are modest. All the more admirable. I'm Edith. Edie is fine. As default would have it, the matriarch of the family."

He made obligatory comments about the beauty of the gardens. As they went to the side of the house toward the court, he heard laughing. Guests sat in wicker chairs under sun umbrellas while others stood. Nine women, and he was only the fifth man. Reggie jogged up with a brown-paper package, which he tossed like a rugby ball. "Here you go, sport. You can change in the house. Is that all right, Em?"

A vision turned, not dressed in frills and lace and flounces, but in a checkered cape and suit. The beauty from the tram. No ring on her finger. All this he took in in seconds, time slowing to a crawl. So this was Emily Carr. He shook hands all 'round. Hers was small but strong and said, "I'm your equal." He hated women with dead-flounder grips. Her face, with a hint of lip rouge, bespoke blooming health and the active life of someone who didn't spend the days lounging in chairs, needlepointing footrests, and complaining about "the vapors."

Did she recognize him? Kind amusement shone in her smoky gray eyes. With a nod, she led him to the rear steps. Closer to the house, a girl in an apron was arranging a meal on trestle tables. "Through the kitchen and down the hall, Mr. DesRosiers, you'll come to a small parlor. You will be quite private. It's kind of you to come and buttress up the male side."

"Thanks, Miss . . . Carr." Should he ask her to call him Edwin when they had just met? After all, they had just been to church like most of the city. What would they say if they knew he was half Catholic and half Jewish? It was one thing in liberal Montreal and quite another here.

The large kitchen was anchored by a massive stove and two

iceboxes. The parlor contained heavy horsehair and mahogany furniture, the large windows heavily draped with brocade and lace undercurtains to forbid the sunlight. On the walls were pictures of the late parents, Carr with a long beard and the mother more delicate than the girls. A modest oil still-life of a split melon caught his eye, but he lingered on the subtle watercolor of Indian canoes and the delicate bridge sketch. Hurrying to dress, he was annoyed to find Reggie's trousers an inch too short. At least the black canvas tennis shoes wouldn't slip on the grass like his leather boots.

When Edwin returned, he was called to play doubles with Reggie and Carrie, who greeted him warmly. His partner was Lizzie, a few years older than Emily. From the corner of his eye as he stood ready at the net, Edwin noticed one young man paying special attention to Emily. He had a thin face with close-set eyes, a weedy moustache, and he looked like a losel. On the old beat, Edwin would have taken him for a punter. Emily and the cur headed toward the sheltered back of the garden, disappearing behind six-foot hedges. Was the presumptuous wretch's hand on the small of her back? Edwin's dark eyebrows arched into a frown, and his spine tightened.

"Ed, look sharp!" A ball hit him squarely above the eyes. As he squinted in pain, he imagined that it could have been worse had the trajectory been lower.

Carrie hurried to the net and brushed a soft finger over his forehead. "My land, you have a round pink tattoo on your noble brow, Edwin. But I think you'll recover. At least you're not a baby like Reggie when dear Cleo scratched his hands to ribbons."

Reggie was doubled over laughing, rapping the racket on the ground. "For certain he's not a ringer. Or are you playacting, buddy, trying to run up the bets?"

The way the matches were arranged, he didn't see Emily for

another half an hour. Suppose she and the rotter had left the party?

When he could, he let Lizzie take the shots. Everyone else whaled away without much strategy. Finally the second serve on a match point fell wide of the line, hopped through a holly bush, and disappeared. "Drat. That's the last ball, but game, match, and set for our team anyway. Go after it, pal o' mine," Reggie said. "These toiling ladies deserve some lemonade. They are positively glowing."

"Oh, piffle, Reggie," Carrie said, tapping him on the bicep.

Where had Emily gone? Edwin wove through a set of hedges and around a fragrant purple butterfly bush. In a secluded spot under a spreading cherry tree sat a young man in a deck chair. The ball had rolled under his footstool. Cushions were piled around him, an afghan on his knees, and he was reading *The Portrait of Dorian Gray*. Hadn't Naomi suggested that it was a bit risqué? The fellow certainly was no prude.

"Hello," the young man said, putting down the book and extending his slender hand. "I'm Dick Carr. Are you enjoying the party?"

Emily and Dick could have been twins. With expressive lips and kind, laughing eyes, they had received the best looks in the family, as if Nature had rationed its charms. Some of the other sisters had the old man's beak.

Edwin responded in kind, then scooped up the ball. "Ed DesRosiers. I'm not much of a tennis player."

"I haven't seen you around. Which of my sisters are you interested in? You're a bit too tender and young for Edie," he said with an impish grin. He was pale and needed a few more pounds. The intermittent cough sounded serious. His hand had been turkey-tendon cold.

"None. I mean, that is, Reggie invited me. But your sisters are very welcoming."

Edwin heard someone yodeling his name. "Did you get lost in there? Come on, Soldier. It's time to put on the feed bag," said Reggie, giving Dick a salute as he trotted up. "Did you meet our fine detective sergeant, Dickster?"

Dick's sharp brown eyebrow arched. "Two law officers at once. A precedent. No wonder crime is so infrequent in the capital city. It dare not show its face."

"Coming? There's a jim-dandy spread," said Reggie, patting his stomach. But Dick held up his book and shook his head.

As the men walked off, Reggie spoke softly. "He's not well at all, poor old fellow. Otherwise he would have been in college. They sent him off to England, but he was too sick. He spent some time down in sunny California with his sisters."

"Tuberculosis, as you said. Do you think he'll make it?" he asked Reggie.

"Maybe if he lived in a hot dry climate. Certainly not here in all the rain and damp," said Reggie. "He'll be dead by the time he's thirty, like Keats—or was it Shelley? Jesus. That's a damn shame."

He put his hand over his mouth as Emily emerged from the back garden. She seemed flushed. A minute later, the weasely man returned with his tacky cap at an odd angle. Was that a spot of lip rouge on his cheek? Damn his hide. If he'd been acting the cad . . . *Maudit*. It was none of his business. Clearly they knew each other well.

The sun was sneaking behind ominous cumulous clouds, and the men were reveling in being waited on by so many ladies. More chairs had been brought out, as well as a few rugs. " 'Clocks, and carpets and chair on the lawn,' saith Hardy," Reggie quoted. "I prefer his novels."

Carrie added, "*Tess of the D'Urbervilles* is so romantic, but it makes me cry. I shall drown my sorrows in this lovely beef."

"Father never had a roast less than ten pounds," Clara said.

"We had ever so much land then. Four acres. A huge vegetable garden and fruit trees, but we've sold off most. Still, it's our little paradise."

Emily took a sip of lemonade. "I miss the old cow in the meadow roaming through the blue and white lilies in the spring, her bag swinging."

"Our Em, that *is* enough." Holding up a warning finger, Edith cleared her throat. As Edwin learned, Alice was determined to become a schoolteacher. Lizzy dreamed of being a missionary. Edith was too much the chatelaine to marry. Yet every house needed a man. Who would do the heavy lifting? Wise investments had guarded the income from their father.

Besieged from all directions, Edwin found his flowered china plate heaped with cold ham, chicken, and tender beef slices, potato salad, and pickles, including dills, mustard, and watermelon. Platters of snowy white bread arrived warm from the oven. Then a red-flannel cake brimming with buttery icing. Canned peaches and cream were served along with a sugar pie made with maple syrup, which reminded him of Montreal. Accepting seconds seemed polite and even sensible. At home it would be Sunday leftovers. Wong always returned after supper.

Emily came over with a bowl of ice cream and a serving spoon. "We could have used a man to turn the crank. My arm was too sore to play tennis. You will have some, Mr. DesRosiers?" Her smile could reduce him to jelly.

"Gladly." Was that a drop of rain on his hand? Could something spoil this idyllic afternoon? He looked up with an inner scowl to the mixture of sun and clouds. They were scudding across the sky as capricious coastal squalls moved in.

As he finished his bowl, he realized that Edith was speaking to him. She had set up a large apparatus. "Honorable guest, can you operate a photographic camera? If you take our portrait, we'll reciprocate." Father Carr, a man of many talents, had been in the daguerreotype business, she explained. The camera was on a tripod. "It's a Carlton. One of the best. Papa wanted chronicles of the family. And the ones of Mother are so precious now that she has passed. He taught us how to use the plates. And heaven forfend that we dropped one."

Everyone stood in self-conscious poses, careful not to move to blur the picture. The department was planning on using photographs ("mug shots") for criminal identification, a first in Western Canada. Edwin had spent some time with the Maynards, Hannah and her husband, Richard, who operated a professional photographic studio on Pandora. Her experimenting with multiple shots to show the front and side view was a thousand times more useful than the old wanted posters.

As they stood static, he noticed the annoying twerp gazing with special fondness at Emily, seated in front of him. Not that faces revealed personality as the physiognomy doctors believed, but when a man looked like a ferret, maybe he behaved like one. His mind was whirling as they watched him. Was this what they called love at first sight? And if so, what about Vicky?

Then rain began to fall in earnest, causing squeals from the ladies. Everyone ran to the veranda, and the second picture was forgotten as Edwin helped Edie move the equipment to safety. He'd like a picture of Emily, but not with this blackguard spoiling it.

Minutes later, he started his trek home, feeling confused. He'd thanked Edie for the afternoon. Reggie had taken Carrie home. After that, he'd probably head for a blind pig. Emily was gone, too. What had that man done or said to upset her? Was he a future fiancé? At least Emily wasn't stuck up. That magical smile and the way her eyes sparkled with intelligence. How could he see her again? Find out what church she went to? It wouldn't be Catholic. Would he be foolish to ask Reggie about his chances? He must be off his trolley to dream about it.

Before he knew it, he had missed his turns and gone all the way downtown to the grand old Customs House, keeping watch on the harbor since 1874. What had Reggie said about that newsboy? He veered down Wharf Street, and where it jogged to Store, a lad stood with the last of his papers.

"Boy," he called and went over, waving off the paper offer. "One of our officers told you to keep a sharp eye for the tattoo man, correct?" He cocked a thumb toward the darkened shop across the street.

The tad nodded. He wore a heavy coat with buttons missing and short pants. The difference in selling a few more papers might better fill his belly tonight. "He did, Sir, and I've been on the job, I have. I followed him down to the dockside when he left an hour ago with a big leather bag. Got into a large rowboat and headed up the Gorge. One Sunday a month, like I said."

Edwin reached for pocket change. "You did a first-rate job, son."

"There were women in that boat. Dressed up fine. Why would a dirty bugger like that be with ladies? He's no ferryman."

# Chapter Twelve

What the boy had seen was mystifying. Edwin sat on the embankment and spent an hour in a twilight world of thought. A lowlife ferrying well-dressed women up the Gorge. To where? Certainly not a prayer meeting. Across the railroad bridge, fragrant cedar fires were burning on the Songhees Reserve and the distant echoes of chanting warred with the fading noises of the city.

A mist was rising, and he could imagine Emily walking across the water to meet him. Beauty, mischief, talent, sincerity, one thousand other undiscovered attractions. When the night chill started to seep into his bones, he rose and turned for home.

As the church bells chimed ten o'clock, he finally turned the corner to his street. Other homes had already doused their lamps and gone to bed. Not his. Lights burned in every downstairs window. Naomi's soiree night. With an interior groan, he let himself in the front door. He could ask her or her friends about Fred Appleyard. Under no circumstances would he mention Emily.

Abraham Rutherford he met coming down the stairs. Everyone wanted to try the new water closet. He wore a green carnation furnished by a local florist. Not long ago, Abraham had seen Wilde in Colorado on his famous American tour. "Every time I cross the border, I use his line: 'I have nothing to declare but my genius.' "

The older man stopped and did a double take worthy of the

great Booth. "Is this the new fashion? Sporting clothes at night? And those shoes. Straight out of Richard Harding Davis. Tell Uncle Ruddy everything." He'd been joking with Edwin since his boyhood. Abraham had been a great comfort to Naomi during that terrible aftermath of Serge's death. His common sense and connections had helped with selling the house and relocating. He held some of Serge's debts as well. Later when Edwin had gone up island to work, Abraham had pulled Naomi from depression. As she said, "Fie on money, good looks, and sex appeal. One of the greatest gifts a man can have is the ability to make a lady laugh."

Damn. Edwin's trousers and boots were at the Carr house. Embarrassing, but it gave him an excuse to go back. Where had his mind been? Only five or six hours ago? It seemed like weeks.

Abraham owned Chez Nous, a *chapeau* shop frequented by Victoria's most stylish ladies. His place snagged the latest European fashions, by way of the City of Paris Department Store in San Francisco. He made monthly steamer trips to freshen his stock and commissioned boys to locate peacock, heron, and egret feathers for his creations, even in Beacon Hill Park, which he strongly denied. As for companions, he lived with his ninety-year-old grandmother, who routinely rapped him on the head with her ear trumpet. He wore a lavender linen suit with a frilled shirt, a silk waistcoat, diamond stud in a dark purple cravat, and pointed Spanish boots with two-inch heels to make up for his five-feet-two. A back brace compensated for the rounded shoulders of a childhood spinal condition. He resembled a gnomish riverboat gambler. Once he had shown Edwin a pearl-handled derringer. Edwin warned him not to expect accuracy beyond four feet. "Unloaded," he said. "Merely a fashion accessory."

"Are you joining us? Your mother was so annoyed at Harry O for playing 'She May Have Seen Better Days' that she broke the cylinder. So we've been having the most divine sessions with a Ouija board. Your mother is conjuring spirits from old Victoria. Tue Guay, kidnapped for ransom and murdered. And Isabella Ross. Mrs. Douglas keeps appearing, too. Lovely woman."

"You're all too modern for me. I'd better turn in now." Edwin faked a yawn to escape.

An uproar came from the parlor. Six regulars, four men and two women. Naomi didn't tolerate female competition. Glasses were clinking, and blue tobacco smoke ringed the air.

"Abraham, you go to the theater. Do you know a chap from the Victoria called Fred Appleyard?"

"Owes me fifty dollars. Is he in trouble again?"

Edwin learned that Appleyard had a girlfriend called Becky Dale. She lived in a rooming house over a haberdasher six or seven blocks up Fort. As long as a detective had one more lead, the game wasn't over.

As Abraham rejoined the party, Edwin made his way upstairs, leaving the noise of the Graphophone talking machine diminish behind him. It was "The Laughing Polka" again. That meant two more hours. When the evening ended, "Home, Sweet Home" began, with everyone "shinging" along, weeping lugubrious tears and rhapsodizing about where they used to live before their "exile" to the island.

Harry Oldham Harrison had been sent to Canada as a remittance man after gambling debts packed him away from London. He had a chin like a walrus and bowlegs, but a gallery of the latest jokes. Giving impressions of local political and religious figures was also one of his hits. His imitation of Amor de Cosmos, now in the asylum, never failed to get a standing ovation. Amor had been deathly afraid of electricity.

As for the others, there was Frederick Rumming, also on the upper side of sixty, who escorted Fanny Moon. Byron Barley, the youngest at forty, had a dubious mining venture near Campbell River. He was always trying to get Naomi to invest, but she refused his blandishments. Raven-haired Byron was as attractive as his namesake, without the clubfoot. Edwin suspected he had a special relationship with Naomi. Then again, there had been many "specials," even a few female models if the sounds from her bedroom didn't deceive his ears. If his mother doubled her possibilities, who was he to judge? The concept pronounced unthinkable by Queen Victoria when the Sodomy Laws were enacted tantalized most men, would they admit it.

If the wine were plentiful, Naomi would tune up her zither and Rumming would start on the mandolin. Once well enough oiled, Byron would tickle the ivories. A large piano shipped at great expense from her parents' home filled one corner, topped by a vase of early daffodils and narcissus. No prudish pantaloons hid the piano legs.

With the music fading downstairs, Edwin palmed a paste of Dr. Lyons powder and brushed his teeth. The rising oohs and ahs meant that Oscar had brought out the magic lantern. He got new slides whenever he went to San Francisco, and that included some titillating poses intended only for gentlemen.

Edwin closed the door to his room and instituted Plan B: wax ear plugs. He'd never been a sound sleeper, and his job was enough to keep him pondering and maundering. In business, he would have been worrying about stock markets, grain futures, uprisings in far-off countries, and government rigmarole. Between Gladstone in England, U.S. president Cleveland (again), and Sir Mackenzie Bowell on his way out with Tupper in the wings, the world seemed alarmingly quiet except for saber rattling from that German kaiser. The old Queen's grandson was supposed to be uniting England and Germany. People were starting to whisper the word "Hun," even with the many local German merchants. He tossed onto his other side as someone started clapping. With a finger, he shoved the plugs deeper and put the second pillow over his head. His feet were hot, a sure sign of insomnia.

The Russians and the Chinese. There was going to be a revolt there. With the long-lived dynasties of the Romanovs and the Manchus, those nations had remained stable on the back of the peasants. How long could it go on? The island felt isolated, a toehold against the mighty Pacific and the Far East. Alaska was an American outpost blocking Canada's north and a stone's throw from Russia. He was starting to count Russian bears padding their way over the iced Bering Strait when he fell asleep. Then he fell into a black vortex where nothing mattered.

A galvanic shock jolted him awake. It seemed only seconds since he had gone to bed, but the clock mocked him. He heard nothing in the house but the gentle trill of their canary Lulu as he shuffled to the bathroom in his bare feet. His gritty eyes were half-closed. They felt tender as raw meat. Where was that eyewash Naomi swore by?

As he opened the door, Fanny Moon stood there, a surprised O on her bowed and wrinkled mouth. Fanny claimed to be in her late thirties (sixty was more like it). Her abilities to parley her "gifts and endowments" from certain gentlemen had led to a nasty shock. One of the wives had hired a thug to assassinate her in a carriage in St. James Park. Fanny escaped with a flesh wound and left by steamer for Panama the next week. Taken overland by train, she completed her journey to British Columbia. The tonic she drank with her pink gins was designed to counteract the long-term effects of the malaria contracted at the Isthmus. Once she had mentioned nearly getting a tattoo on the suggestion of the Prince of Wales. That gave him an idea.

He stepped back as Fanny emerged, her face flushed and freshly powdered until it cracked. She wore a weighty hat with an ostrich plume, and an embroidered linen jacket with enormous mutton sleeves. "Edwin. Lovely to see you. As handsome as ever. If I were a few years younger . . ." Wagging a chubby finger, she pulled him to her ample bosom as a scent of lavender enveloped them.

Edwin stood in his silk underclothes, his arms and calves bare. He'd been used to meeting Fanny at odd hours. Her bright golden hair was thinner as she looked him up and down approvingly. He folded his arms in protective embarrassment.

"Your mother had the most wonderful soiree. The pate. The oysters. The burgundy. I am the last to leave. People simply can't keep up with me. It's in the genes. Rumming went to find a cab to take me back to the hotel." Fanny lived at the Dallas, a three-story crown jewel with a handsome observation tower and metal fencing around the roof. Before Rithet's Outer Wharves opened with its deep harbor, a Dallas porter announced an incoming ship's light. Passengers were rowed back and forth. Fading in popularity with the newer hotels, it was still an embodiment of posh service.

"I won't keep you from your beauty sleep, dear Miss Fanny, but I need your expertise. I know you lived in England and have a much better grasp about things more common to a big city than do we colonials," Edwin said. She was staring at his biceps, which were flexed from tension.

"I'm as flattered as if you were my own . . . brother. Is it a matter of the heart, dearest chuck? About time, I must say. If there's a wedding, you know that I . . ." Her voice droned on, but he nodded, straining to be polite.

"It's a tricky subject for a lady. Have you ever seen or heard about a hexagram tattoo? Not for yourself, of course. Perhaps an acquaintance of an acquaintance."

She narrowed her bloodshot lilac eyes and blinked at the sunshine from the stained-glass window. "*Quelle circonspection*, Edwin. You are growing into a fine man. Ah, a hexagram, you say. What would that be?"

The bathroom mirror was fogged. Perhaps she had run the hot water. "I'll draw one on the mirror." His effort was clumsy but adequate.

"Oh, that kind of hexagram. Why didn't you say so? I haven't thought about that for . . . well, never mind."

Bluffing or covering up some scandal? Fanny liked to keep men guessing.

She hummed to herself as if casting back her memory nets. "Very strange that you would mention that. A shameless *roué* from Bath, what did he say? I can't quite summon details. I must have been a mere girl."

"So recently, then?" He kept his face neutral in a kind charade.

A practiced finger tucked a detaching ringlet into her hat. "George III was still moldering on the throne, poor old duff. And later that Princess Caroline. Scandalous. Our dear Queen has had such a staid and respectable rule, albeit boring. Let me see, it was—"

The front door opened and Lord Rumming looked up the stairs. "Fanny darling? Will you outshine the Venus de Milo herself? Mine eyes dazzle."

"Hello, my Lord," Edwin called.

"Tan tan ta ra! The night shift of the shiftless is leaving now, and the world's business will recommence. Make the way safe for the rest of us, Officer."

Alone at last, Edwin gave himself a quick shave using his father's decorated German porcelain soap cup and brush. He intended to try the new safety razor, and moving too quickly, cut himself. He rummaged in a drawer for the styptic pencil, then stuck on a dab of paper. What had Fanny been driving at? Her drunken ramblings left him frustrated and no wiser.

Downstairs, the ruins of the party littered the parlor and

formal dining room. Glasses and bottles and trays of ravaged food. A red rose wilted on the piano. Meanwhile, as Edwin reached the kitchen, Wong brought the silver toast server and a double portion of ginger marmalade. A soft-boiled egg was cracked open beneath an oozing pat of butter.

Wong spoke very little, preferring nods or head shakes with the occasional hmmmm. "He's very inscrutable. So restful," Naomi would say. "Not like those chattering maids. *Enceinte* before you know it. Men make better servants and have cleaner habits. Women hang stockings everywhere."

Once Edwin had passed him in Chinatown on Fisgard Street in rapid-fire conversation with a grocer over vegetables. Cantonese, not the Mandarin dialect of rulers. Seventeen thousand Chinese men had arrived in British Columbia in the early 1880s to labor on the Canadian Pacific Railway for a dollar a day. They lived in tents or boxcars, hiked over forty kilometers from camp to camp, and lived on dried salmon and rice. Over a thousand had died in the greatest nation-building act in the country's history. Their sacrifices taken for granted, most would never see home again.

# CHAPTER THIRTEEN

As Edwin approached his office, the desk sergeant Frost limped up. He'd saved a toddler from death from a runaway carriage and broken both legs. The force had accommodated to his needs and placed him in a clerical job. The quiet, barrel-chested man with the common touch had a talent for sorting out the drunk and disorderly on weekend nights. Knowledge of the local tongue gave him an advantage with the Natives who brushed against the law.

"Sorry to bother you, Sir, but there's a woman making enquiries. Working class, but good manners. She's very upset. I told her that you would talk to her, but if you're busy, I can find—"

"We work for everyone here, Sergeant, not just the wealthy. Something stolen? Is her man in jail? She hasn't been beaten, has she, and come to take the bugger back?" One drunk Ukrainian had split his wife's lip with a bull whip because she scolded him for tracking mud into the kitchen.

The balding sergeant rubbed his shiny pate and bent forward to hawk tobacco juice into the brass spittoon. "Says that her daughter is missing."

A sharp furrow broke across his forehead. He stepped aside as Brush frog-marched a bearded man in clergyman garb down the hall. The fake reverend had been "collecting" again for a Native orphanage in Duncan.

"How old is the girl? Surely not a child." Abductions were

rare, but they happened in large cities. White slavers were far from a myth. Problem was, they chose their victims well, from the often unloved and unmissed dregs of society.

"Fifteen, but looks younger. Just a little mouse of a thing, the ma says."

Edwin craned his neck past Frost to where a careworn woman in her Sunday best was sitting in a chair in the foyer twisting her hands together. Under the dusty edges of the frayed brown dress, ten years out of style, a pair of scuffed boots peeked in shame, concern trumping pride. A broken set of cherries on the faded ribbon decorated her straw bonnet.

"How long has the girl been gone?" He kept his voice low. These cases often had tragic conclusions. Or worse yet, no conclusions.

"That's the bad part. It could be two weeks now, maybe more." Frost pursed his thick lips in dissatisfaction.

Edwin looked quizzically at the man, but checked his cravat and settled his vest. "Doesn't sound good. I'll take care of her."

He turned and headed for the woman, who looked up hopefully. Edwin introduced himself to "Mrs." Donahue, who wore no ring. Pawned, or a common-law relationship?

"Please come into my office," he said, gesturing with his arm. "It's more private and comfortable."

Her hollowed cheeks betrayed her age and hard life. Edwin seated her, then poured her a glass of water from his pitcher in the corner. She sipped, her knobby hand shaking. He smelled no liquor, a good sign. Why wait so long? Had the girl stolen what little the mother had? Despite the biblical admonition to honor one's parents, some children were cradle opportunists. Edwin did not believe in *tabula rasa*.

He took a small notebook and his pencil, sharpening it with a penknife and brushing the shavings into a pile. "Now, Ma'am, I understand that you are looking for your daughter?"

"My Mary. The eldest? She's been gone for t-two weeks? At least." Her voice wavered like fading birdsong, a touch of echoing guilt and insecurity in the rising of the ends of the sentences.

He cocked his head at the delay. "If I may ask, and no offense, why did you wait so long in coming here?" He remained as expressionless as possible, concerned but nonjudgmental. Perhaps the girl didn't live with her mother anymore. At fifteen, she might have found a job "and all found." Even completing grade six was a major accomplishment in the short and brutish life of the poor. At twelve, boys started in the mines and girls in the mill. Labor laws were a wish.

She put a reddened fingertip between her ravaged teeth at the implication. "Sir, she's been a scullery maid for the last year with the Arbogasts on Oak Bay Avenue. Grand place, she says. Sunday after church sometimes she comes to help with the baby and cleaning. Gives me a share of her wages once a month, and not one miss. She's a good girl. Really, she is."

She didn't seem any closer to explaining, so he focused his eyes on her. How he hated the temptation to blame the victimized. "Yes, please go on. So you last saw her . . ."

"I've been gone to my sister's up Sidney way, sir. She's ill with the fever and needed nursing. Mary's money helped us buy train tickets. Took the baby and two other young ones. Come back and the Arbogasts told me that my little girl's been gone since two Saturdays. The first Monday she didn't report in. They thought she was sick and had stayed with me. Sent a boy after her at home. But no one never answered the door. We was gone, you see, like I said. They as much as said that they thought she'd run off with some man. But that could never be. A mother knows."

"Sounds like you're proud of her. So there was never any trouble at home?"

At this she colored and the corners of her face fell. "Her pa, well, he . . . he didn't pay her no mind. Wanted a boy, truth be told, and cuffed her and me more than once. Then a year ago, he lost his life in an accident at the docks. Good riddance, I say, though I expect God might punish me for that." Her fingers flew into an awkward blessing.

"I see. Sorry for your loss all the same." He looked at his notes, beginning to feel sick. Anything could have happened by now. "Did you inquire at the hospitals, in case she had fallen ill on the street or been hit by a carriage?" Even the indigent weren't left to die in the gutter.

"My boy did. He's ten. The brave little fellow carried a note to the head matrons at both hospitals. No one there like Mary."

"What did—does Mary look like?" Would it be too much to hope that she had a photo? They were a singular luxury for the poor.

She rummaged in her cloth bag. "Happens I have a likeness. She gave it me for my birthday. A visitor to the Arbogasts gave her an extra fifty cents when she ran an errand special."

He took the cardboard, stamped on the back with name of the Pandora studio. The girl looked more like twelve, though her clothes made her older. Her hair was brushed back around her head, fastened with pins at the crown in the latest chignon style. She had sweet, full lips and innocent tapered brows with a brush of freckles across her pert nose. Her white blouse had full sleeves in the mutton style. Lace spilled half way down the front, with a high collar of more lace bias-cut. The photo placed her well above her station. Hannah Maynard gave good value. How touching that she had made the effort, but was that a good sign or an indication of trouble?

"What about friends or acquaintances?" Each answer was making him more anxious as his pulse jumped.

"Never a mention. She was determined to work hard for a good life. After Micky died, we've struggled. I take in washing."

She dabbed at her eyes, the sclera irritated and sore.

He broached the hard part. "Any chance that a young man *is* involved? Girls do fall in love. Even if they are good, churchgoing young ladies."

"She never said nothing to me. I would have known if she was smitten." She thought to herself, shifting in the chair.

"Yes, you remembered something?"

"Only that she was going to have a better place in the household. She was doing so well that she could replace the undermaid in another year. We'd be able to move to a place with two rooms. It's so crowded with all the young ones. Last month she paid half our rent."

"That was kind of her. I see what you mean." But he didn't. Scullery maids earned little beyond their keep. The picture showed her with clothes that weren't hand-me-downs. Had she been stealing from the family? Silver, jewelry? Is that where the extra cash came from? Sometimes it took a while for a wealthy family to "miss" an article. A mental list of pawnshops entered his mind. By the time someone talked to her employer, news might be forthcoming. Sadly for now, it was too soon to open a major enquiry.

"Can you find her, sir? I've been down on my knees praying to Our Lord every night. Is she cold? Is she hungry? I can't help thinking that . . . some harm . . ." She broke down and sobbed, her thin shoulders heaving. She was a broken sparrow, pale and anemic, sacrificing her own food for her nestlings.

Only an iron man could resist such tears. "We'll do our best, Ma'am. I'll alert the officers on the beat. They walk the streets day and night. Not much goes on in this city that they don't know about."

Missing girls were part of urban history. Some turned up pregnant and deserted. Some were butchered by old women with rusty implements. In one case, a girl had fallen drunken from a bridge up the Gorge and lain in the rocky tidal muck with a smashed skull for days before discovery, broken gin bottle in her pocket. Those who had fled abusive parents who beat or raped them were rarely seen again, for good reason. But here was a beloved child in a good position with prospects. There was no way she had been drinking. Pregnancy came to his mind. With the voluminous skirts and dresses, that was possible to hide for a while. As for the father? Were there silver-tongued young men on the premises?

Edwin took the name and address of Mary's employers. "I'll ask the other female servants." Girls often told each other things they didn't tell their mothers.

"Oh, if you would, Sir. I can't go to the family myself. Scant time they would have for the likes of me. They've probably filled Mary's place already. Without her help, we'll be on the street, and no mistake." At that note, fresh tears flowed.

He looked at his notes. Precious little data on a soul. "Does she have any other special frocks for her day off, something she'd wear outside her workplace?" His reasoning was ominous, but he hoped that she wouldn't intuit the idea. He kept his face neutral but concerned. Underneath the desk, his leg pistoned up and down. Despite his ongoing case, he needed to talk to the employers.

"Ay, sir, she favored red plaids. I made her a lovely dress for her last birthday. Her great granny was a MacDonald from Inverness. Six feet tall with carrot-red hair. The men could hardly carry her coffin, t'was said. MacDonalds fought bravely in one of those big wars in the old country. We're a romantic lot. 'Scots Wha Hae' I sang to her in her cradle."

That night his mother was in a restive mood. Wong had been conspicuously absent with a stomach problem. Something about a thousand-year-old egg, though that seemed a figure of speech.

Because of his indisposition, Wong hadn't been able to secure his mother's supply of opium, Edwin suspected. Despite the pipe, lamp, and *yen hanck* tucked in an ornate ebony chest in her bedroom corner, both of them pretended that her weakness didn't exist. That whites indulged was a well-kept secret. New York City alone had over twenty-five thousand addicts, he'd read. The smoker sought solace in dreams and reveries, not violence to himself or others. It was a moral failing Naomi kept in check . . . until times like this.

When he entered from work, she was emerging from the kitchen, wearing one of Wong's long aprons over pantaloons and a linen smock. A tendril of hair had escaped from her 'do, and she stuck out her lower lip to blow it out of her eyes. "Wong's much better. There's yesterday's joint and potatoes, so we won't starve. His cousin Lun came by with a letter from home, and I paid him fifty cents to stay until morning helping him with his . . . well, you know. I'm no Florence Nightingale. The good news is that his fever is down and he's retaining vegetable broth. Canned soup. Can you see me sweltering over a copper boiler with a bloody chicken?"

"I'm glad to hear that."

Finally, they sat to their meager meal, making up the loss with large bowls of canned peaches. Naomi picked at her food. She held out a finger with a plaster. "And I cut myself on the damn can opener. It hurts like the devil. Blood poisoning's around the corner." She inspected her forearm for streaks.

He poured her another glass of the white Bordeaux and topped up his own glass. The atmosphere was nerve-wracking. He was in no mood to discuss Vicky and planned to dismiss with a few words her questions about progress. Now this Mary to worry about.

"How is the painting, Mother?" he asked. As he worked days now, models came and went while he was away. Sometimes she was copying and then "individualizing" the scene with different colors, a languishing cat, flowers in a vase, or drapery, so that each saloon thought that they owned an original. She brooded during the winter, when she painted indoors. The girls "paid" the rent, so to speak, not her *plein air* efforts, Impressionist style.

She waved off his question. "I couldn't concentrate. You know why, so stop being so damned obtuse."

Vicky. Of course. He blotted his mouth. "Sorry."

"Not as much as she is. Tell me what you've learned. Other than the Sooke trip."

Edwin gave a long sigh. She knew where to lodge the knife and twist it. He summed up. "My next task is to track down the stage manager Fred Appleyard. Abraham gave me a lead about his lady friend last night. If only we could piece together where Vicky was living. This murder isn't random. Moving the body takes planning and a carriage or wagon."

Naomi gave a small cough and put down her glass. She tapped a fist over her solar plexus. "That went down the wrong way. I'm a nervous wreck." Then she looked up. "Why is everything taking so long?"

Edwin pursed his lips but kept quiet. She'd had more wine than usual. The edge lacked the dreamy haze of opium that she preferred in her retreat. Then he saw Lun beckon to her from the hall.

"Excuse me, Dear. I'll be back with the tea. Lun needs to . . . tell me something."

*Bring you something.* He finished with rote motions the last sweet peach half.

Naomi returned, the tightness in her face relaxed in anticipation of the later evening. She poured tea for both of them, black and strong. "Lapsang. I feel like something smoky and mysterious." Her mood was rising with the steam.

# CHAPTER FOURTEEN

Fort Street even at eight a.m. was already bustling. Awnings were rolling down and shops opening for the early traffic. Edwin found a beat constable and soon located the rooming house Abraham had mentioned. With Emily on his mind now, and a motive to look sharper, he checked out a haberdashery's window wares. What a snappy fedora. And that nutria fur hat caught his eye. Perhaps a linen "crash" model for summer, but not the bike hat. Too youthful. Bowlers were getting as stuffy as top hats.

The rooms above the shop must have been respectable once. Now they looked like a shabby and perhaps final place to lay one's head. Skirting a broken bottle, he climbed the stairs to a common scene of six or seven paint-chipped doors. What looked like a piece of cooked potato made his heel slip. A feeble gaslight flickered. The city was in the process of changing from gas to electricity. Last year he'd found a sad suicide with rags stuffed around the windows and under the door. Passing quietly into oblivion was kinder for the victim than slitting wrists in a bathtub or jumping head first from an upper floor.

He knocked on the first door and a man in a dingy union suit, pot belly hanging, answered with a snarl, taking a step back at Edwin's size. " 'Chew want, Bud?"

"I'm looking for Mrs. Dale." When the man's eyes narrowed, he added, "Police."

The man flipped a finger to the left. "Third door. Don't know

142

if she's home now, though. She's been coming and going, she has. Nursing some old geezer." With an award-winning belch, he retreated to his lair.

Behind Edwin, a couple stumbled up the stairs. The woman wore a filthy velvet dress that trailed dust. Her eye was blacked and she was holding her arm. "Go on, ya bitch. You already got your quarter. More like a wooden nickel's worth," the sailor said, shoving her in front of him. She bumped into Edwin.

" 'Scuse me," she said, half falling against the wall.

"Go on or I'll give you worse," the man said, raising his hand as Edwin grabbed his wrist and twisted. "Hey, what—"

"Do you live here?"

"Who wants to know?"

"The police. I'll ask one more time, and it's a civil tongue you'll give me."

"He doesn't live here." The woman groped at her ripped neckline.

Edwin set his jaw. "Then be on your way. Or would you rather cool your heels in a nice cell? The admiral of the fleet can bail you out in the morning. Disorderly conduct. Assault of an officer, too, unless I see your arse heading outside."

Grumbling, the man went off, swearing as he got farther away.

"Many thanks, Sir." She made as if to curtsey, but winced. "He's a rough one. I had the price of a supper and should have gone to bed early with this headache, but times are hard, if you knows what I mean."

"I'll choose not to for now. And pick your clients with a bit more care. I don't want to find you in an alley."

As she disappeared into her room, he knocked at number three. A lady in a kimono answered. Edwin stated his business to Becky Dale.

"Ay, he's here like a bad penny. Passed the fever this morning. Nothing more than ague, the doctor said. A bit of worry with the lungs. Can't die of the heart failure without one." Becky gave a small cough. "I suppose I'll be next."

In an interior room a fat redheaded man lay snoring with a patchwork quilt up to his chin. On the table next to him were a pitcher of water, used handkerchiefs, and dark brown medicine bottles as well as a quart of cheap rum, half empty. Fred was, as Serge used to say, *hors de combat.* His bulbous nose and cheeks were a roadmap to apoplexy.

Edwin shook him by the shoulder and even raised him off the pillow, but he was limp as a throttled goose. The reek from the man would choke a goat. Whatever he might say had little value in his state.

"The man's too sick to go to jail for his debts. What kind of a Christian are you?" Becky put up her fists, prepared to fight for her man after all.

Edwin gave her a sharp look. The last thing he needed was for Appleyard to disappear before delivering information. Yet where would he go? The room looked lived in. Family pictures lined the walls and a flat-topped metal steamer trunk had an antimacassar and delicate glass figures.

"I don't give a damn about his debts. I have a murder on my hands," he said. He picked up a water jug and baptized the man. Fred came to with a sputter. Had he been playing possum?

"Don't drown me, you consarned fool. What's this about?"

"Victoria Crosse."

Fred smoothed the oily strands of hair over his bald head. He gave a heroic cough, and Edwin stood back. His resistance to colds was legion, but influenza was something else. "So this is about poor Vicky. Just when she was getting her life back together. A sweet and talented lady, poor lamb."

"Vicky's parents said that she was an actress at the theater."

Fred coughed again. "An actress, aye. She was past prime,

but game enough in some roles. You always need the fifth business, the one who starts the plot boiling. Not great money, but it's a living. They wants the young ones, the ingénues. Or those already famous. Sarah Bernhardt played the Lady of the Camellias when she was fifty-two. Cleopatra not long before that. Makeup and distance work miracles."

"How did you meet her? She's been gone from the city a long time."

Becky perched on a tuffet and buffed her nails, glancing up now and then.

"I was on business in San Francisco before Christmas and met her at a card game in the Tenderloin. She was down at the heel. Some cur had taken all of her savings. Feeling sorry for a local girl, I brought her under my wing, sap that I am." He blinked boiled owl's eyes. "It was all on the up and up. I told her that I could get her on here. Steady wages better than a maid's. Mending of costumes and small parts. I advanced her the fare. Like a Dutch uncle."

Edwin kept his voice even, though he wanted to pummel the man. "I'll bet. So she was working for you at the theater?"

"That's the bitter part. Just a month she put in. After all my trouble."

"Where did she stay?"

"Bunked right here on the daybed in the other room, didn't she, Becky? Then the baggage comes to me with a packet of money end of February. She paid me back, I'll say that much. I never saw her again." He snapped his pudgy fingers and waved goodbye.

Edwin took a note in his book, pressing so hard that the lead broke. "Where did that money come from?"

"Damn me if I know for sure. But a stage-door Johnny's my guess. Like flies to honey. She still had some looks left as well as a mind to pleasure a man. Pardon my bluntness." From across the room, Becky shot him a dagger.

"Any man's name come to mind?"

"Twenty or thirty nobs sniff around the theater. Some live here or Vancouver. Others visiting from the States. I pays no attention, see, 'cause I'm no pimp." He folded his hands like a bishop on his tomb and gave a Cheshire smile. "Now if you'll pardon me, Your Lordship, I'm missing me nap. And, Becks, I need a tad more medicine. I've been a good boy. Be a doll and run down to our friend on the corner."

As he was leaving, the woman put on her cloak and walked out to the hall with him. "He's not exactly lying, but he's not telling you everything," she whispered.

"What do you mean?"

"First of all, he's embarrassed because Miss Vicky wouldn't prime his rusty pump, the old coot. He brought her all this way for nothing in that department. Miss Vicky had prospects, all right. Like she was Lady Muck that last week. New clothes. And there was that cockamamie tattoo." She gave a shudder and rubbed her arm.

His ears pricked up. "What about it? What did it mean?"

"She wasn't fond of it. It hurt like hell. But it was part of the bargain."

"Bargain? What more do you know?" This sounded promising.

"What's it worth?" Her close-set eyes took on a feral look. He didn't blame her. Opportunity didn't knock often for her kind. At least she had Fred for creature comfort.

"Do you know who you're talking to? I could take you to the station. You have no idea what trouble you could find." He felt like a bully, but hard cases need hard treatment.

She stuck out her tongue, then shook her savage curls. "All right. Can't blame a girl for trying. One other thing. She was studying something."

Exasperation got the better of him. "A part for a play. Appleyard said that she had minor roles. So what?"

"Not that. I knows every line in every play. I'm in the prompter's box. This was different. Like for some kind of test."

"What did she say?"

Becky screwed her face up to concentrate, trying a few silent syllables and then rejecting them. Her pupils were enlarged, perhaps from opium or even belladonna—a beauty trick, Naomi had said. "Fay suckatoo view."

"Don't try to gull me. That's gibberish. Is Fay a name? Give me something I can use."

"It didn't make sense to me, either. But there's groups with secrets. What about them Masons? Plotting with signs and symbols and handshakes. Look at that grand palace on Douglas Street."

An elite group of businessmen and politicians belonged to the Masons. The building was smack in the middle of downtown with no privacy at all. If anything was going on there, he'd eat his hat with mustard. "Did she mention an Abbott?"

She curled a lock of hair around one finger. "No names. Seemed that she didn't want to share her fortune with the likes of me, damn her. The trollop said I was over the hill, and after all Fred and I did for her."

They parted at the street. "Ta ta, darling. Keep your powder dry," she said, simpering like a little girl.

Back at the office, it was business as usual. Pickpockets had been busy with another naval ship docked and the swabbies on the prowl with their wages. A pawn shop had been robbed, the window glass smashed. Some large cities used grates over their business fronts. Would that fortress effect arrive here? Reggie had circulated among all the constables and shown them Mary's picture without any luck. With her limited time off, he wasn't surprised that she wasn't gadding about town.

"She's a looker, though. Wouldn't mind a bit of fun with her." Reggie gave a low whistle interpreted the same way in any country.

"You're getting married, and besides that, she's a child." Edwin shot him a contemptuous look. "Women are more attractive for a real man. Don't tell me that you wouldn't prefer Miss Emily, for example, if you weren't shackled already."

Reggie touched a finger to his temple. "You know, old thing, I can't see Em's getting hitched. Far too independent. She may flirt a bit with Jacko—"

Edwin sat up. "Jacko, the one with that ferret face? What's his story?"

"Heading for Alaska, I hear. 'Tisn't for *you* to like him, pal. Get my point? Who can tell what a woman thinks? 'Shall I wasting in despair . . . Die because a woman's fair?' " He poked Edwin in the arm.

Reggie hadn't shown up hungover lately, perhaps adjusting to the prospect of his upcoming wedding at the Episcopal Church. Edwin was invited. His parents had been married in a quiet ceremony by a rabbi with only Naomi's family and a few friends. Then they had left for the magnificent Falls of Niagara, laughing even a decade later about donning India rubber coats, hats, and boots, and making their way to the very edge of the raging cauldron.

"I had a jolly time last night with Clifford. What a wag. His jokes are knee-slappers. Strictly between men, though." Reggie crossed to the mirror in the cabinet and adjusted another batwing tie. This one had polka dots. "Have you heard this one? There once was a man from Nantucket—"

"You told me that last week." Reggie had mentioned the Clifford fellow. He seemed to have pots of money.

"A party in his suite at the Driard. Swell food, too. Oyster pie and champers."

"Lucky bastard. Still, it must cost."

Reggie gave a donkey's guffaw. "Maybe you and I live with mama and papa, but he enjoys his independence, especially with the ladies. His parents have moved out of the family manse to Vancouver. The old grandfather built this palace up the Gorge somewhere. Big and useless. Hell to heat. Cliffie's trying to sell the monstrosity for development, but real estate has cooled since the last panic." His eyes brightened. "But say, we had some fun driving the pigs. Everybody's doing it."

"I beg your pardon." What did a barnyard have to do with a good time?

"It's a game that you hold in your hands. Takes dexterity. Something to impress the girls." He pantomimed the process. To Edwin, it sounded as juvenile as throwing jacks and balls on the sidewalk.

Edwin made his way home by six. As he hung up his coat and took off his boots, sitting down to rub his feet, he was surprised to hear loud noises from the kitchen. The crash of pots and pans blended with powerful Yiddish oaths, an art form millennia old. His mother's favorite curse met his ears, something about an enemy having ten homes with ten rooms with ten beds and rolling back and forth with cholera on every one.

He passed through the dining room. Naomi's hair was flying free and she wore a brush of flour on half her face and ash on the other. Every surface was covered with cooking paraphernalia. Gladdy was lapping up a gravy spill. "What in the world is the matter, Mother?" he asked. "Where's Wong?"

"He was supposed to be back once he collected the laundry. He left around ten and I haven't seen him since. At the stroke of five, when have you ever found him anywhere but the kitchen?" She bit her lip and tossed scabby fall potatoes into a pot of boiling water, recoiling at the splash. "I'm planning a simple omelet with fried potatoes. Damn vegetables have to be boiled first. Can you imagine the complexity? Cooking is time consuming and messy."

The *Woman Suffrage Cookbook* was open on the table, garnished with spills and stains. An open bottle of Barton & Guestier claret sat half empty on the counter. If he didn't calm her down, the evening would be a wreck.

Naomi held up a bandaged finger. "And I burned myself. How am I supposed to paint?"

Wincing, Edwin took off his coat, grabbed an apron, and rolled up his sleeves. After the rubbery omelet and potato mush, they opened a tin of pears for small cheer. But by the time two bottles were empty and they'd done the washing up, it was nearly ten o'clock.

"Where could he be? It must be an accident or maybe he was robbed. If he'd been delayed by something ordinary, he could have telephoned from somewhere or sent a boy." She began pacing the parlor like a panther.

"I could try to find his cousin, but it is late." Who would rob the man? Had he gotten into a fight? Wong was as quiet as paint on a wall. That didn't mean that he wouldn't protect himself and his friends.

She rubbed her temples with a moan. "I haven't the foggiest where he lives other than in Chinatown with three thousand others. And no, they don't all look the same. Not to me."

Edwin rang up the Jubilee and St. Ann's, waiting several minutes before he reached the head nurse's station. Then he tried the police department. A brawl had erupted among a dozen sailors from the HMS *Albert* drunk on shore leave. Wong wouldn't have been embroiled in that. A wagon on fire in a hayfield miles away near Hillside shed no light on his disappearance.

Naomi looked at her son through worried eyes. "You don't

suppose he's been press-ganged and taken off to sea? Ships need good cooks."

Edwin waved off the comment with a barely polite snort. His high-strung mother was quick to panic. It was his job to keep his head and make important decisions. "Nonsense. They don't do that anymore." But he wasn't so sure. Walking the streets had provided a painful education on man's inhumanity to man.

# CHAPTER FIFTEEN

The next morning the kitchen was ominously quiet. A lonely wedge of rye languished in the bread box. No jam. A cheddar rind a mouse might scorn. A can of turtle soup they'd both been loath to open. Perhaps provisions could be delivered. He circled an ad by R. H. Jameson on Fort. Bacon fifteen cents a pound. A fry-up would make an easy supper. He left a note for his mother and a few dollars on the table for expenses they couldn't charge. Vicky's case seemed to have reached another dead end for now.

Like an invisible gargoyle brooding over the scene, the disappearance of Wong smacked him in the face. For an independent adult outside the wealthy community to be gone less than a week wouldn't warrant using departmental resources. Wong was missing, not killed. This would be a priority below Mary Donahue. But to the DesRosiers, seven faithful years of service carried weight.

If the man didn't return soon, Davie Crockett, the house detective, might help. Davie had Chinatown connections with Madame Liang, owner of a brothel. Edwin didn't speak any Cantonese, only a few words of pidgin English from his constable days. Lun was the logical starting place. They had to find him first.

First Edwin stopped at the Chinese hospital, no more than a small wooden hut, a *taiping fang*, or "peaceful room," where traditional medicine could be obtained and a few old men went to die in peace. The Chinese community was in the process of raising money for a modern building via a two-dollar stipend per immigrant. The sole attendant, a stooped Confucian man in a wispy beard, led him through the cramped space, empty at the moment. It was a sad contrast to the care whites received.

When he got to the office, Reggie was beaming. "Old son, we may have new information. It's one hell of a break."

Edwin stopped in the process of hanging up his coat, and smiled for a change. "Don't keep me in suspenders."

Reggie lit up a cigarette and inhaled deeply, blowing concentric smoke rings and cocking his head to admire them. His ylang-ylang cologne was perfuming the office like a brothel. "An anonymous tip, what else? This arrived by post at the department this morning. Frost opened it, and sent it over straightaway." He handed Edwin an envelope. Inside was a paper. Both pieces were ordinary.

"Now if it smelled of roses and had initials embossed, we might have something. I'm not keen on anonymous tips. Usually they're fraudulent," Edwin said.

It read: *If you wants to know who attackt those wimmin and kilt the other, there's a janitor at the Union club. His name is Jack Stevens.* Written in crabbed pencil, the note and envelope had several erasures. The number seven in the address had an odd slash through it.

"Union Club. I'm there all the time," Reggie said. " 'Course you don't see the cleaning staff unless some tosspot pukes. I find it off that he spelled 'janitor' correctly."

"When things are too good to be true, usually they're not. Get a couple of constables and let's go. Brush is around, so bring him. No pistols," Edwin said. "If we need a wagon, there's a livery next door." He turned back to Reggie and fanned the room. "And get rid of that stink, Beau Brummell."

"You're the one with no taste. Carrie gave it to me," Reggie said, combing his hair and smiling at himself in the small mirror.

Assembling in ten minutes, the four of them took off at a brisk walk to the brick club at the northwest corner of Douglas and Courtney. Despite its commanding appearance, the building was notorious for rats and attracted the interest of city officials. Next door were the Victoria Transfer Company stables, a happy breeding ground and grain source. One rat pair could yield a million in a few years. Hay also covered the sidewalks and flies swarmed. On some of the vermin-catching nights, a dozen was common. The day's record for the civic rat catcher was a whopping 120. Those in the know didn't patronize the kitchens.

As they started up the steps, Edwin cautioned, "We may be wasting our time, but let's do it right." He directed the two constables to the rear entrance. "Billy clubs at the ready, boys. He may try to run. I know you two won the footrace at our last picnic, so we're counting on you to catch him and give him a rap if he misbehaves. Don't knock him out. Try the knee first. We don't need the man in a coma."

"Right, Sir!" they said in unison, saluting with their clubs.

At that moment, a cab pulled up and Reggie called, "Hello!"

A tall man in a top hat got out, reaching back for an eagle-headed cane, which he twirled with some talent. His brown goatee added to the Mephistophelian effect. "Reggie. What say we meet at the hotel in a couple of hours? Or a game of billiards? Who's your friend?"

"Actually, old man, we . . ." Reggie stuttered a few unintelligible words.

Edwin grabbed his cohort by the arm. "Come along now, you royal ass."

The man put his hands on his hips and a bemused smile crept over his face. "Well, blow me down . . ." His chuckles made the cabby laugh, as the man opened his wallet for the fare.

Inside they went to the front desk, a walnut masterpiece with a marble top. Edwin turned on Reggie with a withering stare. "For God's sake, man. Don't stop and blab to every idiot you see when you're on a case. Who the deuce was that?"

"That's Clifford Cardinal. We're going shooting birds next week on Mayne Island. Come along if you want. The rates are really reasonable. Room and all meals. I can lend you a shotgun."

The clerk called the manager, who appeared from an office in a trim gray suit with a Prince Albert coat. His monocle focused the sun from an upper window at Edwin's eyes as the explanation proceeded.

He held up manicured hands in beseechment, his tones from sotto voice to tremolo. "Gentleman, *please*. We don't want any trouble in front of the members. This is a very exclusive club. The mayor just went upstairs with several aldermen."

Edwin blew out a contemptuous breath as he tried to control his temper. "We'll be out in minutes. No need to start a panic."

"You'll find Stevens down the stairs to the right. He has a room across from the supplies closet. It has a sign. The man does a decent job, his . . . personal hygiene aside." He sniffed and dabbed at his nose with a lace handkerchief. "Don't shoot any rats at this time of day, no matter what they're doing. And if you could use the rear exit, it would be appreciated."

"We'll do as we please. What's Stevens look like?" Edwin asked. How telling that the man thought they were all armed.

"Bald as a dormouse. Smells about as bad," the bespectacled clerk said. "Don't know if it's his clothes or an affliction."

"One thing more. Does he have Saturday nights off?"

"Gets off after supper. Sundays, too."

Edwin, Reggie, and Brush went down the stairs on tiptoe,

though the old boards creaked. It was cooler below, with a warren of closets and hallways. Feeble light filtered from the half windows in the basement. Edwin directed Brush to wait. The smell was musty, with echoes of damp and the whiff of coal smoke. The cloying smell of overcooked food mingled with the taint of garbage.

They walked quietly down the hall, looking back and forth. Edwin signaled with nods and hand motions. When he reached the doorway of the room across from the supplies, he moved inside. "A word with you, Mr. Stevens. Detective Sergeant Des-Rosiers of the—"

With a curse, a man in overalls jumped to his feet and streaked for the door. Edwin kicked a bushel basket into his path, and Stevens went sprawling, scrambling to his feet and past Reggie. "No, you don't," said Brush, who angled out a meaty hand, caught the man by the back of his collar and shoved him into the cement wall. He went down coughing his guts out. A smell of ammonia hit the air. From his cleaning supplies or was this truly the man the prossies had fingered?

When Stevens got up, a man on each side, he was shaking. Then he belched and touched his solar plexus. A groan escaped as they cuffed his hands behind his back. "Let me get some of my gut medicine. For God's sake, have some pity. I'm in a lot of pain."

"Don't let him have it. Who knows what it is? I've seen some take poison on arrest," said Brush.

"We want you at the station for an interview." No need for details. A young tow-headed boy was peering in the door, a filled coal scuttle at his feet.

Stevens's seamed face contorted as a spasm wracked his wiry body. "My pills," he said as his legs buckled, dropping him to one knee. He pointed to a small box by the bed: *Dr. Wilden's*

*Quick Cure for Indigestion and Dyspepsia.* "And the Carbo wafers, too."

"I'll take them," Edwin said, pocketing the boxes. "We'll consult the doctor, and if he agrees, you can have them back."

Brush had been rummaging in a lone dresser. He hauled out a fistful of black fabric. "Good as signed his own warrant. What are you doing with all these ladies' stockings, you perverted cur? Do you wear their bloomers, too?"

They hauled him up to ground level and down the stairs to the street where the constables each took an arm. A small wagon from the livery had been commandeered.

Back at the station, the officers took Stevens to a bare room in the basement and shoved him into a chair. "I'm not even going to ask you where you were the nights of April thirteenth and twentieth, said Edwin, standing behind the table and leaning forward. "We have your description from the women. Right down to your . . . stomach problems." He intended to move from the assaults to the murder instead of opening with the major charge. That was a more subtle plan.

The man spat on the floor. Brush stepped forward to cuff him in the face. Edwin put up a hand against further action.

"Bullcrap. No one saw nothing."

"That's a confession in itself. You took them from behind, you coward," Edwin said.

"The wages of sin." Stevens's piggy eyes moved heavenward to a crack on the ceiling.

"None of that Bible-beating, you scum. You accosted two women and killed the third," said Reggie, leaning against the wall with an intrigued expression.

Edwin didn't fancy the way Reggie was blundering in like a bull. His job was to shut up and let Edwin handle the interrogation.

Stevens sat in the chair, doubled over from convincing pain.

"Them two, Mamie and Rosie, they're harlots. My ma told me about Jezebels. They're dirty like the rats. I never killed them, did I? That's God's job. Or the pox's. I brought the first righteous warning."

"What kind of a monster are you?" Edwin asked.

Stevens didn't seem to hear. "Filthy things lead decent men astray with their dirty parts. Me mam told me that. She'd be proud of me, sitting with the dear Lord she is."

"I'm not here to waste words on you. Let's move on to Victoria Crosse. Your God will judge you." Edwin placed himself squarely in front of Stevens. His steady gaze meant business.

A curious expression passed over Stevens's drawn face. With a wary tone, he said, "Who'd ya say?"

Edwin hated to hear her name in this foul man's mouth. "Miss Crosse to you. You killed her down by the Belleville Street waterfront two weeks ago on Saturday night."

"Go on. You're not sticking this on me. I heard about her was all." He pointed up to a calendar on the wall. It was from Shotbolt's Pharmacy, a pastoral picture of children playing. "And that night I was on duty. You go check. There was a ruckus in the billiard room. A fight over a wager. Glasses broken. I had to clean up. I was there until eleven rewaxing the wood floor. I could get ten witnesses."

Edwin motioned to the constables at the door. "Take him to the cells. We'll get a confession written up. He'll sign it or I'll know the reason why."

"Hey, who was it peached on me? You didn't just pick my name out of a hat."

Edwin handed him the note. Stevens pounded his fist on the desk before the constable grabbed his hands. "That's a damn lie."

"If your alibi holds up, which I highly doubt, you'll only be charged for the assaults." Something about the odious man's voice rang true, though he hated to admit it. It was an uncanny sense, nothing palpable. That note raised more questions than it answered. Was the person ill-schooled or pretending to be?

Then a light went on in Stevens's eyes, and a deep furrow etched his clammy brow. "Damn. This is the truth and no mistake. The night you're talking about, I got a note from a boy at eight to go to Rithet's Outer Wharves to pick up a package. Straight down Belleville. I was supposed to get a buck for my trouble. When I got there, no one was around and the address didn't exist. Figured it for a bad joke."

"Who would do that to a sweet fellow like you?" Edwin leaned against the wall.

Stevens didn't hesitate. "Spencer Lamrod. He was after my sister last year. Hates me for warning her he's married. Works at the gas plant. He's into stealing anything you want, the little bastard. The stories I could tell you about him and the money he pockets."

"Have you ever seen his writing?"

"Why the hell would I? But I still has the note. I shove everything into these pockets. And you never know when you need a piece of paper." With his head he indicated his capacious overalls. "Go ahead. Look for it."

As low man, Reggie had to search. With his face contorted as if he might pluck out an adder, he probed pockets, turning up matches, small coins, and finally a crumpled piece of blue paper. Its writing was faded and degraded "That's the one. It was just a few words." His face paled as he tried to make them out, but it was no use. "Damn. I had a wet rag in there."

"Don't take us for idiots. For all we know you wrote this yourself," said Edwin, and Brush nodded approvingly. "Get him processed and over to Hillside." Although the original jail had been in Bastion Square, with the increasing felon population, a large facility with sixty-six cells had been built on Topaz Avenue.

"I can read some, but I can't write much more than my name. Ask anyone" were his last words as he was frog-marched out, sniveling like an infant.

Edwin was of a mixed mind. Stevens may have admitted the two assaults, but would a jury convict on Vicky's murder? Was someone playing them for a fool? He rubbed at the back of his neck where a headache nibbled.

"Reggie, follow up on that Lamrod fellow," he said as he thought of Mary Donahue's picture on his desk. "And send a man around to the stationers in case they have any blue paper. See what they use here at the club."

"Use it all the time in the library upstairs. It's cream, embossed with the club's name. That's a dead end," Reggie said.

# CHAPTER SIXTEEN

Far from city turmoil, Anna Bach licked the wooden spoon that her mother had presented after putting her cake into the oven. Chocolate was her most favorite flavor in the whole world. The small farm near Langford Lake didn't enjoy sweets except for homemade toffee, *Pfeffernüsse,* or the occasional apple or blackberry pie. But today was special. It was Anna's *Geburtstag.* She was ten years old. Mother said that ten was the golden age.

"Where's Falk?" she asked her mother.

"Over to the lake to get fish for supper if he's lucky," her mother replied. They had come from the Palatinate five years ago to claim land of their own. The climate was as mild as they'd been promised, though they missed the hot summers. Twice a year salmon from the creeks went to their table and smoker. In the beginning Father Helmut Bach had worked for other farmers and they lived in a neighbor's barn while the cabin was built. Germans had strong work ethics. They were proud of their long heritage and safer here than in Europe. Many relatives had died in the Franco-Prussian War.

"I'm going to help him, Muttie," Anna said. "I finished the mending. And the stitches are really *kleine,* like you want." Sewing was easier than washing. That process took from dawn to dusk to heat the water and boil the clothes outside in the cauldron. And wool took an eternity to dry on the line, or in winter, in the barn.

"Take Fisher. He's always under my feet," her mother said.

Their feisty little dachshund was a good companion, but had a stubborn yen to stray. His breed were born ratters, going down holes, even in the potato fields. They had to keep him from their few cattle or he'd chase them all over the fields and sour the milk.

Ann tied a bright blue patterned kerchief over her golden braids. When she got "an inch or two" older, she could wear them around her head like her mother. "We can't have you getting married so soon," her mother would say with a laugh as she chucked Anna's rosy cheek. "You can't make good bread yet, and that's the first important lesson for a woman."

Fisher was snoozing on a blanket in the corner. He got up reluctantly and shook head to tail when she called. At the last minute, Anna grabbed a piece of dark *Bauernbrot* and added a dollop of their goat cheese, munching as she walked.

Langford Lake was full of small trout and the occasional bass, but eight or nine made a supper. Anna liked them fried in butter with the wild onion. She followed the path to the lake for half a mile, thinking how grown up she felt. Every now and then, her fingers plucked a tasty salmonberry. Then she heard the varied thrush that heralded the berries' ripening. "It is the same bird from Germany," Muttie had said. "But the song is a little different. Listen." Anna didn't remember much about the old country. She had been too little to care about birds.

Finding berries was Anna's job. First came the salmonberries, then the cloudberries, raspberries, salal, and huckleberries red and black, and finally the sturdy blackberry, which lasted into October. Current jelly tasted so good with the tender deer her father shot. Anna felt sorry for the little fawns, but her family needed meat, too.

There was considerable bush to be battled, and her father and brother had worked hard to cut the trees, burn and haul the stumps so that the land could be planted. Even Anna helped with smaller stones, using them for walls or piling them in the middle of a field. Sometimes they took the wagon to the beach to gather seaweed to enrich the fields. Father said that the Natives ate the seaweed, but she couldn't imagine that, especially not the rubbery bull kelp.

Her little ears caught the twitter of a *Wachtelfamilie*. Unlike a plump partridge, they didn't make much of a mouthful. She laughed at the comical way the young ones trooped in line like schoolchildren, their tiny feet moving as fast as a hummingbird's. Males wore the pretty little crown. Fisher chased a covey from the hedgerow into a nearby holly bush. Its red berries cheered over the winter, and they used the prickly leaves to decorate the house for *Weihnachten*.

Where was Fisher? He was always letting his nose guide him, as *unartig* as a beagle, their father said. Naughty boy. More than once he'd been gone all night. How could he run so far on those stumpy legs? Father called him a useless lap dog, but he saved morsels from each meal for the little beggar.

"You'll make him fat, Papa," her mother would say. "Then his belly will hang down and that's not good for his back." Dachshunds had problems with their rear legs. A dog had to earn its keep as a herder, a ratter, or a guard. Or it would be sent to *Himmel*.

"Fisher! *Kommen Sie hier!*" Anna called. Had he followed that game path? She tried to search, looking for his rope collar, but the bramble pulled at her cotton dress. "Ouch!" she cried, pricking her finger and thrusting it into her bowed mouth.

With the lush spring growth, she couldn't see into the woods. The yellow flowers of the Scottish broom had appeared like little butterflies with a faint scent. The gorse she hated. Its huge spines pulled at her.

She sat on a flat rock for a few minutes, trying not to cry from frustration. What a disobedient dog, spoiling her special day. But how could she be mad at him when he looked up with those innocent brown marble eyes?

Anna called and called until her voice grew hoarse. Had Fisher gone to the lake edge and found Falk at his favorite fishing hole under the arbutus? Suppose the dog had chased a deer for miles? She couldn't go home without him. Falk would laugh at her. Muttie would be mad, and even Papa might frown that stormy look. Surely the dog would know his way home for supper when he got hungry. She continued walking an old path to the lake, singing and clapping. Was he getting deaf? He was already nine. Papa said that was old for a dog. Wouldn't it be terrible if he were hurt and helpless? The thought made her lip tremble. But why didn't he bark?

It was still another quarter mile to the lake edge. Go on, stay here, or go home? Falk would come back this way, but perhaps not for another two hours. She squinted up at the sun. Three o'clock. Falk had shown her how to tell the time. Was it her imagination, or did the woods seem to be closing in? She thought of Hansel and Gretel and the witch's scary house. That was a fairy story, but there had been sightings of a mother and two jolly cubs, coming down from the high country after the fresh grass and forage. And where they came, so did the cougars, looking for deer and rabbits. Babies got eaten. That wasn't fair, but it was nature's way so that the strongest would live.

In the bee-loud glade, finally she heard a rustle. There was Fisher, pumping his legs and crashing through the undergrowth. He had something in his mouth? Please not a tiny quail. They were too young to fly. But he never bit down hard. Maybe if the bird wasn't hurt, she could set it free. Or she could nurse it back to health. She knew where to get worms. Her brother used them for fishing. Once they'd kept a sparrow in a little box. It had died, but she'd be really careful. Some day she might be become a veterinary. Could women do that? Maybe a nurse, then. "Fisher, *hier*! Good boy. Give me the little birdie."

Closer and closer he got. Then he dropped something at her feet and looked up with proud, adoring eyes. A red hawk wheeled and streaked downward to grab a helpless bunny. The prey rent the air with its pitiful cries. So did Anna.

# CHAPTER SEVENTEEN

Lamrod had gone east after Christmas to work on the cod boats off Halifax, Reggie had found. So much for Stevens's only defense. No stationer carried similar blue paper. Despite Edwin's doubts, the arrest had pleased the bosses.

Edwin sat in McBride's office with the senior officers standing round, smiles on their faces for once. A bottle of Heather Dew scotch had been unstoppered and generous drinks were being poured. "I don't mind telling you boys that this is a load off my mind," the chief inspector said. "Yesterday the mayor was at me again about the Crosse woman. The Yankee newspapers in Washington picked it up and his cousin in Portland cabled him. Damn yellow-journalist dogs." He clinked glasses with Brush and puffed on his cigar, roiling clouds of blue smoke. "The whole lot of you go home two hours early today. Give the wives a roll in the hay. Three cases solved and the cowardly bastard in the jug. Job well done."

Stevens had been identified by smell by the two prostitutes. He would be arraigned for the murder when court sessions resumed. Then he'd rot in jail until the trial. Bail was out of the question. With the *Daily Colonist*'s story on everyone lips, reinforcements from the Provincial Police might be needed to assure security if the jail's location away from town center wasn't enough protection.

With the scotch sour in his stomach, Edwin felt chafed by the rough edges of the case. Stevens's story about the night

Vicky died was absurd enough to be true. The man was odious, but no one should be railroaded to the gallows. Questions remained. The tattoo. The invisible Mr. Abbott. Vicky's source of cash and that stupid phrase to memorize. There was something oddly familiar about the babble. Could it be another language?

Back in their office, Reggie was giving his shoes a polish, ox-blood lace-up models with a needle toe. "Strictly hand sewn," he said to Edwin. "Why do you wear those heavy old boots like you're still pounding a beat, old thing?"

"Next time you have to run in your fancy shoes, you won't be so happy. They remind me of Chinese footbinding. Whatever about that tattooist? The lad saw him take a boat up the Gorge with a couple of ladies. That spells suspicion to me."

Reggie raised his hands in a helpless gesture. "The store's all closed up. Fellow who rents it out said that the reprobate vanished a week ago. Left everything in place. The owner cleared it out, sold what he could, and left the rest for trash. I was upstairs and down poking around. One my own initiative, I might add. Nearly wrecked my new suit in that filthy hellhole."

"That's a red light in itself. Why leave all that he owned? You should have brought him in for questioning the first time. A change of scene loosens tongues."

"There's plenty of smuggling down by the docks. That shop might have been nothing more than a front. Maybe things got too hot. Occam's razor, Rozzer. Look for the simplest explanation." He smirked at his joke, covering up for the earlier mistake.

Edwin folded his arms in disgust. "Too late now. He's scarpered."

Reggie was due for dinner that night at his fiancée's family's mansion on Pandora. Plans had been made for a June wedding. "This time next month, I'll be an old married man," he added, quickly changing the subject. He ran his tongue around his mouth and frowned. "I'm getting a bloody toothache. God, I hate dentists. Suppose with those pearlies of yours you've never seen one."

Edwin was looking out the window at a Chinese funeral. The eerie music reached him, discordant and high pitched, full of whistles and gongs. Wong was heavy on his mind. He needed to engage Crockett. A quick call to the hotel told him that the man had gone up island to Nanaimo to visit his married daughter. "Damnation," he said, then told a curious Reggie about the faithful servant.

"Anyone would be loco to leave a cushy job at your house," Reggie said, glancing up at the clock. "Why are you still hanging around? Go out and celebrate like Mac said. Find a girl to take to supper. Or would the Mater be vexed?" Reggie shrugged into his suitcoat, flicking a piece of lint from the shoulder. "That better not be dandruff. I need to speak to my barber about a different tonic."

Edwin made no move to rise. Life at home would continue to be chaos. "Stevens threw himself at our feet admitting the assaults. Why not make a clean breast of the murder? And that note looked like a setup."

"Since we could barely read it, how can we be sure? The stockings hanged him like a goose. The papers never got that information. Looks like a sure thing."

"Unless someone from *here* let it slip."

Reggie cleared his throat and a light flush reddened his white cheeks. "I say, pal o' mine. You know what I'm like in my cups."

Edwin locked eyes with him and seized his shoulders. "You damn well better not have spilled."

"Come on, old chum. I don't run with murderers. And I certainly don't discuss my job with Carrie. It's no subject for women."

Edwin picked up his hat and headed for the door. "Then

he'll swing for sure. You know what kind of defenders we have."
Serge would have loved this case. Taking the side of the
underdog and flogging the Queen's counsel gave him a satisfac-
tion beyond the price of rubies. Where had it all gone wrong for
his father, Edwin wondered? Certainly Serge had owed money,
but who didn't, with one financial panic after another in those
days?

Reggie brayed out a laugh. "Then he's a fool to boot. Ten or
twenty years for admitted manslaughter is nothing next to doing the dead man's jig for the amusement of the hoi polloi."

Sergeant Frost hurried in, puffing like a flounder out of water.
His bulbous eyes were growing larger by the second. "Gentlemen, we've had a telephone call from the justice of the peace in
Langford." The JP issued marriage licenses, notarized papers,
and served as a liaison for the Victoria police.

Reggie asked with a snicker, "Some cow get stolen? Or did a
tramp take a cooling pie from a window ledge?"

Frost leaned on the desk with his bulky stomach pushing the
buttons of his uniform. His face passed plum to dark red. "It
. . . sounds serious. A death. Little girl called Anna made the
discovery and told her parents. Good German family."

Edwin and Reggie exchanged glances. "An accident? Put
them through to the coroner."

Between gasps, the man could barely talk. He scratched his
neck, where a stubborn patch of eczema flamed. "They're not
sure. You see—"

The clock tower chimed four. Edwin had hoped to use the
free time to hire a temporary cook to take Wong's place. "You're
not making sense, man. Sit down if you have to. You look like
apoplexy's around the corner."

Frost flopped into a chair, taking deep breaths. A shudder
convulsed his massive shoulders. "All they found was a . . .
hand not far from Langford Lake. Looks like a young girl's, but

it could belong to a young boy, I suppose. Used to hard work. You can tell by the nails and callouses."

"Gruesome. I see why you're upset. Was anyone in the area reported missing? Some feebleminded fellow wander off? It's all farms between acres of bush. I got some tasty venison out there once," Reggie said.

Edwin's glance went to the unopened file on Mary Donahue. In the excitement over Stevens, he'd nearly forgotten about her. What in the name of God would she have been doing at Langford Lake? A train ran through that wilderness to Nanaimo. Could she have gotten off at Goldstream and made her way that far? And if she'd fallen, she'd have been near the tracks. He told them about Mary and showed them her picture.

"She's a beauty. Just a kid," Reggie said, and Frost wiped a tear from his eye, saying that Mary resembled his wee sister, dead of meningitis.

"The time frame could fit." Frost's breathing had returned to normal. He carried fifty extra pounds and often complained about his knees. "Foregone conclusion, ain't it?"

Edwin looked at the fading light outside. "Even sending someone at a gallop, it would nearly be dark. You could survive without a hand, but it's unlikely. So the JP has things under control?"

Frost broke in. "He's dispatched two men to keep watch in the immediate area. He suggested we wait until—"

"That's very rough country, nothing pastoral like the Saanich fields. Steep and deep and the lake has swampy areas. The hand's in safekeeping, whatever it can tell us." Edwin traced a finger on the wall map as he clenched his jaw. Two weeks missing. Chances are she'd been dead when the mother arrived. "Get Jones on board if you can and a couple of constables. We'll meet here with a wagon tomorrow morning at daybreak."

Reggie looked as if he needed a drink. "Jesus, remember a

few years ago when the Chinaman about took off the head of his girlfriend as she leaned out the window on Fisgard? Then the bugger holed up in a coal cellar. That cleaver was wicked sharp."

"Chances are that it's a white man did this, Reggie. Unless you have something constructive to contribute, pipe down."

Reggie tugged an imaginary forelock. "Sorry, Your Lordship. Have mercy on an ignorant peasant."

"With the scavengers, there's a chance we won't find anything more. The thought of asking the mother to identify a . . ." He could still see Mrs. Donahue sitting in his office, shredding her handkerchief, hoping for the best but fearing that she'd never see Mary again. "One missing girl. One young female . . . hand. A plus B. It's going to be hell searching that jungle. Even the original surveyors had a devil of a time."

Reggie narrowed his olive green eyes in thought and struck a match on the bottom of his shoe to light a cigarillo. "Say, my pal Bobby has a bloodhound. Pure bred. Hell of a funny pooch, all jowly and slobbery. I prefer Labs. But bloodhounds are jolly good at this kind of thing, aren't they? What about I ask him to lend a ha—oops there I go again."

Edwin agreed and made a couple of notes about supplies for the next morning's sad task. Reggie's idea had been surprisingly helpful. The man had some brains even if he lacked drive. His father-in-law wanted Reggie to run for the provincial legislature, a soft job with a substantially better salary than police work.

Half an hour later, turning onto his block, Edwin tried to cross the street to avoid Liam O'Neill, but the reporter was too fast, falling into step beside him. "I just got back to town. So you finally made an arrest in the Crosse murder, did you? Sure you have the right fellow?"

"We'll see at the trial." Edwin picked up the pace, but O'Neill stuck close.

The tall lanky man with the ambulation of a displaced stork and bushy red sideburns pushed back his tweed hat. "You don't sound altogether satisfied. I know I'm not. The cases are like chalk and cheese. Admit it, or you're not the copper I think you are."

Edwin stopped and turned. The man wasn't a bad fellow, but he could be annoying. This was their first encounter since he became a detective. Liam would be a better friend than adversary. "Go on, then. What do you know?"

The man shrugged. "Something I heard a few weeks ago. I got slozzled with one of my favorite sporting ladies and she whispered something about sticks."

"Sticks? That's meaningless. What was the context. Some kind of sexual act?"

"A well-kept secret. But she has a lot of contacts. You know how women talk."

"Care to give me her name?" He reached inside his coat for his notebook.

"Not on your life. Besides, she didn't even remember, the next morning."

Shortly after parting company with O'Neill, Edwin found his mother pale and silent in the parlor, drumming her fingers on the chair arm. There were no smells of cooking or any kind of industry. Damn.

Her outfit was the same as yesterday, a Turkish robe cinched at the waist. Usually she was impeccably groomed and dressed, energetic and witty in perpetual salon mode, rarely letting him get a word in when she was holding court. Like a sleek animal shot down in full stride, the light had faded from her face and her muscles were slack. Blue circles pouched under her eyes. Not for the first time, he felt like the adult in the family. Suppose she began scouring the city on her own? She wouldn't dare. "No word?"

She shook her head and picked up a small music box, winding it. "Home Sweet Home" came on. A tear trickled down her face, making a runnel in the powder. Her unraveling chignon drooped across her shoulders in a picture reminiscent of a stage actress "run mad." "I've been beside myself all day, Edwin. I feel so helpless. Wong isn't just our employee. He's a friend. If you were missing, I know he'd . . he'd . . . ." Unabashedly, she swiped the back of her hand under her red snuffling nose.

Edwin poured himself a snifter of brandy and offered her one, but she shook her head. The heat put some heart back into him. First Vicky, and a dubious arrest, Wong missing, and now a new death. Edwin sat down, stretching his sock feet, his big toe poking through a fresh hole. Wong's wooden darning egg would have made short work of it. Soon he'd look as unkempt at the edges as Naomi. "Mother, I know we're turned upside down. But my job . . . I have . . . something to do tomorrow. Probably I'll be back late." This was no time to talk about body parts.

"What do you mean?" She turned her face in confusion. "You told me yesterday that Vicky's murderer was in jail. Some miscreant custodian at the Union Club."

"Maybe yes, maybe no. I've got a man in mind to hire to look for Wong, but he's gone for a few days, and something else very serious has come up. Nothing to do with Vicky. I have to go to Langford very early with a team of men."

"A team. Whatever for? Or don't you trust your own mother?"

The maternal card was not going to work. "A suspicious death in the Western Communities. That's all I know." He touched her arm gently. "You look done in. Get some rest."

She stood up, wounded in fresh fury. "Nonsense. I'm not waiting around. I'll go look for Wong myself. You handle your crisis, and I'll handle . . . ours."

He raised his voice for the first time in years and set down the glass with a bang that splashed over the antimacassar. From his embroidered cushion, Gladdy gave a frightened yelp. Whatever he told her, she did the opposite. How did Serge stand it? "That's ridiculous. I won't hear of your going to Chinatown. White women—"

Her tones were cool and measured as she flared her patrician nostrils. "You are *not* my father, Edwin. I've walked the roughest streets in Paris and Limehouse in London when I was scarcely twenty. First I'll find Lun. As for the rest, money talks in any language. Hire someone for the household if you wish. But I'm not waiting for Hades to freeze. I want action. Now."

"Be hanged, then. There's no talking sense to you. Father told me that." No sooner were the words out of his mouth than he regretted them. She rose slowly, Gladdy at her heels. As a final gesture, she tossed the *Daily Colonist* at his feet. Then she slammed the door, rattling the crystal unicorn he had bought her for Christmas.

He picked up the paper and shook it out, allowing the noise to please him. Ads on page one. "Wanted: by experienced English woman, temporary situation as housemaid." Sounded ideal. The address was 11 Caledonia. No telephone, though. One way or another, they'd have their household set right again soon. But where was Wong?

The next morning Edwin was up before dawn, glad to leave the cold, depressing home after last night's meal of baked beans. He let Gladdy out the back door to do his business. Then he shaved and started a fire in the kitchen stove for tea. The kettle might still be warm for his mother in a few hours. To his surprise, he found Naomi striding down the stairs as he put on his hat and flicked a hair from his shoulder. Her makeup was flawless and totally natural—according to her, the secret of successful women.

"At least I'm trying. I call the hospitals daily. Wong can't be lying in a gutter, can he? Not that you care," she said for an opener.

He turned on her, measuring his anger. "I'm going to swallow that because I can see your state. This is a very small city. He'd have been found by a constable on the beat." Edwin didn't mention what had occurred to him, that if someone disappeared in the city, they probably went into the water. Weighed down, some never came up. There had to be a rational reason why the man was gone. But as each day passed, the safe reasons got fewer.

Shaking her head, she scanned the kitchen for signs of food. "No breakfast again. Stop at the bakery on the way to work and get something. A man can't run on nothing. There will be a grocery order arriving this morning. And where's that city map your father used?"

"Find it yourself, Mrs. Scotland Yard," he said over his shoulder as he left. Department stores had begun hiring lady detectives to prevent shoplifting. Not a bad idea. As for anything that might place them in danger, a line would have to be drawn.

At the station, a buckboard with two horses was parked, a constable with the reins. Down the street came two others in a second wagon. Edwin took the front seat of the first, and Reggie and Bobby Banfiel rode in back, with a lugubrious dog large as a barrel of stout. Blocks of ice waited under tarps and a large canvas shroud was folded in the corner.

"Where's Jones?" Edwin asked, after thanking Banfiel.

Reggie said, "He and the other coroner were gone until the afternoon. But it's not like he's going to be needed at a scene like this. It's the whole outdoors. There aren't any witnesses as far as we know."

"That's what bothers me," said Edwin.

They took the usual route to Langford, crossing the tracks at the junction, but instead of heading out the Sooke Road, they detoured on a dirt track past small Glen Lake and the JP's house. "The hand can wait in the ice house. I don't want to lose any time now that it's light," Edwin said.

The morning was picture-postcard fine, mocking their sad and weighty business. Above an open field, two hawks soared in the thermals, waiting for a chance to grab an unwary vole. An eagle followed, its thin peeping cry belying its majesty. Salmon were flopping up their birth creeks, pale imitations of their prime. Bears would ravage their spent bodies, and the rest would feed chicks and fertilize the rich rainforest floor like the biblical lion's carcass brought forth honey. The cycle of life in death.

Finally they reached an open gate in front of a large, tidy cabin with an addition. A carved wooden sign read *Bach*. "Here's the farm," Edwin said. They pulled into the yard.

A little girl with bright aquamarine eyes was waiting on the porch chalking sums on a slate. She gave them a grin and shook hands with Edwin very seriously, then curtseyed for good measure. "You must be Anna. Can you bring your mother out here?" Edwin asked.

Reggie and Edwin removed their hats and took places on the porch while Anna and her mother sat on a freshly painted swing. The little girl's feet didn't touch the floor. Her platinum blonde braids were tied with red ribbon. She wore a blue patterned cotton frock with delicate smocking. Edwin and Reggie took the glasses of cider Mrs. Bach brought while the rest of the group stayed in the wagon, passing around a canteen and a bag of elk jerky shared with the dog. The horses switched their tails against the stinging flies in these thick lowlands away from the salt air. On a rustic table sat a crock bottle with daffodils.

Anna's proud mother gave her a gentle hug. "You tell them, *Liebchen.* Everything that happened yesterday. Show them how brave you were. Like *Das Rotkappchen* against the bad wolf." The sound of chopping came from behind the house. Far out in the field a tall man plowed with an ox. Farmers had no days off.

Anna swallowed and straightened her shoulders. She spoke with deliberation as if she had rehearsed her speech. "My brother Falk was fishing at the lake, and I was finished with my work, so Muttie said I could go. Fisher, too." At her feet an elderly dachshund licked a paw. Reggie scratched its ears. The dog nosed his trousers, probably smelling Reggie's Lab.

Spunky little Anna told her story without hesitation. She was bright and willing, unhesitant in detail, holding back nothing. Focusing on Edwin, she captivated him in an instant.

Edwin made notes in his pad, noticing that Reggie made none. The rookie prided himself on his eidetic memory, but this was hardly professional. He needed a prod in private. "And you say that you screamed? Until your brother came? Most people would have done the same. Even grownups."

"He told me to fetch Papa because he would know what to do. I ran so fast that I fell. But I got right back up. It didn't hurt until later." She pointed to an abraded knee painted with stinging iodine. "Was Fisher a bad dog, Mister, to act like that? He sticks his nose into everything. But he's not mean. And he doesn't chase the cows. Not much."

Edwin stirred himself to give Fisher a pat, and taking the encouragement, the dog jumped up, placing its paws on his knees. It had a warm smooth skin, and he could feel its beating heart as he gently lowered it. "Fisher was a very good dog. His nose is very smart. Dogs help us track the bad men." He didn't mention that the bloodhound had come into being as a tool for owners of runaway slaves.

While they had been talking, the chopping stopped and a tall young boy appeared. He wore wool pants held by a cross strap, a striped flannel shirt, and short hobnailed boots probably passed down from Papa. His shock of brown hair probably favored his father.

"And this is Falk?" The boy wiped his hands on his trousers, and they shook hands.

"Son, please take the policemen to where Anna found . . ." The mother's voice trailed off and she swallowed, flicking her worried eyes to her daughter. No little girl should have to face such an ugly sight.

"May I go, too, Momma?" Anna asked in a surprisingly bold voice. "I milked the goats. Elsa didn't butt me even once."

Edwin held up a cautionary hand. "You've already done a wonderful job for us, Anna. You would make a very good teacher someday," Edwin said. Reggie pulled wrapped toffees from his pocket and offered them to the girl.

"*Danke*," said Anna, checking with her mother for permission.

Mrs. Bach beamed with pride. "Anna is so good with the mathematics. She learned her times table when she was five. Everything must balance right to the *Pfennig*. Perhaps she will be a bookkeeper for a fine husband with a business in the city."

Edwin and Reggie, along with Falk, returned to the wagons. When the young man said that they were nearing "the spot," they got out and walked. Falk gave a strange look to the dog, Titus.

"*Was für ein*, I mean, what kind of dog is that?" He rubbed the back of his strong neck, burnished brown from the sun. His square jaw was beginning to need a shave.

"A bloodhound, a tracking dog. We got him from the U.S., from Mississippi, way down south. A rare breed around here. I'm thinking of getting a bitch and breeding him," Banfiel said, as Titus planted a sloppy kiss on Falk's cheek.

Banfiel lowered the tailgate and hopped the dog from the wagon. Titus had a twenty-foot rope lead. Nose to the ground and large spatulate feet working, the animal was interested. It went one way, then another, lifted its nose and waffled its jowls.

Then it took off again. Dogs' noses were thousands of times more accurate than humans', Banfiel explained. They could smell traces on the ground and in the air, tell an old track from a new one. Some criminals flung pepper to confuse them or detoured down creeks. Banfiel had said that you could train a dog to follow some smells and not others by using a reward system.

But the dog seemed intent, his mouth wattles fluttering with scent. Whether they would be lead to a body or to a deer carcass was another question. After another few minutes, Titus raised his lugubrious muzzle for a "roooooo." "He's on it now, by God. Good boy!" yelled Banfiel.

Falk smiled and pointed to the ground. "Anna was here when Fisher brought . . . it . . . the hand . . . back."

Edwin turned to Reggie. "Animals a half mile off could have been drawn to the body."

"Do you think this girl was killed by a bear or a cougar?" Reggie asked. "Could it have been an accident after all?" Somehow if they didn't use Mary's name, the death wasn't real.

"Yes, it could have been an accident, but a town girl without a horse or wagon doesn't come out here. Not alone. And not when she has a demanding job. She disappeared on a Sunday afternoon, which was her only time off."

They met one of the JP's men at a path juncture and told him to go home and get some sleep. "Bill's down the way looking around," he said. "It's not a good time to meet a bear. They're after the early grass, hungry and cantankerous before the berries are full out. Cubs to feed, too."

Not long after, they found Bill at a clump of alders, chewing the tender end of a blade of grass. A lantern sat by his side along with a horse blanket. "God, what a night. I'm knackered. I heard brush moving over to the right before dawn," he said, wiping his brow with a neckerchief. His square, honest face bore acne scars.

The constables fanned out. Twenty yards out, the dog located a pile of cougar scat and then a fresh bear dump. The first was marked by twisting hair, tapering at the ends, and the second looked almost like horse dung, mainly grass.

Banfiel stopped intermittently to free the line from bushes and snags. The rest followed, watching their feet for evidence. A scrap of clothes, a shoe, a piece of jewelry.

Titus shot his head up for a moment, then increased his pace. They took off on the remains of an old trail overgrown with salal and huckleberries, and to their consternation, blackberry brambles. Everybody had bleeding scratches on their hands and faces by the time they emerged into a sunny clearing. The dog bayed, straining at the rope. Two hundred yards from the spindly alders and big leaf maples, the shimmering lake flashed its reflections. The air swirled with ominous signs of turkey vultures and opportunistic ravens. They made a gruesome chorus of glee in anticipation of a meal.

In one place, a large cedar had fallen a decade ago, judging from the muted gray of the broken trunk and the moss growth. It had left a root ball fifteen feet into the air and a deep hole, tangled with undergrowth. Hauled off with difficulty, Titus was tied to a far-off tree and given a jerky reward.

"I smell rotten salmon. Common this time or year, but . . . something else," Edwin said, growing pale. They all startled as a huge raven lifted into the air, a long string dangling behind it. A daring crow dueled for the prize.

"Jesus, is that what I think it is?" said Reggie, who stumbled to his knees and vomited. Edwin stepped aside as Reggie's new shoes received a baptism.

# CHAPTER EIGHTEEN

Catching their breath was a problem. The closer they got to the bundle, the worse the smell. Everyone pulled handkerchiefs to shield their noses, with minimal effect. "Should have brought essence of balsam," Reggie said. "Jones recommended it."

"Breathe through your mouth," Edwin said. One small step at a time, holding sturdy roots for balance, he eased himself into the hole. Under a thin layer of dirt was a rag of familiar red plaid. Were those fish scales on the clothing, so far from the lake? From the scrabbling marks in the dirt, a weasel or river otter had been digging. Behind him, the coughs and choking continued. He felt like running, but he was damned if he was going to look weak. How did Jones endure this?

"Stay back," Edwin said. "And for Christ's sake, don't spew on me."

"Party's all yours, Rozzer," Reggie called as he backpedaled. "Wouldn't dream of intruding."

Edwin brushed off dirt, swallowing bile. Why be fastidious since she was being moved anyway? It occurred to him that a camera would be useful, bulky or not. As he knelt, a saturation point reached his olfactory senses, and he began to recover his poise.

The clothing was in shreds. Predators had savaged the soft abdomen, as had scavenger birds. One arm was missing at the elbow with what looked like teeth marks on the small bones. Jones had told him the difference between injuries ante- and post-mortem. Where was the blood? They'd had no rain recently.

At last he girded himself to look at the girl's ravaged face. She was beyond fear or pain, but he blinked back a tear for Mary's unborn hopes and dreams. She was helping her mother as best she could with no thought for her own desires. Her skin was smeared with swamp muck from nearer the lake edge, not here in the drier, peaty forest. Had she been moved by an animal that buried its prey, scuffing leaves over it like the cougar? They might expect hairs on the body. How did she die and who had brought her here? Answer the last question and the rest would make sense.

Rigor had come and gone. Obeying their fecundity, blowflies had begun to lay their eggs. The puckering of the skin signaled exposure to the water. He closed his eyes to better record the scene, a painter's trick of Naomi's.

"Bring the tarps," he called. "Take a good gander in case I need your memory later. You won't soon be forgetting anyway."

With dispatch amid coughs and choking, the men placed the remains on the makeshift litter, lifted it between four of them, and walked slowly to the wagon, nearly half a mile away. The small bundle weighed no more than a hundred pounds. A few more months, and Mary would have become part of the forest floor, moss clothing her bones, fungi her jewelry.

Edwin stood and wiped his hands on fragrant cedar needles, discounting entirely that the poor lass had died in an accident or of natural causes. The murderer knew the landscape. Was she brought here dead or alive? In a wagon or on the back of a horse? Vicky had been moved, too. The similarity in the crimes was definitive. Buried deep, she might never have been found. But the ground was rocky beneath the peaty overlay, territory for picks, not shovels. The killer had taken a gamble and lost.

Stopping by the JP's home on the main road, they collected the hand and placed it on ice with the body. In size and coloration, it was a match. The rest of the arm might never be found.

A sober cortege wound its way back to Victoria with no stops. Dried apples, wifely sandwiches, and a jug of cider were passed around. Titus munched the rest of the jerky. Without him, who knew how long the search might have taken? If Mary's body had disappeared down a deep crevice in the remote hills of the bony island, no hunt could have found her. The killer had been too lazy for that route. What did that failing signify?

Edwin and Reggie dropped off the constables at headquarters and headed for the morgue in the downtown market area. After tying the wagon, he called down for help. Hearing the halloos, Jones appeared in his white coat.

"I just got the word an hour ago," he said, running a hand through his hair as the rising evening wind mussed it. "Thought I was safe with a day off, so I took the train to Sidney to see my brother. Had to turn around at his door. He has the telephone for his dental office."

"You missed quite a day," Edwin said.

"Damn, I wanted to see her *in situ*. You better have a good noggin for recall," he added. "Where's the poor girl's hand? I sure as hell hope it's hers. One body is enough."

"We packed ice around it, not that that helps much at this stage of putrefaction." They went up the stairs, followed by the assistants.

"I'm for home and a bubble bath, Rozzer, unless you two need me," Reggie called, giving a farewell salute. "But not until I have a skin full. Figure I've earned it."

While Karl and another husky aide took the body on a stretcher to the morgue and they followed like mourners, Edwin summed up. "So she's been gone over two weeks, lying out in the water and the woods. I can't imagine worse."

"Try a fire or a body floating for a month in the strait.

Sometimes it tangles in the seaweed," Jones said. Huge rafts of briny bull kelp floated offshore, especially in spring and summer. "Turns to a white, soap-like substance. Try assessing time of death then. It's still better than the one got brought up by a propeller screw a few days ago. Think mince held together by a set of striped coveralls. Could have been any of half a dozen missing men."

Edwin paled but held on as an acid taste fingered his gorge. It was early days in his career. There were years of dues ahead.

"Careful," Jones said to Karl. "Everything on the body is important. With the animals at her, it's going to be a zoology lesson. Ed, you're calling this a murder, I imagine, or you're a greater fool than Thirkstan."

Edwin nodded, reaching inside his gut for a dose of courage as he accepted a graying apron. "My question is, was she killed out there or transported? We might never have found her remains if the German's dog hadn't gotten curious. You know how many century-old bones turn up from trappers or Indians miles from civilization."

"Langford Lake's a damn long trip for a girl with only one day a week off." Jones led him to a table with a tray drain and a bucket and dipper on the floor. Mary's tatters and flesh waited to talk to them.

With gentleness, Jones manipulated the neck. "There's slight bruising. Easy to see on pale skin. Hyoid bones seem okay, though. This is not a strangling victim. That's one big difference from the Crosse woman and the other two attacks. Doesn't mean someone couldn't change methods to toy with us." He turned the body over. "Can't rule out stabbing with all this destruction. Odd, though. She's fish-belly white all over, as if she bled out while the heart was pumping."

"Moved after death, then. Why were the animals so quick to come without blood?"

Jones inspected a scraping tool. "Here's the attraction. Salmon scales. Was she beside the lake or near a creek?"

"A hundred yards off. Looks deliberate to me to attract predators. What about the wounds?"

"Animal damage. Claw and bite marks on that ulna. Postmortem. Cougars love a tasty bite of organs. See the tears and rips on the flaps of skin? They eat their fill and bury the body for later. To a cat, this is a hundred-pound porker and a damn sight slower and less dangerous."

Jones needed that perspective to keep his objectivity. Without the spark of life, people were essentially meat. "And bears don't do this?" Edwin asked.

"Wouldn't say never. They will eat human flesh since they're omnivores, but they don't usually haul the damn body around. That's a cat trait."

"How long has she been . . . like this?"

With tweezers, Jones lifted a few maggots. "Eighteen to twenty-four days. After that you can find an empty puparia, an egg case."

Edwin had seen blowfly activity on corpses. It usually started in body openings like eyes or areas of trauma. Makes sense that they'd head for soft tissue first. "How do you know that?"

"Pal of mine in France sent me a translation of choice parts of Megnin's *La faune des cadavres*. There are eight waves of larval development. This size is mid-pupa." He used a small measuring stick.

After covering her face with a clean cloth, Jones was cutting off the shredded clothing and handing it to Karl, his assistant, proceeding to the lower pelvis and intact legs. Then he stopped at the genitals. Her pubic patch was dark but sparse, typical of a budding young girl. He moved the legs apart. "What the hell?"

"Find something?" It helped that the face was no longer in their vision. Jones must have a core of steel.

"Damn right. She's been ripped open vaginally. She may have been hemorrhaging from the wound."

"The wound? You mean by sexual intercourse?"

"No man has an organ that size, or that hard, pardon my crudity." He picked up a magnifying glass, then probed with tweezers. "See this tiny wooden splinter? Baseball bat. Cricket bat. Jesus wept."

Edwin closed his eyes briefly and remembered the moment. "That explains why there was no blood on the ground. What kind of monster are we talking about?"

Jones shrugged. "When alcohol, drugs, and perversion conjoin with opportunity, the result isn't pretty. You wouldn't believe what people do with vegetables, even bottles. Say she was stupefied, even unconscious. She might have bled where she lay for hours. There are no stomach contents to analyze. Rubbing her with salmon would be an engraved invitation to a predator. In another week or so, he might have gotten away with it."

Edwin's nails cut into his palms as he clenched his fists. "Bastard. Had his ugly way and left her to die. She was a scullery maid, for Christ's sake. It was her first job. Where the hell do I start looking? This is a different scheme entirely."

"What about the family that employed her? Any men capable of this monstrous deed? The crime speaks of madness to me, but there's method all the same."

Edwin stared at the floor, hardly hearing a word. He thought of that innocent smile and the youthful dignity in Mary's picture. "I should have followed up on the disappearance right off. Stupid protocol. We don't take these cases that seriously until . . ." He explained about the mother's delay.

"Pshaw, man. Chances are she was long dead by the time you heard about it."

Jones moved as if to clap a comforting hand on Edwin's

shoulder, then pulled back. His white apron was spattered from his explorations. "Just a live toy. Used and discarded."

"What about this hair?" Edwin pointed to several long light brown hairs adhering to the scraps of cloth near her neck. "Her hair's thick and dark as mine."

"Didn't you say you had a dog with you?"

"Bloodhound. Short coat."

"This may be cougar. It's not dark enough for bear. I might learn more under the microscope. But out there in the bush with a world of contamination . . ."

"What are you going to say at the coroner's inquest?" Edwin wondered.

"Death by misadventure for now. I'm no clairvoyant. One last thing." He turned the body over gently. On the middle of the upper buttocks was the unicursal hexagram. "Surprise."

Edwin used his arm to mop cold sweat from his brow. "The total nerve of it all. He must have been positive that we'd never find the body."

"We're dealing with something very evil here. I don't envy you your job."

"I found light hair on Vicky's body that looked like that. Richards guessed that they might be animal. Didn't make sense to me then."

"That's another science in its gestation period. But with the hexagram?" Jones snapped his fingers.

Leaving the morgue, Edwin started on his way home, ravenous after going without food most of the day. The thought of having to tell Mrs. Donahue depressed him further. Then he smacked his palm against a lamp post to enjoy the pain. If he didn't find someone to help at home, he might as well never return. He opened his pocketbook and fingered the newspaper clipping, then brushed dried mud or debris from his coat and pants.

Eleven Caledonia was eight blocks out of his way. The boarding house had flowers in the front yard and a fresh paint job on the gingerbread trim. A frazzled, red-faced Irishwoman named Mrs. Ryan opened the door. "I'm looking for an English lady who placed a notice in the paper seeking work." He showed her the ad.

The aproned woman glanced at it, then scanned him with a gimlet eye. A large goiter lumped her throat like a parasitic twin. "That would be Miss Millicent Masters. Number five."

He followed her up the narrow stairs. The place was neat and smelled of lemon polish. At the turn, a vase of fresh lilac released delicate perfume. The landlady stopped at the door and knocked smartly. "Miss Masters. Gentlemen for you about a position. He *seems* respectable."

Edwin bit down on his molars. Who had time for this?

The door opened to a pinched face woman in a striped shirtwaist dress. She carried a small book. "Thank you, Mrs. Ryan. Come in, Sir."

The landlady left, conspicuously leaving the door open eight inches. "I'll be downstairs if you need me, Miss."

"I was reading my daily devotional to keep my spirits up. Such a comfort in these troubling times."

"Indeed." Edwin cleared his throat. "I'm sorry to call at this unseemly hour, but I'm on my way home from work. Let me tell our needs and you can describe whether we will be mutually satisfactory. I notice that you prefer a temporary position." He avoided talking about his profession. Why queer the deal?

"I will be leaving for Spokane in two months to live with my sister and her family, but I have a few minor accounts to settle. One's word is paramount." Her accent was British, but not plummy like the upper class. In Montreal, he'd heard many dialects from across the pond, even the rhyming Cockney.

"It's awkward to explain, but our Chinese cook and house-

188

keeper has disappeared. There may a simple explanation, but meanwhile . . ."

"How very strange. I am unfamiliar with the habits of the Celestials. They are more numerous here than in Kent, where my people lived. I wouldn't think that they would be as reliable or clean as a proper English servant." Her *s*'s sounded like *z*'s.

"Doubtless we will find out what happened, but in the meantime we need a replacement. The salary is si—" Her chin rose a tad. He didn't like her already, but needs must. "Seven dollars a week, all found. Will that suit?"

"Ah, the Lord does provide." She kissed the book and set it on a table. The room was spare but clean. A metal trunk stood duty as a table with a few digestive biscuits on a flowered plate. Her clothes hung neatly in an open wardrobe. "As for the cooking, I'm sure I can suit. My dumplings are like clouds, and I makes a fine fruit pie."

"And you are familiar with all styles of English and Canadian food? We have a cookbook my mother prefers. There are two of us."

Her face looked a bit worried. "And your mother is well? I'm not to be nursing, I trust."

He gave an ironic smile. "More than well. She is very independent. A modern woman."

*Modern* made her nose twitch. "And my quarters? Nothing damp."

Edwin suppressed a cringe. This type wouldn't tolerate living in the basement. Wong's things could stay in place. "Certainly, we have a spare room upstairs. It's very . . . airy."

She checked the brass alarm clock on the table. "I can come with you now. That way we can get a fast start. Don't expect fancy fare for supper at this notice. Leave the clean bedding out. No wool, please. I am allergic to that coarse fabric."

Shortly after, they hailed a cab home, Edwin carrying her

cheap cardboard valise. It was determined that she could leave the rest of her things until a cartage man could be hired. Odd that she was inspecting his neighborhood so closely. With only one servant, did she expect a mansion?

"Isn't this a charmer," Millicent said as they walked up to the front door. "It reminds me of my last home on the sea. Ever so cozy."

"Make yourself comfortable in the parlor," Edwin said as he helped her off with her coat. "I'll look for Mother."

Naomi's best cloak was gone. Ed's brow contracted. Not even a note. He thought of offering the woman a sherry but decided not to set a precedent. He took the valise upstairs into the spare room. Happily, the bed was freshly made since the last time Fanny had passed out, gin bottle in hand. He checked under the bed for empties.

Then Millicent followed Edwin into the kitchen, nodding in approval. "Very lovely place you have here, Sir. I admire the new stove."

He waved a hand around the kitchen as his stomach rumbled in protest. A man needed fuel. At least groceries had been delivered that morning, from the empty wooden box by the door. "You must make do for tonight with what's in the larder and in the ice box and the pantry." He took a book off the shelf and handed it to her. "You can't go wrong with this."

From a capacious pocket, she pulled a pince-nez and affixed it. "*The Woman Suffrage Cookbook*. Indeed. Those hounds from hell are a caution in London. I seen them chain themselves to gates. Had to be force fed, the silly geese. What they want to concern themselves with voting for, I can't imagine. However would they know who to pick? But if this is what you and your dear mother want, I'm at your service, I'm sure."

# CHAPTER NINETEEN

With Matron Elizabeth Crawford along for support, Edwin accompanied Mrs. Donahue to the morgue to identify the remains. Sadly, the plaid cloth told the story. For all her small size, like her daughter, she was a woman with mettle. He had expected weeping, but she was finished with that, she told him. Her other children needed her. Crawford put an arm around her thin shoulders with firm but comforting guidance, her own eyes teary. Edwin had never understood the idea of women being the "weaker" sex. They suffered monthlies, then miscarriages or early death for their children. Survival left no time for brooding.

When he asked about the tattoo, her mouth gaped. "Mary would never. Someone must have forced her. Do you think it signifies, Sir?"

"I'll do everything in my power to find out who did this," he had told her when he delivered her via cab to her shabby room. And she had taken his hand and laid it against her chapped cheek as the little children in the household wailed and ran amuck.

"I'll stay to give her a hand. You need a good strong cuppa, Missus, and those little faces need scrubbing," Crawford said.

Mary's meager possessions were with her employers. He kept the cab to visit the large and prosperous brick home of the Arbogasts in the village of Oak Bay. Passing his old home on Michigan Street, he felt nostalgic. His mother, never one for

191

finances and consumed in her painting, had paid little attention to Serge's deteriorating practice. People seemed to prefer English lawyers. The poorly paying cases and the pro bonos came to him. Their last outing together had been a picnic on the Queen's birthday. Serge had seemed preoccupied, feigning merriment. Then a month later . . . But why had the gun remained in his hand? Still, Jones talked of cadaveric spasms where the weapon had to be pried from the grip.

He entered the wrought-iron-fenced front yard and walked up to the wraparound porch. In the back was a carriage house, with two matched bays being curried by a groom next to a shiny brown brougham with brasses gleaming in the sun. There would be the man of the house and this lad. What about older sons?

When the housemaid opened the door and saw his identification, her mouth made an O and she placed a hand on her pigeon chest. Then he was taken to the parlor. The house was quiet, thick carpets on the floor and the heavy curtains drawn. Only the ticking of a grandfather clock in the corner broke the silence. Then the sliding doors were pulled aside by the maid and Mrs. Lillian Arbogast sailed in, ample bosom a prow. Without wasting words, he delivered the sad news.

He thought she might faint, and he reached out to steady her to a chair, taking a stool at a small writing table for himself. Her face sagged as if she had been stricken by apoplexy. Where possible, he curbed the ghastly details. The paper had been discreet. Body in the bush for a week. Everyone knew what that meant.

"Mr. Arbogast and I will send money to her mother. Mary was a very good worker." Her voice was deep enough to be a man's. Some wags called that a whiskey tenor, but she looked teetotaler to her core.

"That would be kind." He paused a moment. The department was calling the death an accident, calling for witnesses who might have seen her traveling. Keeping the public from a panic demanded a narrow line between disclosure and prudence.

"We are as yet unsatisfied about how Mary got to Langford. She needed transportation. No person has come forward. Would you know her habits during her free time?" he asked. It was better to await an answer instead of offering prompts and options.

Mrs. Arbogast wrung her pale white hands for a moment, then straightened her back. "I know that she went to church, not our Anglican parish. I believe she was Methodist. She also attended the Girls' Friendly Society meetings over at Saint Barnabas. And she loved to draw with those clever little hands. She gave me a pencil sketch of my daughter once." She shook her head. "I don't know where it got to."

"Any . . . young men she might have mentioned? Perhaps from church."

"Heavens, no. She was far too young to entertain silly thoughts. I always have the housekeeper give the new ones a good talking to. That way they know what's what."

He made a note. GFS. But what was a reliable churchgoing girl doing in the middle of nowhere? Still, a girl would be foolish to speak to her employer about male friends.

"Did she write or receive letters?"

"I haven't the foggiest. She attended to the mail."

"I won't keep you any longer, but I need to speak to—"

"It is strange, but the other night someone tried to get into the house by the back servant stairs."

"Was anything taken? Did you see the person?" Was this a coincidence, or was someone interested in Mary's belongings? A letter perhaps.

She cleared her throat with some disapprobation as a goldfinch pecked at a cuttlebone in his cage, scattering seed on the Turkey carpet. "One of the under maids heard something on the back stairs about two o'clock and screamed. Then the kitchen door shut. I notified the night constable, and he's keeping a watch."

Finally he was taken to the uppermost attic on the fourth floor, the servants' quarters. Mary shared with another young "girl," actual age aside. Novices got the dirty chores of scrubbing blackened pots in the kitchen, chopping cook stove kindling, hauling wood and coal, and cleaning grates and lamps. The idea was to move up in the hierarchy. For a cook to marry a butler was the top of the ladder. On a larger estate, they might even have a separate cabin.

There wasn't much to see in the garret. A dresser, shared wardrobe, and two single metal beds. Rag rug on the floorboards. The wall had two pictures cut from the rotogravure section of a magazine, perhaps *Blackwood's*. A rose-covered cottage. A Constablian scene with cows withers-deep in lush pasture, church steeple in the background. A tin pitcher stood next to a basin of water and a hunk of coarse brown soap.

Mrs. Arbogast said, "You can tell her clothes in the wardrobe. Chloe is much stouter. Mary did have a pretty little figure. My, she seemed about twelve. I nearly didn't hire her. But she was so willing. Full of energy and eager to please."

"Yes, I saw her picture." Where had she found the money to buy that portrait? He looked up. "Please don't let me take any more of your time. I won't be long. When I'm finished, you may send her things to her mother. Perhaps she has a sister who could use them."

"My girls' clothing goes to the Christian charities. Sometimes they haven't been worn more than twice. Fashions come and go, even in this more remote part of the country." She pursed her lips at him in a conflicted expression.

He had timed asking about the husband until near the

conclusion of the interview. "How many children do you have, Ma'am?"

She blushed, almost coy. "Three daughters, twins of two, and the older is four. The Lord never did send us a boy. Sometimes you must trust in his plans."

"I see. And Mr. Arbogast is a businessman?"

"Indeed. He's been gone the last three weeks on banking business in Portland. I'm just as glad that he wasn't here for the fuss. Such a gentle soul. Makes the maids put spiders outside. Now pardon me, please, I must tell the rest. And it is so hot in here." She made a fanning motion.

As she left, he began his search. Harsh, graying flannel sheets with sewn rips accompanied a threadbare blanket. In the wardrobe, he inspected the dresses on the right side. Black uniforms with a white pinafore. A few plain dresses for church. Underclothes in the dresser—"smalls," Naomi called them. Then under the bed he found a worn Gladstone bag and pulled it out. Inside was a folded brown wool outfit with a golden cord. Sweat was running down his nose despite the open windows at each end of the garret.

A nun's habit? Certainly too small for a monk. He pulled it out, touching it like a rare bird. Methodists didn't have nuns, did they? Had she stolen it? From where? The robe had a cowl and a separate white headpiece, not that he knew the fine points. As he shifted the robe, a set of rosary beads clacked onto the floor. He bent to pick them up. His father had a modest set from the orphanage. Naomi had kept them.

He blinked. Not only was the cross upside-down, the beads were shaped like women's bottoms. They were punctuated by tiny phalluses every ten count. Carved from pink quartz and threaded on a silver chain. He sat on the hard bed to gather his thoughts as nausea rolled over him. Vicky learning lines. Did Mary wear this costume to play act? Why keep it here? Did this explain the attempted break-in?

Someone wanted this costume badly enough, perhaps, to take quite a risk. Who would have the nerve? Linking the tattoos would as much as solve their case. Edwin took the bag with him, puzzling over what to do with it. He had been right when he suspected that Stevens had not been Vicky's killer. But only finding the guilty person would prove that.

The children were too young to involve. The cook, butler, two maids—one older and one Mary's roommate—provided nothing helpful. A gangly groom called Joseph had a crush on Mary. His deep-set eyes bore dark circles and signs of weeping since Mrs. Arbogast had made her rounds. The man had a small room over the carriage house, far preferable to the stifling attic.

"I see that Mary's . . . passing has upset you," Edwin said in a gentle voice.

"She were a fine girl. Not for the likes of me, though. Told me that right off." He rubbed at his jaw, where a few red pustules ripened. At his age, Edwin was already off up north on the fishing boats.

So the young man had the usual inclinations. More than one servant girl had found herself in a family way in upright Christian mansions.

"She said, 'I'll be gone from here in a few months. I've got expectations. I may even take art lessons,' " Joseph relayed to Edwin. "But all the girls think like that. Silly cows."

"So she had no gentleman callers?"

Joseph shook his large head, a spray of freckles across his nose giving him an innocent look. "That's not allowed here, Sir. Not unless you're going to get married very soon and then leave. House rule. That's not to say she couldn't have met someone on the side. Once when she was supposed to be at Saint Barnabas, I saw her walking toward Beacon Hill Park."

Edwin gave Joseph a cool and assessing look, but couldn't

find a chink in his demeanor. Yes, he had access to horses. But he couldn't have taken their carriage, and most likely he was on call every day for his services. "Is this the only carriage?" Edwin asked.

"There's the dog cart, sir. For the kiddies." He pointed to a small, two-wheeled vehicle made to carry no more than a milk can. In a pen at the side of the carriage house, a Saint Bernard lay, massive head on paws.

"Where does the dog sleep?" If in the house, why didn't he bark at the intruder?

Joseph smiled. "With me. We're buddies. Caesar's getting a bit deaf, too."

As for the Sunday that Mary vanished, Joseph was laid low with a lumbago attack from heavy lifting. Mrs. Arbogast's nose had been out of joint because they had to take a "dirty" cab to church.

Edwin walked home in a funk, studying his feet more than his path. Art lessons. Girls' Friendly Society. One person might help with both avenues. He hadn't even collected his clothes since the tennis party. What must Emily think of his lackadaisical manners? Did she understand the pressures of the job? But first they had to find out what the hell this nun's habit and blasphemous rosary involved.

# CHAPTER TWENTY

The next morning, Edwin found himself at the door of one place on the south island where nuns could be found en masse. St. Ann's Academy at Humboldt and Blanchard. The Roman Catholics with their French Canadian missionaries had begun in 1848 with a little school, then built St. Ann's Academy. The chapel behind the main section, moved from its first site, was the first Catholic church in B.C. He walked up the central steps, admiring the view north across an apple orchard, spires of St. Andrews in the distance and, to the left, the modest wooden Church of Our Lord. Across the street stood the massive four-story St. Joseph's Hospital, the city's first. To the west stretched the murky waters of Oak Bay and to the south, Beacon Hill Park. Gathering his courage, he knocked at the massive cedar double door.

"May I help you," said a wizened gnome in traditional black habit.

Edwin took off his hat and introduced himself. "I need some information about an unusual . . . habit we found in an investigation."

The round, expressive face looked quizzical, as if she relished a good puzzle. "We are not cloistered as we are a very active order. Still, we prefer that you wait in the novitiates' garden. Back the way you came and around to your right. I'll call Sister Dympna. It's not quite *terce,* so she should be able to speak to you."

A coroner's jury had brought in a verdict of death by misadventure in Mary's case. No witnesses had surfaced. The habit was one thing, but the rosary? How could he frame the question? *Have you ever seen . . .* Heat flashed across his face at the anticipation.

A roly-poly nun with ageless pink skin came downstairs from a huge corner veranda and joined him on rustic benches underneath a fragrant magnolia tree in full bloom. "This is very mysterious, but of course we are always happy to help the authorities. We attend to spiritual needs and you to temporal needs, though God judges us all in the end."

He unwrapped the outfit from its brown-paper package. The abbess cocked her head like a fat grouse as she examined it. "Oh my. A piece of history, this. The wimple and headdress are very old fashioned," Sister Dympna said, clucking. "The elaborate neck piece and the cape. The small wooden clasp."

"I had no idea that there were so many different habits," Edwin said. "We used to live in Montreal near the Oratory. Out here I'm not as . . . regular as I should be in my religion." She looked like the type who could smell out a lie. Sister Veronica had broken a ruler over his head for not paying attention during mathematics.

Sister's small round watery blue eyes sparkled like the aquamarine in the rosary around her waist. "If you come with me, I can show you what I mean with a peek from outside."

She led him down the trimmed flagstones to a large open window amid the English ivy. "This is our study," she said, pointing to the interior. On the wall was a picture. "*Saint Teresa* by Goya. It's the identical habit. Wouldn't you agree?"

"So Saint Teresa lived quite some time ago?" Naomi attended to Edwin's art and music education. He'd paid more attention to history and rhetoric.

The woman gave an ironic chuckle. "Indeed. The route to

sainthood is long, my son. She lived in the sixteenth century in the province of Ávila, Spain."

"Then this picture is merely an artist's conception?"

"A very faithful one. She was painted in her lifetime." She paused like a precise instructor. "Other artists copied the costume. It is the habit of the Discalced Carmelites."

Though curious, he wasn't going to ask her what that meant. It sounded vaguely chemical or geological. "What separates her from other saints? Aside from their . . . holiness and devotion."

The nun's crinkled face colored and she smiled. "Like many penitents, she inflicted mortifications upon herself to reach a state of ecstasy."

"I see." He met her eyes with a sincere interest. Saying less brought out more.

"In her most famous vision, a seraph drove the fiery point of a golden lance through her heart. This helped her reach the Lord through imagining his pain." Her pantomime left nothing to the imagination, but her girth demonstrated that foregoing tasty food was not Sister Dympna's path.

Edwin gave an internal wince. She smiled a blessing. "But it was a sweet pain, if you can fathom that."

Out of respect and not logic, he nodded.

"Indeed she skated very close to persecutions from the Inquisition, first because her methods were believed to be diabolical, and later the reform she pursued made her serious enemies. She was saved by King Philip himself."

"What might make her an object of interest for a . . . blasphemer?" The rosary in his pocket heated his thigh, or was it his imagination?

Dympna gave a short intake of breath. "So this is your true inquiry. Evil is such a powerful enemy. But the Lord is stronger."

"Sadly, Madame . . . Sister, police work involves sin. But you and I are united on the side of good and justice."

"Divine justice is for Our Lord to decide, Sir."

She spoke slowly, as if she were giving the idea a thorough analysis. "Saint Teresa was probably the most influential female saint. For many, she is an icon to equal the Holy Trinity, a powerful image second only to Mary, Mother of God."

In the distance, a bell rang, and her head turned. "The call to *terce*. I'm afraid that I . . ."

What had he forgotten to ask? He should have brought along another man to this foreign territory. "Of course. May I ask who makes the vestments for your nuns?"

"We do, of course. Some of our sisters are very talented with the needle."

He closed his notebook as his shoulders slumped. "I see."

"But if I may ask, how did this habit come into your possession?"

How could he imply to her that such vestments were used to heighten the sexual experience? "It may have been used in the commission of a crime. A young girl died. This was in her room. There was also a . . . sacrilegious . . . rosary."

Sister gave a sharp intake of breath and her knobby hands suddenly clasped. "That is beyond imagination. I will redouble my devotions. My advice is to seek out secular seamstresses, perhaps those who make costumes for the theater."

"Sister, you would make a good detective," he said, enjoying the brief blush on her papery cheek.

At dinner with his mother that night, he brought up the idea of local seamstresses. She forked in a small piece of chicken from Millicent's fricassee, then reached down and fed a tidbit to Gladdy. Being freed from her labors had given her a slightly better demeanor. "Now shoo. I'm going to have to be strict, little mannie. One must be cruel only to be kind."

"Mother, you were saying."

She took a large drink of Bordeaux. "About what, dear?"

He suspected that, denied the opium, she was drowning her sorrows with overmuch wine. "Someone who sews for the *theater.*" Stressing the last word was as far as he would go. Naomi was under too much pressure.

"You don't need to shout. Madame Pauline knows everything about sewing in this town."

At Pembroke near Douglas, a narrow three-story house with a cedar-shake roof caught his attention halfway down the block. A carriage was drawn up in front and another waiting. The drivers were smoking and chatting. Madame Pauline, arriving from Paris, so she said, had established a wealthy clientele. Her sign read *Dressmaker. Ladies' Tailor.*

Their meeting was brief. Madame Pauline peered down her Gallic nose and referred him to a reconditioned warehouse, where the theatrical crowd took their custom. Edwin detoured back to the department to pick up Reggie and fill him in on the visit to the nunnery.

"Let me see this little bauble," Reggie said, running appreciative fingers over the curves of the beads. "It's almost delicious enough to convert me to Romanism." He made a brief sign of the cross over Edwin, who batted his hand away.

"Reggie, you are disgusting."

"Being an apostate is far more fashionable than being a simple unbeliever like me." Reggie snicked a match on the bottom of his shoe and lit his cheroot, sending up rings he admired. "I've heard about some amazing things the lavender boys do with beads."

"That's one group out of the running." Edwin grabbed his arm. "Let's go."

Dolly Van Klaverin operated out of the top floor of an industrial building on Wharf Street abandoned since the sealing industry shrank. They climbed the wide commercial stairs to the top of the warehouse. Large filthy glass windows obscured the light. An effort had been made to clean and paint, and the faint oily animal smell dissipated at the top floor. Tables were spread with current jobs while three women chatted, stitched, and cut. Apparently they made uniforms for the navy as well, a more lucrative and reliable trade.

Dolly, a chubby woman of forty, handled the brown habit with familiarity. "I made a dozen of these. They didn't require any fine work. The whole point is the rustic style. The lady showed me a color picture from a book."

Edwin's Catholic upbringing twitched. One of the punishments for not paying attention in class had been to copy text from Butler's *Lives of the Saints.* "What book would that be?"

"I couldn't say. It had been torn out."

Edwin and Reggie's eyes met. "And who made the order?"

"It was a few months ago. Let me consult my records." She moved to a large counter and reached underneath for a huge bound volume, leafing through it. Adjusting her spectacles, she said, "Here it is. I remember the lady. In her thirties, red-gold hair, a beauty, if past her prime. She had a tailored suit. Very posh. Nothing like you'd see from theater people. But in this business, money talks."

Edwin's heart tripped a beat. "Her name, if you have it?"

"Here it is. Ann Croft." She gave them a knowing look. "She did hesitate when she said it."

Victoria Ann Crosse. Ann Croft. "And how did she pay?"

Dolly sniffed. "Cash money. There's a discount." She squinted at the figures. "And another four large plain robes with golden braid for cinching. Perhaps for gentlemen."

"You've been very helpful," Reggie said. "This is a fine establishment. Anyone can see that. Do you design wedding dresses?"

"Most certainly. Send your fiancée to me. Bridesmaids, too."

"I suppose you require a cash deposit," Reggie added.

"The Croft woman paid sixty dollars. American double eagles. Not everyone carries those."

Outside, Edwin said, "Even if you're not Irish, you have the blarney about you. Four men's robes. A nice little conspiracy. And a dozen costumes. Looks as if they were expecting more young women."

"Virgins don't come along every day. 'Jewels being lost, are found again. This never. 'Tis lost for once, and once lost, lost forever.' I could have solved Marlowe's murder. It was planned by someone close to the Queen. Cecil perhaps."

Edwin ignored him. "This is making sense. Think about 'abbot' in the common noun, not the proper 'Abbott.' But what do we do about the rosary?"

"Like those nutcrackers. You know, where their legs . . ." He made an open-and-closed gesture with his hand. "I'll ask a few of my libidinous friends. I don't suppose I can take it with me."

"I have faith in your powers of description. It probably comes from the Continent."

"I wouldn't doubt it. My grandfather told me that a good way to woo a woman was . . ." He whispered into Edwin's ear as they stopped to let a streetcar pass.

"No decent lady would permit that."

Reggie grinned, then flicked an errant lock of hair from his forehead. "How do you think I got Carrie to agree to marry me?"

Edwin marched back to business. "That reminds me. I have to talk to Emily. It's possible that she knew Mary, what with the art connection."

Reggie slapped him on the back. "That's my big boy."

Back at the department, Edwin found the Carrs in the telephone book. That Emily herself answered increased his belief in Divine Providence. "I wonder if I might buy you a soda, Miss

Emily. I need to make some inquiries about arts lessons in the community, and since you—"

"It's never too late to begin studies. I'm flattered that you—"

He told her the reason and was happy that she didn't laugh. Could she hear his heart rapping down the line like Morse code?

"How mysterious. I've just finished with my group for the day. This is a happy coincidence. I can bring your . . . clothes and boots, too. I would have given them to Reggie, but I haven't seen him." Why didn't they meet at Hall and Company in an hour, she suggested.

It seemed more respectable than the sordid police station. Who knew what she might see there even in the middle of the afternoon? And would she tell her sisters about the rendezvous? Emily wrote her own ticket, but it would not do to offend Edie, the chatelaine.

So easy. He asked, and she agreed. But it wasn't a date. This was part of his job. Suppose he asked her to a concert or a play?

He was fifteen minutes early at Hall's, at the corner of Yates and Douglas. Emily came in wearing a gay spring frock in robin's-egg blue. She set down a paper bag with his togs.

"What may I bring you, Miss Emily?" He pulled out a chair at a table for two. People were enjoying fountain drinks and ice cream, a world away from the station.

She smiled that wondrous smile, as if they were deliciously alone. Dimples, too. "I *should* have a crushed fruit with ice. But make it a chocolate soda, please."

He ordered two at the marble-topped fountain area with its talismanic spouts for every flavor in the world, jars of chopped nuts and sweet ruby cherries. Signs on the wall advertised their special sundaes: tin roof, banana split, and pineapple. It seemed an eternity while the white-coated young man made them. Edwin wondered if being called a soda jerk was a worse name than Rozzer. The artistic young man moved with aplomb. First came cream, syrup, then a splash of soda water, the ice cream in two balls, topped with whipped cream, more chocolate sauce, and a cherry. A long spoon tucked into the glass and a paper straw and serviette completed the picture.

Setting the sodas down, Edwin waited until they had each had a few sips of their drink, appreciating the tiny formalities.

"I'm trying to learn all I can about a . . . a young girl, Mary Donahue."

Her faced paled and she put down her spoon. "I read about her. What a tragedy. Yet why ever would she have been up in Langford?"

"Did you do know her personally? Not many give art lessons in Victoria. I wondered if . . ."

He explained their doubts about the misadventure. Her hand went to her mouth. One look at those serious gray eyes spelled complete trust.

"She made inquiries through a letter and was going to start taking lessons in the fall." Confusion and sadness furrowed her brow. "It's rare for a servant girl to save money to take art lessons. Most girls want to buy frivolous things. Clothes, ribbons, trinkets."

Emily's dedication to her art reminded him of Naomi, subject matter aside. From the sketches of what he had seen in the parlor, her style was modern, almost ground-breaking. His mother had shown him copies of similar still-life work by Cezanne. Perhaps when this was over . . .

"Still I can't imagine what she—"

A thought struck him. "What about modeling?"

"I've never heard much call for that in this town. We are provincial."

"She looked attractive in her picture. My mother uses models when she paints." His collar tightened. She could have no idea about where most of his mother's pictures went, or could she?

"I'd love to see her work."

"Most of it is . . . sold outside of the city. Anyway, did Mary give you any ideas about where this money might come from?"

"She told me that soon she'd have over ten dollars. I thought she was spinning fairy tales, frankly. Certainly an inheritance would have been out of the question."

"That's substantial for a scullery maid. Even a . . ." He blushed.

"A lady of the streets, you mean. A few of that persuasion do very well in this town . . . so I hear."

Was she teasing? Surely she didn't blame him for the town's notorious graft and corruption.

He returned to his soda. Why did he feel a perfect fool? She was the naïf . . . and he the professional . . . or was it the other way around?

He sipped the tasty dregs as the straw made a rude noise that made them grin. "There's something else. Mrs. Arbogast, her employer, says that Sundays Mary went to church and then to a meeting of the Girls' Friendly Society at Saint Barnabas. If she had a friend there that she confided in . . ." His voice left a question. Small pebbles could construct a wall. If the wall fell, start again.

With a dainty pink tongue that weakened his manly resolve, Emily licked the last creamy foam from the spoon. Not like the kind that laced corsets so tight that a bite of beef made them faint. "I might be able to help you with that."

"That would be terrific. What do you mean?" What a good sport. And so attractive, too, engendering love and devotion at any age. Now he understood the lyrics of "Believe Me if All Those Endearing Young Charms."

Emily wiped her shapely mouth. A trace of lip rouge tinted the straw. "A friend of mine from school calls all the meetings.

Her name is Melodie Campbell. Isn't that a lovely musical name?"

"A pretty girl is like a melody. Do you think we could talk to her?"

"Of course, but she's in Port Townsend to see her American cousins this week." Emily cocked her head in thought. "If the ferry runs, she should be home tomorrow."

Edwin walked her home, reluctant to leave her side. The half hour went so fast that he wished that she lived in far-off Saanich. "Thank you for your invaluable help, Miss Carr."

"You are most welcome. The soda was a treat."

He tipped his hat as she put a hand on her front door knob. "Oh, Edwin."

His heart skipped and he looked at his feet lest he trip and sprawl like an oaf. "Yes, Miss Carr."

"Don't be silly. Call me Emily."

All he could think of as he floated toward Amelia Street was how winsome Emily was. How he'd love to see her first thing in the morning and last at night. Yet police work for a single man was easier. No wife to worry about, but no warm bed, either. And then a little girl or lad with those soft gray eyes bouncing on his knee and growing up so fast . . . What was the matter with him? When he arrived home, it was six o'clock. Waves of a roast beast, as his mother called it, drifted from the windows like ambrosia.

"The Madam isn't here," Millicent said, waving the spoon she carried. "So irregular. All these comings and goings."

# CHAPTER TWENTY-ONE

Earlier that same morning, with the new maid scouring the house like a grouchy mouse, Naomi had assured herself that not one more night would pass before she began to search for Wong. He had been born in the year of the water dog. Each of the twelve animals was also governed by metal, water, wood, fire, and earth. "What are the characteristics for dog?" she'd asked as they enjoyed jasmine tea together in the kitchen a few months ago.

"Dogs kind and supportive. Listeners more than talkers. Know more about you than you do yourself. And finish what they start."

She'd smiled. "Good qualities for a cook." She trusted him like a son with money. Wealth and status meant nothing to dogs, he said.

"What signs are compatible with yours?" she'd asked, learning that dog matched well with her metal ox and Edwin's fire tiger. Ox and tiger, on the other hand . . . problems. Who was she to argue with several thousand years of Oriental wisdom?

Putting those memories behind her, Naomi banged her small fist on the table, causing Gladdy to bark. Then she went to her wardrobe. Caucasians were not forbidden to enter Chinatown, but they weren't encouraged. Most were men in search of opium, a prostitute, or, if they were trusted, a gambling game. White women were another matter. Going in midday didn't frighten her, but everyone knew about Dragon Alley or Fan Tan

Alley at night.

Should she dress as a servant? A poor woman carrying a market basket? People would pay more attention to someone from a better class. A costume plain and serious, not elegant or showy. Dark colors. She selected a suit with a bolero-style jacket in dark blue serge cheviot, billowing sleeves tapering at the elbow. The outer jacket was trimmed with mohair and silk with mixed gimp. The skirt rustled with taffeta and was interlined with crinoline, bound with velvet. "This Milan straw model hat, I think," she said. Ruffles of satin ribbon, flowers, and two rosettes. Nothing too nobby. Into her reticule, pinned inside her capacious pockets, went the ready cash in the house. Seven dollars.

Outside, strolling toward town, she hailed a cab. "To the Chinese arch on Cormorant, please," she told the old driver as she stepped inside.

His rheumy eyes opened like saucers and he paused before closing the door. "Are we stopping for a gentleman, because surely, ma'am, you're not—"

"Puh-lease. Don't argue. Do you want the fare or not? I have no time to bicker." Her withering tone had frozen young Edwin at twenty feet when he was up to shenanigans.

He gave her a disbelieving look, but when she glared back, he resumed his seat and cracked his whip. The dapple trotted off smartly, raising the dust.

Twenty minutes later, she dismounted and paid the fare. What now? Her heart speeded up as she passed under the ceremonial arch built for the governor general's visit in the 1880s, a bold and exotic entrance into a foreign quarter. Shacks and tents in a ravine on Johnson Street had metamorphosed into a bustling hive of stores, a theater, even a school. Over on Fisgard, she knew from experience, was the impressive Chinese Consolidated Benevolent Association building. They represented the community and helped solve local disputes. She'd try there if nothing turned up.

It wasn't that she was afraid. In broad daylight mere blocks from the police station? Fie on the lily-livered. Posture, brains, and pluck would carry her. Straightening her shoulders and taking a restorative breath, she walked on, past grocery stores carrying the special items Wong loved. A box of noxious thousand-year-old eggs lying in straw caught her eye. Flattened roast ducks in a brilliant and unnatural red hung inside. The familiar smell of star anise and sizzle-hot garlic caught in her throat. Bitter melon and long thin eggplant she recognized from their table.

Coming down Cormorant from Government, on the south side she passed Chinese businesses. Sam Chung, Kee, Hing, Lee and Chung. She stopped to talk to a man in a blue coolie costume setting out bok choy, bean sprouts, and ginger root. "Wong?" she asked. When he shook his head in pleasant bafflement, she pointed to her eyes, feeling like a lunatic. He smiled and raised his hands in surrender. Was there another way to pronounce Wong? Did the first name come at the beginning or the end? What the devil was Wong's other name? As conversation washed over her from two chatting grandmothers, she recalled that Wong had told her that there were crucial intonations in Cantonese. Perhaps she was saying something absurd, or worse yet, obscene. *Chin up, Madame,* she told herself.

Naomi walked past displays of clothing, bright silks with dragons, plain blue for work. Shallow straw hats for the sun. Paper kites resembling butterflies. Finally she came to Bossi's Block. The Chinese Boys Methodist School and Mission upstairs had been established with the help of Chinese businessmen over twenty years ago. Immigrants of all ages could learn English. Fate had sent her to the perfect place.

She chose a set of long stairs to the second floor. At the top, the glassed door bore Chinese characters but also English, which reassured her. Inside was a large room of empty desks and benches. A pile of primers sat on a table. The Union Jack hung from a pole. A banner on the wall said *God bless our Sunday school.* Perhaps to accommodate the industrious workers, the school ran at night. On a pot-bellied stove, an iron kettle on a trivet steamed.

A prim lady with a starched ecru bosom bent over a teacher's desk on a platform at the front. Behind her was a blackboard with English numbers and basic words, Chinese underneath. "One" was a horizontal line, followed by "two" and "three," more lines added. "Man" looked like a stick creature with arms and legs. China was represented as a box with a line down the middle, which made Naomi smile. Every nation thought it was the center of the universe. Naomi approached, her heels tapping on the beeswaxed wooden floorboards. The windows were spotless despite the dusty urban commerce.

The woman looked up with a friendly if bemused smile. "Have you come to volunteer? We can always use more English speakers. Did your good minister send you over?"

Naomi took the offered chair and introduced herself to Miss Sylvia Siddens with a very firm handshake returned with the same no-nonsense intent. Naomi liked her immediately.

"Our housekeeper Wong disappeared a few days ago, and I am worried sick." She held up a finger of caution. "He is absolutely the most reliable man I know. His honesty and ethics are impeccable. I've been floundering around making fruitless inquiries until I saw your sign."

Miss Siddens' long face grew serious. "I see. So he has friends or relatives in the quarter? It is not a large place, but so many come and go."

"He has a cousin here, Lun. He must know what's happened, but I don't know where to find him either." A quiver crept into her voice, but she tamped it down.

"Mrs. DesRosiers, you have come to the right place and at the right time of day. Yet you should not be wandering these streets alone. You would be in no harm from the Celestials, but the sailors, the gamblers, the fornicators are another matter. Drunkenness. Debauchery." She placed a bony finger alongside her pointed nose and adjusted her gold-rimmed spectacles. "Let's check the roster for the cousin." She opened a notebook and scanned the pages like an expert. Then she shook her head.

"I'd be glad to pay for your trouble. I don't speak the language." Naomi fumbled for her reticule.

"How generous, but as one child of God to another. The Lord will provide. What you need is a translator. This is a small community with far-reaching connections. Imagine coming across the sea to a new land with a different language. Relatives and friends are invaluable."

Naomi refused the kind offer of tea. Every moment counted. Neither was this the time to confess that she was of Abraham's line. The child of God phrase had been curiously ambiguous.

Siddons disappeared into an interior room. Though Naomi tried to eavesdrop, the raucous sounds of a fire wagon heading down the street drowned out the possibility. She returned with a lanky teenager. With a rough scar from his ear to his chin, he was self-conscious and bowed to her with his hands placed together. Wong had done the same when he had answered their advertisement. She nodded back and extended her hand, which he touched to the top of his forehead rather than shake.

Siddons beamed at her charge. "Ting-Wan is one of our best students and my number-one assistant. He can take you to several places to inquire or leave word. The name of Wong is as prevalent as Smith or Jones."

On their way out of the building, Ting-Wan stopped as they hit the boardwalk. His small face was dead serious, the forehead lightly creased. "Professor Siddens give me strict instructions that nothing happen to you."

For once, Naomi held her tongue. "Of course. I appreciate your care."

He gave a curt bow and stressed his words. "What I say, you do. No questions. Understand, Missus?"

Following her guide, she hastened to keep up with his youthful strides. First he took her to the entrance to a long, dim passage between two buildings with no apparent outlet. "Fan Tan Alley. You stay here, please, on street with others. Safe. Inside is much gambling. Bad women. Worse men. Sometimes arguments."

She'd heard of fan tan. At her soirees, they played mahjong. Naomi had a particularly beautiful ivory set from Shanghai. "Don't worry about me." Her laugh sounded hollow. A pulse pounded in her temple.

Raising a sleek black eyebrow, Ting-Wan folded his arms unless she swore on her mother's grave not to budge. He emphasized his intent by pointing down emphatically and even stamping a foot.

"I swear." She held up a trembling hand in promise.

Time passed in a limbo. The smell of garlic shrimp frying, the briny tang from the sea breeze, a piano tinkling somewhere. A woman's laughter. Chatter of Cantonese. Then more indignant. An argument? Wong had mentioned seven tones. There were no tenses. A person merely used a time word like "today" or "tomorrow." A tiny yellow bird flew by. Wong's finch had died. She'd meant to replace it on his next birthday. So much for good intentions.

Ting-Wan hurried back with a frightened look on his face. He was out of breath, having been up and down stairs, she suspected. "Grandfather Chong say that Lun beaten. Very . . . sick. Break leg."

"What happened?" Her heart jumped. "Is Wong hurt?"

He shook his head. "Maybe Lun say. Please come. Not far."

In dense Chinatown, nothing was more than a few minutes. After passing more alleys, they came to a three-story building on Fisgard Street. Upstairs were balconies with privacy fences. Decorative clay jars held geraniums and marigolds. Checking the number on the door, he took her to the basement, entering a maze, turning this way and that until Naomi grew dizzy from fear and disorientation. Finally they entered a small, barren room with an oil lamp turned down low. The air was thick with damp. On a straw pallet lay Lun, his leg in splints. His head was wrapped in white plaster and cotton. Pray God he wasn't as bad as he looked. Without proper care, people died of complications. He belonged in a proper hospital, and she'd see that he got there within the very hour.

Naomi knelt beside him, noticing a cat was curled up with him, a purring comfort. "What happened to you? Where is Wong?"

"Wong . . ." He struggled with signs but spoke scant English. With his eyebrows and expressions, he appealed to Ting-Wan. Lun's black eyes were wide with terror. He blurted out words that ran together.

Ting-Wan turned to her, shaking his head. "There was a fight. A woman, a debt, I don't know. He and Wong went to help a friend, but they were hurt. Lun fell from balcony. He fears that those in the fight will come back and harm him."

"*Yee shang,*" Lun repeated. Naomi's Cantonese was limited to a few breakfast items like *cha* or tea, *ga fe* or coffee. *Ho* or *m ho*, meaning good or not good, yes or no.

"But where's Wong?" she repeated like a parrot. Was he insensible with a concussion? She looked desperately at Ting-Wan, feeling a hot flash wash over her body despite the room's chill. "I'm not leaving here until I learn where he is."

Ting-Wan spoke in hushed tones, then bent to give a cup of water to Lun, who was struggling to sit up and waving feebly. A dish of broth with chicken meat on a table demonstrated his decent care.

"His hands, Mrs. The English doctor. From the city."

"What about his hands?" Had he been injured? Cut or burned? He earned his living with his talent in cooking, cleaning, mending.

"Now he is gone." Ting-Wan translated. "Island of death."

Lun began to cry, a universal language. Naomi felt her breath stop as the floor moved closer and a great darkness descended. Her last thoughts were of Edwin.

# CHAPTER TWENTY-TWO

A clatter arose at the gate, as Edwin looked out the window in annoyance. He opened the door, and Naomi staggered up the path into his arms as a cab disappeared down the street. "Wong's been taken to D'Arcy Island. We have to bring him back. Tonight before it's too . . ." The words trailed off. She flung her hand back over her head in a stage gesture and began to totter.

"Sit down, Mother, before you fall down." Inside, he tossed aside her hat and led her to a chair. From a bottle of cognac he poured them each three fingers. "What are you talking about? More to the point, where the Sam Hill have you been? Do you know what time it is?"

Naomi closed her eyes and began to rock in the chair, moaning. "It's all been such a shock. And I haven't had a bite since breakfast. Have whatshername make me some strong tea. Brits are cold fish but they keep their heads in a crisis."

He was barely able to make out her words. "I just got home, Mother. It's getting dark. We both need our dinners. You're hardly able to walk anyway. You'd be a liability even if we could go now . . . which we can't. D'Arcy Island, for Christ's sake."

"Curb your language. You won't be so unf-f-ffeeling when you hear what I learned," she shot back.

"Make some sense." He gave Millicent directions for strong tea with sugar. Then he fetched a cold, wet towel from the bathroom and told Naomi to put it over her feverish face. Opening the windows brought cool air flooding in.

With Naomi gaining control, Edwin was told everything that had happened in Chinatown. The crisis in question went back a few years.

In 1891, five Chinese lepers had been discovered in Victoria. At first they were kept captive in a house on Fisgard. One had committed suicide. The truth came out when the *Daily Colonist* blurted the ambiguous headlines: "effective measures" were being taken. Few knew that the first lepers were marooned on D'Arcy Island with only a shack and a supply ship every three months. It was a death sentence. There was no pretense of any treatment. Citizens had been given only reassuring information by authorities about the health problem. Few Caucasians gave it any thought.

"Does he have leprosy? That's the first question. Those white gloves." For a moment he felt queasy. Wong prepared all their food and took care of their clothing.

"Don't be a total fool, Edwin. His cousin swears that it's a harmless condition that Wong has had all his life. Call your doctor friend."

"True. I can't go without a medical man." Edwin went to the telephone. He was as disturbed as she was but dared not show it.

Jones answered. "I'm glad you called, Edwin. I have been meaning to get back to you on Mary's completed autopsy."

Edwin stood up. "You have something significant?"

"I wish I did. At a very rough guess, she died within four days of being found, probably Sunday night. That odd light hair we found . . ."

"What about it?"

"It's not human. That's all I can tell you. We don't have the sophisticated equipment to narrow it down."

"And that's it? Surely there are differences in structure or color."

"Don't tell me my business. The first study of trichology was done in 1857 in France. It had to do mainly with human hair, not animal. A few points stand out. Rabbit hair grows together. It is easy to find deer hair, but cougars aren't that numerous. It's not as if we have a scientific research laboratory on every corner."

That was bleak news. "Something else has come up." He explained about Wong and felt better as Jones explored the possibilities. The doctor would make the right connections. His official status would carry weight.

Naomi had made her way to the kitchen and was directing Millicent to serve immediately. When Edwin came to the table, he said, "In case you haven't noticed, it's high tide. We can't get out to the island until tomorrow. I have some good news, though."

Naomi cut into the slice of beef. She seemed ravenous now that a plan had been made. Edwin noted with approval a very tender roast with mashed potatoes and carrots. Masters had managed very well. Wong usually cooked the roast to death like most English did. A steamed date pudding sat on the side table.

She reached for the wine decanter, but he stopped her, earning a pout. "Fine, then, are you going to let me twist in the wind? What did he say?"

"Jones says that if Wong's had the skin problem for years, with no deformity of the fingers or toes, it's not leprosy."

Naomi took a draft of water instead. "Thank God for small mercy. Not that I'm religious." She reached across and touched his hand. "First thing in the morning, then. I will be ready."

"Mother, no, no, and no. All Jones promised is a small dory. It will be very rough. You'll get wet and catch pneumonia. Remember your weak chest." He swallowed back a lump of meat and tapped his knife on the plate for emphasis. "And what about the lepers? The sight will give you nightmares. This is no place for a woman."

Naomi's eyes narrowed and she got very quiet. An ominous sign. The silence dragged on like an elephant in the room. Or an ox and a tiger. Which would prevail?

"No, and that's final." He folded his arms and sat back from the table.

"Wong is my friend. We are his friends. Masters can prepare food to take." She rose from her chair like a queen. "Tie me up. That's the only way you'll stop me, Edwin. I'll commandeer my own cab, follow you, and jump into the damn boat."

He blew out a disgusted breath of defeat. "Then get to bed early. We'll be leaving at dawn. If you aren't up, I won't wake you. Be warned."

Her answer was to stick out her tongue and serve up the pud.

As the honking of the island geese heading for grain fields broke through his window at five a.m., Edwin's eyes snapped open. Downstairs, a grumpy Masters was preparing breakfast, yawning pointedly and full of put-upon expressions. Naomi insisted on oatmeal, joining him in her dressing gown. " 'Something to stick to the ribs,' your father used to say from his orphanage days. It's no favorite, but I'll choke it down for Wong's sake."

"It's better with maple syrup and cream. Trust me." He doctored his own steel-cut porridge. Juicy pork sausages and toast joined the meal along with cups of tea strong enough to trot a mouse.

Naomi disappeared upstairs, Edwin following. He chose an outfit for action: corduroy pants, a blue cotton shirt and sweater, and, instead of his Aquascutum, an oiled jacket. Short rubber boots seemed wiser than shoes. Wet floorboards could be slippery, and the last thing he'd need would be to fall overboard.

Jones would meet them with a carriage to go to the Saanich docks. It might take as long as three hours to reach the wharf nearest the island.

"Mother, hurry up!" Edwin looked out his window to see the carriage arriving.

Naomi descended the stairs as if making an appearance in *The Importance of Being Earnest.* She wore a plain traveling suit with sensible shoes and a duster. "All ready, even if I feel like a dish clout."

Edwin smiled despite his misgivings. "Don't ever try to change your mother's mind, Son," his father had said. "Make her think that something is her idea. Women are like that." He doffed his cap. "Didn't you mention a waterproof last night? There's my old rubber cape from when I walked a beat. Shall I bring it?"

"Unattractive and hot, but if I must. Your guile is obvious, by the way." She turned and called, "Masters, the provisions, please."

Masters waddled in with a giant wicker basket of food. She also brought another bag of folded blankets. "There's more, Sir."

Edwin tossed his mother an exasperated glance. "This is hardly a picnic, Mother. We're not going up the Nile looking for Dr. Livingstone."

"Wong will be famished. Who knows what he's been given to eat? I've heard terrible things about that place."

As they left, Naomi said, "Masters, we intend to be back tonight, but should darkness fall, we may be forced to stop at an inn. Don't stay up."

"At least it's clearing," Edwin said. They stepped out into a peach-streaked dawn as a surrey clattered, pulled by two handsome white-faced ebony mares. Dr. Jones was waving a sou'wester hat. Then he got down and stood gaping at Naomi.

"Edwin, you didn't tell me that your . . . dear mother was coming. This isn't advisable." The two had been introduced at a band concert in the park a few years ago. When his name came up, her eyebrow would rise. Edwin wondered if his mother wasn't a bit smitten, though older by ten years.

"It's out of the question to try to stop her. Unless you want to try physical force, and you know how women bite and scratch." He deadpanned his expression, but the joke was lost on Jones.

The doctor's mouth moved in silence, then he stuttered, "Upon my word, no, or yes, but—"

"A hand, please," Naomi said, and swept up into the back seat of the carriage. "So nice to meet you again, Doctor, even under the circumstances. I've always admired medical men. My late husband was a lawyer, a rare honest one. Should we survive this ordeal, we must have you to dinner sometime and learn about your most notable cases." She flashed her most dazzling smile and even batted her eyes. Jones turned three colors before recovering his demeanor. In her prime, Naomi's face could have launched a thousand divorces. Autopsies at the dinner table. It was almost as bad as the time Fanny told everyone about her hysterectomy and traveling down a long corridor of light when she was "close enough to feel the warm breath of the Lord."

"There's a pair of mica driving glasses in the rear compartment. They will keep the dust from your eyes."

"We brought a few . . . things. Wong will be starving," Edwin said, and put them in the carriage. It had two broad tufted plush seats and a canopy. Meant for an Easter parade rather than the Saanich wilds with roads just short of corduroy.

"Up, Princess! Up, Lizzie!" They set off at a brisk trot, Jones cracking the whip over the horses' heads in smart fashion. Over to Government Street and north they went. By and by the houses and businesses ceased past Hillside, giving way at last to farms. Not long ago the city stopped at Bay Street.

The day was fining up, blue sky showcasing a brilliant sun. Edwin passed a few words with the doctor. "What do you know about the place? Since the outbreak, we hear little."

"It's a national disgrace. There's a civilized leper colony for whites in New Brunswick. I guess the city fathers didn't want the expense. Hansen's disease isn't very contagious, but the city feared a panic. They got the province to turn over the island."

"Wasn't there a cover-up?" Edwin remembered rumors.

"In the beginning of this sordid tale the city claimed that the island was being scouted for a garbage incinerator dump."

Edwin gave a snort of contempt. His parents had united for once in giving him a belief in the common dignity of all mankind. "Very prophetic."

"The first cases were pretty far gone by the time they were discovered. Disfigured as hell, their faces and limbs distorted. Rough shelters were nailed up, and the lepers were consigned to their doom."

"So it's as bad as they say?" He glanced at his mother, stoic as the bust of Cleopatra. Inside her was true steel, yet this trip would try the courage of a soldier.

# CHAPTER TWENTY-THREE

"A living hell. The medical officer Milne doesn't seem to give a damn. He's more concerned about bad publicity for the city rather than caring for the men. It beggars belief. These poor bastards paid a head tax of fifty dollars to come here. To be incarcerated until a welcome death, then buried on a bleak atoll."

"Is there nothing to be done?"

"With luck the next medical officer will be more humane. To avoid trouble, these poor souls were told that they would be sent back to China for treatment. Another damned lie." They came to a hill, and he clicked his tongue to encourage the horses. A young man raced by on a gaunt nag, stirring up the dust. "Idiot. He's going to run over a child one of these days. We need limits on speed. A woman was trampled on Douglas the other day. Crushed ribs. Punctured a lung and nearly died."

An hour later, they stopped at a small inn near Elk Lake to water the horses and have a cold drink. Women were not allowed inside, but Edwin carried out a flagon of pear cider for his mother.

She was standing beside the carriage, shaking out her duster. On the seat were her white hat and goggles. Her face was streaked, and her eyes raccoonish. "I'm being bounced to kingdom come. We should have come up by boat from Victoria. This looks like the back of beyond." She pulled out a small hand mirror from her reticule and began dabbing at her face with a handkerchief. "Eeeeeeeeeeeeeeeeeeeeeeeeeeeew."

"The peninsula train's all the way to Sidney now." A roar caught their ears as the Woodburner chugged nearby, belching smoke and sparks. Despite the blowback, a comfortable way to travel, instead of feeling each rock in the road. But getting east from the tracks across Saanich to the water was another story. Wong might be unable to walk.

The doctor and Edwin sought out convenient bushes. When Naomi had returned from the privy, their trip restarted. She leaned forward. "What if he's hurt? Maybe the other poor devils are dangerous. Certainly they have no medical—"

"I brought rudimentary supplies. From what I know, the men are too compliant for their own good. Beaten down by the authorities like slaves." He shook his head in disgust. "No white man would suffer this indignity."

She sat back, bracing herself stoically on the side of the seat. Every few miles, a slight cough came from the rear.

"How many men are on the island?" asked Edwin.

"Half a dozen. The number varies according to deaths. It's like the colony of the damned. And they say that we are civilized in Canada." His voice growled with contempt.

They took Mount Newton Crossroad east to the docks for a few miles, passing fertile fields and pastures of fat sheep. "Tell me more about the boat. She's seaworthy? Suppose the wind rises?" Edwin asked. Jones had made arrangements by telephone.

"Just a plain dory. Proudly old girl of the sea. Nantucket to San Francisco. You can't beat them. She carries a load of weight, just not very fast. Belongs to a friend of mine from the Masons."

The Masons again. "Tim, you must know that crowd. Do you suppose there's a chance that any of them is involved in this sordid business with Mary?"

A grin and a guffaw was his answer. "Edwin, those old prunes are about the most sexless bunch I've ever meet. Business deals are all they care about, that and the latest secret handshake. I avoid meetings when I can. They're a mortal bore. There's never been a woman in the building, not even cleaners and cooks."

Finally they arrived at the docks. Weathered boathouses sat on the shore in the sheltered cove. At a small stable nearby, Jones parked the carriage, giving the boy fifty cents to feed the horses a round of oats and alfalfa. "We should be back before dark. In fact, we'd better."

"How did our ancestors cross the Atlantic?" Naomi asked as she stumbled with help into the rowboat. The dory was lumbering but very stable, a plough horse rather than a racer. The baskets were secured under oilskin and there was plenty of room. The floorboards were absolutely dry, a good sign.

"Weight to the back, please. You up front, Madam. Keeps her trim," Jones said, as Edwin cast off the ropes and hopped in. The islands rose from the mist like the enticement of the Lotus Eaters' paradise. But during storms, many found their watery graves in the Strait of Georgia.

Edwin took the first shift. Unaccustomed to rowing, it took him ten minutes to find the rhythm. Aching muscles showed that he'd let himself get soft in his new job. Walking the beat had been healthier. He vowed to order a few Indian clubs and a weight set as well as pass on the next cream pie. When he stopped to wince at his blistering hands, Jones passed over his leather gloves.

A tin bailing can waited under the seat. Waves were only a promise in the satin sea. Intermittent mattresses of floating bull kelp drifted over, each plant twenty feet long from holdfast to bulb end. "Look at that blue heron," Naomi said. The bird was riding the raft, its swordfish beak primed for a tiny stickleback or anchovy. It gave a crabby squawk and lifted off.

Seagulls swooped in the air, diving for herring. An orca fluke surfaced a quarter mile away. Clutching the gunwales, Naomi shivered. "Don't worry, dear lady. They won't attack." The whale jumped into the air and smacked down with its deceptively clownish black and white colors. The tangy salt air revived them from their journey.

Other boats were plying the busy waters. A steamship chugged to Vancouver while another smaller fishing boat charged north. Straight across was Washington State, with Mount Baker in the background. The snow-capped peak floated in the air, a symphony of pastels. A line of volcanoes stretched along the coast from Alaska to California. Every year the shifting plates gave a shudder. Tribal tales said that not that long ago a huge tsunami had borne down on the island, wiping out communities that did not go to higher ground. What would happen to the growing cities when the next quake arrived?

Halfway, Jones took over the rowing. Gingerly the men changed places, bracing themselves on the thwarts. Edwin was sweating, a good feeling. Maybe he'd join the departmental cricket team after all. Emily could come to the games. Inviting her would be a great excuse for contact.

Meanwhile, D'Arcy emerged into clarity, two islands, one large and heavily wooded and the other tiny and uninhabited. A makeshift pier with rings for tying up lay against the shore. "Poor beggars would take any boat they could to escape this hell. All this way to work on the Mountain of Gold and they got a rock covered with guano. Devil's Island."

"You don't suppose that they'd rush us?" Naomi asked. From her wide-eyed look, the realities of the mission were taking hold of her imagination.

"Hardly. They're an obedient lot. Afraid of being cast into something worse, as if there were any situation lower or meaner." He shipped his oars as the boat's bottom scraped on the beach scree. "Problem is, what to do with you, dear lady," Jones said.

"What to do with me? I'm going with you." But as she looked around, her shoulders lost their starch.

Jones raised his voice and folded his arms for emphasis. "Edwin, talk sense to her. The camp is no place for a woman. Perhaps you, too, should stay . . ."

"Hogtie *me* at your own risk, Doctor." Naomi's jaw was firm and her eyes flinty.

Edwin laughed. "That might be arranged. But I know your stubborn mind. Just stay clear and let us lead the way. No complaints either, or it's back to the boat quick-march."

Jones scanned the sky, a dark look crossing his domed brow. "I mislike the weather. We'd better get moving. The small boat is a toy in a serious storm." At their feet, froth marked the retreating tide with a pebbly suck. Scuttling crabs and tiny sculpins followed.

They pulled the boat up past the high-water mark, collected the baskets, and started up a low hill on the only visible path between broom bush and scrub. Naomi struggled to keep up, but she maintained a grim smile through clenched teeth. A half a mile later, they reached a clearing with one long building and several cell doors. Smaller shacks were nearby.

The doctor pulled his trusty Remington sidearm from his doctor's kit. "There shouldn't be any trouble. If it were up to me, I'd organize a rescue party and set the poor buggers free."

Naomi laughed. "Quite the Fabian, Doctor. You might enjoy one of my Saturday night soirees. Socialism is one of our favorite topics."

A fire burned in the encampment and quiet forms huddled around its comfort. As they walked closer, one man rose, gave a small cry, and started running toward them. The others wore cloaks and shapeless rags, but his blue cotton pants and shirt were familiar.

"Wong!" Edwin yelled, waving his arms. "Are you all right?"

As Wong slowed in his approach, Edwin could see that his eyes had been blacked and his jaw was swollen. Despite that, he wore a crooked grin.

"Mr. Edwin." Wong held out his arms in a don't-come-closer gesture. His face was contorted with relief.

"I've brought a doctor. Have you been given any food?"

Wong said that they were provisioned with rice and vegetables, and they caught fish with a net. The later arrivals did the work for the others, who were too sick or deformed.

"We have provisions." He looked around. "How many men?"

Wong held up a hand. Five fingers. The white gloves were grimy and full of holes. How anyone could wash on the island? Salt water was brutal to the skin. Piles of fuel from twigs to logs showed that the wretched souls combed the island on a regular basis. What about drinking water?

He saw Naomi move forward in hesitation, instincts overpowering her common sense. "Mother, stay back until Jones has a chance to look at our friend."

"Madame, what about my cousin? How is Lun?" Wong's face mixed relief with worry.

"He'll be all right. I sent him to St. Joseph's. Thanks to his information we are here." Naomi sat on a driftwood log, hugging Edwin's old rubber cape around her for warmth. Waves of pity washed over her expressive face. "I'm so sorry," she repeated.

Jones and Edwin took Wong around back of the long building for privacy. The dispirited men made no move to approach. Opium's sweet, familiar aroma reached his nostrils. Who could blame them? Only in their dreams could they escape their fate.

Wong got a physical onceover, with Jones listening to his

heart and probing his hands and feet. For shoes he wore wooden clogs.

Edwin checked his timepiece and monitored the weather. The wind was rising. Far as they were from the shore, they could see the whitecaps massing. It was too late to set back tonight.

"I must pull up the boat. The tide's coming in like a bitch in heat," he told Jones.

"We didn't count on this storm. The heavens change their mind every hour." Coastal weather, affected by the Japanese current, was capricious. The doctor's confident manner couldn't disguise his shaking hands as he rearranged his black bag.

Edwin took off at a clumsy sprint and was soon at the flimsy dock. Heaving with all his might and using small roller logs, he pulled the boat farther up onto the beach and tied it to an alder. From the location of the highest debris, it would be safe. From the odor wafting to his nose, he was sweating like a longshoreman. At least it was keeping him warm.

When he returned, Wong was buttoning his shirt. His exposed skin was mottled with dark brown and white patches. Other than the pigment, his hands and fingers appeared perfectly normal. Jones had given Wong a salve for his abrasions and clean bandages.

Jones buttoned up his waterproof coat and adjusted his hat. "Vitiligo. Perfectly harmless. These stupid fools. Leaving him here would have been a death sentence. Normally ninety-five percent of people are immune to Hansen's disease. In very close quarters, leprosy can be contagious in a small number of cases, far less than tuberculosis or cholera. With the deplorable sanitary conditions, these men are doubly doomed."

Edwin put a hand on Wong's shoulder. How small he was. How much he did with so little. "It's all right, old friend. We're taking you home." Tears of joy trickled down the man's cheeks.

How would any of them have held up under the circumstances? A stoic acceptance of fate was an Eastern trait.

Jones gave Edwin a concerned glance, speaking loudly against the wind. "The boat's all right?"

Above them, ominous clouds tinged with black hovered like beasts. A rare crash of thunder sounded to the north. "You were right about the conditions. The wind's coming on forty miles an hour. All boats have gone to harbor. We're stuck here tonight."

"The supply cabin is clean and dry," Wong suggested. "The straw is fresh this week."

"What do you blokes do for water?" asked the doctor.

There was a spring about seventy meters off. Other than that, they caught rainwater and stored it in barrels. Over the few years, the resourceful colony had enlarged a substantial allotment with sea soil and fishmeal, making fertile ground for the seed they were given. The crude buildings with glass windows and sturdy doors kept them from the worst elements. Each got a single bed, table and chair, pots and pans and tools as well as warm clothing. The dead were buried in a small cemetery far from the spring. The city supplied the coffins. "Someday their bones can be returned to their homeland," Wong added. "That is their hope. It does not seem likely."

Edwin pulled up more sitting logs and they neared the fire. The five men shuffled aside. Most were covered in cloaks, and they tried to cover their heads against shame. Their hollowed eyes revealed the eternal torment to which they had been consigned. "Tim, are you sure that—"

"I wouldn't endanger us, man," the doctor said. "I'd be more worried about water contamination. Thank God we brought our own."

"Is this how our newest province, a land of plenty, provides for its people?" Naomi asked. "How appalling. Animals take better care of their own."

The doctor spread his hands in a helpless gesture. "Leprosy is relatively rare. That limits the resources that the scientific community is willing to extend. In the early stages the disease can be quelled with chaulmoogra oil, though the side effects are brutal. I learned about ayurvedic medicine when I was stationed in India."

Naomi shuddered and pulled a blanket closer. "How could anyone, Christian, Jew, or Mohammedan, allow this outrage against humanity? I'm going to speak to the rabbi at Emanu-El. They've given generously to other charities. And I'll start a petition for the premier's office. Ottawa should be notified. When I think of what my dear Serge would have . . ." Her voice petered out with weariness.

"Let's get on with our meal," Edwin said. He began pulling food out of the hamper and giving it to Wong, who distributed it. Cheese and meat sandwiches, cold chicken, fruit, bread, crackers, and flasks of water. A bottle of brandy was declined by the men. Wong said that they preferred opium, which they were given on a regular basis, though it dwindled in the final weeks before the supply ship. At this news, Naomi perked up, and Edwin noticed glances between the two. But Naomi merely shook her head. Revealing her secret in front of Jones would have been painful. Besides, there was ample brandy. With bowed heads and gestures, the men gave thanks. Edwin saw a metal cross around the neck of the youngest, barely sixteen. His life was over. His white man's God had abandoned him.

"At least it's not raining," Jones said. "Yet."

The wind continued to shriek, dropping to a low keening, then picking up in whirlwinds. When the last provisions vanished, save for breakfast morsels, Wong showed them the small supplies building nearby the chicken house. The smell wasn't pleasant.

One by one, they went out to relieve themselves. Edwin stood watch while Naomi hovered behind a rock to urinate. "There might be a fox," she explained. "They're not on our island, but we're closer to the mainland now. And bears swim."

"Mother, really. That's the least of your worries."

"It's always easy for you men," she said with a contemptuous snort as she returned, brushing grass from her skirts. From a clean bale, they fashioned pallets to protect them from the cold ground and divided up the blankets. When the wind finally dropped and the rain began to pelt, the gentle conversation of the nearby fowl lent a comforting coat of normality to the darkness.

"My apologies for taking so long, my friend," said Edwin, his arm around Naomi as they huddled against the buffet of the wind through the shed's raw boards. At least it was waterproof, with a clattery tin roof. "But I hope you knew that we would look for you."

Wong shook his head, breaking into a wide grin. "Lord Buddha provided. Now that you have tasted my cooking, you will never want me to leave your blessed house."

All they heard that night was the crashing of the surf. The idea that the boat might break loose bothered Edwin as he took another swig of brandy and passed it to the doctor.

"Stop worrying," Jones said. "Everyone knows where I went. If we're not back tonight for the horses, they'll send a steam launch from Victoria."

Edwin spent a fitful night. Now that Wong had been found, he still had a murderer to find. A perfect crime defined itself by its anonymity. Would Melodie Campbell have anything to add about Mary? Given the number of costumes, more than one person was involved in this conspiracy. Edwin rolled over as Jones and Naomi snored themselves into blissful unconsciousness.

# CHAPTER TWENTY-FOUR

In the light gray dawn, having grabbed no more than two hours' sleep, Edwin went to check the boat. The sea was silken, the wind's temper exhausted, and the craft was safe. Life could be tenuous. Springing a leak, losing an oar, catching a rogue wave at the wrong angle. Working on the fishing boats, he'd had close calls. Even in high summer, the water was frigid enough to kill a man in mere hours when hypothermia set in. For the other nine months, especially the storms of winter, survival depended on getting to shore and sheltered from the sleet and snow. It was hard to fathom that the northern province snugged alongside the panhandle of Alaska.

God, he was hungry. They'd taken no breakfast, giving the remainder to the lepers. How could anyone do otherwise? The wretches had only the next supply ship and a shallow grave for their future.

From the camp, they took a blanket each for Naomi and Wong. The lepers kept their distance, expressing their gratitude in universal pantomimes, patting the heart. One shuffled forward, his club-like hand outstretched in a palsy and feet swathed in bandages. "You are kind," he said, bowing. "They send us food, but our shelters are cold in the winter. All of us worked hard. Please tell them that we are suffering."

It was like returning from the Land of the Dead. Wong explained that the Chinese businesses took up collections. "What a travesty," said Naomi. "They need so little. This isn't why they left their homeland for a new life in Canada."

"Fear and ignorance are a curse on mankind. And these poor souls are dying as fast as they can, as the Dean Swift used to say about the poor in Ireland," said Jones with a bitter smile. "I'll exert pressure on the medical community. Letters to the newspaper would help. A public outcry is warranted. Your petition is a great start."

Edwin took the lead, and the procession back to the boat began. Every few hundred feet, he looked back at the brave contingent of doomed men until they were small dots on his conscience. The prosperous spring-green hills of Saanichton across the water were a mockery of sanctuary.

Shoving off, a wind from the east lifted them, and the miles went quickly. It was as if they were willing themselves out of hell. Edwin rowed the entire way without speaking.

"Now I understand why I was born in the year of the water dog," Wong said. Only Naomi knew that he was making a joke. The water sign merely added foresight and flexibility to his character.

They put up at the wharf, glad to step onto land. Wong and Naomi stayed behind while Jones and Edwin saw to the carriage, making sure the horses were freshly fed, watered, and harnessed before returning for the two passengers. Having spent the night wrapped in blankets on straw, everyone welcomed the plush but dusty cushions of the carriage.

At the central crossing, they stopped at the Prairie Inn in Saanichton. The original Prairie Tavern, built in 1859 on an adjacent spot, had been the oldest island roadhouse. "We need food. Hours lie ahead of us," Edwin said. Wong shook his head and said that a bowl of rice at home would seem like the best feast in a Chinese New Year.

"Whatever you can get, hot, cold, cooked or raw," said Naomi. "I'll gnaw on hardtack and feel blessed."

Edwin and Jones returned with bottles of beer, roast chickens, loaves of whole meal bread with a square of butter, and a pound of cheese. Everyone tucked in, though Wong neither drank alcohol or ate dairy products. Jones purchased a pint of whiskey to warm the journey. The sun had come out, ushering in a clear front, and a brisk wind frothed waves on the strait. Any longer leaving this morning and they would have had to stay another night in purgatory.

"I'll take the reins," Edwin said, "and Wong can ride up front with me."

"Delighted to chat with your mother," Jones said as he changed places and glanced at darkening clouds. "I have rubber curtains to roll right down in case there's a change in the weather."

Naomi entertained them with "Going Home." A rich contralto, she had once studied music for a year. Wong napped beside Edwin, and Jones eyed Naomi with appreciative glances. The lilt of her voice belied the dark circles under her eyes. In the chorus, the doctor joined with his baritone, then started the next song, "When You and I Were Young, Maggie." Within a few days she could muster her influential friends while Jones swayed the bureaucracy. A new chief medical officer couldn't be named soon enough.

Just before dusk, with the beveled-glass carriage lamp lit, the party reached Amelia Street. "When we all meet again, let's try for something a bit less grueling," Jones said, blowing a kiss to Naomi as Edwin helped her from the carriage. She had been sleeping against tufted seats and bore crease marks on her face.

"I thought I would never see my dear bed again," she said. "I intend to bask in hot water until I turn into a sponge. The skin can never have too much moisture. Then I will apply cream and slide into bed."

Wong said a few words to Jones in private, from his gestures, thanking him for his lifesaving efforts. How easily a turn of the wheel of fortune can plunge someone into unfathomed depths, but just as soon raise him up. Edwin was reminded of Vicky and her short run of luck before dying. Could she have been blackmailing a wealthy man? She had the nerve, but Mary Donahue didn't. There was a world of difference between the two. How did their fates conjoin? How many other women might be in danger?

Naomi was mechanically shuffling one foot in front of the other as they went up the front walk. Edwin placed his arm around her stooped shoulders. This ordeal would have taxed a teenager. And to show her face plain as the day she was born must have cost in front of Jones. Straw still decorated her disheveled hair.

"There's a Miss Masters here," Edwin said to Wong. "She was hired on a short-term basis. We gave her a room upstairs so as not to disturb your things. If she's in the kitchen, please tell her I'll speak with her and settle her wages by tomorrow." He had a second thought. "Better order two blocks of ice. We were running low yesterday, and I didn't show her the window card."

Wong took the flagstone path to the back door, picking a peach-colored rose on the way and touching it to his snub nose. Naomi looked at the house as if it were the Taj Mahal. She cocked her head and frowned. "I can't hear Gladdy barking. When we're away, usually he's parked in the front room, looking out the window. She'd best have treated him right, or she'll answer to me." The curtains were drawn, but the little dog had a favorite chaise to stand on, and Wong daily cleaned nose dabs from the windows.

"Strange." Edwin found the front door unlocked. While he sometimes left it that way, a proper English servant should have been more circumspect. He helped Naomi with the heavy cape, then found himself reaching out a hand as her knees buckled.

"Holy Moses!" Cabinet doors stood open. Books and magazines and cushions littered the floor.

"Edwin, we've been robbed!" Naomi said with an ashen face. "Never in all my life. Has Masters been injured? What could they have wanted? We don't keep money around. I have a few good pieces of jewelry your father gave me."

In the dining room, the credenza was open, and large silver pieces gone.

Wong came running from the kitchen. "Bad things. No woman. No puppy." Gladdy was often left in the fenced yard to meander on his business.

"Leave everything for now, Wong. But make a list of anything missing. I'm going next door." Despite his fatigue, Edwin felt renewed by the adrenalin charge.

"I don't give a damn about the silver. My little man!" Naomi rushed to the empty hook on the hall settee cabinet. She turned with despair. "His leash is gone. Do you think they meant to steal him all along? His breed is so rare." She had bought him on a trip to Portland for the royal sum of fifty dollars.

Edwin put his hands on her shoulders. "Go upstairs and get into that bath, Mother. I'll be right back." With the row houses, not much outside passed privately. Everyone knew when the milkman came, when coal was delivered, when the chimneys were cleaned, when deliveries were made, even when a baby was delivered. They also knew when people were away.

His neighbors to the right had been gone for the winter in Hawaii, visiting their son who ran a Dole pineapple plantation. Edwin and Naomi had been watching the place and had a key. Old Miss Ruby Littlepage on the other side seemed the best choice. Her face flashed behind a lace curtain at the window twenty times a day. She had been a teacher at the Craigflower School fifty years ago. Nothing passed her gimlet eye. Time enough to discover what else had been taken. He remembered

Masters scanning the neighborhood, evaluating the place for pillaging.

He whirled the round bell pull. A cat vanished from the window seat, and thumps erupted inside. An apple-doll face in a long print dress with an apron appeared. Miss Littlepage's shrewdness was belied by her harmless appearance. "Little old ladies can go anywhere," she once told him when he talked about following a suspect around the docks where he was picking up contraband. "They are invisible. I would make the perfect private detective. I hear that the larger stores are employing observant and discreet ladies to watch for shoplifters."

"Edwin, how lovely to see you. Please come in and try one of my molasses cookies. Fresh from the oven." She held out a plate.

He stepped in to be polite, but explained that he couldn't stay. Her sparrow eyes brightened when she heard about Masters. She laid a finger alongside her nose. "I wondered about that one. She didn't seem any too friendly when I chatted out the back door putting up the laundry. But I saw you all together, so I assumed . . ."

Edwin nodded, between warm and spicy bites of the best thing he'd eaten all day. "Was anyone else around the house?"

"I had no idea that you were gone, though I did see you and your dear mother in that carriage so early yesterday. I wondered if there had been an emergency because you didn't return. Around midnight, a man came along with that new woman. They had large sacks over their backs and got into a small wagon pulled by a mule. Of course the light was very bad. And that awful storm hit."

Back home, his mother was near tears, lying with her shoes off on a chaise lounge. "The Georgian silver is gone, Edwin. All the cutlery and the serving set, teapot, and hot water pot. It was in my family for a hundred years. Great-grandfather's gold menorah from Alsace."

He frowned. "Anything else?" Then looked at the coat stand. No Aquascutum. His hands clenched. This was too personal.

"I checked the linen closet. They seem to have taken sheets, perhaps to wrap up the goods. And my amethyst necklace, ring, and earrings. Your father gave me those for our tenth anniversary." She wiped a tear from her eye.

"Don't worry, Mother. I know how to track them down. They can't have left the island that fast. They'd probably have sold some of the silver for the ferry fare. We'll get onto the usual dealers first thing by tonight. Blunt takes care of our robbery section."

She sighed. "Wong is safe. We are safe. That is what matters. But poor Gladdy."

# Chapter Twenty-Five

Three days later, most of the goods had been located, but not the thieves. Masters had gone to ground with thirty dollars from a pawnbroker on View Street. Blunt said that she had quite the record and worked in tandem with Christopher Bullock, last known address in Esquimalt, a deserted beach shack.

Edwin was on the verge of leaving as Naomi came down the stairs. She had been up early every day since the robbery, staring at Gladdy's silver brush. "Any news, Son?"

"The boats haven't run in a few days thanks to the tides and wind, but the weather's calmed. Masters may take the steamer to Washington. She has family in Spokane. We have a man watching the daily sailings. Resources are limited. As for our dog . . ." He didn't meet her eyes.

"You mean that . . ." Her hand flew to her mouth and she sat down heavily on the stairs. Food hadn't been her focus since Gladdy disappeared, he had noticed. How could she dream of preparing a canvas and musing about a palette's colors?

"Think about how a felon's mind works. Either she thought she could sell him, or she liked the animal herself. In either case, he's valuable to her." Standing in the foyer, he gave a final pat to his hair and put on his hat.

With a sniff she turned away. "Everyone adores Gladdy. Those love bites. He'll always be a puppy."

★ ★ ★ ★ ★

When Edwin had left, Naomi did some critical thinking. If she hadn't gone looking for Wong, he might still be with the doomed lepers. What was wrong with Edwin? There had to be something she could do. Meanwhile, she dressed and called for a cab to the Methodist Soup Kitchen, a volunteer job once a week.

What had he said about the ferry? She checked the paper for departure times as the clock struck nine. That policeman on watch hadn't met Masters, but she had. Millicent. What a silly name for such a baggage.

When she arrived an hour later at the soup kitchen, she left her coat in the cloakroom, then took an apron. Her job was to serve. Cleaner than working in the kitchen with those bubbling pots, and after what she'd done to a turkey, they no longer asked her.

As she ladled out the baked beans and plopped a piece of bread onto each tin plate, she greeted each man, by name if possible. As the last of the pot emptied, she saw Corky Wells, a former boxer.

He doffed his cloth cap and rubbed a hammy hand over his hair. "Ma'am." She didn't blame him for his crush on her, though in these plain clothes and her sweating brow, she wasn't her own inspiration.

As she finished her shift, she saw Corky taking his coffee mug and plate to the dish station. Perhaps they could do each other a favor.

"Corky," she said, giving him her platinum smile.

"Ma'am?" His eyes went to his dishes as if to say that he had done his job.

"Step outside with me for a moment. I have a . . . proposition for you."

Outside, his face was curious but respectful as she explained about Masters. "And so I need a good strong man to come with me to the steamer station for the next few days. It should take no more than an hour each time, and of course I will pay you for your efforts. Five dollars." No Worth perfume for Christmas.

He blushed. "I'd be honored, Ma'am. Remuneration would be an insult. You should never go down to the harbor by yourself. It's not safe and not proper. There isn't always a constable around when you might need him."

"Precisely. That is why I am asking you, Corky." She looked at him. "Is that a nickname?"

He blushed roundly, toeing the floor with his dusty brogan. "Yes, for Corliss."

"Meet me here tomorrow morning at eight sharp. Bring a cab. Don't be late. A dear dog's life hangs in the balance." She passed him two dollars. "For the fare." A cabby might not stop for him.

As soon as Edwin left the next morning, Naomi got dressed and ready. The cab clopped up to the minute, and not long after, they approached the Inner Harbor. According to the *Daily Colonist,* the SS *Rosalie* left at nine for Seattle. Across the strait to the south, the snow-capped peaks of the Olympic Mountains loomed purple and proud. If it hadn't been for the War of 1812, the Yanks might have claimed all the land to Alaska. America tried during the Pig War to extend the San Juans, but by then Canada had a large footprint thanks to the Hudson's Bay Company.

At the docks, seagulls wheeled in the air, competing for crumbs, while a small crowd was loading. Some were on board leaning over the rails. The fares read *Port Townsend 1.50, Seattle 2.50, and Tacoma 3.50. Reduced rates for round trip.* Naomi took Corky's massive arm and strolled under an awning, leaning against the wall, chin down, peering through her thick eyelashes. Corky was dressed drummer style in a loud green plaid suit, presumably his Sunday best. She hadn't thought to tell him to look inconspicuous. He was chewing on a toothpick, an authentic touch.

From a stand, a tradesman was selling coffee and rolls. How did people get up and moving this early in the morning? Going to D'Arcy Island had nearly killed her. Not that she'd admit it to Edwin.

Corky shifted the toothpick. "See what you're looking for?"

"Not yet." A frown shadowed her ivory brow, and wrinkling her nose, she noticed horse manure on her patent-leather boot. Thank heavens Wong was back. Her eyes scanned the group. Where was that policeman that Edwin had mentioned?

"Say, did I ever tell you about when I was a kid and went to Victoria's first boxing match?" Corky asked with a grin revealing a missing eyetooth.

He had, but how could she hurt the likable sap's feelings? She tilted her face up and locked eyes. "Never. It sounds exciting. Women wouldn't be allowed, I vow."

"It was back in sixty-six. Boxing had a lot of enemies then. We all got on a steamer, heading for Race Rocks. Then we got off near Weir's Farm over by Pedder Bay."

"Really. Weir's Farm. They say that Sitting Lady Falls is lovely." Her toe was tapping, but he wouldn't notice.

"It was George Baker against Joe Eden. By God those were the days. By the hundred and twentieth round, they was staggering around, half dead. Then in the hundred and twenty-eighth, out came a right hand which floored Baker, and in came the sponge and towel."

"Those were the days of real men." She gave his bicep a squeeze and spoke loudly into his cauliflower ear, a trifle deaf.

"Eden got him a belt with a gold buckle. Then back to California he went."

"And that's how you got interested in boxing."

"Yes, Ma'am. I was a lad of twelve. But truth to tell, I wasn't a good boxer even though I could take a punch. By the time I was twenty-five, my beezer looked like this." He pointed to his flattened nose. "But by Jehosophat, it was the life. There were girls who . . ." Suddenly he tightened his lips and gazed off across the water at a shrimper heading to shore.

Naomi saw a very young man in an ill-fitting duck-cloth suit escorting a woman to the waiting room. It wasn't Masters.

As he passed them, Corky raised a brushy eyebrow and cocked a thumb at the pair. Naomi shook her head and collapsed her parasol.

It was getting close to sailing. Naomi scanned the crowd, discounting on basis of sex, age, accoutrements. Where would Masters get two babies in a pram? Yet suppose she were in disguise with wrapped-up dolls? About to despair at the last call for boarding, at last she saw a swarthy man wearing a very familiar overcoat. He was pushing an older man in a wicker wheelchair. Beaky nose. The man had a large, jiggling basket on his lap. Something was poking out. A small whine met her ears, and her heart leaped. "Keep an eye on them," she whispered to Corky, angling her head.

Then moving swiftly but with a casual air, she hustled inside and found the plainclothesman. A young woman in a cloak was saying, "This is a mistake. My husband is Reverend Carroll at First Methodist Church, and he will—"

Naomi stopped between them. "This is not Millicent Masters. I should know. I employed her, and she robbed me blind," she said. "She's out here. In disguise. Come quickly. I can't handle them both even with—"

"Madam, and who would you be?" The man tipped back his hat and squinted in the bright light coming through the windows.

Naomi hissed in frustration. What a numbskull. Yet even in

medical school, someone had to be last in the class. "Edwin DesRosiers is my son. Will you please help us take those two into custody? And be careful, they're dangerous."

Only then did it occur to her what she was saying. Suppose they had a knife or a gun? People weren't searched to get onto a ferry, even to cross the border.

The policeman looked from her to the pair as they walked out. Seconds counted. If this weren't done right, the felons might escape in the crowd.

"Grab him, Corky. That's Edwin's overcoat," she yelled.

"Right you are, Ma'am." With reactions faster than expected, Corky wrestled the man to the ground. Masters jumped up, flung aside the basket and blanket, and was preparing to run. Naomi stuck out a shapely leg and tripped her as the officer pulled up.

"So there you be, Milly Masters. We have been lookin' for you and your Bullock." He pulled out handcuffs and attached them to the man on the ground.

"And now you, too, dearie," he said to Masters as he took out a second pair. "You'll all be coming to the station with me. If you'd oblige, Sir, we can use your strong arms for a few blocks."

"Always glad to help the law," Corky said, whistling for a cab for Naomi.

The basket sat on the ground, ignored in the melee. "Gladdy!" Naomi cried as the little dog nosed aside the cover and leaped into her arms. From the new collar and fresh brushing, it had been coddled. Gathered around for the entertainment, people burst into laughter and cheered.

# CHAPTER TWENTY-SIX

Edwin could hardly blame his mother for playing detective. She was two for two. Edwin gave his precious coat a onceover, and retrieved the terra cotta marble from the pocket, rolling it in his fingers. It was a talisman, a message from beyond the grave . . . or it was nothing. Would a few more threads pull together this ugly tapestry? He gave his unruly hair a last comb and flicked a piece of lint from his dark gray jacket as he whistled for a cab. Melodie Campbell was back.

Emily was waiting outside her house, face shining in the sun's rays. Most women of her class favored the pale and sensitive look and doted on parasols. Emily's new species looked a fellow in the eye. Serge had told him that it took a strong man to love a strong woman, but that the struggle was worthwhile "if it didn't kill you."

"Melodie's meeting us at the Poodle Dog. They have a special lunch for forty cents. Was that all right? You said to choose."

"Of course." *Dear girl,* his heart whispered. For a minute he wondered if he had spoken the words. He directed the cab to take them to Louis Marboeuf's restaurant. Emily wore a fetching casual suit with spring colors of pale green and light cerise, the same as the salmonberry blooms in wild hedges along the way. Women were amazing. How lovely her hair looked, or was it the smile complementing any outfit?

The popular restaurant was downtown on Yates. Inside, a tall girl was waving at them beside a table set for three.

"Em, as beautiful as ever." The women moved in for a quick female embrace. Edwin missed the Montreal greeting of a kiss on each cheek, but Anglos were so reserved. He hung up the coats and joined them in time to pull out chairs. A light scent of lemon verbena came from Emily, rose madder from Melodie. They were both grinning at him as time stood still. He signaled the waiter.

The olive-skinned man with a white apron presented menus, recommending the special: chicken pot pie with vegetables. Edwin raised an eyebrow at the ladies' glasses of claret, included in the price, but after all, they were grown women. Were people wondering which was the couple? An embarrassment of riches.

"So is this your new beau, Em?" Melodie asked with a wink. She wore a boyish sailor top with a flared skirt.

What had Emily said about him? He took a sip of his wine to cover his embarrassment, but it went down the wrong way and he coughed. He felt twelve years old.

Emily slanted her shapely eyebrows and gave a mock slap to her friend's hand. "You are such a tease, Melodie. I've told you what the *De-tec-tive* needs to learn from you. He's a busy man and probably has to go arrest someone this very afternoon with handcuffs and leg irons. Tell him about the Girls' Friendly Society and Mary."

Melodie nibbled at a cuticle. "It's not like I know a secret or anything."

"Of course, dear. But go on. Little things can be important. Isn't that true, *Detective*?"

"Mary had very few acquaintances, so even those who knew her slenderly might have helpful points." The restaurant was filling. Suppose one of the fellows saw him gallivanting about with two young women on a workday. He ran a finger around his collar and took out a notebook. Mixing business with pleasure was awkward. How could the girl know much anyway?

With a sip of wine, Melodie's mouth puckered. "Oo. That's too sour. I liked sherry better."

Emily nudged her. "Stop lollygagging. Start from the beginning and don't get off track."

Melodie looked from one to the other. Then she folded her hands and her chocolate brown eyes grew serious and troubled. "I'm the president of our Girls' Friendly Society at Saint Barnabas. We try to be welcoming to girls of all . . . classes. It's a Christian duty. Mary came to our meetings for a few months, and then stopped. Nothing to do with us. We liked her. Honest. And we're not stuck up. When I saw her on the street a few weeks later, she said that she had something better to do that night. She acted kind of mysterious. Butter wouldn't melt."

"Any ideas what it might involve?" Edwin shifted. His suspicions were pointing in a very sordid direction. Nor could he tell them what had been found without breaching protocol. Talking to the good Sister about that habit had been difficult enough.

Melodie finished her wine and gave a small hiccough. She took a drink of water, then another. "Golly, this is embarrassing."

Emily pushed forward the sugar bowl. "Mother said a spoon of sugar. It works."

Half a minute later, Melodie continued. "She needed to find girls."

Emily and Edwin shared a wary look. "What for?"

Melodie waved her little hand. "Something about a club. And helping out. Maybe she meant serving or something. Poor girl didn't have an education."

He could tell from the disguised shock on Emily's face that she grasped the same point. "And did anyone else in the group agree to go?"

"Oh no, indeed. They thought it was very queer. I think she

needed her head examined to risk her position working somewhere else."

The waiter arrived with the steaming trays. As the girls chatted, Edwin spun his mind gears. Mary had only one valuable. Bawdy songs called it a "purse." Some base but wealthy men despoiled girls for their own particular pleasures. Jones said that she had hemorrhaged. Did the other robe prove that she was looking for another acolyte? And yet she'd been found in her dress with no apparent blood on it. He was getting closer to the solution.

Edwin took a chance. "Did she . . . did she mention getting a tattoo?"

Melodie burst into laughter. "A tattoo? That's very low class. What in the world for?" She looked at Emily, and they turned in confusion to Edwin. He'd crossed a line.

He hemmed and hawed, talking about cases crossing and threads and blind alleys. "Forget that I mentioned it. Please. And thanks for your information, Miss Campbell."

After they had eaten and were about to leave, Melodie turned to Emily. "I forgot to bring this to you. You wanted to run the pigs."

That stupid game Reggie had mentioned. Was Emily interested in that? He thought that she had a better head on her shoulders.

"It's all the rage now. Everyone's doing it." Melodie pulled a small box from her pocket. It had round marbles and little holes in which they rested. An image of pigs and a farmer with a staff was printed on the outside.

"It's clever, Melodie. Does it take long to learn?" Emily asked.

Melodie rotated it, biting her lip with concentration as she manipulated the marbles into the holes. "I've been practicing, Em. There's one marble gone, but I added a black one."

"May I see that please?" Edwin picked up the box. The

marbles were terra cotta with tiny spots. Identical to the one he had found with Vicky. "Intriguing. Are they for sale in town?" he asked.

"I daresay not. My uncle brought it back from the States. It had a marble missing when he gave it to me a few weeks ago. It looks funny with one that doesn't match."

Emily smiled. "Just a different pig in the litter. Think of it like that."

Melodie giggled. "You smarty pants."

Edwin wanted to take immediate custody of the box, but how could he ask for it? "My colleague has been talking about this game. What's your uncle's last name?"

"Clifford Cardinal. My mother's brother. He's always given me the nicest presents." Melodie yawned, showing perfect white niblet teeth. "Uncle Cliff is very well off. But not stuffy like some rich people."

Edwin cautioned himself, not moving a facial muscle. "And his family? He sounds too eligible to have escaped the charms of a young lady."

Melodie said with a pout of consternation, "He's never married. I wonder if he'll ever settle down. His parents died a few years ago. But he's so handsome and charming, too. All my girlfriends like him. Lots of times he's given me a ride home from the GFS in his buggy. It's a Columbus." She elbowed Emily. "Emily intends to marry a poor man, don't you, pet, just to be obstinate."

Emily struck a pose of mock offense with her hand on her chest. "Melodie, you are acting like a brat. Anyway, we'd best be going. Don't you think?" The clock on the wall showed one-thirty.

Edwin needed a few more facts. "Reggie pointed him out at the Union Club once. I thought I saw the same man at a horse auction up in Saanichton. Is that where he lives?"

"He has a suite at the Driard. Uncle Clifford likes to be in the center of things. Concerts, the theater. He could never stand living out in Hicksville." She stood up with a bit of a wobble. "I've been naughty to have wine at lunch. Don't ever tell Mama. How about we go for a walk to get decent again, Em? Thanks for the meal, *Detective*."

Edwin tipped his hat as he watched the girls stroll off arm in arm. There were probably several games like that in Victoria, but how many had a marble missing? Reggie socialized with Clifford. Perhaps the answers had been under his nose.

# CHAPTER TWENTY-SEVEN

Reggie was at his desk for a change, reading *Maggie, a Girl of the Streets*. "This is even better than *The Red Badge of Courage*, but damned gloomy. Get this lingo from New York City: 'You're outta sight.' " He slapped his knee.

"What's that supposed to mean?"

"Lovemaking, what else? It's a compliment like 'buttercup.' 'Honeybun.' You need to get with it. Can you even dance a two-step? Bet you're a waltz man. No, wait, the minuet."

When Edwin didn't answer, he shut the book and frowned. "McBride has it in for me. Says if I don't shape up, I'm canned. Who the hell cares, anyway? Once I take the vows, my dear father-in-law will have something lucrative if boring for me to do at head office. Father's idea about getting into politics is too much trouble, and it doesn't pay much. There's only one slight problem."

"What's that?" Edwin had little time for Reggie's dipsomaniacal ups and downs.

"Carrie has given me the gate. We were supposed to go to her cousin's violin recital last night. *Eeeee, awww, scriiiiitch.* A fate worse than death, and I lost all track of time at the club. I was down ten bucks in a poker game, and you know me, old chum. She's absolutely refused to see me anymore. And dammit, Edwin, I love the girl. I didn't realize it until now. Just like the poets say."

"You'll make up. She's decent enough to love you in spite of yourself. Get some flowers and candy and go down on your knees like in romantic novels."

Reggie blinked. "Do you think that will work? Sounds soppy."

"I guarantee it. Now listen. There may have been a break." Edwin sat down and related what he had learned, drawing the lines from Vicky to Mary to Clifford.

"That silly pigs game. There wasn't a black marble when I first saw it. How about that? But Cardinal? Do you really think so? I'll be a hornswoggled fool." A flash of concentration crossed his brow.

"I never figured Stevens for Vicky's murder. He's too stupid to have made up a story about the errand. Be honest for once in your life and tell me if you passed on information to the bastard." He stared at Reggie as if he were in the dock. Was this how Serge had felt as an attorney?

Reggie stood abruptly. "Absolutely not. What kind of village idiot do you take me for." Taking a look at Edwin's narrowed eyes, he added, "Never mind."

"We never told the papers about the method of the murder, Reggie." He placed the marble on the table. "Luring Stevens from the club the exact time and vicinity where Vicky was left. All at night. Remember that boy where Vicky was found heard two male voices. The killer may have had an accomplice. And the name 'Abbott' or 'abbot.' The costumes explain that. Does Cardinal stutter?"

"Of c-course not." Reggie's face grew deadly serious as second thoughts got the better of him. "Usually when I over-imbibe, I pass out quietly like a good fellow, but—"

Edwin folded his arms and drilled accusing eyes into his friend's insouciant face. "So you did tell him about the first two girls and that stocking."

Reggie's voice wavered. "Damn it, old man. Maybe I might have . . . dropped a word or two. But I mean, who would suspect

. . . let down my guard . . ." Blotches of embarrassment spread over his face.

Edwin pounded the table and an ink well spit dark blue drops onto the blotter. "You've jammed up this case nice and proper, you ass. Did you ever hear about imitating a crime? Playing copycat?"

"Like with the Ripper, you mean. They'll never solve that in a hundred years."

Edwin took out a pencil and foolscap. "Tell me what you know about the man. I don't care if we're here until midnight. The least you can do after buggering this up is to make sure the case is settled right and proper. He's been damn smooth."

Reggie's lower lip pooched out, then he balled his fists. "He's loads of fun, but I wouldn't cross him. He puts himself first. Says what he thinks will work over the truth. Very fond of Machiavelli's *The Prince*. Better to be feared than loved, that kind of thing. Cliff's very learned. That Rabelais quote and the tattoo sound just like him. I just never—"

"And no family?"

"Clifford is an only surviving son. His younger brother drowned at ten. He has an older sister, and she got her share years ago and lives in Chicago. His parents are dead. Never had to work a day in ye olde salt mines, unlike yours truly."

"And where did this famous family fortune come from?"

"Grandpa Blennerhassett on the mother's side owned a fleet of sealers. He made his money when pelts were at a premium. Later the rumor went that he did a bit of smuggling." He took out his watch and wound it in a nervous gesture.

"Now we're getting somewhere. Clifford has rooms at the Driard. Clearly that's not where these meetings or parties or rituals take place. Where did dear Grandpa live?"

"I told you. In Casa Loma, of course." He spoke as if everyone knew the name.

Edwin's pencil stopped. "Where the hell is that? Italy?"

"It's a big mansion down the Gorge. Maybe ten acres of land. All closed up for years. Impossible to heat. And no one will buy it. A white elephant. A good museum if you like god-awful mock Gothic architecture."

"How far up the Gorge? Past the backwards falls?" The tidal phenomenon was a favorite tourist attraction.

"Damn right. Clear out in Portage Bay. More than an hour's row for sure. Less by a fast horse."

"Anyone keep an eye on it?"

Reggie held up a wagging finger. "He's too cheap for a caretaker. A farmer takes the hay. That lowers the taxes. Agricultural allotment. It has everything, Clifford says. There's a ballroom, library, wine cellar, even a chapel."

"A chapel." Fanny's point about the old English club. Blasphemous philosophies had quite the cachet for jaded people. A virgin or two would be premiums for their fantasies. But virginity isn't a renewable resource.

Reggie snickered at the observation. "He's pretty close-mouthed, but he's made a few comments over the years about special parties."

"If you tell me you've been there, I'm not going to believe you."

A burro's bray from Reggie. "I almost got invited once when he was boiled as an owl on absinthe late one Saturday night. Normally he's under control. But he stopped himself. Then he looked at me ever so strange and said, 'You're much too upright a man, Reginald.' " Reggie cocked a thumb at himself. "Me, upright. That's a chuckle and a half."

"That reporter O'Neill mentioned rumors about a Sticks Club. Any ideas? What do sticks have to do with anything?" He felt foolish asking Reggie, still . . .

"Your lack of formal education is appalling, Rozzer. It must be Styx, the river in Hell. Bloody brilliant name, eh?"

Edwin drew his hand along his jawline with its four o'clock stubble. Snippets of memory from Mary's body returned. The shuttle coursed the loom, making another row. A pattern was emerging. "Didn't you say that you went hunting with him?"

"Right-o. On Mayne Island. He took his golden retriever so that we could get our ducks. Lunkhead of a dog." He tapped his temple in a universal gesture.

"Golden retriever, eh? What do they look like? A Labrador?"

"What do you know with your sissy mutt? We're talking about men's dogs. Goldens have long hair. Labs have short hair, Mister. They're both a bit strong on the nose. Oily coats."

Thoughts were begging to be connected. "Remember that hair that we thought was cougar?"

Reggie got a sick look on his face. "He left her in the bush like garbage? Jesus. That's cold."

"Mary's death was an ugly accident, which I suspect Clifford covered up. As for getting rid of the body, it's not that far from the upper Gorge over to Langford Lake." He went to the wall map and traced a route with his finger.

Reggie stood up and his voice cracked in anger. "Things like that make a decent man sick. When I think of little Carrie . . ." He bit his lip and narrowed his eyes like an adder ready to strike.

"Jones is sure that Mary's death came before Vicky's. Now maybe I understand why. She may have blackmailed him or at the least, threatened to expose him."

"Murder will out, dear old Chaucer says."

"Old lags are plentiful. Young virgins like Mary would be harder to turn. Vicky was well past her prime, but a good judge of women. They probably needed someone to make the arrangements. The clothes, the tutoring."

"Old boy, it's coming together now that we have a different

perspective. That European seven in the Stevens note. I've seen him sign for drinks. He was sent to Germany for school as a lad. That's where the mother's family came from. Bad Hasen-pfeffer or someplace. One of those cure-all spas. That dueling scar on his temple. The bloody coward probably did it himself."

"They'd need a very private place, but not that far. Remember what the lad told me about that tattooist taking a boat up the Gorge?"

"I wouldn't be surprised if he's feeding the crabs at the bottom of the bay," Reggie added.

"Each danger ramps up the excitement. It's like Krafft-Ebing says of forbidden fruit. They're confident that they'll never be identified. It's time to find this lair of serpents and destroy it."

"What's our plan, then? Call out the troops?" He smacked his fist into his palm. "Carrie may take me back if I pull off a coup."

Edwin had never seen Reggie so eager. *Louche,* Naomi would have described him. Now he was turning from Savile Row to Scotland Yard. "If we start making enquiries about the club, he may go to ground. We need reconnaissance." A noise in the hall made him lower his voice.

Reggie's fuzzy eyebrows creased the bridge of his long pointed nose. "Then what? I don't follow."

"We must be certain before acting. I'm going to Casa Loma."

"But really, chappie, how can you—"

Edwin's answer came with a low growl. "Not as an invited guest."

# CHAPTER TWENTY-EIGHT

Clifford was in Reggie's capable hands for the evening, against the possibility of an unscheduled trip to Casa Loma. How many other men wearing those large robes were involved and who were they? Moneyed, of course. Married, probably. But this wasn't an enterprise to confide to even the most discreet valet. Blackmail was a reality. Each man had to be equally culpable for all to be safe. They were each other's best insurance. A cabal.

Edwin borrowed a small cedar canoe from Songhees Joe on the reserve across the bay and paddled up the Gorge that evening, just past nine. Colorful mallards, cormorants, and small black ducks were scudding on the water, and the occasional eerie lament of a loon warbled the stillness. He portaged around the reversing falls, an obstacle to navigation about which the city had been dithering for years. Poking around the tax rolls had given him the property location of Cardinal's castle.

When he glimpsed the turrets in the distance, he nosed the canoe into the first sheltering bushes. Ten unkempt acres, including at least three hundred feet on the waterway. Set far back on a gradual slope, the house's expansive lawn had gone to hay. In its day, it might have been quite the baronial palace.

A large boathouse grayed in aged planks sat on the water, surrounded by weeping cypress and ancient willows trailing their skirts. From there, Edwin crept through the hay cover to the house and observed as he waited for total darkness. Brooding against the sky, it suggested the setting for a sensational novel like *The Monk*. Massive gray stone stretched three storys with turrets on each corner and twenty-foot mullioned windows. The roof was beaten copper, green from rainforest verdigris. Fifteen chimney pots, a day's work for servants before central heating. A crescent moon shattered itself in the lozenge windows. Apparently the home boasted ten bedrooms, three parlors, a music room, conservatory, and a small family chapel. Hedges at the lower level were wild and scraggly, any attempt at topiary long abandoned.

Closer to town, Casa Loma might have attracted thieves, but the property was surrounded by high metal fences and a locked gate, Reggie had said. At the once-proud portcullis entrance was a set of stone steps. The formidable front double doors with the tarnished lion's head knocker could have resisted a battering ram. Cobwebs and dead leaves lined the doorsteps. The massive hinges and locks were covered in rust. Was this a fool's errand, Edwin wondered?

Through what windows he could peep by pulling himself up to the ledge, desultory furniture was shrouded in white sheets. The servants' quarters would be on the uppermost floors, the kitchens in the cellars. Slowly he made his way around the house, keeping to the shadows. The only doors were locked and cobwebbed, presumably servants' and delivery entrances. It took fifteen minutes to circle the massive building. He had lit his police lantern but kept it shrouded.

Then he came to a wing where a smaller addition with clerestory windows twenty feet high gave him more frustration. At the end was a rose window. The chapel. The once holy place would be a perfect site for Clifford's obscene revels, both in spirit and in fixtures. The windows were heavily curtained to forestall noisy neighbors, though it was a hundred yards to adjoining properties. He couldn't reach the window ledges seven feet up. Worst of all, no door. The chapel was entered from within the house. How the deuce could he get in without breaking a window?

An old barn sat two hundred yards off, next to a carriage house. As the shy moon crept behind clouds and hid, Edwin loped over. The barn doors were nailed shut with two-by-fours. At the carriage house, he noted an anomaly: a single wagon track in the packed ground. In or out? He flinched as a flurry of nesting pigeons blasted from a large broken window in the loft. The roof was moss covered and spavined at one end. Its peak was laced with decades of birdlime.

Edwin stood stymied, short on time and patience. What about the boathouse? If the group had come in by water as the boy had suggested . . . Yet surely that would be an inopportune meeting place.

He crept back to the boathouse where huge doors abutted a foot above high tide. A side door gave him a glimmer of hope. Moss on the stone walk had been trampled and then covered with pine duff. His glance returned uphill to the mansion, and his eye caught something. White poles in the ground held ramshackle bird houses. Five. In a straight line every hundred feet right to the chapel area.

An underground tunnel from the boathouse. Smugglers employed such ruses from time immemorial. Perhaps the patriarch Blennerhassett himself. Consumed by the concept, suddenly he heard the sound of a barking dog coming closer. A large beast with an angry baritone. Leaving the lantern, he pulled himself into the embraces of a Garry oak tree. Out of the shadows charged the Hound from Hell, nearly two hundred pounds of Great Dane. It leaped at his hanging leg, ripping fabric with snapping jaws and pearly teeth. Edwin felt something wet and painful on his exposed calf. The dog's eyes blazed with blazing pitch. Edwin pulled his billy club.

The animal was not at fault. And if the dog screamed in distress, its owner would follow. He clawed himself as high as he could. The animal leaped again. This time he got a bootlace and chewed it off. Then came a far-off, two-fingered whistle like the kind Edwin could never master as a kid.

"Dulcinea, Dulcie, where the devil are you? Come on then, my pretty girl." The man started clapping, and with a surly growl, the dog wheeled and disappeared.

Then all was quiet. His heart hammering, Edwin took a couple of deep breaths, and returned to the boathouse side door and its conspicuous padlock. The old sergeant had taught him a few tricks, enough to find an inconspicuous way in. If he didn't find the proof he sought, he'd feel an absolute ass. Worse yet, a killer might go free.

Opening one side of the lantern, and pulling out a set of picks, he started on the elderly lock, which bore traces of fresh oil under the leather cover. Something in this derelict boathouse needed protection. Working more from feel and sound, he thought of his mentor. "Close your eyes like a blind man," he had said. "Gently, gently. Did you never make love in the dark, man? My wife's a shy lass."

Finally the lock snicked free and he slipped inside, closing the door behind him. The boathouse was built over the water, and the timbered moorings inside plashed with the current's rise and fall. Against a side wall were a long table of woodworking and chandler's gear as well as storage cabinetry.

He found his way to the back, following footprints in the dust and making none of his own. A wooden panel stopped any progress, but the lantern flickered as he moved it over the seams. Gingerly, he tried each square inch. Was that a slight give? At last it moved aside on a balance. Beyond was a flight of ten stairs leading to a bricked passageway. On he went, every so often the flame burning brighter under an air duct. At the end, steps led upward.

The carved oak door was unlocked. Moving a velvet curtain, he pushed into the dark church, no doubt ashamed to whisper its deeds. Two rows of pews faced an altar with three silver candelabras of tall black candles. A crystal chandelier dangled from brass chains. The black altar cloth sat beneath reredos of carved ivory with a life-size Christ upside down on the cross. *Got him!* Victorians did not take kindly to these horrors, even if theatrical. Once it would have been a burning offense. Now it would destroy Clifford's family name and those of his conspirators.

He felt transfixed. The stained glass windows were heavily draped in red velvet. One held a gallery of pictures of nudes, including Naomi's portrait of Vicky from a local saloon which had closed five years ago. Overlooking all, the rose window wept bloody tears.

Behind the pews stood dedicated cases with ceremonial paraphernalia. Dainty silken whips, including a velvet cat-o'-nine-tails. Titillation more than torture. An embroidered black banner read *Fais ce que tu veux*. Do what you want. Now he understood the atrocious accent of Appleyard's woman. *Fay suckatoo view.* At the time, even understood, the sentence would have made no sense to him. Playing blasphemous games had effected a murderous price. How did it fit together? How many belonged to this satanic club?

At one side was a baptismal font with an empty champagne bottle. A censer on a staff exuded the smell of pungent incense. Pegs on a side wall lined up familiar brown robes, along with more identical phallic rosaries. Silver chalices and a paten for black communion wafers waited on the altar. On another table was an ornate leatherbound book. Names were inscribed in a fading red ink or . . . perhaps blood. Abbot John, three friars, four sisters. Brothers in crime wealthy enough to afford this kind of liaison. Government official, a judge, perhaps even a clergyman? Aliases part of the game. His heart raced as he picked up *Lives of the Saints*. St. Teresa's page was stuck back in. Her pious hands begged forgiveness while her eyes searched the heavens in ecstasy. Though no loyal Catholic, he would not fail her charge.

At the back he parted curtains hiding three monastic cells, each with bed, dresser, candle, and chamber pot. A copy of *Gargantua and Pantagruel* by Rabelais lay on a bedside table. On the wall framed in gold was a scroll proclaiming holidays based around the ancient pagan calendar celebrating the equinoxes and solstices.

Time to shake the rat's nest.

# CHAPTER TWENTY-NINE

"Gad, old thing. I wish I'd been with you last night." Reggie had been canvassing boat-rental businesses on the Inner Harbor. He crossed his legs in foppish fashion to read his list to Edwin. All had gone well with Clifford. They had been gambling until dawn in Dragon Alley.

Edwin had no patience, with what little sleep he'd gotten after paddling back to Songhees Joe's and returning home. "Let's see where we are. Stevens is in jail for Vicky's death. The coroner's jury ruled Mary's murder 'misadventure.' As for us, the commissioner told McBride to aim all resources at a gang targeting houses of the wealthy by night. They slip in a lad through an open window, and he lets in the thieves. A couple of bankers are mad as hell."

"Sunday or nothing, then." Reggie rubbed his hands together fast enough to kindle a fire. He was thriving on their action.

Edwin's shoulders ached from exertion, and he smelled vaguely of liniment. His calf didn't look septic, but it hurt like blue blazes. "He doesn't own a boat. Are you sure?" The boathouse main door had been nailed shut.

"Said not three times. Lucky he thought I had been drinking. He was beginning to get suspicious when I confessed that Carrie wanted to go for a ride in the moonlight, and could he get a girl and join us?" Reggie flipped to the last page in his notebook. "Now hold on. The last place I went caters to parties who want to go up the Gorge. Picnics and such. The chap says he's taken several cloaked men and young women up to Portage Bay. Lets them off at night and returns just before daybreak. I made it sound like I wanted recommendations." He added details.

"And I don't suppose he gave a name for the inquiring party."

"Money speaks louder than names." He leaned forward and shut the notebook. "Fits the bill for Clifford's height, weight, hair color. A toff, the man said. That diamond-eyed eagle cane. The usual rental is for party of eight. Four couples, I make it, not that he cares."

"Then we'll have to work fast. I've got two men lined up. It's going to be risky. But I couldn't get more without raising suspicions with McBride."

"Capital! What were the odds at Agincourt? It's quality over quantity. Who's in?"

Sergeant Borg had taken a knife meant for Edwin when he was a constable and they had been breaking up a brawl. Constable Croft was thirty-five and lived with his mother and seven Persian cats. His dark blue uniform carried the proof, and he was teased for it. But he was a departmental wrestling champ, fighting above his weight.

Edwin had a theory of how Mary had been recruited to this infamy, and it wasn't pretty. Melodie had said that her uncle often took her to and from the Sunday afternoon meeting of the Girls' Friendly Society. A fine hunting place for Clifford. A missing girl from a poor family would raise no ripples. That she had aspirations clinched the bargain.

Mary's gruesome death was unlikely to be blamed on a sophisticate like Clifford. But no doubt he'd been in charge of the body disposal. To know that a powerful man was in your debt could send many things your way in a thriving town. Contracts, zoning, import laws, a blind eye to a high-class brothel.

What role had Vicky played in this obscene charade? Mother

Superior? He hated to think of her taking advantage of innocent young girls, but some women were willing to take a quick path to wealth, especially when it might be their last chance. Clifford had covered up by fingering the odious Stevens. The discovery of Mary's body with the tell-tale plaid dress hadn't been expected.

Reggie had a cat-licking-cream smirk as a yawn stretched his mouth. "I was up half the night carousing with Clifford to get him to relax his guard. He took me over to his tailor's and I got fitted for a couple of ruffled shirts."

"Playing Scarlet Pimpernel? Acting is easier than police work, my friend. You may be in the wrong profession."

"*Toujours jolie,* dear Rozzer. We all need to use our best talents." Reggie tapped his cigarette in the ashtray.

Edwin aimed a pencil point at him. "You look to the left whenever you tell a lie. Haven't you noticed?"

Reggie turned his gaze to the window. "I looked away because I've been trying to give up the filthy habit. Carrie insisted, but everyone knows that coffin nails sooth the nerves. Ask Jones."

Edwin pulled out a paper with time calculations. "So what about Sunday night? Can we be sure the group will meet?"

"He's not available every third Sunday, I know that much. Today we went to Hudson's Bay and he made a whopping order for champagne magnums and cases of liquors. I was on the other side of the room admiring a Bordeaux, but I heard him say the wharves for delivery. At the boat rental place." Then Reggie began singing, "Cruising down the river."

The cover story was plausible enough to sound true. The four of them would be in a bachelor boating party celebrating Reggie's upcoming wedding. While they were rowing past the mansion on that Sunday night, they'd discover a shore fire threatening the boathouse. What could they do but land and sound the alarm? Even as the law, they needed an excuse to search. Inside, they would head for the chapel. One way in. No way out. Edwin began making rudimentary maps.

# CHAPTER THIRTY

"What in God's name is that shirt all about? Is the circus in town?" Edwin asked Reggie Sunday as they met at the docks on Wharf Street where the rental boat had been secured.

Reggie struck a pose. "It's madras. Dark blue batwing bow tie. As the ad goes, it is the 'coolest.' Only a confident man can wear bowties." Borg made a limp-wristed gesture, which Reggie returned with an Italian salute, doffing his fedora.

"Everyone ready? Batons? Extra cuffs?" Edwin asked as they pushed off. Pistols would have damaged their cover story. What kind of lawmen couldn't handle flabby civilians? The boat fit six and was rowed briskly by four, steered by one, leaving another at the front. The Red Ensign flag with the Union Jack in the corner flying from the stern supplied a patriotic touch.

The boat contained baskets of food and ample wine and spirits, but nobody had imbibed, not even Reggie. Edwin threatened to check his breath. "I say. That is going too far. Have you thought about getting into management?" Reggie whined.

Croft tugged at his oar with so much gusto that they asked the burly man to slack off. "The case may become as famous as the Whelan murder. And here we are on tap for it, lads." On Christmas Eve 1890, a young shop owner in a long white coat and plug hat startled Larry Whelan, a guard at the site of a Roman Catholic cathedral that was under construction. A kerfuffle about the raising of the Fenian flag above the derrick had increased tensions. Tempers remained high about the Irish separatist organization. The shaky guard had shot innocent David Fee in the heart.

The famous "Hanging Judge" Matthew Baillie Begbie had sent the jury back several times about their verdict of "murder, but unpremeditated," which to him seemed "insensible." Manslaughter had been the final "acceptable" judgment.

As they rowed, they sang ribald songs that Reggie had learned punting on the Cam. "The Gelding of the Devil," and then "Oyster Nan."

> *As Oyster Nan stood by her Tub,*
> *To show her vicious Inclination;*
> *She gave her noblest Parts a Scrub,*
> *And sigh'd for want of Copulation*

A fine party they made, rowing up the tidal inlet, waving their boaters like carefree buffoons on a spree. Tardy picnickers and late evening strollers hallooed back. A girl on a bicycle rang her bell. A retriever chased a stick into the shallows and roused a mallard into flight.

"I've got a knee-slapper, boys," said Reggie. "A randy old man from Drumrig," he began.

Borg continued, "Met a widow he wanted to . . ." And so it went.

After circumventing the falls, they passed under a bridge as the last of the small lots disappeared and larger tracts emerged at the edge of town. Then they glided under the Four Mile House bridge and around the bend to their destination. Edward remembered the tasty beef he'd enjoyed there. Today's preparations had left time for only cheddar and bread.

Near dark they swept silently into the huge inlet of Portage Bay. Through the trees up the gradual incline Casa Loma waited. Few people came this far, and the area was free of traffic. They pulled up under the shelter of a sweeping willow tree which had spread its branches in front of the boathouse. Croft crept ashore and kindled a small fire of dead leaves and twigs at the side of the building as the evening breeze rose. They communicated with a sequence of innocuous whistles. Borg had taught them the Peabody call of the white-throated sparrow.

Croft was fanning the blaze, piling on dry cedar duff to create smudge to alert the neighbors. On such a clandestine mission, they needed an "excuse" to inspect the property if a building were in danger from "rascally lads." It would make sense to go down the tunnel to sound a warning to the house. Flames from the dry grass in the rising night wind could move like lightning.

"Peabody. Peabody." The game was on.

When Edwin reached the old boathouse door, the lock hung loose on its hasp, an excellent omen. Clifford and his crew were getting careless. They should have waited before daring to meet again. But an addiction could not be denied. The men crept forward with their shielded lanterns. "Leave your hats. Too distracting," Edwin said.

Edwin pushed aside the panel. Croft stayed behind blocking the stairs, his billy drawn. "I say, that is clever," he whispered as they peered down the long corridor. Sconces held lit torches along the airshaft.

When they got to the end, they waited, relying on hand signals. From inside came the sound of social merriment. Solemn chants were intermingled with riotous laughter, popping of corks and clinking of glasses. Edwin flipped open his timepiece. It was his father's solid gold Elgin with a sailing ship on the back but cleaned of the specks of blood from that terrible day.

Two a.m. seemed like a good witching hour. The boatman had told Reggie that he usually returned for the party just before dawn. Liquor would be down to the lees. Catching them in flagrante would double their confusion. Nothing is more help-less than a man with his pants off. Conversation ebbed, even with a few giggles and the odd roar. Then all was quiet except for the ticking of each officer's timepiece.

"They've gone to the rooms," Edwin said. "Remember the diagram. The chapel is blocked off from the house. Croft is waiting at the other end of this tunnel. There's no way out for them."

Reggie grinned in the flickering shadows, his lantern turning his cherubic face diabolic. "Like shooting fish in a barrel."

Borg said, "Back East we had these lamprey eels—"

Edwin shoved a hand at him. "Quiet. We need another hour to be safe."

"Dammit. Sorry, fellows. I have to drain the old potato," said Reggie. Edwin didn't doubt that he'd had a few drinks from his flask when his back was turned.

Reggie tiptoed down the corridor and turned to the wall, with a sigh and a splash at his feet. No sense of timing, thought Edwin. It would serve him right to piss on his oxblood lace-up needle toes.

"It's been awfully quiet up there," Reggie said at one minute to two. "Almost like they're gone."

"Passed out, I'd say. But someone will wake up to meet the boat at the dock."

What about the ladies? Their reaction could range from faint-ing helpfully or scratching like cougars. Edwin had raided his mother's closet for soft silk cords to tie their hands.

"I plan to tickle a couple of beauties in the course of duty. This may be my last hurrah before the tying the knot." Reggie shifted. "Curses. My foot's asleep."

Borg snickered. "Take care that you don't grab a poxy one, lad. Your new wife won't thank you if she has to take the mercury cure."

"You know something about that, Borg?" Reggie asked, rubbing his foot back to life.

Edwin growled softly and did a knee bend. His leg was cramping from tension. "You brainless bucks. Stop butting antlers." He took a last look at the time from under the glow of the torch. "Let's go."

# CHAPTER THIRTY-ONE

Having tried the door earlier, Edwin knew that it didn't squeak. Slowly the crack widened until he could see inside the dim chapel. Behind him, the other two pressed forward, one hand on the shoulder before him. The altar candles were guttering. Each of the three rooms had a curtain drawn and bore a faint flickering light. A fat man slept in the first pew, bullet-shaped bald head on an altar cushion as his chins wobbled. A whale of a catch. McBride's older brother, Malcolm. He wouldn't be any trouble. Unless he had come armed. How many times had he shoved his bulk around the department bragging about his carriage business, showing a wicked set of brass knuckles confiscated from a Lascar by his grandfather?

Edwin motioned to Borg. "Cuff him first. He'll be in a stupor." A soft snoring came from the man and only partially covered by his monastic robe, he shuffled pudgy legs in his sleep. Red wine had spilled down his white shirt front. The smell of frankincense wafted over along with cheap perfume, hair oil, and the gamy odor of sex.

Gently Borg maneuvered Malcolm's hands in front of him. The tenor of his wheeze changed, but he was out like a cooperative baby. Then they crept to the rooms. Hearing the erotic joys of the others was likely part of the enjoyment.

"He's helpless. There's one for each of us now. Take the men first," Edwin whispered. He'd wedged a chair under the door to the tunnel. The interior door to the house was blocked by a massive carved oak cabinet.

Edwin was behind Borg as he entered the first room, where a couple lay asleep. It looked like Alderman Grey. The girl nestled at the side of the bed, her arms around an expensive doll whose eyes opened in ironic surprise. Scarcely fifteen, she seemed unconscious. Another innocent from the streets. Her thin arm in the brown habit made Edwin swallow the flames of ire. He felt a faint pulse and smelled alcohol. Perhaps mixed with laudanum to help her forget the abuse. He took one hand of the man's and secured it to the iron bedstead. "Dear chick. Come to papa," Grey muttered, rolling over. Then he blinked his eyes open and sat up. The girl still didn't move.

"Hey, what the—" Borg slapped a hand over his mouth and gave him a light tap with the billy.

"Nighty night," Borg whispered, blowing on the end of the club.

In the second room, Reggie pulled a man by his collar but he wouldn't waken. The woman was over thirty, her arms like pipe stems. "Get up, you," Reggie said. Before they could stop her, the woman gave a strangled cry.

Edwin headed for the last cell, next to the outside wall. He and Reggie looked at each other. "Clifford," their lips said without sound. Then McBride began thrashing and kicked over a lantern. While Reggie and Borg scuttled to beat out the spreading flames, Edwin pushed toward the last curtain.

On a plush bed with velvet covers, a woman huddled in a corner, a silk quilt around her shoulders. The window was open. Edwin looked out with a curse. A form in a white nightgown and boots was bounding across the grass, disappearing in the blackness under the trees.

Edwin launched himself outside, eye on the man. With luck, he'd catch the tricky bastard in minutes. He didn't notice the ten-foot drop, but his ankle did. He fell with a thump into a boxwood bush, flailing in pain. In the distance he heard a dog howling. There was a whinny, and then the muffled clops of hooves. So Clifford hadn't come with the group. Of course he had an escape route.

Borg came to the window. "I can still catch him. Let me drop down."

"He's on a horse. It's no use. Get one of those curtain ropes and haul me back up." Edwin rubbed at his boot as he gritted his teeth. The ankle wasn't broken, but it was as bad a sprain as he'd ever had. He retched up bile from pain.

Inside, all the candles had been lit. Three women and three men sat in the pews, their faces a mixture of shame and cold fury. The youngest girl was beginning to come around, moaning for her mother. The next older had an arm around her, sharing a blanket. The oldest bit her lip and pushed back a long strand of mousy blonde hair, her face frozen with a world-weary expression.

"DesRosiers, you stupid b-b-bastard. Do you know what you're doing?" Malcolm said, moving next to him. His breath was as foul as the grave. "My b-b-brother will see that you're off the force. All we're doing here is having a b-b-bit of fun."

"I'd advise you to say nothing more. This will all be taken before the judge in the morning. The girl is underage, for one."

His porcine eyes narrowed, but Edwin detected a tremor in his jaw. "You didn't find *me* with a girl. These trollops came here of their own free will. You're on private property. How dare you trespass?"

Alderman Grey said, "Shut up, you ass. We'll have our solicitors on this soon enough."

The last, a prominent banker named Chatters, sat with his head in his hands, whispering, "My wife. Dear God."

Edwin spoke evenly. "I don't give a damn if you tup sheep in your spare time. We know that this site and the abominations

which happen here are connected to at least two deaths."
McBride's stuttering reminded him of what little Ben Conrad
had heard.

Croft had joined them, shutting the door. His disgusted gaze
took in the hellish museum, walking to the altar and shaking his
head. Croft was a Bible Christian and disliked the high-church
trappings.

Reggie said, "We must get to Clifford's rooms."

"That can be done faster from the department. I doubt he's
gone back there anyway, except to pack." He turned to Croft.
"Get to the next property and find the first available telephone.
Have them send half a dozen constables, Eliza or another
matron from Hillside, and a couple of wagons. Send three
armed men to the Driard. This place will have to be under
guard until this room is sorted out. There may be critical
evidence about the two dead women. And if you can arrange
for horses for Reggie and me, do it."

If Clifford had one badger hole, he had another. Staying on
the island would be impossible. His money could take him a
long way.

The older woman stepped forward. She had dressed in a long
woolen cloak against the chill. "I'm Susie Baker. I've no stomach
to spend any time in a prison. I'll tell you everything if you
make it worth my while in court. So will the other two . . .
ladies." She shot them both stern glances. "If they know what's
good for them."

The youngest, her hair braided like a schoolgirl, had tears in
runnels down her powdered face. "But, this was my first night. I
don't know nuffink."

Susie confirmed that. "I took over from Vicky. Betty here is
new, like she said. Bonnie's only been to the last two nights. We
didn't meet for weeks when things were hot."

Edwin gave her a long, hard look. It would be the only route to the bottom of this ugly business. "Spill what you know." He took her into one of the rooms so that the rest wouldn't hear her story.

She sat on the bed and kept her voice low. The candlelight revealed that she once had been a handsome woman before a thickening of age. Her flowing chestnut hair was her glory. Clifford had discarded her for the younger girl.

"Clifford and I had our jollies. Then he brought in his friends, so we needed more girls. He met Vicky at the theater and brought her in. Mary was an 'accident' in his words. I wouldn't call it that. McBride's as cruel and unnatural as he is a fat turd." A shudder ran over her, and she sobbed. Edwin gave her his handkerchief.

He touched her shoulder gently. "She bled to death, did she?"

"In that room over there." She pointed to the middle curtain. "I cleaned it myself. Like a charnel house it was."

"How did her body get to Langford Lake?"

"There's an old coach house with a wagon. Clifford took her under a load of moldy hay from the barn. I expect he might have set the wagon afire somewhere to get rid of the blood."

Croft spoke up. "That wasn't far from the Six Mile House. Thought it was some lads up to no good calling out the fire department. Came close to spreading to dry fields."

"And what was . . . Vicky's part?"

"She was our abbess, did the organizing. Fair liked it in the beginning with the money flowing and the play acting. It was a lark until . . ."

"Go on," Edwin said. He wanted to know the timing.

"If a woman agrees, she knows what she's in for and takes money twice as fast. But Vicky wouldn't stand for using under-age girls. And that's what the men wanted. Younger and younger. They paid premium for virgins. When Mary died, McBride was pie-eyed and randy as a cock. Just couldn't get it up. She was dead out when he took the bat to her."

His stomach turned. "Vicky saw that?"

"Never. She was down with the flu that night, or she'd have stopped him."

"So Vicky didn't know."

"Not until later. Cardinal claimed that Mary quit. I told her the truth. That's what started the fight at his rooms. He strangled her there. Then he took her down the back way with McBride. They left her over on Belleville Street at night. Like she'd been walking the streets. What could I do about it? He would have killed me soon as look at me."

"And this?" Edwin pulled the marble from his pocket where it had now become a talisman.

"That silly game. I have a feeling Vicky nipped it to spite him." As they returned to the chapel, she looked at Edwin as if she still didn't trust him. "What's going to happen to the girls, to me?"

"That depends on how honest you are. If they weren't a party to the deaths, they have little to fear for the long term."

"I would have murdered him myself for the poor chicks he's ruined." She pointed at the other two. "Betty's been around the block. But Bonnie doesn't even have her monthlies yet. Pa ran her off unless she came across. Easy pickings."

"You all knew what you were in for," Edwin said. The shadows and thin tracings around her eyes reminded him of Vicky.

"Try being born a girl into a poor family and see how far you get. It's a man's world and no mistake."

"You'll be taken to the station and then sent to Hillside Jail until it's determined if bail can be set. But given your status as a material witness, don't count on it. You're safe there anyway. Conditions are better for women."

"Aye, I've seen those cold walls before."

Reggie returned with two requisitioned horses outside from the neighbor's stable. The man ran dry goods stores in Victoria and Sidney. "You should have seen him, Edwin. What a sporting chap. He was chuffed to help the police. Say, there are advantages."

An hour and a half later, they found Clifford's rooms on the Driard's top floor. The door was open, and two constables stood outside. "Not a sign of the wretch," one said.

"I figured as such," Edwin said. "Let's see what we can find."

They proceeded through an anteroom and then pulled aside a double door to the sitting room. A small breakfast nook adjoined a butler's pantry. Little if any cooking would be done here, only tea made from a gas jet. A hall led past a bathroom and bedrooms. This was one of the hotel's best suites, second only to the Royal. Plush Turkey carpets, French Empire furniture with torchères, wainscoting and flocked wallpaper. A warbling raven in a gilded cage added a bizarre touch. Edwin set it free and watched it fly toward the new Parliament buildings. Ravens were lucky birds, not intended to be captives.

The master bedroom had a gigantic bed with walnut furniture and erotic East Indian pictures on the wall. "Wonder where the dog is?" said Edwin.

"He boards it in a kennel across town. Only uses poor old King to hunt," Reggie said, turning his head around to figure out one copulative position. "Look at those gymnastics."

One bedroom functioned as a dressing room. Rows of suits and coats lined one wall. In the corner were pieces of matched leather luggage with a gap of two. In a desk drawer, Edwin recognized the same blue notepaper that had accused Stevens.

"Men like that have a thousand snake holes and cash in a hundred banks. He may even have hopped a boat to San Francisco. He could take the train to Nanaimo and cross to the mainland. We'll put a man at the stations downtown," Edwin said.

"Find out which boats are leaving and send telegrams to the destinations. He can be caught landing at the docks. If he's smart, he headed to Anchorage. I know I would be." Then Reggie held up a warning finger. "Timing could be a problem, old bean. The town will be crowded, what with the Queen's birthday today, so Monday and Tuesday for the parades and the water festival. Everybody on the peninsula will be here, and likely a few Yanks. I was going to take Carrie before we—"

"McBride will have to recuse himself for his brother's investigation. Chatters and Grey will get their lawyers out of bed. Grey is finished in this town for being with the underage girl. I hope McBride swings." Edwin yawned. "I need a few hours of sleep before getting to the office."

"I'm staying up to celebrate. A couple of sherry flips and I'll be fine. You're getting old. When she hears about this, Carrie will have me running to buy her ices every hour tomorrow."

By early afternoon on Monday, information from the docks revealed that a man with Clifford's name and description had taken a private room on the steamer *Patrick*, bound for Los Angeles. "We've got him," the commissioner said to Edwin, bringing the news. "The American police will nab him for extradition."

Edwin gave it some thought. "Why give his own name? That's plain stupid."

"All the better for us. If you haven't heard, McBride has taken an early retirement. Wise path. Brush will move up the ladder." The commissioner clapped Edwin on the back. "You've earned a day off tomorrow. Your methods were a tad unorthodox, but results count. You still have time for some of the fun. Parties on every other block, and naval celebrations and games in Esquimalt. Have you got a girl?"

"Yes, Sir!" Edwin said, unable to suppress a grin. Across the room, Reggie had barely managed to hide the ice pack for his head. When their boss left, he replaced it and closed his eyes as he leaned back in his chair.

The *Daily Colonist* was on his desk and Edwin ran a finger down the festivities he hadn't attended since he was a boy. Then he rang Emily. As her unmistakable voice answered, he nearly froze, but delivered his invitation. "I'm sorry for the short notice, and I understand if you have plans," he said. "Would you be free to spend the day tomorrow at the celebrations?"

"I'd love to. May I bring anything? We've had a picnic today and there's plenty to—"

"I wouldn't hear of it," he said, looking at the paper. "I'll drop by Ross's." The front-page ad was giving him an appetite. Saratoga chips, potted meats, oranges, biscuits, cakes, Brie cheese. "I'm as good a provisioner as any woman."

Later that evening, Edwin sat smoking one of Naomi's aromatic cigarettes on the back porch, parsing the case. When would that steamer land? What if Clifford got off the boat before it docked? Maybe he was a champion swimmer. If only they had put a man outside. He flexed his ankle. Still swollen. Naomi had wrapped it tightly after a soak in Epsom salts.

Should he get champagne to show Emily how special she was? Where was that weasel from the tennis party? Frozen to death in Alaska, he hoped. If that cad had done something to make her unhappy . . . Perhaps Carrie knew her. Girls confided in each other. He daren't ask. It was all so problematical.

# Chapter Thirty-Two

Edwin was on a dangerous side of giddy Tuesday morning. Wong had instructions to clean and spruce his best outfit. An entire day with Emily. A consummation devoutly to be wished. After bathing, he put in a fresh blade and shaved, then slapped on the lightest tap of Florida Water. Brushing and rebrushing his hair left him unsatisfied. A dab of Brylcreem showed that double cowlick who was boss. Thank God he'd had a trim that week. Bumpkins with bowl-cut hair were hardly Emily's equal.

He sat reading the paper with his toast and chunky marmalade. The important regattas had occurred yesterday. Mayor Beaven had commandeered a barge for friends and associates. Private receptions with strawberries and cream along the Gorge at private homes had made a gala celebration, even if the sun had not graced the festivities. The James Bay Athletic Association held an "at home." The rich and middle class rubbed elbows with the trades, and the poor found a few hours of joy. Pickpockets lurked at the edges, despite the extra officers in high-traffic areas.

The Royal Navy "bluejacket" crews from the HMS *Royal Arthur* and HMS *Satellite* raced their heavy ships' boats on a two-and-a-half mile course around Deadman's Island. Several ten-oared cutters ran fouls from the congestion on the water. Then came the twelve-oared competitors and the fourteen. Edwin's favorites were the single sculls. Wouldn't it be fine to know Emily was watching him race? Maybe next year.

The Indians joined the tribute to the Great White Mother. The Cowichan teams excelled, and a prize of five silver dollars was awarded for each blade on the forty-foot canoe race. The Fifth Regiment supplied the latest music, improvising during a tandem race by playing "Down Went McGinty" as a canoeist was dunked.

No one would miss the upcoming star event, a sham battle. The Royal Navy was Victoria's pride. It anchored the province to the nation.

The grandfather clock chimed ten. Up early, Naomi was reading a novel downstairs. Wong had the house back to normal and even Gladdy had lost a few ounces. The usual gang was invited to a gala midweek soiree that night. Edwin hoped that he'd be home very late, but he supposed that such liberties wouldn't agree with Edie Carr.

"Exciting novel, Mother?" Edwin said as he gave his paisley ascot a final pluck in the hall mirror. He was wearing white flannels and a new cotton sweater from Geo R Jackson. "*The Woman Who Did*. What did she do?"

His mother waved her hand. "What she pleased! Every woman doesn't have to get married to be fulfilled. They can *do* just like men. Will I live to see the vote? It's already arrived in New Zealand, and they're such provincials. Your father would have been marching with Mrs. Pankhurst."

"Conservative parents have liberal children. And vice versa." Edwin sighed, determined not to get embroiled. "I won't let you down when the time comes. In fact, I will come and smash your chains with a sledgehammer."

She got up and gave him a hug. "This movement will free men, too. You'll see."

"I'd gladly be a slave for the right woman." He held out his mock-manacled wrists.

Wong came in with the picnic basket. Naomi peeked under

the snowy linen cloth. "How many people are you feeding? Are you taking a cab downtown? What's this all about?"

"I'm going over to Emily's."

"Emily who? That Carr girl you mentioned once?" Her tones were exaggerated, rising at the end. "Do you want to smell like a sweaty donkey by the time you meet? Not to mention a piker when her comfort is concerned."

"She likes to walk. And bicycle. Last year she and her friends took the train to Duncan and rode their wheels ten miles on coach roads. They stayed overnight at the Cowichan Inn. She has plans to go to Ucluelet to draw and paint."

Her face bloomed at the thought. "She sounds independent. Like an Amazon. I like that. But what about your ankle?"

"I've got a tight wrap on it. And Emily's no Amazon. She comes up to here." He raised his hand to his shoulder. "Perfect for her size."

One talented eyebrow raised half-arch said a thousand words. "I'll give you the once-over, Mr. Perfect. Your father would have."

She got up and put a hand on each of his shoulders, looking one way and then the other with a coy smile at the corner of her expressive mouth. "Everything looks operational. Good work on that stubborn hair. That's a new sweater? I trust I am to meet your paragon *some* fine day."

He ran a finger around his collar against the tightness of the moment. She'd never let up on the teasing. "We're only new friends. I'd feel . . . strange being so formal. Meeting the family is tantamount to a proposal."

His mother's trill followed him out the door. Women who *did*. Things were changing so fast. Only four years to the new century. Canada hadn't even been a country when the last one turned.

Taking Naomi's advice, Edwin hailed a cab and went the

back way to Carr Street, over to Cook and south as the driver suggested. Roads were jammed as crowds gravitated toward the waterfront. A stroll in nearby Beacon Hill Park, then lunch. After that, they would be hard pressed to elbow across the Point Ellice Bridge to Esquimalt for the mock battle. Hours lay ahead. What would they talk about? Certainly not his job. He could look into her eyes forever in silence.

He caught his breath to see Emily standing by her gate, a fresh red rose in her shiny brown hair with an attractive 'do that complemented her heart-shaped face. She pinned a pink rose into his buttonhole as his cheeks flamed. Naomi had said that flowers had messages. Why a different color for him? Reggie's favorite saying about "the face that launched a thousand ships" took on new meaning. Maybe he could borrow a poetry book and learn a few crackerjack lines. What scribblers did she like? Was literature appreciation different for a woman? "That's a lovely outfit," he said, lost for words.

"It's a bicycle suit," she said, twirling. "Five pieces, plus leggings and cap." The blue water-repellent cloth was edged in leather. "I'd prefer a divided skirt, but Edie won't go that far."

From behind a hedge she pulled two bicycles. Edwin paid the cab fare and added a generous tip. His chest expanded in pride and anticipation.

"Yukon models," she said. "One's my brother's." The boy's model was black with forward dropped handlebars and the other ivory with a mud guard. Each had a capacious woven-willow basket on the handle bars. "The lunch can go here," she said.

What a good idea. He'd hardly wanted to be toting their food over his arm all day like a marketing woman. But he looked down at his creamy flannels. Emily's mirth was obvious, and so was her preparation. "Your costume is fine," she said, pulling an apparatus from her pocket. "These clips will keep your pants safe from the chain." He swallowed as she fussed with him. "Say, is your ankle all right? You seem to be favoring it."

"A work injury. It's practically . . . perfect." Especially with your magic fingers. He couldn't resist dropping a few points about the raid, but skipped the salacious parts. "We expect to make an arrest when Cardinal reaches his destination."

"It sounds ever so exciting, Edwin. I'm glad women can be safe again. But those innocent girls. And poor Melodie. What must she think? We don't get to choose our relatives."

On her lapel, a gold pin of a deer winked a ruby eye at him. "Beacon Hill is our best bet. It's going to be madness in town."

Could she read his mind? "That's what I thought."

They transferred the lunch and set off. Edwin hadn't ridden anything since his rusty wheel fifteen years ago. Richard's was lighter and had a hygienic seat instead of the uncomfortable racing style.

The park abutted the Carr property. Soon they were skimming across gravel paths, dodging the occasional duckling. The park had been named for two beacons used by navigators to avoid the treacherous Brotchie's Ledge out in the channel. In the 1850s the land had been set aside with amazing foresight and became Victoria's own in 1882. Recently a lake and stone bridge had been added with formal garden, Garry oaks, and winding pathways. The April bluebells heralded a rainbow of colors leading into fall chrysanthemums and hydrangeas.

After making the tour, avoiding children running about with hoops and balls, then gazing across the strait at Washington State, they settled under a huge tree and spread their picnic. Emily had packed a cheerful checked cloth with matching serviettes. She picked a multicolored chestnut bloom for a centerpiece.

"Is cider all right?" he asked. The store had been sold out of bubbly. Would she think him cheap?

"Our island's own champagne," Emily said. "Neither would it do to get tipsy when Edie's at the gate." She arranged the feast with an artist's touch. "You must have emptied the shelves! Medjool dates, too. My favorite. And sugared walnuts."

So far so good. He gave her a warm smile. What could they talk about next? He couldn't recall the last time he read a novel. She'd probably enjoy *The Woman Who Did*. Then again, those ideas were a bit forward.

Two horses and riders clopped past, posting in their trot. "I don't ride much, but when I do, I prefer to gallop and feel the wind in my hair," she said.

"I have a horse. Peggy, I mean Pegasus, is stabled up on North Park." Why did he say Peggy? It sounded silly for a man's mount. "Did you see any of the festivities yesterday?" he asked, to change the subject.

"Actually not. My sister was sick and I had to babysit," Emily said. "That's why I'm glad you invited me. I missed the Indian canoe races. They're always so colorful and exciting. Sometimes I go to Songhees and paint *en plein air*. The outdoors is my favorite studio."

He listened to each word, drinking in her beauty. "My mother paints, too, but you might not approve the subject."

"Reggie told me about her work. It's not easy being a woman artist. I admire her for sticking to it. Like Mary Cassett. Too many jolly babies for my taste, but she'll be famous someday." Emily speared an errant curl and pinned it back.

He cleared his throat. "And your sister. She's fine, I trust?"

"Only a megrim. Runs in the family."

Emily pointed out the resident peacock. It strutted its stuff, flashing its tail, then gave an ear-piercing shriek. "He was a very sad bird. Oh, not this one, of course. But his great, great grand-father. It's a risky life but better than being behind bars. How awful that he has no mate."

When the food was tucked away, they sat against a massive cypress and compared notes about the puffy cumulous clouds. Emily saw a galleon. Edwin found a rabbit eating a carrot. The childishness of the age-old game contrasted with his horrors of the recent weeks. "What about those new moving pictures? They had their first performance in New York City this year. It all started in France. Of course, what doesn't?" she said.

"They've come a long way since the Leonard-Cushing match in New York when everyone had to look through his own Kinetoscope." He didn't mention that a San Francisco operator of the scene-flipping machine had been arrested two years ago for showing pictures "alleged to be indecent."

"There's piano accompaniment, too," Emily said. "I can't wait until they come to Victoria. Edie predicts that they will never replace the thrill of the stage."

Emily looked at her chatelaine watch. Was she bored with him? Had she remembered something? A supper appointment? Reggie was right about ladies driving men crazy. You never knew what they were thinking. If so, perhaps they were the superior sex, as Naomi implied.

"They say that the sham battle will be the best ever," she said. "If we leave now, we'll have time to get over the bridge and up the hills for a good view of Macauley Point. They used to hold military maneuvers here in the park, but a naval battle is much more exciting."

"Splendid idea. Shall we go?" Inside he breathed a sigh of relief. All was unfolding so naturally.

They pedaled back to Carr Street, then up Government. An exponential number of people had finished lunch and were converging in the harbor area. As they clattered across the old James Bay Bridge, they stopped to look east toward St. Joseph's Hospital. The putrid bay carried a rainbow of effluent on its mud flats. To his surprise, Emily looked nostalgic. "Once this was a beautiful spot where the Indian canoes slipped through the marsh grass. Then came Pendray's Soap Works, Kanaka Row's refuse. How I long for those days. Why can't they fill in the bay and build a palace looking out to sea? Like Kubla Khan did in Xanadu."

"You have an amazing imagination, Miss, I mean Emily. That's why you're an artist instead of a police officer." They could barely breathe, and she was imagining the home of an empress. Naomi would like her.

In the crowded bustle, they had to walk their wheels. Tomorrow everyone would return to work. A banner year to have an extra day's holiday because of the Sunday.

As they passed Johnson Street into Chinatown with the colorful lanterns and red and gold banners, Edwin thought of Wong and his fortunate escape. He was spending the day with Lun, who was back in his rooms. Then it was Cormorant, Fisgard, and Herald. No cab could have navigated this crowd.

When they hit Pembroke, Emily said, "Let's cut over to the Rock Bay Bridge. I love that old fossil, even if it creaks with age. I sketched it last year standing across the bay." They passed the gas works and reached the Store Street intersection.

"I saw the painting in your home. A perfect likeness," Edwin said, as they braked to avoid a dog cart. The big Newfie was pulling a boy and small beer barrels. Saloons would be doubling their orders. A streetcar operated by the Consolidated Railway & Light Company passed as they crossed, and they stepped aside. Why had he said "likeness"? Maybe she didn't favor the representational style.

"I stuffed myself at lunch, but we must be burning off pounds," Emily said.

Edwin nodded, but alert from instinct, he didn't like the groaning sounds of the bridge as the car clanked by. It was fully loaded with about sixty people, and reminded him of a sow covered in squirming piglets.

As they turned onto Work Street, the crowds jostled for position. More people jumped on the trolley as hands reached out to hold them, adding to the hilarity.

"Look how crowded the trams are," Emily said, touching his arm. "Every standing place is taken, even on the platform. They're hanging onto the sides. I've seen them go off the tracks when the lads put rocks in the way. The cars are so light."

Number 16 came lurching along, only minutes behind its brother. "They're on the roof, the idiots. What's the matter with that conductor?" Edwin said, frowning. But what was he supposed to do? Stop the car and haul the extras off? Why not just start a riot?

Smells of roasting meats from vending carts filled the air, along with ladies' perfumes and the cigar and pipe smoke of their escorts. Children were playing tag and shouting, while the youngest were rolled along by parents or older siblings. Emily admired a double pram with twins. "Twins didn't run in our family. Can you image double the diapers?"

Edwin cleared his throat at the image. As an only child forced to grow up quickly, imagining Gladdy's needs was all he could manage. In the distance he saw the mansion of Point Ellice House on Pleasant Street north of the bridge. Prime Minister John A. Macdonald had been entertained there by Peter O'Reilly and his family. The mansion grounds included acres of gardens, a lawn tennis court, and a croquet pitch as well as barns and smaller outbuildings sloping down to the boathouse.

"Will we make it?" he asked Emily.

"About a quarter to two. We have plenty of time." They looked at the car, swaying like the galleon in the clouds. Sounds of laughter and singing grew louder as the people surged across the bridge. It was still some distance to the vantage points. Emily had raised a cautious eyebrow, a touch of fear in her merry eyes. "Maybe we should wait until that car gets over. I'm afraid it will tip on us."

Continuing on, they passed Bridge Street, then Turner and Pleasant, stopping at the juncture with the Point Ellice Bridge. The first span had opened in 1861, linking Victoria and Esquimalt. This updated version was eleven years old and had run the streetcars since 1891 when the west line went in.

Preoccupied with the car and their safety as well as his throbbing ankle, Edwin was only half focusing. In front of him, a man wheeled as someone bumped him. "Take care, you fool," the familiar voice growled. His face was clean-shaven, but despite his shabby clothes, there was no mistaking the eagle cane.

Edwin stopped in his tracks, his front tire nudging Emily's. "It's so jammed," she said. "Why don't we wait over by that lamppost until the worst of the crowd clears the bridge? Or get a cup of tea. I could use the ladies room."

"Stay here!" he said, gripping her shoulders for emphasis as the bikes leaned against the railings. "Don't follow me. That's Clifford. I must get him."

The overburdened street car was entering the bridge behind carriages and walkers, some arm in arm. Clifford wormed forward, shoving his elbows like oars, but he couldn't penetrate the crowds. As his feet left the street for the wooden spans, Edwin was closing in. Clifford pushed aside a clump of pedestrians and reached out for the handrail. Shoved from behind, Edwin fell to his knees.

"Clifford, you bastard!" Edwin yelled. "You'll never get off the island."

As the car reached the center of the bridge, a terrible groan emerged from the whipple trusses in the middle of the six-hundred-foot span. The flooring rose like the blades of a jack-knife. The car shuddered and began to turn on its side. Unaware of the chaos in pursuit, the earlier car reached safety on the western end. Behind it, a carriage and a bicyclist splashed into the dark water. Number 16 broke through the last timbers and plunged toward the bottom of the harbor. Horses screamed in their traces and people cried in terror. Pandemonium broke out as two sections of bridgework collapsed onto the stricken car.

# CHAPTER THIRTY-THREE

Horrified at the carnage, Edwin watched Clifford bobbing in the roiling current, swimming clear of the wreckage. Was there no end to the man's luck? Nearby him a young boy struggled. From the shore a woman yelled, "My son Philip! Save him, somebody!"

Treading water, Clifford glanced at Edwin, turned to the boy, and put his arm under his head. Another man tossed a rope loop. Clifford secured it around the boy's shoulders and pushed him to safety. Then with the high tide running, a huge log rushed down the channel like a battering ram. It struck Clifford's head with a pulpy sound, and he disappeared under a pink spume. Edwin waded in to pull a woman to safety. Swept by the torrent, Clifford floated down channel, turning and turning in the frothy waves.

The juggernaut of destruction wavered between panic and despair as people struggled to conceive the wreckage. Edwin imagined at least a hundred in and on the car. Not long ago, an investigation had been undertaken into the safety of the bridge. What had ever become of that?

Edwin joined the other men and a few women trying to reach those who flailed above the water. Below in the chaos of wood and iron few could survive, even with bubbles still emerging. The racing water of the high tide was compounding the confusion. He stripped off his sweater and jumped in, paddling toward the strugglers, grateful for the clips securing his trousers. People along the Gorge, from the Grants on up, were setting out from their boathouses in small punts, sailboats, even rafts. Men assisting in the docking of the schooner *Penelope* were among the first to arrive. Wails and keening filled the air in a symphony of horror.

"I knew it. I knew it," one man said. "The cursed bridge has been creaking all day. It was just a matter of time. Oh my sweet Jesus. The humanity."

"Is there a doctor? Fetch some brandy!" a woman called. "Sheets for bandages!" A dog ran past with a turkey leg in its mouth. Toddlers, unsure if this was part of the theatrics, were giggling as their parents clutched them to their breasts.

The horses pulling the unlucky carriage in front of the trolley struggled in the shallows, their animal cries rending the heart. In their panic, the poor beasts would flounder until they drowned or someone cut the traces. Chances are they had broken legs or fatal chest wounds from the splintered wood.

Those on the spans still standing froze in fear. Dubiously safe where they were, they watched with terrified eyes. A huge Indian canoe paddled by two men was first across from the Songhees.

Of the victims outside the car, some had jumped to safety, only to be hit by murderous debris. Those inside were under the roiling surface, water pouring in the open windows, and heavy beams crushing them. Except for the fallen sections in the middle, the rest of the bridge held.

Edwin swam after another man with a bleeding temple, pulling him to the shore. Then he went back again and again until he lost count. A young woman stepped out of her heavy skirts and plunged in to bring two children to safety. On his knees, a clergyman clasped his hands in prayer over a still female form while a man sobbed at her side, one fist pounding the ground.

From the watery tomb, the bubbles had ceased their pleas. Had it been but twenty minutes? It seemed a century.

Finally Edwin crawled onto the grass, exhausted, coughing up the polluted water he'd swallowed. Emily hurried over, her face a mask of concern. "Drink this," she said, handing him an open bottle. "The women went to the nearest saloon and brought back whiskey. Others fetched blankets. There wasn't much else we could do. The fire brigade's on its way. Perhaps they can pull some of the timbers. But for most it will be too late. God have mercy on their souls."

Edwin drank deeply, wiping his mouth, uncaring of the dribbles down his undershirt. He was almost too cold to speak and weak from shock. The liquor would warm him, but he needed his senses.

"A day that will never be forgot. Victoria has lost so many." She seemed to recollect something. "Before the collapse, what did you say to me? Do you realize that you could have been—"

"Clifford Cardinal. The man I've been after. He killed Victoria Crosse and had a . . . hand in Mary's disappearance."

"I was watching. He stopped his escape to save that boy." She pointed to the binoculars hanging from her neck. "His face was . . . a pulp. No one could survive that."

Screams had turned to moans and steady weeping, except when a fresh tragedy shrieked announcement. Every few minutes, a relative summoned from elsewhere in the city rushed to the waterfront.

A passing elderly woman spoke in quivery tones to Emily. "Word's going out to telephone Mayor Beaven at McCauley Point. Those with loved ones in distress will want to know as soon as possible."

"Captain Grant brought all the men at his gathering. The . . . bodies are being taken up to the lawn and covered." Emily pointed down the harbor.

From afar, the expansive lawn looked like a battleground. Large and small forms were lined up. Ten, twenty, thirty. Some faces were covered. Clangs of Engine Number 1 turned heads as Chief Deasy and the fire brigade arrived, fanning out to help raise the debris as only draft horses could.

"Oh God, Emily. There must have been a hundred killed. I should have done something to stop that car." Edwin ran his hand through his filthy hair.

She shook her head. "Half that, they think. Still, some are not yet recovered. As the tide drops, they'll bring divers."

A voice made them start. It was Jones, suitcoat off and sleeves rolled up. "Edwin, were you caught in that hell?" He noticed Emily. "Pardon, Ma'am."

Edwin told him about Clifford. "Aye, it won't pain me to have him on my table. I'd like to discover what made him so evil. It will be my pleasure."

"There was yet a seed of good in him," Emily said. "Melodie told me that he had a younger brother called Philip who died of typhoid. That was the name of the boy whom he rescued, his mother said."

"What will the city do?" Edwin wondered aloud. "The scope of this tragedy unhinges the mind." But British Canadian mettle would proof. Already the wheels were turning.

"Coroner Crompton will have an inquest starting at eight tonight at police court at the city hall. Nothing more can be done for the dead. Let's hope those spared recover with good care. I'd best go now and help the living for a change. The naval surgeons have arrived." Jones hesitated before he left. "One more thing. That number sixteen is the same damn car on the bridge when it sank four feet three years ago. The company swore that the span was strengthened. Others claim that the test drill holes were never filled. It's been a little time bomb."

"Lawsuits will bankrupt the owners, and the city will bear blame for the overcrowding," Edwin said. "Small comfort for the bereaved."

By six o'clock, Edwin's clothes were almost dry. He and Emily had been helping as the bodies were organized on Grant's lawn. "You should go home now," Edwin said as she brought hot coffee from the house kitchen to the workers. Wagons were bearing away the dead, some to the morgue and others to already overcrowded funeral parlors. A few parents had already taken home the broken bodies of their children. Who could say them nay?

"I suppose I had better get back. My family will be frantic if they've heard the news," Emily said. "You can use my brother's wheel to get home."

"Thanks. I'll take good care of it."

She gave a little wave and went to the fence where they had left the bicycles. Her face was smeared with dirt and sweat, her clothes would never be the same, and she looked like Venus emerging from the sea in a scallop shell.

"And Emily . . ."

She climbed onto the saddle, rubbing her nose in a heart-breakingly young gesture, before giving a little sneeze. "Yes?"

"You've been wonderful."

Those dimples came to the rescue. "You, too."

Edwin headed for a saloon for something to eat and drink before the inquest. Despite working on nothing since luncheon, he had no appetite. But a glass of beer, a few pickled eggs, and half a loaf restored him. Using their telephone, he called Naomi. The delays were significant since the operators were jammed with requests.

"Edwin, are you a ghost? Tell me you weren't anywhere near that bridge. The news has been shouted all over town." From the tremble in her voice, he knew she'd been worrying.

"I'm fine, Mother. Emily as well. It was indescribable. So many. So fast." He told her not to expect him until very late, or even the next morning. Then he laid his head on the table and dozed for half an hour.

Bone weary, rousing himself with leaden legs, he headed for the inquest. Crowds pressed on all sides, many muddy and wet from rescue efforts. With the effluvia from factories and other businesses that pumped swill into the harbor, as well as rotting vegetation and fish remnants, the mud along the banks stank to the heavens. Edwin had no coat, and one sleeve of his shirt had been ripped off by a snag. A trickle of blood down the biceps had dried. He felt in his pocket for his father's watch. It had stopped at 2:13.

At the city hall door, hapless constables were linking arms to hold back the crowd. Voices, high and low, were raised in fear and fury.

"My wife was killed. I have a right to be here. Someone's to blame."

"I'm searching for my mother. Has anyone seen a white-haired woman with a calico dress?"

"I'm sorry, but the occupancy limit for the room and corridors has been reached. It's unsafe to let anyone else in except those who have a direct business in the inquest." The corporal in charge looked for help, no match for the pressing numbers. Sweat dripped down his face from the heat and humidity. Edwin began moving toward him. Someone had to control the mob, or more would be hurt.

With ever-increasing jeers and grumbles, the crowd pressed forward. Then Big Tom Knox clomped down the main stairs in his boots. He won the caber-tossing event at every Hibernian celebration. Tom stood six-feet-six and had the stubborn disposition and body of an ox.

"Dinna ye ken the Queen's English, you lot? Someone leaves, someone can come in. Anyone I have to lay my mitts on will be in police court tomorrow for obstruction. Consider this a reading of the Riot Act."

Edwin climbed onto a table next to Tom. "He's right. I'm Detective Sergeant DesRosiers. All the coroner's doing in there is assembling his jury. Then they will be leaving to visit the . . . victims at several locations. There's nothing to see or hear tonight. Tomorrow and probably many days after, the evidence and opinions will be presented. Go home to your families. Come back tomorrow when we have more information. God bless, and say a prayer." Religion hadn't mattered much to Edwin, but he wasn't Everyman.

"Thanks, Guv," said one constable. Mumbling among themselves, half of the crowd moved off and the rest sat down to wait, poleaxed but compliant.

Inside the chambers, Edwin could barely find a place to stand, jostled and squeezed. The body odor in addition to the toxic mud made the torpor unbearable. But those beyond comforting deserved an explanation.

Coroner Crompton read the names of the nine men chosen at random to serve on the jury. As they took a rear exit, Edwin followed down the street and over to Hayward's to see the first dozen bodies. They were laid out on tables, boards over chairs, and even on the floor. No funeral parlor was equipped to deal with such numbers. As the jury filed by, each pale face was revealed, a stunning array of men, women, and children, of all ages and complexions. War must be like this, Edwin thought. To their credit, the good men and true held themselves together, though some that knew the victims firmed their lips to form the names. Among the dead were a boilermaker, a blacksmith's helper, a bootblack, a chipper at the Albion Iron Works, and even a harpist.

Then it was on to the public market. Another thirty to forty corpses lined up like cordwood. "What a damn dump," one man said with disgust. "It's a disgrace to our city."

Crompton pinned him with a look. "Then help us convince

the city council to build quarters at the new Jubilee, man. My complaining hasn't done a tinker's damn. If this crisis doesn't do it, what will?"

At 8:45, the jury assembled back at the police court. The heavy crowd had thinned. In very few hours, working men and women had to rise to go to their jobs. Earning a living elbowed aside the need to grieve.

When everyone was seated, Crompton took his place in front of the jury. "You have witnessed forty-seven souls gone to meet their maker, gentlemen, including Conductor Talbot and Motorman Farr, who died at their posts. Pray God that no city sees another tragedy like this. One of the reasons we are here tonight is to begin understanding why this happened and what can be done to prevent it. Mayor Beaven has already shut down the other bridges on a temporary basis."

The jurymen shuffled their feet and muttered amongst themselves. Some held small notebooks or paper and pencil in their fists.

Crompton said that the body of a girl had been taken to her home at Windsor Street. Though the jury could go there now to view the body, he itemized at least half a dozen still missing.

A light had been obtained to focus on the night rescue efforts. Due to the enormous weight of the tangled ironwork, not much would be accomplished until the next day, when powerful equipment could be located to raise the timbers.

"Under the circumstances, gentlemen, I suggest that we adjourn for the evening and reconvene here at two p.m. tomorrow. We have a terrible job ahead. May the Lord give us strength to honor the dead and comfort the living."

Edwin was sitting in the last row, about to nod off when Jones came up. "I'd give you a ride home in my carriage, Edwin, but we're going to be handling the autopsies all night so that the bereaved families can make arrangements for their loved ones. You look done in, man. And that arm needs attention if you don't want it to go septic from the harbor filth. Any kind of alcohol will do, inside as well as out."

Edwin stood with some difficulty. His thigh was aching where a timber had grazed it. He weighed the advantages of going home. For a minute he imagined that he'd sleep in his office on a mat that they kept in the wardrobe. But his clothes needed changing, and Jones was right about infection.

An hour later, hardly knowing how he navigated the streets on his borrowed wheel and senseless for the better part of a bottle of brandy, he was tucked into bed by Naomi.

# CHAPTER THIRTY-FOUR

Edwin forced open his bleary eyes. A nightmare came to life as events stuttered across his memory. He couldn't stomach breakfast, instead downing a noxious preparation from Wong. *Kuding* tea, a bitter tisane laced with ginseng to "purge excessive *yang*" and generate fluids. Then he dressed with minimal care and walked outside. The glare from the sun made his head threaten to burst. Back inside for a glass of headache powders, he drank a pint with slow deliberation, trying not to gag.

Not trusting his shaking hands, he stopped at Sulo's, where the barber shop door was draped in black. Wreaths of mourning were sprouting like mushrooms. "God, man, you smell like a distillery. What you need is a long hot sauna and then a cold water bath. That's the way we treated hangovers in Finland," Sulo said.

"I'm feeling better," Edwin said, relaxing under his capable hands.

"Did you have any loved ones at the bridge?" Sulo asked. "My second cousin Eino is still missing."

"Sorry to hear that. I'm still learning about people who had said that they were going to the harbor and then didn't. Maybe your cousin will be lucky."

"Ah, he's a black Finn. Near hangs himself every winter with the depression. Death's a blessing for those few."

At City Hall, Edwin could barely elbow through the mob. The crowd was either looking for information or making complaints, as if they weren't fortunate enough to be alive and unhurt in the midst of the slaughter.

"My aunt's body was robbed right on Grant's lawn. Damnable vultures! What are you going to do about it?" a woman in a black bonnet screamed, shaking her fist. Others were demanding updated lists. The tide had come and gone and was returning. Bodies in a still-water lake would normally sink at first, then rise rump first. But with the currents and debris, not to mention the voluminous and buoyant clothing women wore, anything could happen. The cold bottom of the harbor would retard gas formation. A surfacing body might be dashed into unrecognizable jelly against the relentless roar of the waves on the rocky shore or float clear to Puget Sound.

"Let's hope there's been a mistake, Ma'am. Purses and pocketbooks were put into safekeeping at Captain Grant's boathouse. One contained three hundred dollars," the sergeant said gently. "Come up and I'll take your particulars. My condolences about your aunt." He gave Edwin a what-can-you-do look. Despite the good nature of most people, every catastrophe brought opportunists. Edwin had seen one accused thief hustled off in irons to an express wagon. The crowd might have torn him apart.

A clerk had brought a standing bulletin board and was setting it up in the lobby to post messages. Rumors were flying.

"San Francisco Bridge Company denied liability. Can you imagine the nerve?"

"My brother blamed bad welding. Cheap bastards."

"There's some as should hang for this."

Around five that evening, Jones called. "We've got Cardinal. A shrimper saw his body floating on a kelp bed off Otter Point. His head's a mess, like you told us. Guess what's on his back shoulder?"

Aside from a crab, Edwin couldn't imagine.

"A unicursal hexagram." He paused. "His inside pocket had a letter of credit to a San Francisco bank. Someone boarded that steamer under his name. His accomplice will be arrested for obstruction of justice when he docks."

"Just deserts," Edwin said, but not enough to keep two women from dying. Fresh depravity would take the place of the infamous Styx Club. His job was to keep the balance. What had Serge said? "All that is necessary for evil to thrive is for good men to do nothing."

He opened the abandoned morning paper, where survivors were telling their perilous stories in gruesome detail. Telegrams were jamming the offices. Condolences from the mayors of Vancouver, Nanaimo, Spokane, even Toronto. Mainlanders were especially panicked about their island friends and relatives. Only a few bodies hadn't been located, and perhaps never would be. The miracle was that more had not died. At the bottom of the page was a notice from J. Wenger's on Government Street offering to clean and repair salt-water-damaged works. Edwin made himself a mental note to see if his precious keepsake could be saved.

People would say that this day would never be forgotten, but it would fade even in a generation. An epidemic. A war. A great ship going down. But on the grounds of the Crosse farm would be a granite marker to someone who had stamped her imprimatur upon his boyish heart. Vicky had paid a high price to be "the woman who did."

# ABOUT THE AUTHOR

**Lou Allin** is the author of the Belle Palmer mysteries, set in northern Ontario, and the RCMP Corporal Holly Martin series, set on Vancouver Island. She also has written *That Dog Won't Hunt* in Orca's Rapid Reads editions for adults with literacy issues, and in 2013 she won Canada's Arthur Ellis Best Novella Award for *Contingency Plan*. She's done two standalones for Five Star/Cengage, *A Little Learning Is a Murderous Thing* and *Man Corn Murders*, set respectively in the Michigan Upper Peninsula and in Utah. A former B.C./Yukon vice president for the Crime Writers of Canada, she lived across from Washington State on the Juan de Fuca Strait with her border collies and mini-poodle. Lou died of pancreatic cancer on July 10, 2014.

MN
NW

6/16